SOL
A Silver Ships Novel

S. H. JUCHA

This book is a work of fiction. Names, characters, places, and incidents either are products of the author's imagination or are used fictitiously. Any resemblance to actual events or locales or persons, living or dead, is entirely coincidental.

Published by S. H. Jucha
www.scottjucha.com

ISBN: 978-0-9905940-0-00 (softcover)

First Edition: July 2016

Cover Design: Damon Za

Acknowledgments

Sol is the fifth book in *The Silver Ships* series. I wish to extend a special thanks to my independent editor, Joni Wilson, whose efforts enabled the finished product. To my proofreaders, Abiola Streete, Dr. Jan Hamilton, David Melvin, and Ron Critchfield, I offer my sincere thanks for their kind support.

Despite the assistance I've received from others, all errors are mine.

Glossary

A glossary is located at the end of the book.

-1-

Jodlyne crawled on her hands and knees through the air shaft, the cool rush of air chilling her thin body, making her shiver despite the exertion. The circular, one-meter diameter, metal ventilation shaft nested inside the walls of the enormous spoke, extending a hundred meters from the space station's core through the inner wheel to the outer wheel. A fine layer of dust coated the inside of the shaft, making it easier for Jodlyne's wrapped hands and knees to slide along.

Two years ago, at the age of eleven, Jodlyne became an orphan. The United Earth (UE) militia caught her parents running supplies for the station's rebels. Judged guilty, they received life sentences to work the ore borers in the asteroid fields. Word reached Jodlyne that her parents weren't even granted the small favor of working at the same outpost.

Rather than be taken into the militia's custody and shipped via freighter to an inner-world, UE-run orphanage, Jodlyne ran away. While the militia searched for her, she discovered an air vent in a utility corridor's bulkhead that was detached at the bottom. The vent swung up to accommodate her small frame and she crawled into the dark, sliding down the passages, until she lost her way.

In the pitch black, with the air cooling her body, Jodlyne sat absolutely still, knees drawn to her chest for warmth, trying not to cry and listening to the militia call back and forth as they searched for her. Hours passed and she sipped water and chewed on meal bars, fighting the urge to pee.

After what seemed like an eternity to Jodlyne, a voice hissed at her from the darkness. "You gonna sit there all day or you wanna come with me?"

Jodlyne hadn't seen anyone, but she heard scuffling and then saw a small glow light shining on a scrawny butt, which began fading away. Stuffing her water jug and a half-eaten meal bar into her pack, Jodlyne had scurried after the fading light.

Today, Jodlyne was still following the slender flanks of Edmas, the boy who had found her that day. The fliklight pinned in her hair fluoresced the bands of reflective cloth affixed to Edmas's coveralls and the dashes smeared on the walls, which the young rebels used to guide them through the station's extensive ventilation system.

Jodlyne's heart was thumping in her chest. Edmas had picked her for the raid, and it was to be her first. Her teenage mind spun fantasies of being with Edmas, who was two years her senior and the leader of the tunnel rats. She touched the gun strapped to her thigh for the hundredth time.

The tunnel rats lived to harass the UE militia, crawling through the ventilation system from the inner ring to the outer ring to pop out and ambush militia patrols. They tagged the troopers' visors with their pellet guns, blinding them, and then swiped their stunstiks and anything else that could be grabbed before dashing back into the air tunnels. Jodlyne had practiced incessantly with her pistol in every stance and from every position she could imagine until she was considered one of the best shots among the rats.

At the end of their air vent, Edmas eased opened the cover whose bottom was unattached. The vent ended in a utility corridor rather than the station's main passenger corridor. Edmas motioned Jodlyne up beside him, and they lay together for warmth in the air vent's mouth, listening for the footfalls of militia boots.

Sometime later, a nudge in Jodlyne's ribs woke her, and a dusty hand covered her mouth. She flushed with embarrassment that she had fallen asleep, but Edmas's body had been a warm blanket after the seemingly interminable crawl through the incessant stream of cool air.

Edmas held a finger to his lips, which Jodlyne could barely discern in the dim light that penetrated the vent's slats, and he signaled her to crawl deeper into the vent. Jodlyne wriggled backward as quickly and silently as she could, hearing the muffled sounds of Edmas following her. He had no sooner spread an old piece of dirty cloth over their heads to conceal them, than a powerful light played off the tunnel's walls as the militia patrol sought to catch any tunnel rats off-guard.

Seconds later, the light switched off, but Edmas cocked an ear, listening intently to ensure the patrol had walked on. He tugged on her jacket, crawling quickly back to the vent cover, and Jodlyne hurried to keep up with him. Edmas was already in the corridor, holding up the cover, when Jodlyne reached the opening and slid silently to the deck.

Creeping down the corridor, their wrapped boots served to muffle their approach as they followed the sound of the patrol's fading footsteps. At the corridor's tee, Edmas peeked around the corner to find a militiaman waiting for him. The patrol had set a trap with one man noisily walking on and the other lying in wait.

Jodlyne watched Edmas throw himself across the corridor to land on his back as sleeper darts from a stunstik struck the wall above his head. Her training took over, and as the ambusher rounded the corner into full view, Jodlyne snapped out her pistol, dropped to one knee, and peppered the trooper's visor, blinding him.

Edmas frantically waved her back to the vent, but the footfalls of the second patroller were fast approaching as he raced to the rescue of his comrade. The man Jodlyne blinded was stumbling around, shouting and cursing the rebel rats. His visor was covered in a matrix of paint and bonding material that glued his visor shut. He was alternating between swiping at the visor trying to clear it and yanking on his helmet to pull it off, but for safety's sake militia helmets were attached to the upper torso armor via a mounting ring

Jodlyne shook her head at Edmas, who was still waving her off. She backed up a couple of meters and laid down her pellet gun. Swiping the cover off her head, Jodlyne shook out her fine, blonde hair around her shoulders and held her hands up in surrender. She glanced at Edmas, who nodded his agreement and quickly crawled backward to wedge himself into a doorway set back from the corridor.

The second militiaman came sliding around the corner on his knees, but he hesitated when he spotted a young, blonde teenager with her hands in the air. Puffs from Edmas's pellet gun sounded in the momentary quiet, and a second visor was effectively covered and sealed.

Edmas rushed forward and kicked the legs out from under Jodlyne's target. While the trooper was down and disoriented, Edmas unsnapped his utility belt and grabbed his stunstik. He hurried to Jodlyne and snatched at her shoulder, but she jerked free to scrabble forward and grab her head cover and beloved pistol before she sprinted after him.

Edmas was waiting at the vent cover and boosted Jodlyne into the tunnel's mouth. She scurried down its length as fast as she could, the coded dashes on the walls guiding her, until Edmas called a halt. They sat side by side, laughing at their successful raid against the UE militia, who held sway over the outer ring of Idona Station.

* * *

"Patrol attacks are rising, Captain Yun," Lieutenant Patrice Morris reported. "We had five attacks around the wheel yesterday. None of our people were seriously injured, more embarrassed. They were robbed of stunstiks, web belts, and other gear. It's all kids."

"Kids grow up to be rebels, Lieutenant. Don't forget that. Implement four-man patrols immediately. Let's see how the little rats handle those odds."

"Yes, sir," the lieutenant replied.

UE militia was housed in the administration section of Idona Station's outer ring, but their numbers were such that they didn't have adequate forces to effectively patrol day and night even a quarter of the huge ring. The rebel stronghold was the inner ring and the core, which gave them control of the station's critical systems, including its giant fusion reactors, and the enormous size of the station allowed the rebels, mostly tunnel rats, to surreptitiously visit much of the outer ring with impunity.

This had been the status quo for several generations, but lately moods were shifting, and the rats were becoming brazen. And the mood was echoed by the citizens of the station, who no longer ducked their heads as they passed militia patrols, but more often stared back.

"Anything else?" Captain Yun asked quietly.

"Nothing, Captain," Lieutenant Morris replied.

This was a frequent daily exchange, and not just between the captain and the lieutenant, but between senior militia and naval officers and their direct reports throughout Sol's outer rim. The entire system had witnessed the historical return of the *Reunion*, and everyone waited restlessly for the much-anticipated announcement from the Supreme Tribunal of the explorer ship's exciting discovery, but nothing was heard. To add to the general unease created by the lack of information, Speaker Garcia, the leader of the expedition, was not seen or quoted in the media after the *Reunion* made Earth's orbit.

But nothing was more disquieting to UE forces than the nonappearance of the battleship, *Hand of Justice*. Days passed after the return of the *Reunion,* then a month, and the more time that slipped away, the edgier the men and women of the naval forces and the militia became. Scuttlebutt had it that the UE ships had discovered aliens with the capabilities to destroy the UE's fiercest war machine, and now the aliens knew the way to Earth. Fear was creeping through the UE's vaunted forces.

Among the bridge crew of the rim's patrol ships, it seemed one eye searched for rebels running the blockade and the other eye kept watch beyond on the asteroid fields where the *Reunion* had made its faster-than-light (FTL) transition into the system of Sol.

-2-

The Haraken fleet sailed out of the deep dark two days out from the outer asteroid field that ringed the star called Sol. The distance was precautionary. The fleet decelerated and came to a halt while the SADEs mapped the Earthers' system — stations, surface colonies, planets, moons, and ship traffic.

Alex Racine, the Haraken president, was pleased to see that the data correlated favorably with the UE scientists' information. The Earthers were comfortably settled in cabins below deck from Alex and Renée's suite aboard Haraken's largest fighter carrier, the *No Retreat.*

In preparing for the fleet's launch, Alex hadn't intended to be traveling on the carrier, but in an imitation of the circumstances of Haraken's first traveler test, his people had revolted and arranged alternate transportation. Alex boarded his traveler, the Haraken gravity-driven fighter-shuttle, bound for the *Rêveur*. At least, that's where Alex thought he was headed. However, instead of descending into *Rêveur*'s compact bay, the cavernous bay of the *No Retreat* greeted him.

"Welcome to your flagship, Mr. President," Captain Miko Tanaka said proudly, saluting Alex.

"Captain," Alex replied tersely, returning the salute. He turned to Tatia Tachenko and asked, "Any other changes in our plans that I should be aware of, Admiral?"

"Negative, Mr. President. Ships, captains, and preparations are as you requested. It was a strategic decision to locate Haraken's intelligence resources aboard our most formidable ship," Tatia replied.

<Julien, I would have thought at least you would have warned me,> Alex sent his thought via his implant to his friend and SADE, a self-aware digital entity housed in a human avatar, who stood beside him.

<I can't share with you, Mr. President, what I don't know,> Julien replied privately to Alex.

The two individuals, human and SADE, took the measure of the four females who faced them — Renée, Alex's partner; Cordelia, Julien's SADE partner; Admiral Tatia Tachenko, and Captain Miko Tanaka, who stood resolutely in front of them.

<An intelligent human would withdraw gracefully, facing such formidable forces,> Julien sent to Alex.

<Well, we wouldn't want to appear foolish, would we?> Alex replied to Julien. "The *No Retreat* it is," Alex announced, which caused the three humans to breathe quiet sighs of relief, having expected Alex to object to his being overruled. Cordelia, on the other hand, had calculated the probabilities were in their favor that Alex would relent.

* * *

When the SADEs confirmed to Alex that the collection of the system's telemetry was complete, a large group gathered around the *No Retreat*'s expansive holo-vid. Surveying the size of the audience, Alex had to compliment Z, the third SADE traveling with them, on his efforts to design and build a holo-vid that was in proportion to the carrier's massive bridge.

"There, Mr. President," Olawale Wombo, the ex-Earther scientist said, putting his finger into the holo-vid, which responded by enlarging that territory of space to the degree his finger was held there. "Your pardon, Mr. President," Olawale said when he realized the audience was left with a display of a small portion of a planet's surface.

"I, for one," Priita Ranta, Olawale's associate said, "am glad that Haraken technology does not extend to teleportation by way of their holo-vid. Olawale would have us sucking frozen gases on Neptune at this moment."

Olawale's compatriots tittered good-naturedly at their friend's consternation. It was the same predicament for all the UE scientists, who had deserted the Earther explorer ship and sought asylum with the Harakens merely forty-eight days ago. Haraken technology continued to astound them at every turn. But if anyone could enjoy being surprised and confounded by a world of technological advancement the likes of which could only be imagined, it was seven scientists.

"Not to worry, Ser Wombo," Alex said, resizing the holo-vid with a signal from his implants, the Méridien devices embedded in his cerebellum. Whereas most, meaning nearly 100 percent of the population of Méridien and Haraken carried one implant, Alex carried two. It was a consequence of his birth on New Terra, a world far removed from the Méridiens' advanced civilization, his development as a mathematics prodigy, and the receipt of his implants as an adult that enabled Alex to disregard standard practices and adopt his first implant at a phenomenal pace.

Implants were the common means of communication among the *Rêveur*'s survivors, who were the last remaining passengers on a Méridien liner that Alex rescued. Alex hadn't received the structured, step-by-step, implant training every Méridien child received. To him, the useful rules were the ones he chose to create and write. Implant to implant there wasn't an equal to the power that Alex could wield, to the detriment of some, to the relief of the Harakens, and to the pleasure of one, Ser Renée de Guirnon.

"Proceed, Ser," Alex said to Olawale, indicating the reset holo-vid view of Neptune and its surrounding satellites.

"This is Idona Station, of which we spoke," said Olawale, pointing to a small dot and careful to keep his hands out of the holo-vid.

Alex enlarged the display of space around the station. "Julien, a summary, please."

"The station is a pre-grav build, consisting of a core, housing energy plants and utilities systems, surrounded by multiple rings, which maintain gravity with a constant spin," Julien replied. "However, the station isn't spinning now, which implies it has been upgraded as Ser Boris Gorenko indicated."

"If you would, Julien?" Boris asked, indicating the station. Julien increased the holo-vid's magnification until Boris nodded to him. "When we left Sol's space, the UE militia was housed in a small section of an outer ring. Commerce under the citizens continues to operate there too, and the rebels hold the inner ring and the core."

"That's a huge station," Tatia noted, studying the telemetry details in her implant.

"Idona Station was built as the transfer center between the rim's asteroid belt miners and the outer worlds," Boris added, his knowledge having accrued from his two sons, who had served in UE naval forces. "Many of these miners have lived their entire lives between Idona and the belt, mining, refining, and delivering the finished products to the station. The station's outer ring hosts, or at least it used to host, a tremendous number of brokerage houses that buy and resell the miners' metals and liquid gases to other colonies, stations, the outer planets, and to Earth. Freighters and passenger ships journey inward from the station but rarely travel beyond."

"Julien, what's the status on the present commercial ship traffic?" Alex asked.

"For an outward location, the freighter traffic is quite high, with ships taking routes between the station and the inner planets and other ships journeying from the belt to the station and returning. Liner traffic appears to be at a minimum," Julien replied.

"Personnel movement to the station ceased for many years after the station's takeover," Boris continued, "and many owners and their families abandoned their shops for a safer life elsewhere. The station's resident population has never recovered. Estimates are that the outer ring is somewhere at one-third of its previous height. But as Julien noted, the station is still a heavy shipping transit point. Crews take breaks there ... freighters load and unload ... none of them bothered by the rebels."

"It's certainly an odd revolution," mused Yoram Penzig, who was the resident philosopher and psychotherapist of the UE scientists.

"What about military ships?" Tatia asked.

"One significant presence, Admiral," Z replied. "Utilizing our historic Terran records, this ship would be classified as a destroyer." When the audience stared at him, waiting, Z added. "About one-third of the *Hand of Justice's* power ... no fighters and a significant reliance on missiles and rail gun fire."

"Enough power to destroy the station," Tatia murmured.

"Indeed, Admiral," Z affirmed.

"There are several patrol craft, Admiral," Cordelia added. "They are small, carrying perhaps ten to twenty personnel and capable of interdicting freighters and boarding them, presumably for inspections as our new friends have indicated."

<Thank ... young ... miss,> Olawale attempted to send to Cordelia. When he saw the SADE turn toward him and smile, Olawale shrugged his huge shoulders in apology. The scientists obtained their implants 35 days ago and were still learning to cope with the new manner of communication. Olawale had tried to thank Cordelia using the term he had first given her of "young miss" even after he learned her true century-plus age.

"This has been going on for decades?" Alex asked. "Why has neither side gotten the upper hand?"

"It became a stalemate between the militia and the rebels from the day UE forces landed on the station," Yoram explained. "The operating personnel, working in the outer ring, fled to an inner ring, joining the people running the station's support systems. They sealed the massive transfer doors of the spokes that connect rings. Then the rebels threatened to blow the station if the militia attempted to breach the doors."

"The station is strategically that important?" Alex asked.

"Yes, Mr. President," Boris said. "The UE, especially Earth, is dependent on the metals and gases mined in the asteroid fields, and the entire transfer and shipping process of those resources depends on this station. The Supreme Tribunal had no choice but to acquiesce and order the militia to hold."

"The situation is complicated by the civilians in the outer ring, Mr. President," Nema said, despite the scientist's advanced age she had become a great admirer of Alex and not just for his presidency. The situation presented moments of pleasure for Renée, teasing Alex by inquiring as to the well-being of his latest admirer. "The UE naval forces patrol the area around the station, interdicting those who attempt to help the rebels, while ensuring the safe passage of UE ships, personnel, and goods. The problem for the militia is that goods for the rebels are snuck in by freighters to legitimate shop owners, who in reality are rebel sympathizers."

"The inner wheel possesses extensive food production farms and water treatment systems, which are critical assets for the rebels, and the entire outer ring, including the militia and UE ships, depend on that purified water source," Priita explained.

"That's our target, people," Alex declared. "Now, I wonder if the Earthers still know how to play the game of poker?" he mused, and Julien smiled and sprouted a croupier's visor, imaged by the holo-vid capability of his synth-skin. He had begun displaying the visor when he played cards with Alex. You would think a SADE, capable of calculating the variances of each hand of a card game would hold the advantage, but Julien found an equal in Alex in the games. As Julien would often say, "The tendency of a certain New Terran to prevaricate at will disturbs the laws of probability."

* * *

"Thé, Admiral?" Renée asked Tatia, who had dropped by Alex and Renée's suite late that evening.

"No, thank you, Ser. This won't take long," Tatia replied.

Alex came out of the sleeping quarters, tying his robe around the waist. "And what can I do for you this evening? Is it Admiral or Tatia?"

"Admiral, Mr. President. I would like you to consider an alternative strategy. The SADEs' telemetry indicates that most of the UE warships observed are not FTL-capable. At least, they do not have the winged configuration that appears to signify FTL-capable."

Alex offered Tatia a seat, and he took one across from her. Renée moved behind Alex where she could rest her hands on his shoulders. Tatia was reminded of her Méridien partner, Alain de Long, who exhibited the same habit when they were in private, his hands always seeking to touch her. It had been disconcerting, at first, for Tatia, who was a tremendously independent and private person. Now, after years together, she wouldn't have it any other way.

"Our UE scientists were convinced a fleet would come to the Confederation, which got me wondering how they would accomplish that when the scientists also stated that the UE possessed few FTL-capable ships," Tatia continued. "When I examined the telemetry in detail, I found several winged-shaped battleships and some enormous winged vessels." Tatia turned on the salon's holo-vid, and Alex leaned in to examine one of the gigantic ships on display.

"What is it?" Alex asked.

"According to Z, this ship has a wingspan over 60 percent greater than a battleship but appears to possess none of the bay and port configuration of the warship."

"So what's it for?" Alex asked.

"We have a rearward view of one of these ships," said Tatia, who changed the holo-vid view.

"Are those bay doors? If so, they're big enough to accommodate … ships," Alex said, looking up to see Tatia nodding.

"Giant FTL-capable ship carriers," Tatia announced. "That's how the UE intends to spread its forces. It's quite inventive. It saves the effort and cost of retrofitting or replacing the war fleet."

"So what's your suggestion, Admiral?" Alex asked.

"If we take out these ship carriers, the UE battleships might be able to reach our system, but they won't have any support ships. One quick strike against these carriers and the UE will spend a decade or two replacing those ships," Tatia urged.

Alex stood up to pace while he thought. "These ship carriers are staged around Earth. The UE naval commanders will see us coming and take measures to protect them. The concept involves a great deal of risk … fighting our way in system, the battle itself, and then fighting our way back out."

Alex continued to pace and Tatia waited patiently. "I admit your idea has merit, Admiral, but I came here to stop a war not start one. We'll continue onto Idona. Thank you and good evening."

"Wouldn't be doing my job if I didn't offer you alternatives. Good evening, Mr. President, Ser," Tatia said, turning to leave.

<And a fine job it has always been,> Alex sent privately to Tatia, who paused at the cabin door and acknowledged Alex's compliment with a touch of two fingertips to her brow.

* * *

In the morning, Cordelia would transfer to the *Last Stand*, Haraken's first and smaller carrier, to organize the launch of two probes Alex required.

Before she left, Cordelia was able to enjoy a final meal time with Julien. Not that the two SADEs would eat, but it was their habit to be present at meals. Cordelia was in the president's suite with Alex, Renée, and Julien when their scheduling apps signaled meal time. Too easily isolated by their implants, Méridiens treasured meal time for its face-to-face reminder of what was important — one another. Alex offered Renée his arm, and, to Cordelia's delight, Julien offered his arm to her.

That Cordelia's synth-flesh sensors reported the contact of Julien's arm, and her deeper sensors signaled the pressure was immaterial. That her partner, a shy one as any you might find in a human pair, wished to demonstrate his attachment to her brought many of her ancillary programs to a halt. It was a moment to carefully record, to treasure, to play over and over in the centuries and perhaps the millenniums to come.

The morning would pass too quickly for Cordelia, but by 9.75 hours, she was aboard the *Last Stand*, prepping the probes. The first was a smaller FTL relay sent on a ballistic course toward Neptune. Its path was calculated by Alex's inventive g-sling program, which he had developed while hauling ice asteroids from the far asteroid fields of Oistos, his home world's star.

The SADEs still marveled at the incredible precision with which a human-designed program achieved ballistic accuracy when using a tug to sling an asteroid toward a celestial body, not that they hadn't made subtle improvements on the program since coopting it from Alex's Tara, his original computer on board his explorer-tug, the *Outward Bound.*

There wouldn't be time to allow a ballistic course for the second probe. It was loaded on board a traveler, piloted by Captain Darius Gaumata, who had persevered in the first fight with the Earthers, which had been termed a contest by the now-deceased High Judge Patricio Bunaldi. But the detestable contest had cost Darius the life of his good friend, Sean McCreary. In his dark mood, Darius was hoping a UE pilot would be foolish enough to intercept him on the way to or from his destination, Earth's moon, despite his orders to avoid contact.

Darius would land his traveler on the moon's Earth-face and open his hatch to offload the probe. A traveler's shell, created by the alien species, the Swei Swee, depended on harmonics to harness gravity waves, which drove the ship and powered its devastating energy beam. The fighter's dependency on gravitational waves limited its use to in-system deployment and necessitated its shell remain completely intact for it to charge the alien crystal-power systems created by the Nua'll, an alien race that had kept the Swei Swee imprisoned for generations until Alex rescued them.

* * *

While Cordelia readied her probes, Z transferred to the *Rêveur*, where he had stored his "toys."

When Alex landed aboard the *No Retreat,* Tatia told Alex that all of his orders, save the change of his flagship, had been executed as he had requested, and she couldn't be accused of inaccuracy. That Z and she had added their own plans would have been news to Alex, but not surprising to him. Since their beginning together, Alex had come to think of Tatia, the ex-New Terran major and ground pounder, as his weapons master.

When the Assembly approved Alex's plan to take the Haraken fleet and journey to Sol to sue for peace with the UE's Supreme Tribunal in hopes of preventing a war, Julien sought out Tatia and Z. "What plans are in progress, Admiral, Z, to ensure our survival, and how might I be of help?" Julien asked.

"We have a particular challenge, Julien," Tatia replied. "Allowing the UE explorer ship, *Reunion*, to return home was morally right, but it hurt us strategically. The Earthers took with them a great deal of tactical information about our fighters — acceleration, maneuverability, and our beam weaponry."

"We must create new strengths," Z added.

"My greatest concern is that the Earthers will make diplomatic overtures to draw us out, and, as they have amply demonstrated, they will employ treachery," Julien replied.

"If they offer Alex an opportunity for a diplomatic solution, he might accept it," Tatia said. She was angry at the thought that the Earthers might exploit Alex's greatest vulnerability, his good heart.

"From our leader, I would expect nothing else," Z replied, "Without our president's sense of justice, there would be no Swei Swee on Haraken, there would be no travelers, and there would be no freedom for us, the Haraken SADEs."

"To answer your question, Julien, we have plans to teach the Earthers a severe lesson if they pretend diplomacy but intend treachery," Tatia said.

"There is much to be done before we leave, Julien. It will be good to have your help," Z replied. "The probabilities are high that our president will have need of tools that will allow him to deal with the Earthers from a position of strength."

Julien considered himself a pacifist in the general sense of the word. But under the circumstances, he believed that Alex needed every advantage he could get to aid his efforts to prevent a war, and, if unique tactical weapons were required, there were no more devious individuals to turn to than Tatia and Z.

-3-

Cordelia set the timeline for the fleet's advance when she signaled Alex that the ballistic-launched probe would be in position at Neptune in forty-five hours, a day and a half by the Harakens' chronometer.

<Admiral, we're headed inward. Launch the traveler ahead of us as soon as it will collect power,> Alex sent. Then in a second comm, he sent, <Julien, coordinate with the SADEs, start the fleet moving for Idona.>

An ancient, three-cornered hat appeared on Julien's head. When Julien's emotional programs played a significant part in his reactions, he couldn't resist a virtual hat. It conveyed his mood to others without communication. This time it was a tricorne, borrowed from an image of an ancient Terran revolutionary soldier and was adorned on one side with a circular, gold pin, embossed with an "H."

Julien linked Cordelia and Z, and the SADEs coordinated to execute Alex's order. The captains accelerated their ships, and the fleet drove for the huge asteroid field surrounding Sol's outer perimeter.

Once the Neptune probe was in place and while the fleet was still on approach for Idona, Alex used the comms information gathered at Méridien to beam a direct signal from the probe to the UE destroyer deployed near the station. Alex intended for only Tatia to be with him on the vid comm so as to prevent the commander from focusing on Haraken's exotic Méridiens, and that only after an audio comm was established.

In the days leading up to the fleet's arrival at Sol, Julien readied the Harakens for open contact with the Earthers by monitoring the UE scientists' language syntax and pronunciation and consuming the various text stored on their readers to assimilate a translation program for the Harakens to upload into their implants. The Earthers' language was more similar to the New Terrans' Sol-NAC language than the Méridiens' Con-Fed language. Overall, it was quite easy for the Harakens to understand

and speak to the Earthers. The translation application in their implants only aided the quality of those efforts. "It's a lot easier than learning to whistle to a Swei Swee," a senior tech was heard to say.

* * *

"Captain, we have an incoming, directed transmission, unknown ID ... and Captain, it's coming from Neptune," the comms officer of the UE destroyer announced.

Captain Reiko Shimada eyed her comms officer with doubt. The UE had no stations or ships in the direction her officer was indicating.

"I swear, Captain, that's the direction of the signal," the comms officer persisted.

"All right, I'll bite. Put it on." When the comms officer nodded at Shimada, she said, "This is Captain Shimada of the UE destroyer, *Conquest.* With whom am I speaking?"

<The *Conquest*?> Tatia sent to Alex. <Trying to make a statement, are they?>

"Greetings, Captain. I am Haraken President Alex Racine. I would speak with the superior individual aboard your ship."

"I am the senior person aboard, and who did you say you are?" Instead of a response to Shimada's query, her central bridge monitor lit up with the image of Alex and Tatia.

"I find a visual offers a much clearer explanation. Doesn't it, Captain? I repeat ... I'm Alex Racine, Haraken's president, and this is Admiral Tatia Tachenko."

Shimada had always been aware of her slender and short stature among the UE's space forces but had worked hard to overcome any negative views of her capabilities because of it. On her screen were humans who each massed three or more times her weight, but, despite their size, nothing about them, stance or expression, suggested aggression. Shimada leaned off cam and mouthed to the comms officer to record, but he whispered back, "Sorry, Captain, they have control of our comms."

"You seem to have me at a disadvantage, Mr. President, technologically, at least."

"My apologies, Captain Shimada, but I have much to accomplish in a short amount of time."

"May I ask where you're calling from, Mr. President? I'm hoping this is one hellacious long-distance call." When the strange president chuckled at her joke, the tightness that had gripped Shimada's stomach eased.

"Our fleet is inbound into your system. We are through your asteroid fields and will be arriving at Idona Station within a day," Alex said.

"Yet, your comm signal issues from the direction of Neptune, and we've received no reports from our miners in the fields," Shimada challenged.

"You will in time, Captain," Tatia said. "We sent a comm probe ahead of the fleet to facilitate communications ... FTL comm system, you understand."

Shimada was about to open her mouth to speak, but out of the corner of her eye, she caught her comms officer mouth the words "FTL comms" and then nod his understanding. Suddenly, several pieces clicked together for the captain. "Would you be the people who the *Reunion* discovered, Mr. President?"

"We would. How is Speaker García? A most disagreeable man, I have to admit," Alex said.

"Actually, we haven't heard a word from him," Shimada found herself admitting.

<Interesting,> Tatia sent Alex.

"What about our battleship, the *Hand of Justice*?" asked Shimada and saw, for the first time, tension radiate from the two heavy-massed individuals.

"Your High Judge Bunaldi chose to challenge our sovereignty, Captain," Tatia replied. "He and his people aboard that ship paid the ultimate price for their aggression. We're deeply sorry it came to that, but he left us no alternative."

When Alex saw the jaw of the slender captain tighten, he asked, "Did you have people on the battleship, Captain?"

Shimada would have wished these strangers banished to the nether worlds, but the president, despite his enormous size, had a gentle manner about him. She unclenched her jaw, and replied, "A younger brother."

Of all the responses, Shimada might have expected, what she saw wasn't one of them — both individuals crossed hands over hearts and bowed their heads. She waited but they held their pose. Finally, Shimada cleared her throat, which had threatened to close up on hearing of her brother's loss, and said, "I accept your condolences."

Alex raised his head, but before he could press on, Captain Shimada beat him to it.

"So you're here in our system. Are you declaring war on the UE, Mr. President?"

"Exactly the opposite, Captain. I'm trying to prevent one. And on that subject, I need your station."

"You know I can't let you have it, Mr. President. It's my duty to prevent that."

"I thought as much, Captain. So I have a demonstration for you, and a line of dialogue you might offer your superiors to keep you out of trouble. But first the demonstration. You will see on your screen, a small asteroid about the size of one of your patrol vessels. Watch carefully."

Shimada and her officers had their eyes glued to the monitor when the asteroid disappeared in a cloud of dust, rocks, and expanding gas.

"Captain, the guide detected an object moving across the face of Neptune," Shimada's second mate reported. "It was traveling at ... one moment, Captain ... it was ... sorry, Captain. The guide reports the object was traveling at 0.91c, and an energy source initiating from the object struck the asteroid."

"Impressive, Mr. President," Shimada said, trying to keep her voice calm and controlled. "Would you care to explain what we've just witnessed?"

<A very competent and cool commander,> Tatia sent to Alex. <I like her.>

"That was one of our fighters, Captain, what we call a traveler. I brought a few ships full of them to ensure I'm given the opportunity to be heard by your Supreme Tribunal. Now, as I said, I need your station. My suggestion is that you pull your destroyer back about 1M kilometers inward of Neptune, along with your patrol ships, and you tell your Tribunal that since we came to offer peace, you thought it better to let the Tribunal communicate with the aliens than start a war with them."

Shimada had to smile at the president's description of themselves as aliens. That's exactly what the entire UE populace was thinking the explorer ship found. Shimada was running down the options in her head. The fighter's velocity as reported by the ship's guide was incredible, and it possessed an unknown beam weapon. If the Haraken president spoke the truth, he had ships full of them. *Not to mention, the president didn't have to show me his demonstration,* Shimada thought. *He could have sent a squadron of his fighters and blown my ship into space debris before we sounded battle stations.*

"Suppose I agree to your request, Mr. President. May I ask some questions?"

<Oh, I really like her,> Tatia sent.

When the president nodded, Shimada addressed her first concern. "You might not be aware, but we have militia aboard the station." Before she could continue, the admiral had held up a hand to forestall her.

"We are aware of the situation aboard Idona Station — your militia, the civilians in the outer wheel, and the Independents ... I mean the rebels in the inner wheel and core," Tatia replied. "That's why we've chosen Idona Station as our starting point. We wish to speak with all of your people."

"I do not command the militia, Admiral Tachenko. Major Lindling does, and he will not be a willing participant in your schemes."

"All we need you to do, Captain, is relay our entire conversation, in your own words, to the major. We will handle the rest," Tatia said.

"One more point, if I may. Unless you have a means of shortening your comm lag time to Earth, you will have a difficult time communicating with the Tribunal. That's where they're headquartered."

"We have that subject covered as well, Captain," Tatia replied.

"Of course you do," Shimada murmured and then in her command voice, "Very well, Mr. President, I will pull my destroyer and patrol ships back the distance you've requested. It will take several days for some of my patrol ships to pass inward of Idona Station."

"So long as you've informed your officers to proceed without any aggressive action on their part, Captain, all will be well. And Captain, should you or your patrol ships need supplies or emergency services, do not hesitate to comm. Open broadcast is fine. We'll always be listening."

"May I recover my crew from Idona, Mr. President?"

"Certainly, Captain," Alex replied.

"Mr. President, Admiral," Shimada said, saluting the superior ranks. It felt appropriate, and the admiral responded with a sharp salute. Her first academy training officer once told her that a superior who couldn't return a proper salute was a danger to his people — someone who played at being an officer.

"Comms, get me Major Lindling," Shimada requested. When she failed to get a response, she repeated the request in a power-laden command voice, which caused her bridge personnel to jump to and appear busy.

"Aye, Captain," the comms officer repeated loudly, a little too loudly.

Watching the reaction of her bridge personnel, Reiko Shimada realized it wouldn't take long before the entire ship and the station, for that matter, would know that the aliens had come, and they were human — mostly.

* * *

With the asteroid fields behind them, Z, who had the fleet's advance position in the *Rêveur*, signaled Julien and Cordelia, relaying the positions of the UE's patrol vessels.

<Admiral,> Julien sent, <Z reports that we have a problem with the patrol ships.>

Tatia froze in the middle of her discussion with Commanders Lucia Bellardo and Franz Cohen and held up a finger to forestall their conversation. <Go ahead, Julien.>

<At our rate of acceleration, Admiral, we will pass many of the patrol craft, which are on vectors to rendezvous with the destroyer. At the same time, the destroyer is proceeding to Idona Station, presumably to collect the crew.>

<So, we will find our fleet boxed between patrol craft at our stern and the UE destroyer to our front.>

<Precisely, Admiral.>

<Thank you, Julien,> Tatia replied, closed the comm, and signaled Sheila. <Commodore Reynard, as we follow the president's timetable, we are passing the UE patrol ships, and the destroyer is making for Idona. I need a trailing and a frontal force around all three ships. The numbers are up to you. Try not to scare the locals.>

Tatia refocused on Bellardo and Cohen and said, "Commanders, I'll leave you to it. You'll have incoming signals from your commodore. Good fortune," Tatia said and left, making her way to the carrier's bridge. She was taking these actions in stride and breathing easily. After heavy losses at Niomedes against the *Hand of Justice*'s massive wing of fighters, Tatia feared that Alex might not allow her the time necessary to repair the large number of damaged travelers that Sheila reported, but to her great relief Alex relented.

On the way through the asteroid fields, Sheila and Tatia had held several vid conferences. During one of them, the admiral apprised Sheila that the *Rêveur* carried a single traveler. Sheila had raised an eyebrow in query at the liner's lack of travelers, but Tatia had just replied "Z" and shrugged her wide shoulders. Now, Sheila hurriedly signaled her wing commanders to launch protective forces, including a request to the *Last Stand*, which was second in the fleet's order, to cover the liner from that carrier.

After Sheila's comm, Wing Commander Ellie Thompson began arranging the protective shield for her ship, the *No Retreat*. She was another individual who was pleased that the time was granted for the Swei Swee to repair the battle-damaged fighters. Ellie smiled to herself as she recalled the eventful morning.

The flight crew was preparing the launch of the first traveler from the *No Retreat*, shortly after it had made Haraken's orbit, its bays full of travelers with nicked, dinged, and cracked shells. Ellie claimed the privilege of first launch and was on the way to the bay when she heard swift and nearly silent footfalls behind her. It was movement only two individuals she knew could execute.

Ellie whirled around, drawing breath to shout, when she was almost bowled off her feet by Étienne de Long, who had wrapped her in his arms, squeezing her so tightly she could barely breathe. His embrace surprised her, for while Étienne was an ardent lover in private, he was quite reserved in public. But as he held her, all thoughts fled her mind, and she lost herself in his embrace.

<My heart, welcome home,> Étienne sent.

<It's wonderful to be home, my heart,> Ellie replied. <Ride with me! I'm taking the first traveler to the Swei Swee.> Ellie could barely contain herself as she walked arm in arm with her beloved to the launch bay.

When Ellie landed at the shell construction base near Alex's home, she settled the fighter onto its grav cradle and found a committee waiting for her — Alex, Renée, Tatia, Sheila, Mickey, Alain, and the SADEs.

"This will be a day for public demonstrations, my heart, and one of them is long overdue me," Ellie said and winked at Étienne before she scrambled down the traveler's hatch steps and adopted a purposeful stride toward the group.

Walking directly up to Alex, Ellie announced, "I have a personal message from President Gonzalez for you, Mr. President." Then Ellie laid a deep, long kiss on Alex. When she pulled back, she took a moment to catch her breath and announced, "The message is from Maria, Mr. President, you have her sincere thanks for your protection of New Terra ... but, um ... the delivery was all mine," Ellie said, grinning at Alex.

<Ah, my love, you shorted Ellie after our first traveler test, and she has waited nine years for redemption,> Renée sent privately to Alex. <Perhaps, you should be more generous with your affections. Then again ...>

Alex didn't bother to respond, but he did catch Étienne's grin. The escort sent, <We'll make a Méridien of you yet, Ser President.>

Alex threw a comradely arm around Ellie's slender shoulder, saying, "Let's see what the Swei Swee must repair."

Passing Sheila, Ellie gave her superior a big grin. When she heard Maria Gonzalez ask Sheila to give Alex a kiss for her, Ellie pleaded to deliver the message. "He owes me one, Commodore," Ellie said, and both knew she was referring to the aftermath of the critical and successful first test of a Haraken traveler. Sheila, a New Terran who had been with Alex since the beginning, had received a generous kiss on the mouth, while Ellie, who had great expectations, had received a chaste kiss on the forehead.

While the humans and SADEs conversed, the Swei Swee matrons swarmed over Ellie's traveler, examining the damage and warbling their laments at the nicks, gouges, and cracks the vessel's shell suffered.

Mickey was prepared for the dilemma he thought the matrons would face. When a traveler shell was built, the first female laid down some shell compound on the bow's frame crosses. The material was masticated from minerals the young females prepared and was mixed with additional material the matrons chewed. As the Swei Swee spit dried, the matron tested her work by clamping her mouth parts on the piece of shell, blowing firmly, and producing a harmonic. The females picked up the sound and tuned their keen sense of vibration to it. All subsequent work was done to preserve that original sound. It was the harmonic nature of a Swei Swee shell that enabled a traveler to intercept gravitational waves so efficiently.

However, the damaged traveler Ellie landed was only charging at 32 percent capacity, and its true harmonics were corrupted. As the *Rêveur*'s chief engineer, Michael "Mickey" Brandon had also been with Alex since the beginning, and he had become the de facto person for all things traveler related.

Once the Harakens discovered the Swei Swee method of tuning a shell, Mickey engineered a unique method of interrupting the shell's integrity to build in hatches, and he kept a library of every shell, tagging the traveler with a code number and linking the code to a harmonic recording in his database.

<Ready, Mr. President,> Mickey sent.

Alex let loose a shrill, high-pitched whistle, and the First scurried across the cliff top, his six legs tearing up lumps of grass as he raced across the 40-meter distance. His 3-meter length and snapping great claws still gave pause to humans and SADEs alike, but not Alex.

Ellie smiled at that memory of the committee freezing, including herself, while Alex released her and hurried to greet the First, the two of them whistling some unknown concert. The First held out his great claws and Alex formed fists and thumped down on top of them with a resounding thwack. Alex had looked around for Mickey and laughed when he found the engineer waiting back with everyone else.

Mickey's embarrassment showed in his grin as he hurried forward with his device. Alex worked for several minutes to communicate to the First what they were attempting to do, but, in many respects, the worlds of the Swei Swee and humans were still far apart. Finally, Alex whistled for the First's eldest mate and she, with her blunted claws and scarred back from her years of forced labor mining resources for the alien race known as the Nua'll, had hurried to the Star Hunter First, as Alex was known among the hives.

Alex led the matron over to the traveler's bow, placed Mickey's device against the foremost point, and played the harmonic recording. The matron placed her mouth parts against the bow, but she failed to duplicate the sound. Her four eyestalks moved from the recording device to the bow and back to the First. She warbled her confusion.

Alex thought for a moment and then played the recording again, whistling "affirmative." He pointed at the bow and whistled "negative" and then walked along the shell pointing at the dings and cracks, two sets of eyestalks following him.

The audience waited while the First and his mate communicated, then hopes rose when the matron loosed a shrill whistle and the females crowded around her while she whistled and warbled her instructions.

Humans sat down in the grass to wait, while the SADEs remained standing, locking their avatars in place, and the Swei Swee First hunkered down beside Alex, who leaned on his shell to watch. Ellie had a memory of watching three pairs of eyeballs, Alex and the First's, following the lead matron as if it was some sort of sporting match.

The Swei Swee were faced with an entirely new challenge but devised a means of solving it. The young females prepared their batches of shell compound and passed them to the matrons, who added their contributions. Then the damaged areas were patched or filled and allowed to set. The First's mate would swing a couple of eyestalks at Mickey, who would play the recording, and she would test the traveler's harmonics, whistling further instructions to the hive's females. Step by step the Swei Swee fine-tuned the traveler while repairing its damage until the mate whistled success, and the females joined in chorus.

Alex hurried over to the mate and held out his fists. It was a rare gesture for a female to be invited to a greeting of claws with a First, much less the Star Hunter First, and the matron whistled her appreciation and held up her blunt, scarred great claws. Alex thumped them firmly several times, which, for a moment, confused the matron, but when the First whistled his appreciation, the females joined in a chorus of tribute to the mate.

A pilot flew the traveler back to the carrier, and two more fighters, hovering above, landed. After the first traveler was repaired, an assembly line followed, a tech taking over the device playback and matrons substituting for the First's mate.

The First whistled his concern to Alex about the absence of the Hive Singer, and Alex assured him that Mutter was safe, but hunters still roamed the stars. The First was momentarily placated, but as he watched the long line of travelers requiring repairs, his confidence faded. The Star Hunters demonstrated dominance when they defeated the Swei Swee in their dark travelers and showed their cleverness when they aided the Swei Swee in defeating the Nua'll. But the number of damaged travelers said his People's protectors fought great hunters and would soon leave for the hunters' star. He was concerned for the Star Hunter First's safety — should he and his people be sent to travel the endless waters, so might the Swei Swee meet the same fate.

* * *

Darius was a deeply disappointed man as he stepped onto the traveler's small bridge to relieve his backup pilot. They passed hosts of ships on the passage inward to deploy their package, a probe, and the count increased the closer they got to Earth, but no one had attempted an interception.

"Upset we're being left alone, Captain?" Lieutenant Sanders asked when he saw Darius's disgruntled expression. The traveler carried not only the two pilots but a crew of four, who would ensure the probe's quick launch.

"Foolish, I know, Sanders," Darius admitted. "I'm surprised the commander requested me in the first place, considering the mood I've been in since we lost Sean."

"We lost a lot of good people at Niomedes too, Captain," Sanders reminded him.

"True. Maybe it's time I screwed my head back on straight."

"Couldn't agree with you more, Captain," said Sanders, offering his friend a cheeky smile before going back to join the crew.

<I think the captain's going to be all right now, people,> Sanders sent to the crew, and the men and women breathed a sigh of relief. Their mission was dangerous enough without having a captain who was itching for a fight.

Darius ordered Sanders and the crew into environment suits as he donned one of his own, and the entire group strapped in as their traveler closed in on the moon's Earth-side face. As Darius decelerated the traveler, it finally attracted attention and several patrol ships accelerated to intercede, but at the UE's ships relatively slow velocities, compared to the traveler, they would be late to the fête, providing the crew was able to launch and activate the probe in time.

"We will have 0.12 hours to drop the probe, Captain," Sanders said.

"Should be enough time," Darius replied. "Too bad we can't just kick it out the airlock."

Sanders glanced at his friend, who had made the first joke of the entire trip, since, to accommodate the probe, the traveler's small emergency airlock was removed, but Darius was concentrating on his telemetry as he sought to locate an open area to land on what was turning out to be a very crowded moonscape. *That's a good start, Darius,* Sanders thought.

"For an inhospitable place with no air, there are more domes here than I've seen on any rock in the Confederation," Darius commented. "The Earthers must really love their moon or maybe it's the view of Earth."

"It's a spectacular view," remarked Sanders, who took a moment to increase his helmet's telemetry view of the planet. Little could he know that the blue, green, and white marble below him had centuries ago been colored in much more browns and grays than he would have believed, its population in those dark times about to descend down a path of near extermination.

<Get ready, crew,> Darius sent. <Touchdown in fifteen from ... now.>

Implants synced to the countdown and hands fingered their seat restraints, ready to jump on the last tick. Their captain hit his mark, and the crew leapt from their seats. A woman crew member signaled the hatch open and jumped through it, forgetting this moon's lack of gravity. Safety concerns had caused the crew to tie themselves together and anchor the end of the line to the inside of the hatch, which enabled a crewman to pull the woman back from her flight meters away from the ship.

Two other crew members activated the grav-sled on the probe and worked it through the hatch. Implants sent views to one another to guide the sled, which was forced to squeeze through the hatch opening. Once on the ground, the senior crewman signaled the probe, but it failed to respond. They lost precious time diagnosing the problem before they managed to activate the probe. Immediately, four legs unfolded from the probe's body and while the crew held it in place, bolts were fired deep into the moon's rock to anchor it. The crew scrambled back into the traveler, while the probe finished deploying, including activating a self-destruct program if the Earthers thought to tamper with it.

<Should be hot, Captain,> the senior crewman, a burly New Terran, sent.

Darius signaled Julien and received an immediate affirmation. With no more time for conversation, the crew closed the hatch and strapped back into their seats, signaling their readiness.

"How we looking, Sanders?" Darius asked as he launched the traveler.

"We lost that nice comfortable window, Captain. The patrol ships have us bracketed, and the word from the admiral is they are armed with an assortment of small missiles."

"Best way out?" Darius asked as he concentrated on a spiral pattern to build up velocity.

"Keep heading the way you're going, Captain. I don't think these craft are optimized for an atmospheric entry." Sanders was rewarded with a grin on his friend's face, who acknowledged the suggestion with a nod of his head.

Darius kept the traveler in an ever-faster spiral as he headed toward Earth. The patrol ships shifted vectors to intercept him, and both pilots tracked the launch of several objects from the planet.

"Ships?" Darius asked.

"Negative, Captain. Missiles, multiple launches ... make that tens of launches," Sanders replied calmly.

Darius signaled his controller and assigned priority evasion to the missiles, and secondary priority to the patrol craft behind them, notating his final destination — Idona Station. Then he sat back in his seat and tightened his webbing. "Now we're in the hands of the SADEs," Darius said.

"As good a place to be as any," Sanders acknowledged. It was a true Haraken sentiment.

The traveler's evasion programs activated and sought a way through the numerous obstacles in its path. Humans might have thought to seek an opening between the patrol ships behind them rather than face the dangerous missiles clawing free of Earth's gravity well to reach them. But controllers aren't human, and they were built by the SADEs.

In several ticks, the controller ran several hundred options through its kernel seeking an optimum outcome for its occupants, its highest priority. Option selected, it dove the traveler at max acceleration toward the planet,

Earth's gravity well lending the fighter enormous charging power for its drives.

Pinned in his pilot's chair, Sanders sent, <Don't think this would have been my first choice. By the way, Captain, I'm wondering if it's getting exciting enough for you now?>

<Sanders, you can be an irritant. Now shut up and let me soil my environment suit in peace,> Darius returned as his crossed arms clung to his webbing and tried to minimize the pounding his body was taking.

The controller utilized its tremendous velocity to shoot past the missiles before they could change vector to intercept it — step one accomplished. Now it sought to ease the fighter out of its earthward plunge without damaging its occupants. Algorithms calculated that the ship's inertia compensation system was 6 percent over maximum limits, and the controller would need to push that by an additional 3 percent.

Fortune was with the crew. Had they been over Earth's Rocky Mountains, Alps, or Himalayas, the traveler couldn't have pulled out of its dive quickly enough without harming its passengers. As it was, it skimmed across the Pacific Ocean, sending a giant wave of water spreading out from either side of its path.

A quick check of telemetry told the pilots that they had evaded the ground-based missiles and patrol ships, as their traveler shot out of Earth's atmosphere into the cold, safe embrace of vacuum.

"Don't think the president has to comm the Supreme Tribunal," Darius quipped. "I think we just made the announcement for him that the Harakens are here."

Sanders looked at his friend and let loose a belly laugh. "Good one, Captain," he said, slapping him on the shoulder. "Welcome back to the land of the living."

-4-

Earth's Supreme Tribunal met in its private chambers located in a quiet mountain retreat in North America's Rocky Mountains, in an area once called Colorado. It was a secret location known only to a few select people. The critical and only subject of the meeting was the extensive media coverage from the previous day — a mysterious ship appeared and deposited a device on the Moon, missiles were launched from the planet but the ship evaded them, and then there was the infamous footage caught by a freighter crew. The strange ship was recorded shooting across the surface of the Pacific Ocean with the tremendous wakes created by its passing, and the images were sold to a major media broadcast company.

"The images of the unknown ship match those recorded by the *Reunion*," Kwan Woo stated, laying her tablet on the antique, wood table around which the Tribunal was seated. Woo was elected by the space and militia leadership to sit on the Tribunal and, previously, had held the position of rear admiral.

"We should send for Captain Lumley," said Giuseppe Lucchesi, "I have questions for him."

"Now, you have questions for him," Woo said and chuckled. "It was you who insisted the captain and his crew be held incommunicado and the announcement of their discovery kept quiet."

"That last part is moot," said Ian Brennan, whose chair on the Tribunal was filled by a vote of the corporate giants of the new UE order. "The entire system's population is probably guessing, and rightly so, that these are the aliens that they've been worrying about, and that we've known about them all along."

Giuseppe Lucchesi leaned back in his chair. He carefully adjusted a button on his black robe to buy him time to consider his response, but refrained from running his finger under the ever-tightening and chafing upright collar. Lucchesi was dressed as the other two tribunes were, but he required his tailor fabricate a new robe every few months to conceal his growing bulk.

"What's done is done," Lucchesi finally said. "We must consider our options under the present circumstances."

Brennan and Woo shared a quick glance. They were the pair who kept Lucchesi's ilk in check. His position was filled from among the UE high judges, and every one of them was a true believer in the UE's strict principles of absolute control. To them, the world was black and white, innocent or guilty, and a person was either a UE believer or a rebel.

"I don't think we have any options, at this point, Tribune Lucchesi," Woo said. "All we know is a fighter matching the description of those seen by the *Reunion*'s crew entered deep into our system, evaded our best efforts to capture or destroy it, and ... oh, stopped to drop us a present on our Moon, which we know nothing about, and it did this without firing a shot."

"Fear is racing through our people, and we haven't a plausible story to sell to put a better twist on the situation," Brennan added. He was tired of arguing with Lucchesi. The man had a one-track mind and was as far removed from reality as Brennan could imagine. The days of the fundamentalist United Earth were long over. To a degree, there was stability; at least, there were no more wars. Now, it needed commercial growth, and the kind that wouldn't endanger the progress made recovering the Earth's environmental health.

"We tell the people what they need to hear," Lucchesi stated smugly, adjusting his bulk on the too firm chair. He hated the fit and slender physiques of the other two tribunes.

"And what do you suggest that is?" Woo asked.

"That we are investigating the phenomenon," Lucchesi replied. When he found himself the butt of his compatriots' laughter, his face flushed a deep red.

"The phenomenon ... as in a singular and unique occurrence? Maybe it doesn't occur to you because you didn't bother reading my original report," Woo said, leaning forward on the table. "Captain Lumley stated that the Haraken fighters were launched from a carrier. The vessel seen in yesterday's media reports is too small to have made the light-years' trip that our explorer ship crossed to return home. My concern is that the appearance of that ship means we might soon be facing a fleet of these strangers' carriers and their fighters."

* * *

A day later and long into the night, Brennan and Woo sat in a private room, discussing the newly released reports, summarizing the UE's growing problems, which were now compounded by the arrival of the strangers.

"How bad is it?" Woo asked.

"It's bad, and it's going to get worse. Figures for global public works and UE factories indicate another 3 percent drop this year."

"Same problems," Woo asked.

"Same problems, Kwan," Brennan acknowledged. "Our conscripted labor force is aging, and the number of new recruits drops every year."

"You mean the convicted," Woo corrected. "Call them what they are."

"Fewer rebels arrested; fewer criminals caught. It amounts to the same thing. Our giant socialist and judicial experiments are running out of credits."

"How much time do we have?"

"If we do nothing, the projections are that we have fifteen to twenty years."

"That's all?" Woo exclaimed, sitting up quickly to prevent choking on her drink.

Brennan shrugged his shoulders. The corporations had elected him to the Tribunal to watch the numbers and keep the UE financially healthy, and he had been trying to tell this story for years. Brennan hadn't gotten either of the tribunes to listen until he pulled Woo aside and sat her down for an entire day and showed her the numbers.

"It can be extended for decades if we slowly cut down on public projects, shift people to the factories, and keep their output up," Brennan said.

"What about the forces?" Woo asked. Part of her job was to ensure the resupply of the naval and militia forces, including the costly replacement of aging ships.

"You're going to have to tell the admirals and generals to make do with fewer ships and smaller forces, unless they want to start seeing their people's accounts shorted."

Woo hung her head in her hands. "I'd rather eat a stun dart, Ian, than deliver that message. Same timeline?"

"About the same," Brennan replied. "The sooner you start; the smaller cuts you can make. Keep them gradual, and you can hide them longer."

"So do our new visitors have any effect on these disastrous numbers?" Woo asked.

"That one's easy. If these people start a prolonged war, we will run out of missiles and rail slugs long before we can possibly win," Brennan said, toasting Woo with his glass and slugging down a healthy swallow of aged cognac.

* * *

The Tribunal convened again days later. This time the members sat in their high-backed seats in a forbidding chamber, their ornate bench positioned high above the chamber's floor. Captain Francis Lumley occupied an old-fashioned, three-quarter, circular witness stand, forced to stand much as an accused would be required to face judgment.

"Captain, review the footage cued up on the tablet in front of you," Lucchesi demanded. It was his privilege to prosecute those facing the tribunal, but, over the years, Brennan and Woo had sought to erode much of the man's pompous interrogation methods.

Lumley scanned the crewman's footage taken from a Pacific freighter. The familiar fighter's hull of blues, greens, and whites gleamed in the bright morning sun. "This was inevitable," Lumley said, a smile spreading over his face.

"Remember where you are, Captain," Lucchesi reminded him, but he was disappointed that his warning didn't wipe the smile from the captain's face.

"Why was it inevitable, Captain?" Woo asked, noticing Lucchesi's knuckles whiten as he gripped his tablet, angry over the usurpation of his interrogation.

"We've became complacent," Lumley replied. "We defeated the rebels ... to a large extent ... so we thought we were invincible. Turns out we're not. We met our match at Méridien and angered some very powerful people. Looks like they didn't bother to wait until we returned to their worlds, they came here first instead. I thought they might."

"Why did you think they might?" Woo asked, intrigued by the captain's line of thought.

"First, Speaker García, and then High Judge Bunaldi, treated those people with the same lack of grace they've always demonstrated to our people. They pushed and prodded, and, when they didn't get their way, they resorted to cheating in a life-and-death contest. When that didn't work, they tried brute force, and that cost them dearly. I think our visitors, if these are the Harakens, believe in personal honor and a deep commitment to the well-being of one another, and they perceive us as disreputable. They're here, Tribunes, taking away your initiative. And, at this point, you can believe you'll have to prove any goodwill intended on the UE's part, because the Harakens, if it is them, certainly won't believe you can be trusted in diplomatic negotiations."

"We've received a report from Captain Shimada. Her destroyer, the *Conquest,* is based at Idona Station. Check your tablet for her file. It's under her name. I would be interested in your speculations," Brennan said.

Captain Lumley found the file and opened it, reviewing the text report and the visual telemetry. It occurred to him that the tone of this Tribunal meeting was different from his first, which had been a condemnation without an opportunity to defend himself. This meeting was different — an interrogation, yes, but an earnest desire to hear his answers.

"Your records indicate you faced ships like these seen in Captain Shimada's report," Brennan pressed.

"Yes, I see three ships here," Lumley replied. "We met the largest one in the Hellébore system. It dumped 256 fighters into space like some sort of automation system — very eerie. The next smaller ship seems to be made in the same design. I would estimate it would hold at least 128 fighters ... we never saw this one."

"So you don't know what ship or ships defeated the *Hand of Justice*?" Woo asked, hoping to glean a piece of valuable intel.

"May I ask what actions were taken, if any, against the fighter that you showed me earlier?" Lumley asked.

"We ask the questions, Captain," Lucchesi stated officiously.

"Patrol craft tried to intercept it and chased it from the Moon toward Earth," Woo explained, ignoring Lucchesi. "Missiles were launched to bring it down, but it evaded all our efforts, dived into our atmosphere, and raced across the Pacific at an incredible speed before making for space again. Telemetry tracked its velocity past Venus's orbit —"

"At 0.91c," Lumley finished for the tribune. The number delivered to him by the *Reunion*'s guide had shocked him. "Incredible technology," he finished absent-mindedly.

"What are your thoughts, Captain?" Brennan pressed.

"My thoughts are that those ships at Idona are definitely the Harakens, who have brought 350 to 400 of these incredible fighters to our system. Probably not enough to win a protracted war, but enough to make certain we listen to what they have to say. I certainly wouldn't want to face their fighters with anything less than a very powerful fleet, and then you should be prepared to lose most of it, even if you do win," Lumley replied.

"And just how are we supposed to have a discussion with these people, Captain? They have stopped at Idona Station," Lucchesi asked with a sneer, happy to find a hole in the captain's logic. But his enjoyment was short-lived.

"Tribune Woo, you said the patrol ships chased the fighter from the Moon?" Lumley asked.

"Yes, it deposited a device on the Moon. We investigated it but haven't disturbed it as yet ... not until we can understand its nature a bit better," Woo answered.

"No need, Tribune. I can tell you what it is," Lumley replied with a big grin. "Soon you will get a comm from, my guess, President Alex Racine of the Harakens. You'll be able to talk to him in real time. The package on the Moon is a present from him. It's an FTL relay comm."

Lucchesi longed to object to the captain's summation, but a glance at his fellow tribunes found them nodding their heads. The captain's logic had made sense to them, so he closed his mouth.

Lumley was also nodding to himself. He was loyal to the UE concept that sought to balance humankind's commerce with the needs of the people, but not its manner of doing so. And despite the Tribunal's absolute power, he decided the tribunes could benefit from some advice even if it meant the public works for him. "Tribunes, you'll pardon my presumption, but when President Racine comms, I would advise you to listen carefully and deal honestly with him. He's not like anyone you have dealt with before. High Judge Bunaldi discovered that, to his detriment."

"You're presumptive, Captain," Lucchesi replied, "but we will take your words under advisement. Go now. You'll be kept on the grounds. We might have need of you later."

"What about my crew, Tribunes?" Lumley asked.

"Depending on the developments with these —" Woo began.

"Harakens," Lumley supplied.

"Yes, Harakens," Woo continued, "during the next several days, providing their device does provide some sort of functional FTL communications, of course, we will no longer require your crew be held incommunicado."

"A final word, Tribunes, if I may?" Lumley asked. "When you say things like 'providing their device does provide some sort of functionality,' I must stress that everything the Harakens do, they do well. My debriefing stressed that they have developed artificial intelligences who are walking among them. That demonstrates their technological capabilities."

"Well, Captain, we have your report stating such," Lucchesi said. "But these so-called SADEs have yet to be proven to our satisfaction. Who knows what sorts of mind games were perpetrated on you and your crew? You're dismissed, Captain."

After Lumley left the chamber, Lucchesi announced in a strong voice, "I say we deal with these people in an expedient manner. They only have three ships, and one appears to be a passenger liner. We send a couple of battleships, a few cruisers, and a number of destroyers and wipe them out. Problem solved."

Brennan stared at Lucchesi for so long that after a minute he forgot he was still staring. It took that long for him to regain control of his temper and refrain from striking the idiot.

"What did you not understand from our two interactions with Captain Lumley?" Woo finally asked. "We don't know what defeated the *Hand of Justice*. Captain Lumley reports the Harakens have beam weapons. What's the range? How powerful are the beams? Is the entire system going to watch footage someday of our fleet being annihilated before it even engages the enemy? One of their fighters made it from Idona to Earth in record time and evaded all our efforts to capture it. One fighter!"

"In simple economic and political terms, Tribunes," Brennan announced, "the UE can't afford to lose a significant portion of its fleet by making poor and uninformed assumptions about the Harakens' armament. Funds are tight, and if our forces are severely curtailed, the rebels will have years to strengthen their positions while we rebuild our fleet." What Brennan didn't say was that he feared there wouldn't be sufficient credits to rebuild the fleet.

"I agree with Tribune Brennan," Woo said. "Captain Lumley is confident we'll receive a call. I say we wait and listen to what the Haraken leader has to say."

-5-

After a great deal of wrangling with his staff, during which time Alex considered his presidential powers had somehow been reduced, a plan was concocted to take over Idona Station. The concept, which was Alex's idea, was still intact. But his staff chose to entirely reconfigure the approach to the station, and the final plan did not involve Alex being the first to step off a traveler as he had suggested.

Tatia and Sheila coordinated the loading of passengers and troopers on the travelers and the overwatch flights, ensuring their best commanders were providing protection. The first group, the trooper-loaded travelers, would encircle the station, landing simultaneously in bays scattered around the outer ring. The second group of travelers, acting as fighter escorts, would ring the station and face outward.

Launched from the fleet's ships, the travelers bore in on the station, and the SADEs went to work, using the information gleaned at Méridien concerning the Earther communications systems and protocols. Once they had access to the comms throughout the space — ship systems, militia comms, and station intercoms — Julien signaled Alex.

"Captains, militia, and personnel in and around Idona Station, I'm Alex Racine, president of Haraken," Alex announced as graciously as he could. "We are here at Sol because your people entered our systems, treated our people with disrespect, and then tried to use force to convince us of your government's righteousness. To our great regret, hostilities escalated until a confrontation was forced, and it required we eliminate your battleship, the *Hand of Justice*."

Aboard ships and the station, it clicked for many listeners. The mystery of the *Reunion*'s return, without the *Hand of Justice*, was solved, but not to anyone's pleasure, except for the rebels, who were cheering as they listened to corridor speakers that had been silent for decades, crackle to life.

"Your leaders aboard the *Reunion* heeded our warning, and the ship was allowed to return home without harm," Alex continued. "At this time, we have need of a temporary location while we negotiate a peace with your Supreme Tribunal. Idona Station has been chosen. There will be a slight inconvenience for all of you while we execute a landing. Soon afterward, you may resume your activities, with a few exceptions, of course."

Alex paused for a moment, and when he resumed his tone had hardened. "The instructions I give you now must be followed carefully for your safety and ours. We intend no one harm, but we will absolutely protect ourselves against any perceived threat. Captains, if you are in a bay or in dock, remain there; if you are on an approach vector, come to a zero delta-V relative to the station immediately and hold your position."

A grin crossed Alex's face as he considered his next instructions. "Now, for our friends in the militia aboard the station, we politely request you retreat to your headquarters and remain there. No exceptions. While we have a tendency to use stun guns if we feel threatened, we are likely to employ plasma rifles if we spot a militia uniform outside your headquarters."

Captain Yun and Lieutenant Morris glanced toward Major Lindling. The senior officer wore an ugly scowl and stared at the comms speaker as if doing so would silence the voice pouring forth. "Plasma rifles," Patrice Morris mouthed silently to her captain, worry written across her young face.

"To the owners, operators, and station personnel in the outer ring," Alex said, "Stay in your shops or rooms. Do not venture into the outer corridors for any reason. Finally, to the rebels in the inner ring and core ... I ask pardon for my use of the term; I have been given no other word by which to address you. Please stay in your areas for now. We will meet with your leaders soon. You have my word."

The tunnel rats slapped one another on the shoulders and punched arms. Jodlyne was hugged in joy by Edmas, and her teenage heart thundered in her chest. The rebel leaders exchanged looks, and more than one tear was shed in hope that the long fight might be over.

In contrast to the rebels' reactions, Major Lindling grabbed the comms speaker and ripped it from the wall. Captain Yum calmly switched the output to a secondary speaker next to his position. The major might wish to curtail the announcement, but Yun desperately wanted to hear everything the president had to say.

"To all, our entry and securing of the station might take several hours," Alex continued. "We have no intention of disrupting the commercial enterprises of this station while we are here. In fact, if we can help it flourish, we will do so. We will broadcast an all clear when activities can be safely resumed, with a list of exceptions that I mentioned previously. Proceed now to do as I have asked. You risk your safety and the safety of others for noncompliance."

While Alex broadcast his message, his people were performing multiple jobs. On board the fleet's ships, telemetry monitored all UE ship positions and the status of the station's docks and bays. Haraken captains, Sheila, and her staff monitored those views and that of the travelers' positions.

A UE freighter captain was dissuaded from continuing his approach, by three travelers who stood off his bow, their noses pointing at him. Watching the foreign ships travel backward only meters beyond his ship at his velocity scared him witless, and he screamed at his pilot to cease their approach.

One of the station's bay doors opened and a sleek yacht lifted from the interior's deck only to discover two travelers hovering just outside. Within moments, the pilot settled the yacht back onto the deck, and the bay doors slid closed.

The SADEs gained control of the station's operating systems for the bays — doors, cam views, ship statuses, and airlock controls. Julien signaled Tatia of their control, and she proceeded to make her own announcement to the station. Crews and passengers were warned to vacate the bays and given a time limit, by the station's clock. When the time passed, Tatia signaled the pilots who comprised the travelers' inner circle, and the SADEs opened a bay door for each ship.

* * *

Haraken pilots eased their travelers into the open bays. The doors remained open for their exit, which would soon follow. The fighters settled to the deck, hatches opened, and troopers poured out. Each wore an environment suit and was armed with stun gun and plasma rifle, such was the level of distrust of the Earthers, especially that of the UE militia.

The SADEs, each descending from a separate traveler, checked for electronic weapon emplacements and pronounced their bays clear.

The enormous Haraken carriers and the mass of strange ships surrounding their station, compounded by word that no ship was being allowed in or out of the station, finally convinced every person aboard the station to heed the Harakens' warnings. Not a single life was lost as the travelers landed.

When Tatia received the all clear from multiple sources, she let her irritated president up from his seat. Troopers were the first to pass through the airlocks accompanied by a SADE, if one was with them, and they ran reconnaissance, while the SADEs checked air quality and searched for contaminants, chemical and biological.

<I would recommend upgrading the station's air filtration system, Admiral,> Julien sent, <but other than that we can detect no danger.>

Once troopers and passengers had exited their craft, the traveler pilots eased out of the station's bays and joined the circling fighters to maintain the perimeter.

The SADEs had downloaded maps from the station's control banks and shared them to eliminate the Harakens wandering aimlessly through an unfamiliar station.

<Okay, people, you have your maps,> Tatia sent on open comm, <take the shortest route to the outer ring's main deck and spread out. Troopers, stay in groups of three, and stay in sight of the groups on both your flanks.

The SADEs calculated the curvature of the outer ring and the maximum distance between individuals before they would lose sight of one another due to the curvature. Multiplying by three, Tatia had come up with the minimum number of troopers she voted to take. Alex had objected to what he saw as an invasion, but those supporting Tatia, which was just about everyone else on Alex's staff, had their way. The SADEs and the twins had demurred from expressing an opinion, preferring to maintain positions of neutrality.

The troopers gained the station's main deck with its wide but empty corridor. They glanced about them, and it didn't matter whether they were Méridien or New Terran in origin, they all had the same thoughts. The corridor, despite its spacious size, was in a sad state of disrepair. Refuse, here and there, was tucked along its edges, surfacing was peeling from the overhead and upper bulkheads above the shops, and every few meters signs of moisture accumulation could be seen. From the shops and sleep quarters, the faces of the fearful and the curious peeked out.

Alex and Renée were surrounded by a mass of bodies. Tatia walked directly in front of Alex, acting as a shield, and the twins, Étienne and Alain, flanked Renée. Z, wearing his Cedric Broussard avatar, an immense New Terran design that rivaled Alex's mass and was armed in multiple ways, walked closely beside Alex.

The group was packed so closely together that Alex grew irritated at being bumped and jostled every time a noise was heard. Several times, the group froze so quickly that Alex bumped into Tatia's broad bottom. On the third occasion, Renée intervened before Alex's temper got the better of him.

<Wouldn't the two of you,> Renée sent to Alex and Tatia, <prefer to perform this particular act without clothes?>

Tatia glanced back at Alex and recognized the signs of a president ready to explode. <Okay, people,> Tatia sent to her group, <add a meter-and-a-half spread before the president fires us and leaves us behind on this sad excuse for a station.>

Implants seamlessly calculated distance by way of signal strength, and the troopers spread out away from their principals. A young girl, watching from her father's shop window, opened her mouth in an "oh," reminded of a flower blooming in a time-compression vid.

Tatia moved farther forward, but the twins stayed in position. Alex could accept that, but he eyed Z, in his Cedric avatar, who still hugged his side.

<You have beautiful eyes, Ser President,> Z deadpanned in response to Alex's stare, which broke Alex into a fit of laughter, requiring he brace a hand on Cedric's enormous shoulder.

<Julien and Cordelia,> Alex sent to Z as he caught his breath.

<Most intuitive, Ser President,> Z replied. <Julien said I was not to leave your side, under any circumstances, and when I pointed out you had the authority to order me away, Cordelia gave me several responses to offer as I saw fit. Although she explained the concept of absurdity, I was unsure how to apply it to her selections, so I chose the first one on the list.>

<And there you have it, Z,> Alex sent, <absurdity in its truest form.>

Z considered that for a few ticks, and the concept crystallized for him — an arbitrary relationship; no mathematical definition. He had participated in the idea without realizing it. His booming laughter echoed Alex's previous fit, and it froze the protection detail. No one had ever heard Z laugh in this manner, but it ended as abruptly as it had begun, when his protection algorithms resumed priority. The face of Cedric immediately smoothed, and his eyes resumed tracking the surroundings.

<I believe the world of the SADEs will intrigue us to the end of our lives,> Renée sent to Alex. It was one of those rare moments when Renée knew by Alex's expression that she had said something that troubled him. <Tell me,> she sent.

<I was thinking of Julien when I'm gone,> Alex sent back.

<He will miss you for the rest of his life ... and a long one it might be, but he will have Cordelia just as I have you.> Renée slipped her hands into Alex's and briefly laid her head against his arm. Around them the protection detail was on high alert with tension running deep, but Alex and Renée were a lifetime away, imagining their end and the SADEs living on without them.

* * *

<Admiral,> Julien signaled, <we've reached the militia's doors. They're locked down as we expected.>

Julien's team was the last to report to Tatia, but then his group had the farthest to walk from their traveler to reach their target. Tatia and her extended detail had only just reached the militia's doors on the opposite side from Julien. The Harakens hadn't encountered any opposition to their landing. It could be suggested that a strange human race that could destroy a UE battleship was to be feared.

Alex caught Tatia's glance and said to her, "Why are you looking at me, Admiral? I presume you and the SADEs have concocted some method of neutralizing the militia. If you're waiting for my permission, you have it."

Tatia grinned and nodded, signaling Julien and Z to proceed. The SADEs, each on their side, faced the massive doors that the militia had installed for their protection and attacked the militia's control systems through the comms system, which were interconnected with bay, dock, and station door controls as well as the militia's data systems.

Z located an operation's database for the militia's weapons maintenance, downloading the specification manuals and schematics. The files detailed their stunstiks and pellet air-compression rifles, used for crowd control, and Z shared his prizes with Julien.

Julien stripped the weapons schematics apart, including the ammunition, searching for weak points. He located one in a small chip that activated the firing mechanism on both weapons and passed his observations to Z. The two SADEs designed a nanites program with an extremely short lifespan to prevent interference with any other such chips that might be on board the station.

Z signaled his three associates, and the troopers stripped off their heavy packs, none as heavy as the 230-kilo pack Z carried, which to his Cedric avatar was inconsequential.

Alex and company watched in amusement while Z squatted on the deck and began assembling his machine.

"It's a miniature GEN machine," Renée exclaimed.

"Precisely, Ser," Z acknowledged.

The GEN machines were originally designed by Julien to help the New Terrans elevate their technological capabilities in order to produce the materials needed to repair the Méridien starship, the *Rêveur*, recovered by Alex. The products produced by the GEN machines marked the beginning of the crossover of Méridien technology to Alex's people, the New Terrans.

Z finished his machine's setup, added the newly designed program, loaded the machine with a pouch of generic nanites, and then sat absolutely still while he waited. As the time began to extend, Alex sat down beside Z to wait, and Tatia allowed the troopers to take a break, all but three, who were ordered to stand watch. She didn't consider communicating to the twins. The escorts would do what they considered best to protect their principals regardless of what she requested.

At 1.4 hours later, a soft chime sounded and Z extracted a small canister from the GEN machine, loading its contents into what resembled a plasma rifle, which was connected to a compressed air canister.

<Z, what's the isolation quality,> Alex sent. A moment later, he heard from Julien instead.

<Mr. President, I have been studying the layout of the militia's section. They have made heavy modifications to this section that they occupy and chose one that does not intersect with any of the station's central spokes. Air systems are isolated as are several other support systems. Z and I have programmed the nanites for a one-hour lifetime, and the nanites will only assemble on the target chips once several factors are met before they deactivate the chips on the militia's weapons.>

Alex linked Tatia and Z to his comm with Julien. <You're good to go, people.>

Z stepped up to the heavy door and activated his rifle. Rather than a short blast of plasma, a focused tip of constant energy soon cut a small hole through the heavy metal door. Z pulled back his rifle, yanked off the tip, and dropped it. When the plasma tip hit the deck, it sizzled, evaporating in a puddle of condensation. Several troopers winced at the thought of touching the extremely hot tip bare-handed.

Z sprayed a small canister of nitrogen on the hole, cooling it. Then, inserting a different tip on the rifle's open bore, Z pressed the barrel back into the hole. The group heard the sound of compressed air releasing as Z emptied his nanites canister. A countdown clock appeared in their implants, and Z pulled back his rifle, plugged the hole with a sealant compound, and began packing up his equipment.

Alex took Renée by the hand and walked over to a clean and dry portion of the corridor's bulkhead. He sat down, leaning against an upright, and Renée snuggled up next to him. Within several moments, both of them were fast asleep. Tatia and the twins regarded their two principals and smiled, shaking their heads.

When Alex's implant clocking app chimed the end of Z's countdown, he signaled Renée, and the two of them regained their feet. <Ready for entry, Z, Julien?> Alex asked.

<Ready,> both SADEs returned.

<All right, everyone,> Alex sent to the two teams on either side of the militia's doors. <I want a calm entrance, not a martial one. Everyone sling or holster your weapons.> When the people around Alex hesitated, looking to Tatia for confirmation, the team received a thundering <now> that reverberated through their implants and their minds, and every trooper jumped to obey.

Tatia offered Alex a cocked eyebrow. <I would have loved to have been able to issue an order like that to my New Terran troopers. Guess I just lacked the right equipment.>

The twins shared grins, enjoying the opportunity to experience the power of Alex's twin implants. Having been with Alex when he first received his implant, adopting it at the incredulous rate he did, the twins had witnessed greater and greater demonstrations of his implant capabilities with the passage of time. On one such occasion, Alex had mentally manipulated the fingers of two crew members via their implants to pull the triggers on e-switches simultaneously, allowing the *Rêveur* to exceed its drive restrictions and escape from certain destruction from the dark travelers rapidly closing in on the liner.

<We want a relaxed entrance,> Alex sent, <casual, nonthreatening. Am I understood, people?> Alex waited until he had received every affirmation, noting the twins failed to reply. At least they had holstered their stun guns, but they edged close to Alex and Renée. <We're ready, Z, Julien.>

* * *

After hearing the Haraken president's announcement, Major Lindling ordered his troops back to the militia's headquarters and ordered the doors sealed on every deck level. He assembled his people in the large open space on the main corridor deck. The space was intended for administrative use, but it now housed the militia's staging area and the armaments lockers. Every trooper was armed with a stunstik and a crowd-control rifle, but on the major's orders the troops had removed their helmets. Expecting their enemy to come at them from two different directions, the rigid helmets, which were connected to the shoulder and chest armor, would have restricted the troopers' views.

Major Lindling was ranting, swearing up a storm at his superiors, the Tribunal, and anyone else he could call to mind. Over the years, he had made multiple requests for heavier weaponry but had always been refused. The excuse was always that he and his people faced little danger. *How wrong they were,* the major thought for the umpteenth time in the last three hours.

When a point in one of the corridor doors began turning a bright red and a small hole appeared in its center, Major Lindling ordered his people into defensive positions. They had unhooked desks and other furniture from the deck and piled it high. The hole wasn't enlarged, and after nothing more happened, everyone relaxed and the major went back to fuming.

"What's with the hole?" Lieutenant Morris whispered to Captain Yun. Idona Station had been her first posting, and now she had thoughts that it might be her last.

"Doesn't make much sense, Lieutenant," Captain Yun whispered back. "They have an air hole. They could gas us at any time."

"Maybe they don't want to hurt us," Morris whispered back. The captain's scowl told her not to voice such absurd thoughts.

With most of the militia coming close to nodding off from the long wait, the heavy doors on both sides of the administrative space suddenly and silently slid open. The troops scrambled into defensive positions and held their collective breaths. Then, without fanfare, the militia watched an odd-looking collection of individuals stroll in with armed troopers backing them.

"Fire," Major Lindling yelled.

Alex hit his people with an implant pulse designed to stall their movements for just a moment, to prevent his people from reacting. Even the twins received the pulse. Later, the crèche-mates would compare notes, discussing what they should do in the future if it happened again. The oddest question would come from Étienne, who would ask his brother, "How was it for you?"

As Alex expected, nothing happened — no stun darts were fired; no pellets flew their way. The militia continued to pull the triggers of their weapons several more times and even began checking for ammunition loads.

Incensed, Major Lindling yelled, "Attack!" He climbed over the barricade of office furniture, brandishing his rifle like a club, and Alain, released from Alex's brief implant pulse, calmly shot the major with his stun gun. Unfortunately for Captain Yun, his training kicked in and he followed his superior. The captain now lay crumpled on the deck beside the major, felled by Étienne.

Tatia glanced at Alex, who stood with his hands clasped in front of him, waiting, and she chose to withhold further orders to her people.

The militia's troopers, looking decidedly uncertain, turned to regard Lieutenant Morris, who was crouched behind some chairs.

"Lieutenant," a sergeant whispered, "you're senior."

Lieutenant Morris stood, her legs visibly shaking, and eyed her senior officers lying comatose on the deck. Faced with the task of command,

Patrice Morris chose to be guided by her own initiative. For the first time in her brief career, she had no immediate superior; she could act as she believed the militia should have always behaved. "Put down your weapons," she said, but her order came out rather weakly. "Put down your weapons," Patrice barked loudly when no one had obeyed. Weapons clattered on the deck in response.

Patrice Morris scanned the two groups of strangers standing in front of the militia's barricade and picked out a large individual with clasped hands that one group was carefully arranged around. It was the two beautifully identical young men, flanking the large individual, who had dropped her superiors.

Lieutenant Morris placed her pellet rifle on the deck and awkwardly climbed over the barricade of chairs, walking as steadily as she could toward the large Haraken, *make that immense,* she amended, the closer she got to him. That a soft, lopsided smile formed on the face of the man she hoped was the president, caused her, for no reason that came to mind, to smile shyly in return.

<Ah, my love, you have such a way with women without even trying,> Renée sent privately to Alex.

<A good thing, my love. If I pursued them earnestly, I would be a miserable failure,> Alex replied.

Patrice stopped in front of the Haraken and extended her hand slowly. "I'm Lieutenant Morris, Sir. I would like to surrender the station to you, and I ask for clemency for my people."

"As Haraken's president, I accept your surrender, Lieutenant," Alex replied, shaking her hand.

Lieutenant Morris glanced down at her hand, seeing it enfolded inside Alex's considerable one, but she didn't flinch; just stood looking at their hands for a moment.

<Release the child's hand, my love, before she swoons to the deck. It would not be a propitious moment for her new command,> Renée sent to Alex.

Lieutenant Morris watched the president turn and beam at the incredibly attractive woman next to him. Patrice could sense the intense emotion shared in that moment between the two Harakens. *Would that someone would look at me like that someday,* Patrice thought.

"Well, Lieutenant Morris," Alex said, snapping the young woman's eyes back to him. "What do you think of your station?"

Lieutenant Morris was prepared to plead for the lives of her troopers. This certainly wasn't a question she was expecting, and the president appeared to be waiting for a sincere answer, and she scrambled to provide him one. "Sergeants Hanford and Diaz, step forward," she ordered firmly.

Two senior sergeants moved without hesitation, easily vaulting the barricade, and hurried to snap to attention before their lieutenant. But their eyes flicked from her to the president and the stun guns strapped to the legs of the twins, who returned their glances with calm determination.

"President Racine is inquiring into the status of our station," Morris said. "Please update him on dock and bay usage, maintenance, and systems problems."

Alex stood patiently while the two sergeants droned on for a while listing problem after problem, before he finally held up his hand. "Quite a mess you have on your hand, Lieutenant," Alex said. "I suggest you get started."

"I beg your pardon, Mr. President," Morris said.

"Sir," Sergeant Diaz, the enlisted men's senior noncom, said, saluting Alex, "we will be happy to get started on these projects immediately, and we appreciate your lenience with the troops." When his lieutenant remained dumbfounded at what was transpiring, the sergeant scowled slightly at her and flicked his eyes at Alex, which finally galvanized Patrice.

"Yes, thank you, Mr. President. We'll prioritize the work, but with our small number of troops, it will take many months, if not a year, to complete the entire list, and there is the question of adequate parts and supplies," Morris said.

"Not to worry, Lieutenant," Alex answered with a generous smile. "You'll have a great deal of help as soon as I speak to the rebels."

"The rebels, Sir?"

"Yes, Lieutenant, or don't you believe they have a stake in the welfare of this station?" Alex asked.

"Yes, they do ... but, President Racine, they don't like us," Morris replied. That her comment elicited smiles and a few snickers among the president's people bothered her, but not as much as the prospect of facing the rebels.

"Then I suggest you be extra nice to them, Lieutenant. I won't tolerate fighting. That's a walk through an unconnected airlock. Am I understood?" Alex asked.

The man's commanding tone galvanized Patrice Morris to jump to attention. "Yes, Mr. President," she said. "One more question, Sir. Do you wish to collect our weapons?"

"Negative, Lieutenant, they're inoperable," Alex replied. "Now get this place cleaned up and your doors open on every deck. I want your section to look like an administration and aid location before today ends."

When Alex turned away, his people flowed out of his way in a manner that indicated they knew he was going to turn, and they knew where one another stood. *Weird,* Morris thought. "Well, Sergeants, you heard the man. Jump to it," Morris ordered.

Both sergeants gave Lieutenant Morris big grins and slapped each other on the shoulders as they began issuing their own orders. Patrice Morris leaned against an overturned shelving unit to brace her shaky legs. Nothing in her training had prepared her for this situation. Before the administration doors had swung open, she was sure she was dead. Now, she thought there was hope, at least for today. *Tomorrow's another thing,* Patrice thought.

-6-

"You wanted the station, Mr. President, and now you have it." Tatia said as they walked back down the main corridor, leaving the militia busy resetting the administration offices. "How long are we planning to stay?"

"At Idona?" Alex asked.

"At Sol?"

"How long would you be willing to stay, Admiral, if it continued to keep Haraken safe?" Alex asked in return.

"But, what's the plan, Alex?" Tatia complained.

When Tatia reverted to using Alex's first name, he recognized the symptoms of growing frustration on his admiral's part and stopped to give Tatia his undivided attention.

"What do you see, Admiral?" Alex asked, waving his arms around him, indicating the entire station.

Knowing Alex and she were about to have one of their strategic-tactics conversations, for which they were famous, Tatia gave his question careful consideration. The station's deterioration was evident, but that it had been allowed to reach this condition, considering it sat at a key system's crossroad, according to the UE scientists, made no sense, economically speaking.

"I see a stalemate between enemies … a totalitarian government and a rebellious faction," Tatia answered.

"Now, how has that condition affected Idona?" Alex asked, his eyes staring intently into Tatia's.

"The station's deteriorating conditions reflect a situation in which no side is in a position to win. It's a stalemate to the detriment of both sides."

"Precisely, as the SADEs would say," Alex said, slapping Tatia on the shoulder, creating a resounding thwack. "I admit I didn't see past our landing, but the station's condition gave me an idea. We can't win a war against the UE, but maybe … just maybe … we can win a peace with the people of Sol and force the Tribunal to the bargaining table."

"Just how do you expect to make that happen?"

"The tribunes will succumb when we overpower them with prosperity," Alex said, winking at her, walking off to catch up with Julien, whom he saw exiting from a side corridor.

Somehow, Alex had thought he had answered Tatia's question, but, at the moment, she was fairly sure that either she hadn't heard it correctly or hadn't understood it.

Étienne and Alain hurried to keep pace with Alex. Having overheard Alex and Tatia's conversation, Alain quipped privately to his crèche-mate. <Definitely a madman.>

<Wonderful times, brother,> Étienne replied, and the twins' faces lit with infectious grins.

* * *

When the UE explorer ship, *Reunion*, returned to Sol, exiting FTL and heading in system, a second mate on a docked freighter at Idona had passed a secret transmission to the rebels, and a buzz raced through the community. But a second message passed to the rebels that the *Reunion* was running silent, refusing all hails by ships and stations, was met with confusion and anxiety.

During the following days, news of the *Hand of Justice* was expected, but the battleship never appeared behind the explorer ship. Rumors from freighter captains and station shop owners were passed to the rebels that aliens were discovered in a far distant world and might have destroyed the UE battleship. Speculation ran rampant about the future of the UE, having disturbed a powerful enemy.

Over time, the rumors faded, except for one story that took root and persisted. It originated from Earth after the *Reunion* made orbit and the crew was transferred planetside, which gave it credence. It read, not aliens — humans.

To the rebels, this possibility was exciting. Humans out among the stars represented a hope, and the rebels discussed and argued as to what these humans might do and whom they might side with if they visited Sol. Questions without answers provided endless hours of debate. Would the UE send fleets back to the new humans' worlds? Would the absence of the fleets offer an opportunity for them? Could this be the time to retaliate?

The truth of the matter was that the system's remaining rebels held only pockets of resistance aboard stations or in underground colonies, and they were woefully weak after long decades of fighting, worn down by a war of attrition. Retaliation was a dying hope for them, a dream. The time had long passed for the rebels to defeat the UE with force.

The average Earther was a different creature, not outwardly rebellious against the government but harboring no love for the UE. Many had lost family members or friends to the UE's harsh policies. They performed their daily jobs faithfully and kept their heads down. Some only thought contrary opinions about the UE, and others crept carefully across the restriction lines to deliver messages and supplies to rebel outposts.

As time wore on following the *Reunion*'s return, rebel excitement dampened, the stories becoming stale and repetitive — until a few days ago. A station restaurant owner passed a message to a tunnel rat, Edmas, to deliver to Nicolette "Nikki" Fowler, the leader of Idona Station's rebels. Nikki's grandfather was Idona Station's last legitimate station director before he fled the outer ring to take up residence in the inner ring as the UE militia landed. The restaurateur's message was brief but shattering: alien ships were spotted entering the system and were headed for Idona.

Nikki reread the message several times. She was a proponent of the argument that the distant humans might represent hope for the rebels. *Be careful what you wish for, Nikki,* she thought. *You might just get more than you want.*

Finally, Nikki passed the message to her second, Vic Lambert, for him to distribute to the tunnel rats, who acted as the rebels' message runners. The rebels hadn't trusted the comms system since the day Nikki's grandfather sealed the connecting doors leading to the outer ring and threatened the militia with the destruction of the station if they touched the doors.

* * *

Nikki and Vic were speaking to the aeroponics department head, who was pleading for more shipments of water and nutrients for the food banks, when the bulkhead speakers crackled to life. The rebels ducked into a crouch, searching for adversaries. In their minds, there was no other reason for the speakers' activation than as a ruse by the militia to disguise their breach of the connecting doors.

Before Nikki could order her people into defensive positions, she heard, "Captains, militia, and personnel in and around Idona Station, I'm Alex Racine, president of Haraken." She and the others listened intently to the message, fear and hope entwined in their thoughts. Then, when the president addressed them, cheering broke out so loudly that Vic had to scream for quiet to allow Nikki to hear the rest of the announcement.

"The surveillance room," Nikki shouted when the message ended and broke into a run. Rebels jumped aside as Nikki raced down the corridors.

Over the decades, the rebels secreted vid cameras at key points in the outer ring to monitor the militia. Nikki found the tiny surveillance room packed tight with bodies and ordered the room cleared. She posted teams to monitor the cameras and call her when the Harakens, as the strangers referred to themselves, entered the station.

Hours later, Vic interrupted Nikki in a meeting. When she looked up at him, Vic nodded in the direction of the surveillance room, and Nikki excused herself to follow him out.

The surveillance room was crowded again, but the rebels made room for Nikki and Vic, having saved a pair of worn-out chairs at the console for them. It didn't take long before the room began overheating as everyone waited anxiously for the moment when the Harakens appeared on the first camera. When they did, there were gasps and intakes of breath as the strangers walked undisturbed down a main corridor.

"Look at what they're carrying," one rebel said. "What fools bring plasma rifles on board a station?"

"The kind who means business," another answered.

"Milt piss, will you look at the size of those people?" Jodlyne asked.

"Jodlyne, watch your mouth," Vic reprimanded.

"But not all of them," the group heard.

"Yeah, some look a little thin … but pretty," another said.

"Pretty? Try exquisite," someone added.

"Him," Nikki said, touching the screen. "That's this group's leader. I don't know if he's the president we heard, but look how they're protecting him."

"Nikki, seriously?" Vic challenged. "You think these people's president would land in the first wave? I'd take bets he wouldn't." No one took Vic up on his offer. Everyone was too busy staring at the monitors.

Silence reigned when the rebels saw the group they were watching stop at the militia's doors. When the Harakens settled down to wait while the huge man assembled his machine, many of the rebels left to sit in the corridor and allow the small room to cool.

Inside the surveillance room, rebels were focusing on their favorite individuals on screen. Two tunnel rats were fixated on the man assembling the machine.

"Milt piss, Edmas. Look at the size of that one guy. He's as big as a patrol boat," Jodlyne whispered.

"Be safe to be around him," Edmas whispered back, "Milts wouldn't mess with us then." The two rats snickered until they caught Vic's scowl.

Two systems engineers switched a monitor to pick up a cam from an opposing direction to observe the machine being assembled. They whispered their conjectures to each other, one engineer guessing it was a breach explosive to blow the militia's doors.

"Can't be," the other engineer whispered back. "They're outnumbered by the militia six to one. They'd lose a straight-up fight unless they're stupid enough to use those plasma rifles. Then you can kiss a big portion of the outer ring goodbye."

"Here they go," Vic announced later when the Harakens' breach operation began. Those waiting in the corridor piled back into the room. But the rebels were forced to wait again when nothing extraordinary happened.

"Gas," one engineer whispered to another. Unfortunately, in the tiny room, everyone heard him, and rebel blood was chilled.

"Milt piss," Jodlyne whispered, and no one bothered to correct her.

Nikki wasn't concerned with the machine or the machine's maker. Her eyes followed the man she thought was the group's leader and watched him lead the exotic woman to the corridor's edge, settle down against a bulkhead, and throw an arm around her as she snuggled next to him. *You're one vacuum-chilled customer,* she thought.

When the Harakens' operations resumed, the militia's doors slid open without fanfare. Doubt and confusion spread through the rebels. Visibility into the administration area was limited, and although the pinhead cameras couldn't transmit audio, the militia could be seen alive and well behind their barricade.

"There goes any chance of rescue," Vic stated soberly when he saw the major shout and the militia raise their weapons to fire.

Nothing happened, and the strangers walked in slowly, with weapons slung. The rebels broke out in loud discussions, and Nikki raised her hand, which triggered Vic's shout for silence.

"Watch carefully, everyone," Nikki said. "There's more going on here than we're thinking. Let's learn what we can."

In the next moment, they watched the major and then the captain jump into view and crumple to the deck.

"What hit them?" an engineer asked.

"Didn't see anything," another rebel replied.

The rebels were glued to the monitors, watching the situation unfold. At the door to the surveillance room, someone was whispering updates to those in the corridor, and the messages were passed along to the hundreds who had abandoned their jobs to learn firsthand about the strangers.

Despite expectations, nothing resembling a fight occurred. But curiosity became disappointment when they witnessed Lieutenant Morris shake the hand of the Haraken leader, eliciting groans from most in the room.

"Bastards, they're joining the milts," Vic swore softly.

"Maybe, maybe not," Nikki said thoughtfully. "Let's wait and see." She wasn't sure that Vic wasn't right, but it was her job to keep her people calm.

* * *

After neutralizing the militia, Alex's mind was churning with ideas as to how to achieve his goal. He ordered the UE scientists transferred from the *No Retreat.* When they disembarked from a traveler, they were escorted to Alex by troopers with slung plasma rifles, not that any of them would have considered firing the deadly weapons and not that the station people would ever know that.

The rifles were carried for their intimidation factor in hopes of preventing the foolish from starting a fight, especially since the Harakens considered the UE forces as prime examples of fools. But, just in case, every trooper carried a stun gun set to maximum.

Alex requested Cordelia and Z find suitable headquarters and asked Julien to remain for an extended discussion, which caused Julien a moment of anxiety. The protective teams were disbanding except for a small one remaining with Alex, Renée, and Tatia.

<You need not be concerned, Julien,> Cordelia sent to him and Z, <I'll remain close to Z. What situations I can't talk my way out of will provide Z with an opportunity to test his protective devices.>

<Fear not, Julien,> Z added. <It will be my pleasure to ensure Cordelia's safety.>

Julien and Cordelia were witnessing ever more blending of the Miranda Leyton persona, Z's undercover femme fatale alternative, in Z's mannerism. The change was welcomed, but it gave both SADEs pause to wonder how much their personalities might be evolving.

"Julien," Alex said, interrupting their communication, "I need an in-depth analysis of this station. The core question is: How do we reinvigorate this place? After Cordelia and Z locate us a headquarters, pull them into your analyses."

"Do I understand that you wish this station to become a profitable, working enterprise, Mr. President?" Julien asked.

"Precisely, Julien," Alex said, laying a comradely hand on Julien's shoulder.

"You do realize, Mr. President, that when the SADEs backed your initiative to come to Sol, our reliance on your strategic thinking was predicated on more than discovering you have chosen to become a station operator." Without waiting for a reply, Julien headed for the militia's administrative office, and two troopers fell in beside him. A straw panama formed over Julien's head, reminiscent of a millennium-ago, Earth plantation owner, and one trooper grinned at the other as he flicked his eyes toward Julien's head.

* * *

Julien walked into the militia's administrative headquarters and sought out Lieutenant Morris.

In the few hours since the Harakens' absence, the militia had returned the place to its original condition, storing their crowd-control rifles, although they still carried their stunstiks.

"What do your men intend to do with those, Lieutenant," Julien asked, nodding toward a corporal who held his stunstik in front of him.

"We … we might have need …" Morris began, and then stumbled to a halt. "Sergeant Diaz!" she shouted.

"Ma'am," the sergeant said, coming to attention in front of her.

"Our guests don't appreciate us carrying our stunstiks as batons. Store them, Sergeant," Morris ordered.

Sergeant Diaz glanced only briefly toward the plasma rifles slung on the Harakens' shoulders and shouted, "Store all stunstiks, now!"

"You realize, mister … um —" Morris began.

"The name is Julien. No mister. Just Julien, Lieutenant."

"You realize, Julien, that we'll be at the mercy of the rebels," Morris said.

"Haven't they been at your mercy, Lieutenant?" Julien asked. "It does make for an argument that the first step one should take when meeting other individuals is their treatment with the best of intentions. It prevents the whole retaliation mindset; don't you agree?" Julien didn't allow the lieutenant to ponder his statements before he said, "Now, Lieutenant, I require a complete overview of the station's economic operations. Might we have the privacy of an office?"

Julien queried Lieutenant Morris for more than an hour, developing an overview of the station's operations, fee basis, and credit flow. What he learned was that the station was practically impoverished. The fees for docking, bays, and ship services that were intended to maintain the station were confiscated by the militia with the majority of the funds funneled back to Earth.

Furthermore, since the militia took over the station, freighter and passenger liner stops had dropped to less than half of their high, from decades ago, so as to prevent adding to the UE's coffers. Instead, ships often met in the deep dark and used shuttles to exchange people and cargo. It was a time-consuming and dangerous process, but the alternative was unforgivable to many captains.

While Julien and Morris were talking, Major Lindling burst through the office door with Captain Yun right behind him. They were brought up short by the stun guns, which were stuck in their faces.

"Troopers, stand down," Julien ordered calmly.

"I'm the commanding officer aboard this station. You people need to deal with me," Major Lindling huffed.

"Other decisions were made in your absence, Major," Julien replied. "My president put Lieutenant Morris in charge."

Patrice Morris, who had jumped up when the major plowed through the door, eyed Lindling, then Julien, unsure of what to do or say. So she stood still and kept her mouth shut.

"What do you mean in my absence? You people shot me," the major declared.

"Circumstances which you precipitated, Major, or did you not jump the barricade to attack my president?"

"If you think you can get away —" Major Lindling started to say, but the words died in his mouth. One moment the man he was speaking to was sitting relaxed in an office chair and before Lindling could utter his next word, the man was standing in front of him nose to nose. Lindling heard an intake of breath from his captain behind him.

Julien studied the major's face for a moment, letting the fear he generated sink in. "I knew a man like you once, Major. He went by the name of Clayton Downing. I didn't like him either. Now, you have a choice, Ser. Work under Lieutenant Morris's direction or we'll find a nice, quiet place to stow you while we're here, but I warn you we might be here quite a while."

Major Lindling scowled and then loosed a low growl as he exited the office.

"How about you, Captain?" Julien asked.

"I'm happy to take guidance from Lieutenant Morris, Sir," Captain Yun said, still trying to process how the human moved so incredibly and uncannily fast. His movement was one thing, but his stop in front of the major was frighteningly sudden and still. *Maybe we only think they're human,* Yun thought.

"Take a seat, Captain," Morris directed as she sat back down. "Julien has questions for us about the station's financial operations. I'm sure that you could add to the discussion."

The two militia officers had just sat back down when they watched the straw hat on Julien's head disappear and a felt fedora replace it.

Julien gave the militia officers a nasty grin. "I do hope that if the major causes any problems or foments an insurrection against the lieutenant's command, it will be dealt with quickly." He was pleased to see both officers nodding vigorously. *I had better warn Alex about the major,* Julien thought.

-7-

Nikki, Vic, and several other rebels took turns monitoring the Harakens around the clock for a full day. They thought their surveillance was being conducted in secret until one of the Harakens, the one wearing a strange head cover, went past a hidden cam, looked up at it, and winked.

"That can't be a coincidence," Vic said. "Do they know we're watching?"

"I suspect they know and don't care," Nikki said.

"Look at that far monitor on the right," a rebel said. "The one with those two milts."

The room's occupants leaned over to peer at two troopers, who stripped off their uniform shirts, exposing the top of their unitards.

"What are they doing?" Vic asked.

"Those two have been standing beside that resurfacer for the longest. I think they're reading the instructions."

The room burst into laughter at the image of the two troopers bent over a tablet and flicking through pages.

"I don't see a primer machine," said another rebel. "Do you think they would be stupid enough to start resurfacing the bulkheads without stripping and priming first?"

"These are milts," Vic replied, an undercurrent of anger evident. "Who knows what they're capable of screwing up."

Suddenly the central monitor's view of the militia's admin doors blanked, and the man Nikki had identified as a Haraken group leader appeared on the screen. His voice issued from the room's speakers, which were part of the station's comms system.

"I'm Alex Racine, the Haraken president, and I would like to speak with your leader."

"Can he see us?" Vic whispered to Nikki, who pointed to a cam in the room's upper corner next to the comms speaker.

"I'm Nicolette Fowler. My friends call me Nikki, and I'm the one you want to speak to," Nikki replied.

"Excellent, Ser Fowler, may we meet and discuss our mutual interests?" Alex asked.

"Why would we trust you, President Racine? You think that just because you have the militia pretending to do some maintenance we should be swooning at your feet in thanks?" Nikki asked. She expected protestations or some clever response from the president but was surprised when the big man simply shrugged his shoulders and said, "Actually, can't think of a good reason why you should trust us." Now, Nikki wasn't sure what to say or ask.

"May I present my case?" Alex asked. When Nikki didn't respond, Alex began anyway. "I believe that we need each other. The militia isn't sufficient in number and is not skilled enough to accomplish my goals. I need many more skilled personnel. You, on the other hand, need access to the outer ring, food, and supplies."

"Let's back up, Mr. President," Nikki said. "Why are you here, and what do you want with this station?"

The camera view widened, which shocked the rebels that the Harakens were controlling their cam systems. In the extended view, the rebels saw a broad woman in uniform seated beside the president.

"I'm Admiral Tatia Tachenko, Ser Fowler, and I find it amusing that you should be asking the president the very same questions I asked him just yesterday. Admittedly, I didn't understand his answer. Perhaps you will have better fortune."

Nikki and Vic exchanged momentary glances. It occurred to both of them that they were ill-prepared to deal with the Harakens, whose manner of speaking and attitudes were so far removed from their culture.

"To be candid, Ser Fowler, it's against my nature to see any ship or station in a state of disrepair," Alex said.

"A spacer," Nikki said.

"Guilty," Alex replied. "Captain of an explorer-tug."

"An explorer-tug captain who rises to the position of president by your age," Vic challenged. "What did you do? Find a bunch of people and declare yourself president?"

Vic's comment generated a great deal of laughter, which the rebels heard over the comms speakers. It was clear that there were many more people in the room with the president than were in the cam's view. Nikki kept her eyes on President Racine, who appeared embarrassed by Vic's accusation.

"It's a long story, Ser Fowler, best saved for another time," Alex replied.

"You still haven't answered my questions, Mr. President," Nikki said.

"The simple answers are that I'm trying to prevent a full-scale war, and I'm planning to use this station as a proof of concept."

"What concept?" Nikki asked.

"That peace leads to greater prosperity than war."

"Peace between who ... your people and the UE?" Nikki asked.

"Why no, Ser Fowler, between your people and the UE," Alex replied.

Again, Nikki found herself without a reply. She stared at the screen, but in her mind images from the last several days played — the president's announcement about what the UE had done while in his world, his regret at destroying a battleship, the taking of the station without a single death, and the militia now attempting to clean and repair the station, as poorly as they were accomplishing that.

"Where do you want to meet?" Nikki asked flatly. Her comment elicited a melee of discussion around her until she held her hand high, which shut it down.

"I've established my headquarters at an engaging location called the Last Stop. We had to open and restore it before talking up residence, and I apologize that I don't know who to pay for our accommodations."

"That would be my grandfather's place," said an engineer, who stepped behind Nikki.

"Then we will owe you the credits, Ser. Please see me at your earliest convenience, and we will arrange the transfer," Alex replied.

"With whose credits and how?" Vic challenged again. "Our people have never had accounts or credits, for that matter, and our ancestors had their accounts confiscated when they fled the militia's landing. And what type of credits could you have that would be of use to us?"

"All good questions, Ser, and I will be happy to explain those to your satisfaction when we meet."

"Mr. President, a station spoke exits into the outer ring 19 degrees, counterclockwise from your location. I'll meet you on the main corridor in thirty minutes by the station's clock," Nikki said, leaving the room, and causing most of the rebels to chase after her.

* * *

The Harakens arranged themselves in front of the massive safety doors that separated the outer ring from the giant spoke that led to the station's interior workings. Each of the two doors was a full 3 meters wide and substantially constructed. The wait extended to an hour before they heard motors engage and gears grind. The doors lurched apart a few centimeters, halted, and then lurched a few more centimeters. The process continued off and on until the doors were open about a third of a meter.

Z stepped up to the opening and peeked through. "Please step back, Sers, while I see if I might be of help." He crossed his arms to grasp the edge of each door in an attempt to pull them apart, and while they creaked in protest, they opened only another third of a meter.

Examining the opening, Z turned his body to place his hands behind him and grasp one door's edges with both hands. Then he levered his body up into the air by planting both feet against the far door. Suspended horizontally by his hands, feet, and back, he shoved. The doors groaned and screeched in protest but began slowly moving. Z kept the pressure up until the door opening was about one and a half meters.

Vic was staring at Z as he released his grip on the doors and stood upright again. "Are you human?" Vic asked.

In Miranda's sultry voice, Z replied, "Oh, my dear, I'm so much more." Then Z quickly resumed his place beside Renée. When Z noticed the rebels were frozen in place, he sent a query to Alex and Renée, who were busy hiding smiles behind their hands. <I thought to keep the rebels off balance, Sers. Perhaps, I miscalculated.>

Nikki took tentative steps through the opening, her eyes scanning for trouble. When Vic failed to immediately follow, several rebels prodded him from behind. One by one the rebels slipped through the safety doors, and then more quickly flowed through until over 100 rebels had poured through the opening.

<Back up, people,> Alex sent on open comm. <Give them room. I don't want them to feel crowded.>

"Greetings, Ser Fowler," Alex said when Nikki stopped in front of him. "I'm President Racine."

Nikki eyed the huge hand held out by the president. A lifetime of experience told her to run away and seek the safety of the inner ring. She couldn't conceive of any good coming from this meeting, except now the safety doors they depended on were breached and probably stuck open for the foreseeable future.

Alex continued to hold out his hand even as his arm began to tire.

<Patience, my love,> Renée sent privately to Alex. <She has waited all her life for a moment such as this one. You can hold out your hand until she takes it.>

Nikki let out a slow, long breath, and resigned herself to fate. She was tired of the fight and hoped for a better future for her people and herself. She slipped her hand inside the president's and received a warm, friendly handshake.

"Ser Fowler, I see some of your people are carrying stunstiks," Alex said. "For the safety of your people and mine, I must insist we collect them."

"Who says we're staying?" Vic growled, stepping forward toward Alex. His movement elicited subtle responses from Alex's people.

"We're staying, Vic," Nikki commanded, having caught the movements of those intent on defending the president. "Unless you're prepared to close the safety doors that he … or she opened," Nikki added, indicating Z.

It was at this moment that two rebel engineers on the periphery of the crowd spotted the same two militia personnel who they had seen previously on the surveillance cams improperly applying the resurfacing machine.

"Hey, you two milts, stop that," one engineer called out, which drew everyone's attention toward the engineers and the militia.

Only eighteen and twenty, the young militia cowered as the engineers strode toward them and readied themselves to accept their due — a severe beating.

<Stand still,> Alex sent to his people. He eyed Nikki, who in turn was watching him for his reaction. In fact, both groups, Harakens and rebels, were torn between watching the engineers bearing down on the militia youths, and the two leaders staring at each other as if each one was waiting to see who would make the first move.

"Where'd you get this machine?" one engineer asked the two militia youths. "And stop cringing. You'd think we were going to beat you. That's something you milts do."

While the eighteen year old stammered out corridor and storage room numbers, the second engineer called back to two rebel techs to join them. With an imperial hand, the first engineer waved the youngest milt to lead on, and the six men walked off down the main corridor. Everyone could hear one of the engineers lecturing the militia on proper resurfacing procedures and the need to strip, seal, and prime the metal surfaces first.

Nikki spared a brief glance at the retreating backs of the six men and then looked at Vic, who said, "Okay, I guess we're staying."

"Everyone," Nikki shouted, "give up your weapons — stunstiks, fighting blades — everything. Now!"

The troopers moved among the rebels thanking them politely for turning in their weapons.

"We'll need to process your people, Ser Fowler," Alex said. "With their identities, we can create station accounts for them, pay credits for their work, and —"

Before Alex could finish, Vic interrupted, saying, "Nikki, we're moving too fast. How do we know —?"

But Vic was cut off by Nikki's hand held up to his face. "President Racine, could you tell me how you took over militia headquarters without killing anyone?" The question had been nagging Nikki. It wasn't just the method the Harakens used; it was why they had done it that way.

"Certainly, Ser Fowler," Alex replied. "But I can't take any credit. The SADEs did all the work with nanites targeting the chips in the militia's weapons."

"I'm sorry, what? SADEs? Nanites?" Nikki asked dubiously.

"That's another long story, Ser Fowler, one best saved for another time. If you and I could sit and speak, Ser Fowler?" Alex asked politely. "My people need only a name and a profession from each of your people to begin the process I spoke of earlier."

"All right, Mr. President. Let's talk, but Vic comes too," Nikki replied.

"Certainly, Ser, and if you could have two of your senior engineers and your head of food production accompany us, it will make our meeting much more productive."

As it was, requesting some additional senior people to accompany Nikki was moot — most of the rebels trooped after them, wanting to hear firsthand what the alien president had to say. During Alex's meeting, he found his statements were consistently confusing the rebel leaders. His mind was racing ahead with ideas that might energize the station, and they were still trying to come to grips with their newfound freedom and what the future might bring.

At one point, Nikki held up her hands to stop Alex. "Wait, wait," she said. "What about the future? Say we help you fix up the station. What happens when the UE comes?"

"That's the point, Ser," Alex replied with a generous smile. "I want the UE to come."

"See what I mean, Ser Fowler," said Tatia, sitting beside Alex. "You hear his words, but then again, you don't."

-8-

"What are you prepared to do about this?" Major Lindling demanded during his call to Captain Reiko Shimada aboard the UE destroyer *Conquest.*

"I sympathize with you, Major, but if President Racine put Lieutenant Morris in charge, I'm in no position to contradict his orders," Shimada replied.

"But you have a destroyer, Captain!" Lindling cried out.

Captain Shimada took a deep breath before answering the major. That she thought the man was an ass did not change the fact that on Idona Station he was the senior militia officer as far as the UE was concerned, regardless of what the Haraken president had done.

"Major, maybe you haven't reviewed the data on these strangers' fighters. At least we believe these are fighters because of the way they behave, even though they don't look or move anything like ours. The Harakens have the numbers on their side, and their fighters are incredibly fast and maneuverable. One false move on my part, and I believe my destroyer and all aboard would be space dust."

"Captain Shimada, you do realize —"

"Apologies, Major, but I have an incoming call from President Racine. We will speak later." A small smile spread on Shimada's face when, on her hand signal, the comms officer cut the connection. *Who would have thought a call from the enemy would be so pleasantly timed?* Shimada thought. Despite the impression she gave Major Lindling, Shimada was in constant contact with Lieutenant Morris, but she would have been surprised to know that what she thought were private conversations were carefully monitored by the Haraken SADEs.

"And to what do I owe this unexpected call, President Racine?" Shimada asked when the comms officer signaled the audio connection was ready.

"I trust you and your people are well, Captain. Do you require any assistance from the station?" Alex asked.

"President Racine, pardon me for pointing this out, but for a conqueror, you have no idea how to act," Shimada replied.

Alex could hear the smile in Shimada's voice. He appreciated the level-headedness and no-nonsense attitude of the captain. *Not very UE-like,* Alex thought. "Perhaps, I've been watching the wrong vids. You might help me out by recommending something."

This time Shimada couldn't control herself, and she burst out laughing at the idea of educating the Haraken president on how to be mercenary. When she regained control, she said, "You know, Mr. President, I can't cooperate with your enterprise … if rumors are true. It would mean my head."

"But you already have cooperated, Captain. Your destroyer with all crew aboard retreated from the vicinity."

"That decision I can defend."

"So be it, Captain, but I do need your help on another matter. I need you to contact the Supreme Tribunal for me."

"I can send a message for you, Mr. President," Shimada said. "What do you wish me to say?"

"That's not what I'm requesting, Captain," Alex replied, "We have an FTL relay on the Earth's moon. I want you to comm the Tribunal as if you were in Earth's orbit. My people will handle the technicalities." Alex waited for a response, but he heard nothing. "Captain?"

"Sorry, Mr. President," Shimada finally replied. Her comms officer had mouthed "FTL comms" to her twice as if he hadn't heard correctly. "This is a bit much to process. I would like to help, but I don't have direct access to the Tribunal. The best I could do is place a comm to naval headquarters on Earth and request access, but even that might not work."

"Why not, Captain?"

"They would probably think it's a hoax or that I'm an impostor."

"Please try anyway, Captain."

Alex left the next steps in the hands of the SADEs, who intercepted the captain's comm and routed it through the FTL relay on the Earth's moon as Shimada contacted Earth's naval headquarters.

Naval comms techs challenged Shimada several ways to ensure they were speaking to the captain of the *Conquest* stationed at Idona. They had been warned to expect a comm from Idona, even though the idea seemed ridiculous. The Tribunal was still keeping the foreign device deposited by the Haraken fighter a secret.

Identity confirmed, the captain was passed up the chain of command, and then transferred to the Supreme Tribunal's location. At that point, Julien notified Alex that the captain's comm had reached the intended audience, and the SADEs had identified the Tribunal's physical location.

* * *

The comms officer on duty at the Tribunal's retreat expected to speak to Captain Shimada. Instead, he heard, "Greetings, Ser. This is the Haraken president, Alex Racine. I would like to speak to your Supreme Tribunal."

"One moment, Mr. President," the officer replied. Opening a private channel to the Tribunal's chambers, he announced, "Tribunes, the comm you're expecting is happening. You've a call from the strangers at Idona Station. The man on the comm says he's President Racine of the Harakens."

"Ask him to wait a moment while we assemble," Tribune Woo ordered. "And hustle Captain Lumley to our chambers immediately."

The tribunes hurried to gather around a comms monitor and seated Captain Lumley behind them to quietly advise. When they were ready, Woo signaled the comms officer, but instead of the audio comm they expected, the Harakens commandeered both vid and audio signals.

"Greetings, Sers. You have been given my name. How may I address you?" asked Alex, whose head and shoulders filled the tribunes' monitor.

"And Captain Lumley!" Alex exclaimed. "I'm so pleased to see that you made it back safely. How is our mutual acquaintance, Speaker García?"

Lucchesi and Brennan were flummoxed by their inclusion in a two-way vid transmission and the president's quick switch in topics. On the other hand, Woo, who had studied Lumley's reports in detail, had taken the captain's advice about whom he expected would call. Intellectually, she was as ready for the president as she could be. When Lumley looked at her for permission to respond, she nodded encouragingly.

"I'm well, President Racine," Lumley replied. "I wish to thank you again for sparing my ship and my crew."

"Always willing to accommodate a reasonable man," Alex replied with a smile that never reached his eyes. "And how is our unreasonable friend?" Alex pressed.

Woo nodded to Lumley to continue, and the captain said, "There was an accident aboard the *Reunion*, President Racine. Speaker García did not survive."

"Hmm … I wonder what exchange High Judge Bunaldi and Speaker García are enjoying now," Alex mused for his audience. "Probably regretting their hasty decisions. Ah well, to business, Sers."

"What do you want with our station?" Lucchesi demanded.

"And you would be —?" Alex asked.

"I'm Supreme Tribune Giuseppe Lucchesi. These are my colleagues … Tribune Ian Brennan and Tribune Kwan Woo," Lucchesi said, puffing up in his chair.

Alex took in the tribunes' robes so similar to the high judge and wondered what had given rise to the affectation. "Tribune Lucchesi, you remind me of an Earther I met. By any coincidence, are you an ex-high judge?"

"I have that honor," Lucchesi said.

"Thought as much," Alex replied, but the look on his face said he wasn't pleased to hear it. "Well, you asked a question, Tribune. I intended to use your station as a resting point, while I decided my next course of action, but I've changed my mind."

"Changed your mind about what?" Lucchesi asked.

"I've decided to make Idona my temporary headquarters while we speak about our mutual problem. Did you know your station is in horrible disrepair? How can you let such a strategic exchange point lapse into such a sad state?"

"We have it on good authority, President Racine, that the station is being properly maintained," Lucchesi replied. He hated letting the president continue to lead the discussion, but the man refused to stay on topic. *Like talking to a mindless idiot,* Lucchesi thought.

"That's interesting. Perhaps you'll believe your own people." The vid on the station's end widened, showing a nervous Lieutenant Morris sitting next to Alex. "By the way, I have placed Lieutenant Morris here in charge of your militia. She is much more levelheaded than your Major Lindling ... a most disagreeable and unreasonable man."

Morris nodded at the tribunes and cleared her throat, twice. She summarized the station's financial trends for the past three decades — docking fees, bay fees, service fees, and distribution of those funds. While she spoke, Cordelia ran a series of vids that the repair teams were collecting of pre- and post-repair jobs.

"I'm sorry to report, Tribunes, that much of the funds for station maintenance has been diverted," Morris said, ducking her head.

"Diverted where?" Ian Brennan demanded, leaning forward onto the table.

"Your Major Lindling and his family have become wealthy individuals, while your station suffered," Alex said. "From the records we've recovered, the past four senior militia officers have all participated in the looting of station funds. When was the last time any of you sent an accountant to check on station finances?"

Lucchesi and Woo looked at Brennan, but he was staring with disgust at Woo.

"I see," Alex said. "Well, at this rate, you probably would have lost this station to catastrophic accident in another decade or so. As it is, I've decided to turn it back into a going concern."

"Looking at those images, I would surmise, President Racine, after decades of neglect, you don't have the workforce to manage the extensive repairs that have accrued," Brennan challenged.

"Oh, but I do, Tribune Brennan, with the shop owners, the militia, the rebels, and my people working side by side, we're making great progress," Alex replied.

"What?" Lucchesi cried, disbelieving he heard correctly. "The rebels?"

"Um … I meant to clarify that, Tribunes," Morris stammered. "In the recordings you saw, most of those working with the militia aren't stationers. They're … um … they're rebels."

"It's actually working out quite well," Alex said cheerfully. "We've had a few incidents, but nothing more than fistfights."

"And you expect us to believe this?" Lucchesi asked.

"It's as the president says, Tribune Lucchesi," Morris replied respectfully. "My people have been assigned work details, and we are cooperating with the rebels, the station personnel, and the Harakens."

"How many of your people survived the fight, Lieutenant?" Woo asked. "And I presume that Major Lindling and Captain Yun are dead."

Alex gave Morris an encouraging smile, which Woo interpreted as the victor lauding over the captured.

"Major Lindling had us build a barricade in the main corridor admin area and ordered us to fire on the Harakens when they breached our admin doors," Morris explained.

"And?" Woo pressed.

"Nothing, Tribune. Our guns were rendered inoperable. Something about nanites," Morris replied and shrugged her shoulders. She appeared apologetic and confused.

"Nanites, Sers," Alex said. "Just another piece of technology we possess that triumphs over your great forces. We don't need size to defeat you. Although, we have twenty-eight more carriers, just like the two here at the station."

Alex's people kept their faces carefully schooled, but implant comms were burning the air.

"Julien, what is our latest fighter total?"

Julien calculated the minimum number of fighters that twenty-eight nonexistent carriers could land and came up with approximately 13,000, but he decided to join in Alex's game. "As of the latest count, Mr. President, we have 32,319 fighters."

<My, how my forces have grown,> Tatia sent to the room's Harakens.

"Apologies, Julien," Z added, "but that number doesn't take into account the pending production of the newest version of our fighters."

"True, Z," Cordelia chimed in. "Production will be completing 116 fighters a day by now."

<Okay, let's not get carried away,> Alex sent, cautioning his people. "Incidentally, Tribunes, every one of our fighters can traverse your system indefinitely, without resupply of fuel or armament, and our pilots can trade off to eat and rest."

Woo glanced at Lumley, who shrugged his shoulders as if to say it was possible.

"So you've advanced technology, you've a powerful military force, and you have our station, Mr. President. What's next?" Brennan asked.

"What's next is we negotiate a resolution to rectify this incredulously poor diplomatic start by your people. We negotiate a peace."

"There's no reason that can't be accommodated," Lucchesi replied, smiling.

"And there lies the problem, Tribune Lucchesi. I don't trust you," Alex replied, leaning toward the vid pickup. "Your two most senior people, the speaker and the high judge, were two of the most duplicitous men I've ever had the misfortune to meet. And, I have it on good authority that they are symptomatic of your political hierarchy, which puts me in the difficult position of deciding how to deal with you three."

"I would like to know how you can make statements like that without even knowing us. Good authority, indeed!" Lucchesi replied.

The Harakens' vid pickup opened wider. Arrayed behind Alex was a group of senior people.

"Olawale!" Lumley exclaimed, forgetting in whose company he sat and jumping up.

"Francis, my friend," Olawale said, standing as well, his huge smile a blaze of white in his dark face. "It's good to see you well."

"That Ser Wombo and these other senior scientists would rather risk fortune with a strange civilization than stay with their own people speaks volumes, Tribunes," Alex said.

"If you can't trust us, then why even come here?" Woo asked.

"To prevent you from sending a fleet to my worlds," Alex replied. "If we see any sizable fleet forming or ships heading out of system in the same direction as our worlds, for whatever reason, we will destroy them. No warning; no questions asked. In the meantime, I'll continue with my experiment."

"And that experiment is the station," Brennan pursued.

"Exactly, Tribune," Alex replied.

"After you repair it, then what?" Woo asked.

"You don't understand, Tribunes. I'm not going to just repair this station. I'm going to return it to prosperous operation."

"But for what purpose?" Lucchesi asked.

"It's a lesson for you, Tribunes. When you figure it out, please comm me. Have your comms personnel place a call to Idona Station as if it was in your planet's orbit. Our SADEs will do the rest. I'll be in touch," Alex said and cut the connection.

Realizing he was still standing, Lumley sat back down, a small smile on his face. He couldn't be happier for his friend, Olawale, who had found the better way of living that he was hoping to discover.

Lucchesi shoved back his chair and hurried his bulk out of the room as fast as he could. He had no desire to participate in the after-comm analysis he was certain his colleagues wanted him to join.

"Are you hungry, Captain?" Woo asked. "We would like you to join us for some dinner and extended conversation."

* * *

Lumley was allowed to eat his entire meal in peace, and a generous meal it was. Dessert and a port were served and consumed before the conversation began.

"Could the Harakens have twenty-eight carriers of the size reported at Idona Station?" Woo asked Lumley.

"Consider, Tribune Woo, that the *Reunion* entered a system with a reportedly single colony of just a half million people and one of those monster carriers was present. A single carrier on station, armed with 256 fighters, for one small colony," Lumley said, posing the rhetorical question.

"My guess," Lumley continued, "is that the *Hand of Justice* met several of these carriers at New Terra. Twenty-eight carriers and tens of thousands of fighters spread among their home worlds would suggest why the president has the assurance to come light years to our system with only two carriers."

In the quiet that followed Lumley's statements, the captain took the opportunity to ask the question that drove him to be on his best behavior with the tribunes. "What about my crew?"

"The Haraken president's call, a no-delay comm from Idona Station to Earth, will be around the globe by morning, if I know my military grapevine," Woo said. "There's no more need to hold your crew. They'll be released in the morning. We'll expect their cooperation, of course. The story will be that isolation was necessary to ensure that no microorganisms were carried back to Earth after contact with the aliens."

When Lumley's eyebrow rose in question, Woo amended, "After contact with these distant humans."

"Why resurrect the station? What's the lesson we're supposed to get?" Brennan asked. He looked at Woo, who just returned his stare, before Brennan turned to regard Lumley.

"I can't say that I know what's in the president's mind, but I could hazard a guess," Lumley replied.

"Do educate us, Captain," Woo said, gesturing toward Lumley with her crystal glass of fine vintage port.

"I would like to be forgiven in advance for what I'm about to say, Tribunes." When both nodded to Lumley, he put aside his glass of port and leaned on the table. "I believe the president came here as he said to prevent our fleet from arriving in one of his systems without his foreknowledge. It's the sort of smart strategic move that I think he would make, but now he's stuck."

"What do you mean stuck?" Brennan asked.

"The Harakens strike me as honorable people, so I don't think they'll be the ones to start a war, even though they might well be the ones who end it. Problem is they find us despicable and corrupt. So how do you start a dialog with people you can't trust?"

Lumley sat back in his chair and regarded the two tribunes, who appeared lost in their own thoughts. He didn't have a clue as to the answer to the question he just asked, but he hoped he had presented the Harakens' conundrum properly.

"By not employing dialog," Brennan said, suddenly sitting upright and spilling his port. "You don't talk; you do." He looked expectantly at the table's other diners. "Don't you see? The president has had the inside story on us from the beginning … first from our over-ambitious high judge and speaker and then from our scientists who defected. So when the president takes Idona Station for his headquarters, he finds a perfect example of our systematic failures — people rebelling against harsh policies, corruption of militia officers, and critical infrastructure repairs ignored — the works."

"The images of the station before repair were appalling," Woo agreed. "I wonder how many other locations we have that are in as bad a shape as the station, which we are completely ignorant about."

"Probably more than we care to contemplate, but that's not the lesson we're supposed to be learning. The captain gave us the clue," Brennan said, hoisting his glass to Lumley. "The Harakens are honorable people. Look at the president's goal and how he intends to get there. He's teaching us that if you remove the strife between our people and give them a common goal that supports their welfare … watch what happens."

"Do you think that he can succeed?" Woo asked.

"I have no idea, but let's face it," Brennan replied. "We're out of our depth here. President Racine might as well truly be an alien. His mindset is worlds away from ours … no pun intended … and his people possess technology that we can't even conceive."

"So what if we learn this lesson … unite and things will be better?" Woo asked, shaking her head at the preposterousness of it all. "What could we do with it? We can't replicate it. No one would accept this concept coming from the Supreme Tribunal."

"Maybe you won't have to worry," Lumley said, leaning back into his chair with a grin.

-9-

Twenty-eight carriers wasn't the only lie Alex told the Tribunal. Progress on the station wasn't proceeding as smoothly as Alex might have indicated. In fact, there were many more complications to sorting out the issues on board the station than Alex and his people could have conceived — everything was far from copacetic.

To begin with, the rebels suffered from a lack of quality medical care and insufficient nutritional intake. Some of the rebels displayed symptoms of genetically inherited diseases, and others suffered from ailments and accidents, displaying arthritic joints, poorly healed multiple fractures, and severe burns.

In preparation for the journey to Sol, Terese Lechaux, the Harakens' senior medical expert, ordered the medical teams to initiate the manufacture of large quantities of medical nanites. Her intentions were to be prepared for her people's treatment.

Terese was observing vid streams of the rebels as they emerged into the outer ring, courtesy of the SADEs' transmissions to the fleet, when the sight of a young boy with burns along one side of his face and into his scalp galvanized her. She organized her people and commandeered three travelers, which were landing at the station within hours and were filled with medical teams, equipment, containers of medical nanites, and GEN machines. Julien was conscripted to assist Terese in reprogramming the medical nanites, which were set for a 180-day lifetime in order to cure some of the rebels' more obstinate medical problems.

A little-used medical facility was commandeered by Terese, and Haraken crew began clearing out the outdated medical supplies and equipment, replacing it with the fleet's surplus stock. Once the facilities were ready, Terese waited impatiently for the first patients to arrive. She intended to service every rebel, even the healthy, using the medical nanites to bolster their health. However, despite sending medical personnel to collect the first groups of rebels, none arrived at the medical station.

<Ser, do we have a problem?> Terese sent.

<Apologies, Terese, but the rebel leader, Ser Fowler, is not allowing her people to be treated,> the *No Retreat*'s chief medical officer, Darrin Hesterly, sent back.

Terese hurried to the meeting hall, working her way through the rebels lining the corridor and up to the table where the main constituents sat.

<Incoming,> Tatia sent to Alex, who looked up to see his flame-haired medical expert striding purposefully toward them.

"Pardon me, Ser Fowler, we need to deal with an important issue before we continue," Alex said.

"You're Ser Fowler, I believe," Terese said firmly to Nikki, her hands on her hips and an impatient look in her eyes.

"Allow me to present our chief medical adviser, Ser Terese Lechaux, Ser Fowler," Alex said as diplomatically as he could. "She obviously is ready to help your people with medical issues."

"We've just met you," Nikki said. "I have no idea what medical experimentation you wish to perform on my people."

"Medical experimentation —" Terese replied hotly, which caused more than one Haraken within earshot to wince. Fortunately, Terese was interrupted, before she could continue.

"Ser Lechaux, allow me to help," Wombo said, stepping forward. "Ser Fowler, my associates and I are UE scientists who left the explorer-ship *Reunion* while it was in the Haraken system. We've received medical treatment from Ser Lechaux and her people, and I can tell you that your people will be most carefully treated and will enjoy health improvements that you can't imagine."

Wombo explained to Nikki the ills that the Harakens had cured for him. The other scientists joined in and related their personal stories of ailments cured by the Harakens' amazing medical technology.

"Okay, okay," said Nikki, raising her hands to back off the elderly scientists who had crowded around her and urged her to reconsider her decision. With the scientists eagerly sharing their ages, Nikki admitted that they did not look their advanced ages and possessed robust, healthy glows.

"I better not regret this," Nikki said, staring intently at Terese. "You can start with the worst cases, but know that I'll be closely monitoring your efforts."

"I would have started with the worst cases, Ser Fowler," Terese replied, locking eyes with Nikki. "But I will treat all your people. I can do no less." Terese spun around and left as quickly as she had arrived.

"Bit of a whirlwind personality there," Nikki said quietly.

"You have no idea," Alex and Tatia said simultaneously, and they shared small smiles, relieved the issue was easily resolved.

<Thank you, Olawale,> Alex sent.

<Pleasure,> Olawale managed to send after a few moments through his new implant. Mental messaging was new and tricky for the scientists, who had filtered every thought throughout their lives immersed in the dangerous political atmosphere the UE fomented.

The scientists were constantly concerned they'd send uncensored thoughts to their new hosts. To complicate matters, their visuals often selected the message recipients. In their excitement, they sent messages to everyone in sight instead of the intended individuals. To the scientists' relief, the Harakens found each sharing amusing rather than taking umbrage over the faux pas.

* * *

Another immediate requirement for the rebels was a substantial increase in the quality and quantity of their food intake. Cordelia supervised the offloading of a third of the fleet's food dispensers and stocks. She selected three closed restaurant locations, equally spaced around the station, and the fleet crew went to work opening the sites, cleaning them, and installing the dispensers and the food stock tanks.

The food supplies were insufficient to feed the rebels for more than three-quarters of an Earther year, but it would be long enough to ensure their return to health and see an increase in food shipments to the station.

In an insightful move, Cordelia collected the first individuals completing their medical treatment in Terese's clinic and took them to the meal room.

"Jason," Cordelia said to the young boy, who had been badly burned. The medical nanites would need several Earther months to replace the badly scarred skin, restore the scalp's follicles on one side of his head, and give little Jason a full head of hair. "I'm going to teach you and your friends to order your first Haraken meal. Then all of you will teach anyone else who has received medical treatment, but only those who have visited the medical clinic. Am I understood?"

"Why can't we share it with anyone now?" Jason asked.

"Sometimes you have to do things that appear mean in order to actually help people. Medical treatment for your people is critical. This is one way to ensure they'll receive it. Are you willing to help me do that?"

Jason nodded reluctantly as did the other seven rebel children accompanying him.

Cordelia turned around to demonstrate the food dispenser and explain the menu selection process. Z had added a simple visual-touch display that Earthers could access since they were without implants. A young girl, no more than eight, hurried to the side of the dispenser and stared at Cordelia's mouth.

"That's Ginny," Jason said, pointing to the little girl. "She can't hear, but she can read your lips."

"Hello, Ginny," Cordelia mouthed silently, and the girl's face lit up in a bright smile. Cordelia picked her up and sat her on the dispenser's shelf so she wouldn't miss the instructions. Despite the children's desire to select some of the more exotic menu items for their first meal, Cordelia gently guided them to foods packed with the nutrition the young rebels needed.

Seated at a long, bench-like table, it didn't take long to make the children converts to Haraken food. Their first tastes were tentative, the second tastes less so, and then silence reigned as food was shoveled quickly and efficiently.

<The children are eating,> Cordelia sent to Terese.

<Is it going well?> Terese inquired.

<One is reminded of our dear president at meal time.>

<Excellent, then they should be healthy by tomorrow,> Terese sent.

Cordelia heard Terese's uproarious laughter, which was only silenced by the closing of the comm.

It didn't take long for a group of passing rebels to spot the children plowing through trays of food and sought to join them. Cordelia barred their way and signaled to the medical nanites she hoped to discover in their bodies. None were present.

"Jason," Cordelia called out, "these people haven't been to medical yet. What should I do?"

"You have to go to medical first," Jason called out, barely taking time to point with a spoon before he went back to shoveling his food.

"That way," a little girl pointed with a fork before she too resumed cleaning her plate.

One of the older men might have argued, but his compatriots deserted him, heading in the direction the children had indicated, and he reluctantly trotted after them.

"Well done, children," Cordelia said. She came to the side of the deaf girl, who with her back to the door failed to grasp the entire exchange, and gently stroked her hair. The little one smiled up at her and returned to devouring her food.

* * *

Immediately after Julien's interview with Lieutenant Morris, he commandeered the station's financial programs and computers, freezing out all remote access. Julien's initial investigation provided Alex with the information the president shared with the Tribunal concerning Major Lindling's diversion of station funds.

<Good tidings, Mr. President,> Julien sent. <Further analysis of the station's funds reveals that the major's last transfer was from the service fee's account to his personal account. He didn't have time to transfer the funds off station.

<I take it that he won't be able to do so now,> Alex sent back. When silence greeted Alex's message, he sent <Apologies, my friend, so much is happening so fast.>

<Understood, Mr. President. The SADEs will not fail you in your new role as station master,> Julien replied, sending an image of Alex sitting in an ornate, high-backed chair and playing with a replica of the station, tossing it repeatedly in the air. That Julien received just a brief laugh before the comm closed told him the pressure Alex was under to make a success of this odd venture.

Julien transferred the major's funds to the station's general ledger account and left a single credit in the officer's personal account. Then he sent a short summary sheet of the station's accounts to Alex and returned to setting up an account for each rebel. To Julien, it appeared an exercise in futility, considering the limited economic future for the rebels, but he had faith in Alex's intuition.

* * *

Alex shifted again in his chair, trying to find a comfortable position. Despite his crew locating the widest station chairs they could find and removing the arms, the final result was terribly inadequate, and Renée ordered some wide-bodied, nanites-driven chairs from the fleet's ships to accommodate the New Terran-born Harakens while they were on station.

"I've some pleasant news," Alex announced to Nikki and Vic, seated across the table from him. The large rebel audience, who had attended their first meeting, was gone, which Alex appreciated. Now, only some of the senior rebel figures attended the ongoing meetings with Nikki and Vic. The exceptions were two scrawny teenagers, who often sat or stood near Z and rarely took their eyes off him.

"The militia didn't have time to make the latest transfer of credits off the station, which leaves the station with a nice surplus," Alex continued. "We will be sharing half of those funds among your people, Ser Fowler. Call it a down payment on reparations. The remainder will be used to pay station personnel salaries, maintenance services, and for amenities my people use."

"How much will you be keeping for yourselves?" Vic asked, his chin jutting out and his eyes narrowing.

<Easy, my love,> Renée sent. <These people have built up a lifetime of distrust. Yes, this man is a fool, but don't let him disturb you.>

"Will station accounts be made available for our review, Mr. President?" Nikki asked, attempting to diffuse the tension between the two men.

"I would certainly think so, considering," Alex said, a broad smile replacing his frown.

"Considering what?" Nikki asked dubiously.

"Did I not mention this? How forgetful of me, Ser Fowler," Alex said, his grin becoming even broader. "I'm appointing you the station's new director. I believe your grandfather held the post before he fled the militia to the inner ring with the core of the rebel faction."

"How can you know that?" Nikki asked incredulously.

"My people have been collecting information from your people and sending it to me," Alex replied, tapping his temple.

"Did we not tell you there was much more to discover about the Harakens?" Olawale said to Nikki. He had opted to stand in a corner rather than suffer with the narrow station chairs.

"Okay, fine. You're learning our history. Then you should know that my experience is limited to the inner ring and core. I know nothing about the outer ring … docking and bay fees, ship service fees, owner leases, and … and everything to do with the outer ring," Nikki said, waving her arms to indicate the entire station's outer face.

"Then you will need help, and I've arranged for that," Alex said, crooking his finger at someone behind Nikki and Vic.

The rebel leaders looked around to see Captain Yun walking toward them.

"Oh no, not him!" Vic yelled, standing up and knocking over his chair.

"Sit or leave, Ser," Alex said quietly.

Nikki took one look at the president's face and ordered Vic to sit down. Vic was torn between continuing his objection and obeying his leader. Finally, he righted his chair and grudgingly sat back down.

"Captain," Alex said, motioning him forward. "It's my understanding, Ser Fowler, that Captain Yun understands the financial workings of the station's outer ring quite well."

"And just how are we supposed to keep an eye on him?" Vic demanded.

"Two of our SADEs will have ultimate control of the station's financial systems and will approve all credit transfers," Alex replied.

"You mentioned that word once or twice before, Mr. President. What's a SADE?" Nikki asked.

<These are the moments I live for,> Tatia sent to Renée.

"They are my friends ... very unique entities that you might call artificial intelligences or AIs. We call them self-aware digital entities or SADEs."

"Milt piss," Vic said, leaning back in his chair with disgust at the lie that was being foisted on them.

"Mr. Lambert," said Yoram Penzig, the UE scientists' diminutive philosopher, who was sporting fresh hair growth over a bald pate that hadn't seen hair in decades, "it's understandable that you have doubts. What's amazing to me is that you're unwilling to learn if those doubts are proven true or false"

"So is one of these AIs here, or do you keep them in a box?" Vic asked, snickering.

"I'm present," Z replied.

"You?" Vic said. His mouth dropped open at the thought that the huge man wasn't human.

Nikki glanced toward the scientists, who were clapping and smiling.

"Another one," Olawale called out, thinking that the Cedric avatar and voice marked him as a SADE they hadn't met.

"On the contrary, Ser," Z replied in Miranda's voice. "You met me at meal time aboard the *Rêveur.*"

"Z … and Miranda … and Cedric," Wombo exclaimed. "How many versions of you are there?"

"There's only one version of me, Ser, but I have many avatars. However, Miranda is an alternate persona," Z said. *Most of the time,* Z thought.

"Nice voice trick," Vic said, unconvinced. Before he could blink, Z was at his side, yanking him out of the chair, and holding Vic's head to his massive chest. Struggle as much as Vic might, it was in vain. His head was locked in an inhuman, vise-like grip.

Nikki glanced at the president, who appeared entirely unperturbed by the actions of one of his men.

"Stop struggling, human, and listen carefully," Z demanded. The voice he used was as surreal as was his avatar's strength.

Vic chose to obey, seeing that he had no choice. He waited to hear the rasp of lungs and the heartbeat of a human, but after moments he heard nothing. He twisted his head to better place his ear on the man's chest and the grip on his head lessened. Finally, Vic stood up, staring incredulously at Z. "You … you don't have a heartbeat and you don't breathe," he stammered.

"Perhaps now, human, you begin to understand," Z said. "Now, sit and learn before our patience runs out with your child-like mouthing."

<Never gets old,> Tatia sent to Renée.

<Too much, Ser?> Z privately inquired of Alex.

<He's quiet now. That works for me,> Alex sent back.

"Milt piss, a robot," Jodlyne said, stepping up to Z and poking him gently in the ribs to see what he felt like.

"A robot? No, little one, I am the great wizard, Oz," Z said, paraphrasing one of his favorite ancient Terran stories. He smiled at the little rebel who had been shadowing him with her friend for days.

"Absolutely zounding!" Jodlyne gushed, staring up into Z's face.

"How many SADEs are with you?" Nikki asked.

"I believe I met one," Captain Yun said. "Would he be called Julien, Mr. President?"

"Yes, among other things, Captain," Alex replied, a small smile crossing his face. "The third is Cordelia. It will be Z and Julien who will control the financial accounts and ensure the station's credits flow as you request. Congratulations, on your new position, Ser Fowler," Alex said extending his hand.

Nikki was stunned. Her objections had been swept away by the Haraken president's planning. She glanced up at the president's partner, Renée, who smiled and winked at her. *These people might be more dangerous than the militia,* Nikki thought, shaking the president's hand to accept his offer.

* * *

With their experience as directors of the Harakens' Central Exchange, it was a simple task for the SADEs to manage the station's flow of credits — docking and bay fees, ship services fees, leases, personnel salaries, etc. However, Z did lodge a complaint with Alex about the antiquated computer applications the SADEs were forced to use.

"Then build your own financial system," was the phrase Alex threw off to Z as he hurried to his next meeting.

Z requisitioned one of the carrier's spare controllers and, within several hours, installed it in the station's central control offices. While Z set up the controller's applications, Julien and Cordelia upgraded the station's myriad terminals with new software.

The improved system was a delight to owners and operators aboard the station, who witnessed complete transparency of their accounts. Ship owners and captains could check the cost of docking and service fees in advance and order/approve services as needed from any terminal.

Credits began flowing through Idona Station as smoothly as water, and, most important, people knew exactly what services and supplies they were receiving and approving for payment.

-10-

Word passed from captain to captain, ship to ship, from the far asteroid fields to the outer rim's innermost colony — strange humans accompanied by artificial intelligences had taken over Idona Station, backed off a UE destroyer 1M kilometers inward, disarmed the station's militia without any loss of life, freed the rebels, and opened the station for business.

It began as a trickle, which became a stream, which grew into a flood.

Freighters were the first to respond, offloading shipments of food, fertilizing minerals for the Idona food production beds, clothing, bedding, and other personal supplies — all for the rebels. Then freighters and passenger ships brought the descendants of shop owners who had fled the militia when the station was overtaken and were intent on recovering their families' assets. Many people hoped to reopen their shops, especially if Idona might prosper once again.

People from all walks of life stopped at Idona — store owners with credits; individuals spending their last credits to make for the asteroid fields' mining operations; wealthy people aboard their yachts, curious to see the strangers; and criminals, who were attracted to any opportunity.

For the rebels, the growth was a bonanza. While some hired on as station maintenance and ship services personnel, many of them took over their grandparents' abandoned shops, restaurants, and sleepovers. They found the SADEs willing to extend credits for equipment and supplies to get their enterprises started.

Julien and Z were close to draining the station's accounts to finance the rebels' shops and their positions as the station's new employees, before the inflow of credits exceeded the outflow. That trend accelerated when Nikki, in her capacity as station director, reinstituted the station's full range of services and their associated fees, which the militia had failed to maintain, due primarily to the lack of station personnel.

Ore-freighter captains from the asteroid fields, who sympathized with the rebels, accepted the restored docking fees now that the credits weren't going into the militia's pockets. As for the returning shop owners, the leasing fees were an expected part of doing business, and the wealthy … well, they had credits in abundance.

* * *

Tatia saw trouble coming from several directions the busier the station became and worked to head off the problems. She ordered Mickey and his engineering people to upgrade the sensors at the docks and bays. The Haraken sensors could detect bio, mech, and tech paraphernalia, as well as explosive material.

Unfortunately, time was against the Harakens. The enormous number of bays and docks surrounding the station's outer circumference and stacked on multiple levels made it impossible to complete the number of installations in order to stay ahead of the ever-increasing growth in visitors.

Tatia suggested that Mickey focus on bay airlocks. In her opinion, trouble would come from the independent operators, who flew an assortment of small ships, which required bays to access the station. The freighters and liners, which would use berths on the docking arms, were thought to be the lesser concern.

More than one thrill seeker, who landed in a station's bay, was challenged by Haraken troopers when they set off the airlock sensors. On the first infraction, their stash of fun chemicals, weapons, or whatever was confiscated, to be returned on their exit from the station. For second infractions, and there were a few slow learners, the airlock simply failed to open on the station side, and the offending individuals were informed via a pleasant message recorded by Cordelia that they were unwelcome on the station and then wished good fortune.

Subtle issues arose from those who set off the sensors because of their bionic prostheses. After a careful scan cleared them, many of these people, talking to the rebels, discovered the stories of the Harakens' impressive medical technology. Their requests for medical aid became a sore point between Alex and Terese. She wanted to offer services to anyone who could be helped, and Alex adamantly refused.

"If we offer miraculous cures for the ailing, Terese, we'll be inundated," Alex said. "We can't start this and then stop once we leave."

"Then why are we helping the rebels? Let's just refuse medical services to everyone," Terese replied hotly.

"I need the rebels to turn this station around, and I need them healthy. Your medical services are partial repayment for what they've suffered under the UE."

"Is that your last word on the subject, your highness?" Terese asked, her face a hot mask.

When Alex nodded, Terese whirled around and marched back into her clinic in a huff. Alex, just as dissatisfied with the discussion as Terese, spun around, and Étienne neatly stepped out of his way.

<It's good not to be president,> Étienne sent to Alex.

<It's good to be anything but the subject of Terese's ire,> Alex returned.

<It has been a much-discussed subject that our medical expert's hair is not naturally red,> Étienne replied.

<No?> Alex asked.

<No,> Étienne sent, shaking his head. <It's thought that it's been turned that color by the force of her personality.>

The two Harakens burst into laughter as they walked along the corridor, and Earthers again witnessed Harakens simultaneously reacting without a conversation being overheard. It fed the rumors about the strangers, rumors of all types.

* * *

Intense, but often unnoticed, painful moments transpired daily for some of the older rebels. They were parents, who were quietly searching for their children, now often full-grown adults, who had been secreted from the inner ring when they were newborns to live with friends in the outer ring, giving the children an opportunity for better lives. Couples and often a single parent surreptitiously observed their lost children from the cover of utility corridors, nearby shops, or passing in the corridors, tears often clouding their eyes.

In one incident, a strapping young man stopped to aid an elderly woman, who seemed to stumble at the sight of him.

"Are you ill, grandmother?" the man asked solicitously, supporting her arm.

"It will pass, son. Thank you for your concern," she replied, savoring the assistance of his strong arms. She took heart — she had given him that chance at health. The mother smiled up at her son, so straight and tall, and patted his hand. "Such a generous boy," she said and moved on, never minding that she had been mistaken for an elderly grandmother.

* * *

As the station filled up, Tatia faced her most difficult challenge — maintaining the peace. Several fistfights had broken out between militia and rebels, and the guilty parties were handed over to their prospective superiors, Nikki Fowler and Lieutenant Morris, for disciplining. However, soon ship crews got into trouble, and petty criminal acts came to light. As these issues continued to pile up, Tatia sought out Alex for his recommendations.

"Well, Admiral," Alex replied, "I see these incidents falling under the purview of martial law."

"Martial law?" Tatia asked.

"Yes, Admiral. In a sense we are invaders and have taken over this station by force, imposing martial law, and you are our military's highest-ranking authority. The issue is yours to resolve."

"That's quite logical, Admiral," Julien added, which earned him an evil stare from Tatia. In response to her glare, Julien's headgear transformed into a gunner's helmet, encasing most of his head.

Stuck with the problem of dealing with the station's lawbreakers, Tatia borrowed a page from the UE and created a version of the Supreme Tribunal, except her panel was composed of five judges — a rebel, Nikki; a militia officer, Patrice; a Haraken, herself; a UE scientist, Priita; and a station sleepover owner, Desmond Lambros, who was a respected businessman.

The judges devoted two mornings every seven days to hear the charges against the accused and the testimony of witnesses. In most cases, the judgments were fines to be paid to the station or the aggrieved parties. In rare cases, the lawbreaker was expelled from the station, forced to take the next ship, freighter, or liner leaving the station, regardless of the ship's destination. These latter cases and their sentences were quickly circulated among crew and visitors, and the stories drastically curtailed the number of graver offenses.

In one of the precedent-setting cases, a freighter captain docked his ship, accepted services, but refused to transfer the required credits. Services were suspended, and the captain was told to vacate the dock until the matter was settled, but the captain refused, insisting the fees were unfair and should never have been raised. Furthermore, he demanded his complaint be heard by the station's new judiciary panel.

Nikki, the lead judge, agreed to hear the captain's argument, knowing that ship captains and owners would be being paying close attention to the outcome of the review.

At the appropriate time, the freighter captain and eight of his crew came through the militia's admin doors. They were a rough-looking lot, who were obviously used to getting their way in the wild spaces of the belt.

Patrice wanted to warn the members of the panel to be careful as the captain and crew closed on their table when suddenly the nine men rushed at the judges.

Providing security for the panel, Z felled three of the spacers, the twins accounted for two each, and the captain and the second mate were unfortunate enough to reach the judges' table.

Z signaled for Terese and her medical staff, who arrived and examined the fallen freighter personnel. Terese pronounced most of the crew as simply unconscious and would only need time to recover.

"Except for these two," Terese said, pointing to the captain and the second mate. "They will need medical treatment to repair their broken bones and organ bruising."

When Z, the twins, and the four other judges turned to regard Tatia, Terese cocked an eyebrow at her.

"It was self-defense," Tatia proclaimed, "and who knew these spacers were so fragile?"

* * *

The Harakens constantly filtered out the thrill seekers, criminals, and known assassins, who attempted to board the station. Militia records did an exceptional job of identifying many of the nastier cases, and they were arrested and incarcerated to await transport to Earth. It was only afterwards that most criminals realized that disarming the militia didn't mean making them inoperable.

A promotion-seeking destroyer captain, Borden, and a militia major, Faring, planned a subterfuge that intended to catch the Harakens by surprise. From millions of kilometers inward, a wealthy businessman's yacht, the *Lazy Pleasure*, which was headed to Idona, was interdicted and confiscated by the patrol craft of the destroyer *Vigilance*.

Major Faring loaded the yacht with heavily armed militia, placing a lieutenant in command. Of the yacht's passengers and crew, only Captain Alicante was kept aboard to handle comms and docking.

Many days later, the *Lazy Pleasure* approached Idona and the yacht's captain, with the lieutenant standing closely behind him, commed the station and requested a docking berth.

"*Lazy Pleasure*, I have your dock request," the station's militia sergeant replied. "Please supply your ship's identification codes, and I will activate the beacon at your dock."

"Acknowledged, Idona," Captain Alicante replied. "Transmitting vessel ident now."

The sergeant's system matched the ship's code to the militia's records of the luxury yacht, *Lazy Pleasure*. "Identification received, Captain. Your berth is level 2, dock 18. Beacon is active on your ident."

"Thank you, Idona, message received," the captain replied and signed off.

Alicante eased the yacht into its assigned berth. Docking lasers playing off his hull sensors guided the ship into its final position. Station services personnel, most of them rebels, extended the gangway and sealed it to the hull's airlock hatch.

"Ramp secure, Captain," the ramp operator commed. "Please access station maintenance for a list of services. Order what you need, and transfer your credits."

"That's new," Alicante replied without thinking.

"Upgrades courtesy of the Harakens," the operator replied. "Enjoy your stay on station, Captain."

"What now, Lieutenant?" the captain asked.

"Now, Captain, you and I stroll down the gangway and ensure all is quiet. And remember, it's not lieutenant; it's Mr. Livingsworth. I'm a cousin of the yacht's owner. You're guiding me to locate services for the yacht's other guests. Act casual, but remember that if you give me up, my needler will end you first," the lieutenant said, patting his waistband.

A natty jacket borrowed from the yacht's owner and complementing the rest of the lieutenant's casual attire hid the small but deadly weapon that fired high-velocity darts, which injected fast-acting neurotoxins into the body.

After passing through the yacht's airlock, the two men strolled down the gangway, looking like old friends. Finding the docking corridor empty, the lieutenant was emboldened until two slender men with weapons on their hips walked around the corner.

"Station security, Sers," one of the men announced. "May we see some ID?"

"Is this how things are done now?" the lieutenant replied. "The good captain identified our yacht, and I'm a cousin of the owner. Surely that's enough identification."

"Captain," said the second security agent, extending his hand.

Alicante reached into his jacket pocket and extended his identification to the agent, who didn't bother to produce a reader. He just stared at it for a moment, and then said to his partner, "Confirmed."

"Now yours, Ser," the first agent said to the lieutenant.

"This is ridiculous," the lieutenant declared hotly. "I left it on board. Are you going to make me go back just to prove I am who I say I am?" When neither agent replied, he let out a snort of exasperation. "Come, Captain, I've already grown tired of this sad excuse for a station, with its obviously freaky visitors. We're leaving."

The lieutenant reached for the captain's arm, but he never finished the movement. Alain pulled his stun gun and dropped the man where he stood.

<I don't believe that was necessary,> Étienne sent to his crèche-mate.

<He was irritating me,> Alain replied. <Besides, you had the privilege of stunning the last two.>

"Step aside, Captain Alicante," Étienne requested, as a huge man came swiftly down the corridor, carrying an odd-looking machine.

"How is your airlock accessed, Captain?" Z asked.

"Biometric. Please, follow me, sir," the captain replied, hurrying up the gangway ramp. A smile crossed his face at the thought of his subterfuge's successful outcome. He had affixed an emergency code to his ident signal that he sent to the station. It would have come up on the militia's monitor as "hijacked."

Alicante opened a small hatch and placed his hand on the faceplate, which read his palm's surface blood vessels and pressure, confirming the captain's identity and that he was alive.

When the hatch opened, Z set his GEN machine in the airlock and activated it. Stepping back out, he ordered, "Close the outer hatch, Captain, and open the inner hatch."

Once the captain complied, he was invited to return to the corridor where a trooper waited to escort him to the Haraken leaders. Farther down the corridor, he passed ten more Haraken troopers, armed with stun guns.

"Sir, you must tell your people," the captain said urgently. "There are thirty armed militia aboard that yacht."

"For now, Ser," the trooper replied good-naturedly. "Soon there will be only thirty confused and unarmed militia aboard your vessel."

While Z's nanites were busy disarming the militia's weapons on board the *Lazy Pleasure*, the captain met with Alex and told the story of the destroyer that interdicted his yacht and kidnapped his people.

"Admiral, send some of our travelers inward to locate this destroyer and retrieve our good captain's people. Then chase this destroyer farther inward. And, Admiral … please try not to start a war."

"What's the good of being admiral, if you can't start a fight with anyone," Tatia replied, throwing Alex a cheeky smile as she left.

"Did she mean that?" Alicante asked dubiously when Tatia left.

"Relax, Captain. Your ship will soon be cleaned of militia vermin, and your people will be safely recovered in a few days, if I know my admiral."

* * *

Tatia assigned Deirdre the task of recovering the yacht's people aboard the *Vigilance*. The commander launched her traveler squadron and Tatia waited until the last moment before she called Captain Shimada aboard her destroyer to share the story of the *Lazy Pleasure*.

"Please inform Captain Borden that my fighters will be on the *Vigilance* before he can get up speed. He has two choices, a good one and a bad one. The good one requires that he hands over the yacht's people and heads far inward," Tatia said.

When Shimada contacted Captain Borden and Major Faring, the officers were crestfallen to hear their ruse had failed and surprised to learn retribution was swiftly headed their way.

"In the words of the Haraken admiral, Sirs," Shimada said, "'My commander will be happy to let the captain fire his primary engines without turning over the yacht's passengers. Then when it pleases her, she'll take the engines out and leave the destroyer to drift in whichever direction it happens to be heading.'"

Shimada had deliberately made the call voice only. She knew she wouldn't be able to conceal her mirth, watching the officers stupidly debating their options.

Faring argued for firing the engines and attempting an escape, until the navigation officer pointed out to Captain Borden that a squadron of strange ships was bearing down on them. Neither officer knew which was more unnerving — the swirling fighter squadron, circling their destroyer like a pack of menacing carnivores, or the single ship that sat nose to nose mere meters off their bow. Shimada had warned them that these were the fighters that likely had destroyed the *Hand of Justice*, a warship many times the size of their destroyer.

"Captain, we have a call," the comms officer announced. "The signal direction indicates it's coming from that fighter at our bow."

"Audio only —" Major Faring called out, only to see a helmeted face appear on his monitor. He glanced angrily at the comms officer, who shrugged his shoulders in apology. His comms had been hijacked.

"Sers, I'm an extremely impatient woman, especially with idiots," Deirdre announced. "And since you exemplify humankind's lesser intelligences, I will keep my statements simple. Put yacht people in patrol ship. Send vessel to Idona. Then go far away from us. Do I make myself clear? Nod, if you understand."

Both officers slowly nodded their agreement, each one overwhelmed by the force and skills the Harakens were exhibiting.

Deirdre and most of her squadron shadowed the destroyer until it was well on its way inward. Two of her pilots escorted the destroyer's patrol ship until it docked at Idona, and a group of grateful Earthers were united with their captain to share their tales of the Harakens.

-11-

Weeks after the Harakens overtook Idona, Brennan called a meeting of the Tribunal and requested Captain Lumley be brought from his quarters to attend.

"We're here, Tribune," Lucchesi said, miffed at being called away from one of his most pleasurable pursuits, dining.

"It's time that you were made aware of certain aspects of the UE, Tribune," Brennan replied.

"Should he be here?" Lucchesi asked, pointing a laconic finger at the captain.

"Tribune Woo and I have already shared this information with Captain Lumley. We wanted his opinion as it pertains to Idona Station," Brennan replied and watched Lucchesi's neck and face flush. He didn't bother waiting for Lucchesi to vent his infamous temper, just continued. "Since the Harakens have taken over the station, the estimates of the economic changes are staggering. Much of this is extrapolation from indirect observation, but I judge it to be accurate for the sake of our discussion. Ships arriving weekly at the station are up 400 percent; passengers staying on at the station since the Harakens arrived are estimated to be 5,200; and the net transfer of credits to the station is estimated to be 14 million."

"And your point, Tribune?" Lucchesi asked.

"Tribune, are you not aware of the income we have been receiving from such rim stations as Idona?" Woo asked. "Up until the Harakens arrived in system, Idona's revenue was paltry. But recently, we surmise Idona has already surpassed the average traffic and credit flow of our largest stations by over twice, and this has been accomplished in an incredibly short period of time."

Brennan took the opportunity to lay out the economic constraints that the UE was facing and how long the Tribunal had until it became evident to the public. "The Harakens are aptly demonstrating that our entire way of governing is an economic failure."

"This is why I argued for the aliens' destruction the moment they entered the system," Lucchesi said, pounding the table with a pudgy fist. "But the two of you wouldn't listen."

"A little late now," Woo replied. "Word has been circulating through the fleet that we have one destroyer captain standing off, refusing to move on the station, and another destroyer captain and major who are being chased inward after initiating a fool attempt on the station."

"What happened?" Lucchesi asked.

"Same thing as happened when the Harakens took over the station," Woo replied. "Somehow, the militia was disarmed without a shot fired and taken into custody."

Lucchesi heaved his bulk out of the chair, which creaked in protest, and ranted about the weakness of the military and the failure of the corporations. He accused everybody, except the judicial system, of incompetence.

"When you're ready to continue," Brennan said, "I have an idea I wish to discuss."

Lucchesi welcomed the excuse to sit back down, but he did his best not to show it.

"I plan to invite myself to Idona. I wish to see exactly what's going on and see if what the Harakens are doing can be replicated by us," Brennan explained.

"That's treason," Lucchesi sputtered. "You're consorting with the enemy!"

"What he's trying to do, Tribune," Woo said calmly, "is see if he can find a way to rectify the UE's financial woes. Or weren't you listening? We're going broke. Our methods are bankrupting us, and the Harakens … in our system and with our people, by the way … are making credits faster than any station or colony we run."

"I'll be taking Captain Lumley along," Brennan said. "His relationship with Administrator Wombo should buy me enough time to present my credentials without landing in the militia's brig or beaten to a pulp by the rebels. Then again, the rebels are probably most incensed at the high judges and the military," Brennan added with a grin.

"I see you two have already decided on your course of action without my input," Lucchesi said. "Fine. Go pursue your foolish scheme. If we don't hear from you every week after you arrive on station, I will gladly request to have your post filled." Lucchesi left the meeting in disgust, intending to return to his meal but found that he had lost his appetite.

Within a half hour afterwards, Brennan and Lumley boarded a shuttle and left for orbit. Woo had a naval clipper standing by for them. Clippers were the smallest and fastest passenger ships the UE built and were dedicated to transporting senior naval commanders from point to point.

* * *

Lucchesi brooded over Brennan's plan for days before he decided to confront the tribune about his intentions to visit Idona. Discovering that Brennan had left with Captain Lumley soon after their last meeting incensed him, and he requested a meeting of the enclave of high judges.

Six days later, Lucchesi departed his shuttle and traveled secretly to a building located in the Appalachian Mountains of what was once the US state of Tennessee. Inside, fifteen high judges, who were nominated by their compatriots, comprised the judicial enclave, the body that elected their tribune. They were acutely aware of every detail that Lucchesi was privy to. This meeting was not for the purposes of updating the enclave.

"Judges, I've come seeking approval for a plan of action," Lucchesi began. "We are in danger of having our very way of life undermined by these strangers if we let them continue to infest Idona Station."

"What do you need from us?" a high judge asked.

"Connections," Lucchesi replied. "I believe only direct, overt action will prevent these strangers from undermining what we've achieved." Lucchesi was careful not to repeat what he had learned from Brennan concerning the UE's economic state of affairs. "We need senior naval commanders with connections, officers who can pull together a sufficient number of warships to exterminate the Harakens. That will prove to our people, especially our military, that these invaders are not invincible."

"You recognize, Lucchesi, that if members of this enclave were to have such connections, ones I dare say required decades to cultivate, these individuals would no longer be of value to us once you employed them in your scheme," another high judge remarked.

"We have this one opportunity. We must destroy the invaders now before it's too late," Lucchesi argued.

"Why now?" a third judge asked. "They are small in number and hold one station. They can do little else."

Above all else, Lucchesi dearly wished to prevent sharing with the enclave the dire economic news he had heard. His fear was that they would blame him for the UE's potential collapse. That would be his death sentence. *The Harakens … their archaic attitude of goodwill will get me killed,* Lucchesi thought.

The mood of the enclave was swinging against Lucchesi, and he was left with no choice. He laid out the UE's dire economic future in detail for the judges, and then added the note that several station and colony directors were journeying to Idona to see for themselves what was being accomplished.

"It's my feeling that we will soon see a rebirth of the rebellion, but it won't be isolated groups of ineffective rebels, it will be entire colonies and stations seeking a new way of operating," Lucchesi said. "There is the distinct possibility that many senior military commanders might be joining them. If this happens, we will lose control of the UE. We won't have the military might or the economic power to regain control."

The room was utterly still when Lucchesi finished until the spokesman for the enclave announced, "Leave us, Lucchesi, while we deliberate."

The high judge of the UE Supreme Tribunal sat in an antechamber like a schoolboy waiting to be disciplined. Lucchesi ran through the conversation with the enclave several times in his head, reconsidering his every word. In the end, he believed he had no other choice but to say what he had said.

The UE was headed for a cliff, driven by the makeup of its society, a model which appeared to have run its course. If Lucchesi was honest with himself, the Harakens were only hastening the end or perhaps showing the people a different path. Regardless of which it was, the aliens' actions were derailing the UE, and, more important, could potentially strip the power of the Supreme Tribunal and the high judges.

To Lucchesi, this latter result was the cruelest part. He couldn't conceive of living any other way than in the opulent manner in which he was now accustomed. For the seemingly hundredth time, he wished oblivion for the Harakens' intervention in UE affairs.

"The enclave is ready for you, Tribune Lucchesi," a young man said, dipping his head and waving an arm toward the enclave's entrance.

"We've reached a consensus, Tribune Lucchesi," the spokesperson said. "We will give you one name, who will have the seniority to assemble the necessary forces, but on one inviolate condition. You will speak to no one about your scheme except this individual, who will execute this endeavor as he sees fit. If it fails, and it is our hope that it won't, then you will resign your position, citing ill health, and we will nominate another in your place. Are we clear?"

"Yes," Lucchesi replied. "I thank the enclave for their support." An imperial wave of the spokesperson's hand sent Lucchesi exiting the chamber. In the antechamber, the same young man held out a small piece of paper to him, but when Lucchesi reached for it, the note was snatched back.

"Only look, Tribune, and commit it to memory," the man said and held out the paper again.

On the note was written "T. Portland."

After Lucchesi returned to the Supreme Tribunal's hideaway, he searched militia and naval records for the name, locating an Admiral Theodore Portland. His next step was fraught with difficulty. He had been warned to involve no one in his communications with the admiral.

Lucchesi waited until the early morning hours of the following day. A new comms operator had been transferred to the Tribunal hideaway two days earlier, and Lucchesi sought him out. The young man was flattered by the tribune's attention and eagerly worked to demonstrate his equipment. When Lucchesi requested a comm to Admiral Theodore Portland, the comms operator accessed an application on a computer monitor, and, within seconds, he located the access and routing codes for the admiral.

"All that's required, Tribune Lucchesi, is to enter these two codes here and here," he said pointing to his comms station. "When ready, you activate the record function on this panel and speak into this pickup."

"The admiral will then receive an encrypted message, I presume," Lucchesi asked.

"Absolutely, Tribune Lucchesi. The admiral must enter his personal code in order to be able to read the message."

"How are replies routed to me?' Lucchesi asked.

"All messages for you are routed to this comms center, Tribune, unless you wish otherwise," the boy replied.

"What if I wish all messages from a single person routed to me in my chambers?" Lucchesi asked.

"Simple to arrange, Tribune. On the control board, I input your name here, the access code for the individual, and the code for your chamber. After that, all messages from that individual will be sent to your chamber's comms console," the operator replied, a broad, innocent smile on his young face.

"Thank you, son. Now, I need to send a private message. This will be an opportunity to see if I've been an apt student of your generous tutelage."

The comms operator gushed at the praise and eased out of the small control room to leave the tribune in private.

Lucchesi entered the access codes for Admiral Portland, and then, tapping the record function, spoke his carefully composed message, stopped the recording, and then tapped the lit send icon. Afterwards, he programmed messages from the admiral to be routed to his chamber console.

As Lucchesi left the control room, he generously thanked the boy for his help, laying a friendly hand on his shoulder. It was the least Lucchesi felt he should do for him. In the morning, the young comms operator would be arrested for treason, and, for that charge, the sentence was death.

* * *

Admiral Theodore Portland, better known to his subordinates as Tyrant Portland, was working through his message queue in his stateroom aboard the battleship *Guardian*. His personal code unlocked his console, but the fifth message in the queue required a little-used code for communication with UE superiors.

What have we here? Portland wondered as he entered a second code and played Tribune Lucchesi's message. He played it twice again, and then instead of erasing the message as directed, Portland moved it to a private directory. Leaning back in his chair, his fingers played a silent tattoo on the tabletop, while he considered the request.

A judicial tribune's request couldn't be considered a lawful order for a naval admiral. For Portland, it would need to be issued by his superior, the senior admiral of UE naval forces, Space Admiral Li Chong. But Portland owed much of his career's advancement to the patronage of the high judges, and lately the enclave itself, and the opportunity to engage and defeat the invaders was a sweet siren's call to his burning ambitions.

Despite the assistance his career had received, Portland was by no means without skills, experience and cunning among them. He was aware of the rumors about the strangers' technology and knew that he would need to bring his entire fleet to bear. The challenge was how and when to move an entire fleet from Saturn to Neptune without lawful orders.

Having almost as many moons as Jupiter, Saturn's moons hosted fifty-two extensive underground colonies and domes, and the populace hid the greatest concentration of rebels. Portland's fleet was constantly interdicting freighters and liners attempting to sneak supplies to the rebels, and he was ruthless with the sympathizers his ships caught.

Pulling up Sol's planet chart on his monitor, a sly grin spread across Portland's face. Saturn was approaching an alignment with Neptune, which happened about 5.6 times during Neptune's 164.8-year orbit of Sol. Portland considered it an omen that heralded his triumph over the invaders.

But the admiral still needed an excuse. Checking the planet positions again, Portland would have giggled if he wasn't a conservative man by nature. Mars, where Space Admiral Chong was stationed, was on a far pass of the sun from Saturn, and the Earth was nearer Portland's position. It meant communication times to the space admiral and from the space admiral to the Tribunal would be maximized. His message to Chong would take almost twelve days, and certainly the admiral would want to check with the Tribunal before considering any action against Portland. That would add another four days each way for every message sent.

Immediately, Portland issued orders for the recall of the fleet's patrol ships and to ready the fleet for maneuvers, emphasizing each ship was to be at full armament load. Then he sat back and considered his message to Chong.

-12-

<Mr. President,> Julien sent, <a UE fast transport vessel has landed in the station's bay. None other than Tribune Brennan is aboard with Captain Lumley.> When Alex didn't immediately respond, Julien added, <The tribune doesn't have an appointment, Ser. Shall I send him back to Earth?>

<Smart of the tribune to bring Lumley,> Alex replied. <Julien, meet Brennan personally. Escort the tribune and Lumley on a slow tour. I want him to see the station. Take Z with you for innocuous protection … no troopers.>

<Understood, Mr. President.>

<Oh … and Julien, if he's wearing his tribune robe, have him change into something civilian. That goes for Lumley too … no uniform.>

<Acknowledged, Ser.>

Alex continued examining the holo-vid, which had been transferred from the fleet's stock for his use. Z installed an FTL transmitter to allow Alex to communicate independently with the fleet and pull data from the carriers' databases and the seeded probes for the holo-vid's display.

The UE scientists were continually educating Alex and Tatia on the system — planets, moons, colonies, domes, stations — the complete and partial domination by the UE militia. The moons of Jupiter and Saturn, totaling more than 100 bodies, held the greatest concentration of rebels, who were mixed in with the general population.

A couple of hours later, Alex received Julien's message. <I believe the admiral's warning would be "incoming,"> Julien sent.

Alex looked at the door and the scientists followed suit, recognizing that Alex had received a message.

In the corridor, Julien gestured to a door, which slid open, and Tribune Brennan walked through it with Lumley beside him. As directed, both men were wearing casual Earther attire, which seemed out of place on the station, where most people wore some sort of variation of a ship suit, uniform, or the more creative civilian wear of the outer rim.

"Francis," Olawale called out loudly and ran to greet the captain by picking him up in a huge bear hug.

"Easy, Olawale. After surviving everything I've been through in the past few months, it would be ironic to die from the greeting of a friend," Lumley replied, but the grin on his face said he didn't mind the enthusiastic welcome.

"Captain Lumley," Alex said, walking around the holo-vid, which he deliberately left on, to greet the captain. "It's a pleasure to see you in person again. Is your crew well?"

"They have been released, Mr. President. It seems the word is out about you, and their incarceration has no more value."

"Good to hear, Captain. Although, to my mind, there was never a need to imprison them," Alex replied, and slid his eyes to the tribune to drive his point home. "Tribune Brennan, so generous of you to bring the good captain to visit with his friends. Will you be staying long or are you just dropping the captain off and returning to Earth?"

<Mr. President, your ire is showing,> Julien sent.

Alex shook off his pique and offered both men a smile. "But where are my manners? Please come in. I was just being educated on your solar system … the habitats and the players … you know … the conquerors, the conquered, and the rebels."

Lumley hurried forward, fascinated by the holo-vid, and Olawale and he huddled while the scientist explained how the device worked and what they were seeing.

Brennan leaned over to study a remarkably clear view of Saturn and some of its moons. "How old is this image?" Brennan asked.

"You're looking at a real-time image, Tribune," Tatia replied.

"Since Saturn is on a near pass, it's about three days old then," Brennan guessed.

"Is that what real time means to you people?" Tatia asked, a frown forming on her face. "We've had time to drop probes throughout your system, Tribune. The image you're looking at is real time."

Brennan looked over at Lumley, but it was Olawale who offered the tribune an apologetic smile and an explanation. "If I was to say, Tribune Brennan, the Harakens are more advanced than us in many ways, I would be so woefully understating the truth."

The tribune was trying to grasp the reality of the Harakens' incredible technology when he absent-mindedly reached out to touch the life-like image of Neptune.

"Careful, Tribune," Tatia warned. "You don't want to destroy Neptune." A round of laughter followed Brennan's quick snatch of his hand back from the holo-vid, a shocked expression on his face. "Apologies, Tribune. I couldn't resist," Tatia said.

"Tribune Brennan, let's take a walk, while Lumley gets reacquainted with his old friends," Alex said and swung a hand toward the salon's main door.

Brennan's exit to the corridor was a mix of stuttered steps as he followed the president and took in the entourage who accompanied them in a precise turning of bodies even though the president hadn't requested their presence. Adding to the thoughts churning through his mind was the incredible variety of the Harakens — some enormous like the president, his admiral, and the gigantic one called Z — some displaying an other-worldly beauty such as the identical twins, who flanked their group, their eyes searching the crowded corridor for signs of trouble.

"Have you been to the station before, Tribune?" Alex asked.

"Actually, never, Mr. President, but I've seen militia vids as late as five years ago. I must say that what you've accomplished here is a —"

"Revolution," Alex supplied.

"Miraculous, certainly," Brennan said, carefully avoiding Alex's term. "That's why I'm here. Analysis of the flow of ships, people, and credits indicated a statistically significant growth. But I have to say that what I'm seeing so far indicates the estimates didn't do justice to the changes. This is a revival!"

"And what do you intend to do with this information, Tribune?" Alex asked.

Brennan would have explained, but an intoxicating woman swept up to the president and kissed him passionately. Then holding onto the president's arm she extended a hand to him, saying, "Tribune Brennan, I'm Renée de Guirnon."

"A pleasure … uh, Lady de Guirnon," Brennan replied, shaking Renée's hand and taking a stab at her title."

"Actually, we say Ser de Guirnon, but you may call me Renée."

"Renée," Brennan repeated, enjoying the name and fixing on Renée's face. "I'm Ian," he added.

<How to win friends,> Julien sent to Alex and Tatia.

<If I looked like Renée, I could win friends too,> Tatia retorted. President and SADE carefully kept their faces schooled lest they destroy Renée's conversational inertia.

"What do you think of your station, Ian?" Renée asked, releasing Alex's arm and taking Brennan's — just two old friends strolling the corridor and chatting.

"I was just telling the president," Brennan said, looking over his shoulder at Alex, "that I'm impressed, and I want to study what's happening here. I would love to replicate this across the entire system."

"But do you know, Ian, what is at the heart of this success?" Renée asked.

"Yes, I believe I do," Brennan admitted with regret. "I'm hoping to convince others that we should make this station the model for the entire UE."

"Why now, Tribune?" Julien challenged. "Is it because the UE is failing, economically and politically?"

"That's —" Brennan started to say and then stopped. "That's not a well-known fact," he finally said.

"How bad?" Alex asked. The group had come to a halt and formed a small circle around the tribune, forcing the station's inhabitants and visitors to flow around them.

"Twenty years or so," Brennan admitted.

"If you wait until there's an economic collapse, Tribune," Julien said, "your system will descend into chaos."

"There's always that remote possibility, but —" Brennan started to argue.

"A 0.1 percent possibility of avoiding a chaotic end," Z added.

"I wouldn't argue with the SADEs, Tribune," Alex said. When Brennan showed his confusion, Alex said indicating the two SADEs next to him. "Allow me to introduce Julien and Z, cognitive digital entities. What you might refer to as artificial intelligences. Strange term though. There's nothing artificial about them."

Ian Brennan looked across the faces arrayed in front of him — large, slender; ordinary, beautiful; human and artificial — and felt his legs go weak, but he never felt the strike of the deck. When the black mist began to dissolve, Ian felt powerful arms under him, carrying him toward a door labeled medical clinic. Black fading to gray allowed him to identify his rescuer as the president.

Suddenly, another beautiful face with flame-red hair swam in front of his, calling out his name. "How does everyone know me?" Brennan mumbled before passing out again.

* * *

Ian Brennan came back to consciousness on an extremely comfortable medical table. Touching his head, he felt the cool metal of a small device attached to his temple. Shifting onto his side, Ian sensed the table arrange itself to accommodate his new body position. For a moment, he thought the movement under him was indication he might be overwhelmed and about to pass out again, but no nausea or blackness came on. In fact, he felt fine.

"You may sit up, Tribune Brennan," Terese said, sweeping into the cubicle. She examined her medical reader and reached up to remove the monitoring device from Brennan's temple.

“Were you aware of the extent of your thyroid condition, Tribune?” Terese asked.

“Thyroid condition?” Brenan echoed in confusion. “I knew I was suffering lately from fatigue, always tired, but I thought it was just stress, the work,” Brennan replied.

“Yes, I can imagine playing tyrant is extremely taxing,” Terese replied. “Well, you won’t need to bother seeing a doctor now. You’re free to go. I’ve commed the president. He’ll be waiting for you outside. Through there, Tribune,” Terese said, gesturing down a corridor and walking away.

“Wait … won’t I need continuing medication?” Brennan called out.

“Medication? For what purpose?” Terese asked tersely.

“To keep the symptoms at bay,” Brennan replied.

“You’ll have no more symptoms, Tribune. As of this moment, 73 percent of your thyroid function has been restored. Within two more days, it will be fully restored and should remain that way. Be on your way, Tribune. I have people who I prefer to treat.”

Brennan found his way out of the clinic. The president was waiting for him as the red-haired woman had said he would be.

<Do you think it was his near brush with potential demise or his experience with our medical expert that has the tribune looking so confused?> Tatia sent to Alex.

“Well, Tribune Brennan, now that your medical disaster has been permanently averted perhaps we can continue our conversation,” Alex said, indicating they should continue walking.

“That’s what the woman said … the striking woman with the red hair … she said I was cured. But how?” Brennan asked.

“Another of those technological advancements of ours,” Alex replied.

“Do you think that you might share some of these capabilities with us?’ Brennan asked.

Alex stopped and faced the tribune. “First, stop warring on your own people. Prove you can act like a civilized human society, and then come visit us in peace. Maybe then we’ll see about sharing what we know. Come to think of it, I advise you to send the good Captain Lumley. He knows the way … that is, of course, providing the captain doesn’t leave with us.”

* * *

Cordelia left the station's admin offices, intending to join Julien and meet the tribune, who had just arrived. Instead, she heard Jason's young voice desperately calling her name.

"Come quick, Cordelia," Jason urged, running up to the SADE and grasping her hand, unaware that he was tugging on an avatar, to no effect whatsoever. "Hurry! It's Ginny. Something's wrong."

Jason released Cordelia's hand and ran down the corridor, waving for Cordelia to follow, but his spindly little legs weren't anywhere as fast as the algorithms that drove Cordelia. She raced up behind Jason, scooping the boy up in her arms, and moving through the corridor at a speed that frightened humans, Earther and Haraken alike.

"Point the way, Jason," Cordelia said, keeping her voice calm for the boy.

She needn't have been concerned for Jason. The breeze created by Cordelia's pace was blowing the boy's half-scalp of hair back and only accented the smile momentarily plastered on his face.

"Turn here," Jason said, pointing to a side corridor.

With her avatar's weight, Cordelia's feet were unable to maintain traction against the decking for the sharp turn, and she quickly shifted Jason to her right side as her left shoulder impacted the corridor wall, leaving a significant dent in it.

"Uh oh," Jason whispered, looking back at the dent. He directed Cordelia for a few more turns before he cried, "Stop, Cordelia! She's in there!" Jason was pointing to an abandoned supply compartment. The door was slightly ajar. "She won't let anyone come close to her, Cordelia. Not even me, and I'm her best friend. She just cries and holds her ears."

"Stay here, Jason," Cordelia said, setting the boy down gently.

The door was jammed, but Cordelia forced it. The resulting squeal of metal elicited sobs from deep in the room. Cordelia made her way as quietly as she could through the wall of empty shelves, finding Ginny huddled in a far corner, tears streaking her face and hands covering her ears.

The sounds of our world overwhelming you, little one? Cordelia thought. She lowered herself next to Ginny, making as little noise as possible.

In moments, Ginny abandoned her corner and crawled into Cordelia's lap, pulling her legs up to her chest, forming the tightest ball she could.

I've only just become mobile, little one. I've no experience as a mother, Cordelia thought. Searching for information on children, Cordelia was struck by the image of the Swei Swee young, riding the backs of the matrons, and falling asleep to Mutter's lullaby serenades. The centuries-old SADE had been gracious enough to share her extensive library of human compositions with Cordelia to use for her visual art, and Cordelia carried many of her favorites with her. Selecting the gentlest renditions and barely whispering, Cordelia began to sing.

Song after song came from Cordelia's lips until Ginny slowly uncurled and crawled upward to place her partially repaired ear on Cordelia's cheek. Over time, Cordelia ever so slowly increased the volume, and Ginny slid back down into her lap, placing one ear against Cordelia's chest.

The tiniest whisper of feet signaled Jason creeping through the shelves. When Cordelia saw him, she held out an arm, and Jason snuggled in close, timidly reaching out a hand to Ginny, who reached out to hold it.

Cordelia continued to serenade the children until both fell asleep. It was hours later when Julien eased through the open storage door and silently crossed the room to Cordelia. The sight of the two children huddled asleep in Cordelia's arms stopped his processing for the barest of moments. *For the gifts that continue to come our way, thank you, my friend,* he thought.

Julien, listening to Cordelia's soft voice, sat down across from her and the children. In one hand dangled the pair of Earther noise-canceling ear covers Cordelia had requested.

-13-

Space Admiral Li Chong, the supreme leader of the UE's naval forces, having completed three days of ship requisition planning with staff, returned to his headquarters housed in one of Mar's more expansive and well-appointed domes. After exiting the connecting airlock from the transport dome, Chong chose to walk to his quarters.

The admiral's adjutant was careful to keep his distance. This was one of the few opportunities Li Chong had to decompress. He enjoyed people watching and letting the lush greenery, planted along the walkways, ease the tensions created by the duties of his office.

After an enjoyable meal, Chong took his glass of wine to his desk, letting out a long sigh. He expected his message queue would be extensive and it was worse than expected. Pulling up those marked urgent first, he worked for several hours, before the desire for sleep overcame him.

With the demands on Chong's schedule, it was two more days before he opened Admiral Portland's message, which hadn't been marked as urgent. Chong got up from his desk to get another cup of caf, while Portland's message played, but in moments he was hurrying back to his desk to hit replay, listening intently to the message.

Portland was heard saying, "I've obtained reliable information, Admiral. The Harakens are intending to make a play for the moons of Saturn. It's a logical move on their part. Saturn is entering an alignment phase with Neptune. But in good conscience, I can't wait until the Harakens have backed my forces into defensive positions against our moons' colonies and stations. It's my opinion that the only way to handle this problem is to interdict the Harakens before they're underway from Idona. My fleet is headed there as of the time stamp on this message."

Chong's eyes flicked to the message's date and swore enough to blister his monitor's coating. Portland had been underway for over seventeen days. Immediately, Chong opened a message to Tribune Woo, attaching Portland's message to his own.

"Tribune Woo, you should be as shocked by Admiral Portland's message as I have been," the space admiral recorded. "It was my understanding from you that the Harakens were hands off unless they moved inward. Portland indicates he possesses information that the Harakens are planning just such a move. This seems specious to me. I believe Admiral Portland is glory hunting. If you haven't bypassed my command, which I doubt you have, then you had best check your own ranks. Portland wouldn't have made this move without someone putting him up to it."

Chong closed the message and sent it as admiral priority. *What I wouldn't give for some of those Haraken FTL comms probes about now,* Chong thought. He debated sending a recall order to Portland. Even knowing it would arrive too late, he finally decided to do so just to have it on the record.

What bothered the space admiral most of all was the Harakens would soon spot the fleet headed their way, if they hadn't already, and they would have no way of knowing that Admiral Portland's actions were unauthorized by Tribune Woo or him.

"Well, Portland, you always wanted my job," Chong said to the empty room. "Let's just hope against all odds that you're successful. 'Cause if you're not, my over-adventuresome fool, you might end up unleashing the fury of these strangers on all our heads."

* * *

Tribune Woo was in her chambers when the comms operator called about an urgent message he was transferring to her console from Space Admiral Chong. After unlocking it, Woo sat back in bed with a glass of lemon water to listen and then spilled it down her nightgown rushing to sit up and restart the message.

After several replays, Woo sat thinking about Chong's warning that he thought someone in her ranks put Portland up to this action. She knew it wasn't Brennan and his associates. They were keenly interested in coopting what the Harakens were accomplishing. That left the enclave of high judges and Tribune Lucchesi.

Despite knowing that she should wait to confront Lucchesi in the morning, she leapt out of bed, dressing quickly and hurrying down the corridors to Lucchesi's wing. Security passed her through the first two checkpoints, but the man stationed outside the Tribune's private quarters stated that Lucchesi had retired for the evening.

"Tell you what, Sergeant," Woo said, looking up the 30 centimeters to the guard's face and locking eyes with him. "How about I just announce a general breach of security within the Tribunal's domain? Then a fresh set of security will sweep all of you up and sort through who broke protocol. And while they are escorting you off to some deep, dark hole, I'll have my chat with Tribune Lucchesi."

The sergeant's swallow was quite evident before he replied. "One moment, Tribune Woo, I'll let Tribune Lucchesi know you have an urgent matter to discuss."

"You do that, Sergeant, but tell the tribune not to keep me waiting."

The sergeant returned within minutes, ushering Woo into a sumptuous sitting room and quickly vacating her presence. Woo took in the quality of the furnishings and whistled softly. "It appears someone is making the most of their title," she murmured.

Woo sat in one of the plainer chairs, still a plush piece of furniture, and fumed for the additional quarter of an hour it took Lucchesi to appear. Yet, he still looked as if he had just rolled out of bed, tying his robe about his ample waist.

"This is most irregular, Tribune Woo. What's the emergency?" Lucchesi demanded.

"You're the emergency, Lucchesi," Woo replied hotly. She wanted to get off her chair and poke a finger in Lucchesi's ample belly, but during the time she waited, she schooled her thoughts to consider her evidence, which was suppositional, at best. "Admiral Portland's fleet is sailing toward Neptune to engage the Harakens!"

"This is indeed news," Lucchesi replied, "but couldn't it wait until morning? There is little that we can do about it at this late hour." Lucchesi chose one of the most sumptuous chairs in the salon to settle into while he appeared to be surprised by Woo's announcement.

"According to Space Admiral Chong, Portland has no orders to leave Saturn's space, much less to travel to Neptune to take on the Harakens. According to Chong, someone put the idea in his head. My credits are on you or the enclave of high judges."

"That's a felonious accusation, Tribune Woo. I would be careful making such libelous statements," Lucchesi said, pretending a show of indignation. He would have jumped up to emphasize the point, but those days were long past. Struggling to rise would not suit the show of resentment the moment required. "What's your proof of the enclave's or my involvement?"

"None, as of this moment."

"Hah, thought so. You come here, in the early morning hours, throwing about your malicious accusations, all because you have a rogue element … in your military, I might add, and you're seeking to make a scapegoat of the judiciary."

"Don't play your games with me, Lucchesi. I know you're complicit in this, and I will find the proof. What you don't realize is the great mistake you've made. Tribune Brennan's reports indicate Idona has become enormously profitable with minimal problems. It could be a model for the UE, and Portland is about to end that."

"How? By ridding us of the Harakens?"

"You actually think he will win against the Harakens? You're deluded."

"A UE fleet anchored by a battleship, several cruisers, two destroyer squadrons, and loaded with sixty patrol ships … how could Portland not win?"

"For a man of the judiciary, you seem to know quite a bit about this particular fleet."

"Well … well, I read the military bulletins, Tribune," Lucchesi stammered.

"Only there are several problems with your plan, Lucchesi," Woo said, standing to hold up a finger to him. "One, the population has been squeezed economically as far as we can manage without inciting a general revolt. Word is out about Idona Station, and people want to see it succeed … are hoping it will succeed. How do you think they're going to react to the military wrecking that?

Woo moved closer to Lucchesi to make her next point, and she could see the tribune disliked the imperious action, but his ego and his weight kept him pinned in the chair. "Two, Portland just left Saturn uncovered, which allows the single, greatest concentration of rebels in our system free access to freight and passenger drops to support them. What if they decide to revolt against the resident militia while Portland is gone? And, three, what if the Harakens simply pull up stakes from Idona and take over Saturn's colonies and stations? They have the speed to outmaneuver our ships or didn't you read that military bulletin, Tribune?"

Woo watched the emotions flick across Lucchesi's face. This was the moment she hoped to have when she chose to confront him in the middle of the night. What she saw was Lucchesi reconsidering his plan in light of the arguments she just enumerated. *You're guilty, you idiot, of making the biggest mistake with the Harakens since High Judge Bunaldi played heavy-handed with them,* Woo thought. She shook her head in disgust at Lucchesi and marched her small frame out of his salon.

* * *

A senior comms officer was woken in the middle of the night by the head of the Tribunal security. "Up and at 'em, Captain. Tribune Woo needs you on the Harakens' comms as of now! Don't bother taking time to look pretty. The tribune said it's an emergency."

The captain took one look at the head of security, whose jacket was absent and whose shirt wasn't even tucked into his pants. He jumped into a pair of pants, pulled on lined boots, and threw a shirt on. The two men hurried from the officers' quarters to the comms station, where Tribune Woo, dressed in her nightclothes and a robe, was waiting impatiently.

"Ah, you're here, Captain," Woo said in greeting, pulling out the central comms chair for him. "I need to speak to Tribune Brennan."

The captain halted in mid-position as he was rotating the chair to sit. "But Tribune Woo, Tribune Brennan is on Idona."

"It appears I'm the only one fully awake," Woo muttered. "Yes, Captain, Tribune Brennan is on Idona Station, but we have access to the Harakens' FTL probe. President Racine said we could call him anytime. I realize we haven't attempted to do so yet, but this will be a learning moment, won't it, Captain?"

"Yes, Ma'am," the captain replied, resorting to his training in addressing a superior officer, which was exactly how the ex-admiral was handling the situation. He resorted to the notes made by the previous officers on duty when they received the Harakens' calls. The instructions seemed simple enough, if nonsensical. Setting the panel to the codes for Idona Station and bypassing the recording process, he took up the headset.

"This is the Supreme Tribunal calling Idona Station. Come in Idona. Over," the captain announced, feeling every bit as foolish as a cadet at attention in front of an admiral. When nothing happened, the captain started to repeat his message, but was interrupted by a reply.

"Supreme Tribunal, this is Idona Station. Sergeant Hanford on comms. Is this really Earth?" The last was delivered with a heavy streak of incredulity.

Woo motioned the captain out of his seat, and the station security head pulled on the captain's arm to guide him out of the comms room.

"Sergeant Hanford, this is Tribune Woo. I must speak to Tribune Brennan, but you need to get him on comms without raising a fuss or communicating to the Harakens."

"Apologies, Tribune Woo, but all FTL communications are monitored by the Haraken SADEs," the sergeant said.

"This is Julien, Tribune Woo," the SADE said, intent on discovering her desire for secrecy. "What seems to be the matter?"

Woo's plans flew out the hatch. She had hoped to advise Brennan privately and discuss a means of diplomatically breaking the news to the Haraken president. SADE was a word she read repeatedly in the dispatches from Idona — mobile artificial intelligences. Most of the messages contained glowing reports about them, as much about their capabilities as their personalities.

"Julien, I have an urgent need to speak to Tribune Brennan, but you might as well include your president and your admiral," Woo requested.

"Allow me to arrange the conference call, Tribune Woo," Julien replied.

After a long silence on the call, Woo asked, "Sergeant, has Julien left the comms station to organize the conference?"

"Tribune, Julien was never here. I have no idea where he is. Furthermore, it's unnecessary for him to physically locate the president or the admiral. He'll communicate with them through those things in their heads. Only Tribune Brennan will need to be located and brought to a comms station ... and Tribune Woo ... Julien is monitoring this conversation as we speak."

"Apologies, Julien," Woo said. "No disrespect was intended."

"And none was taken, Tribune Woo," Julien replied. "The confusion generated by the lack of knowledge about our technology is understandable."

If Woo had known the thoughts of her comms captain, feeling like a cadet at attention before a ranking officer, she might have realized she was feeling the same way. *Portland, you're a dead man, either at the hands of the Harakens or by my own,* Woo thought.

"Tribune Woo," Brennan said, "I'm here in the president's quarters. Several people are present on this comm."

"I must admit, President Racine, I'm caught off guard," Woo began. "I hoped to speak to Tribune Brennan privately. However, I've just learned from Sergeant Hanford that this will never be possible with your FTL comms system."

"One thing about Harakens, Tribune Woo, we tend toward open communications," Alex said.

"What I'm about to tell you, Mr. President, would be considered divulging a state secret without the consent of the Tribunal. So discussing it with you puts my position, if not my life, in jeopardy."

"Noted, Tribune Woo," Alex acknowledged.

"The reason I'm breaking the seal of the Tribunal is that I believe others have already done that. For reasons yet to be discovered, an admiral, stationed around Saturn's moons, has gathered his fleet and is headed your way."

<Julien,> Alex sent, and the SADE activated the holo-vid and began displaying telemetry from a probe stationed hundreds of millions of kilometers inward of Neptune. "Tribune Woo, please clarify your statement 'for reasons yet to be discovered.'"

Woo cleared her throat softly, knowing she was treading on dangerous ground and about to betray a military commander and his fleet. "No one in the military command, including myself, authorized Admiral Portland to undertake this mission."

"Tribune Woo, this is Admiral Tachenko. What does Admiral Portland believe his mission to be?"

"According to Portland's message to Space Admiral Chong, he believes you were about to make a run at Saturn so he intends to intercept your move."

"Intercept?" Tatia asked. "You mean attack and attempt to destroy us."

"Yes, Admiral," Woo admitted.

"Tribune Woo," Brennan interjected, "while I'm not privy to all that happens here on the station or with the Haraken fleet, I've seen no preparations for an invasion of any other … pardon me, Mr. President … I've seen no plans to move the Haraken fleet from Idona. In fact, all efforts have been concentrated on restoring the commercial capability of this station, and, I must say, the progress has been nothing but outstanding."

"Be that as it might be, Tribune Brennan, Admiral Portland is about to bring that progress to an end. He has a considerable fleet. Let me tell you what you are up against, Mr. President."

"Um … Tribune Woo, that's not necessary," Brennan said. "I believe we're looking at Portland's fleet now. Is that not correct, Julien?" Ian

Brennan had learned enough in his short time on the station that if something seemed technologically incomprehensible, it was best to ask one of the SADEs.

"That's correct, Tribune Brennan, this is a probe's view of Admiral Portland's fleet on approach from Saturn," Julien replied.

"You're looking at the fleet? How?" Woo asked.

"Julien, please," Brennan said, indicating he should reply.

<Mr. President?> Julien inquired. When Alex nodded, Julien explained. "We have had sufficient time for our fighters to seed your system with FTL probes near key planets. The probes have extensive telemetry capability and can relay that information to our comms in real time."

Woo muttered something unintelligible. She was busy filing that piece of information in two places: dangerous technology the Harakens possessed and a potential tool she might borrow to mitigate the oncoming disaster Portland was fomenting.

"So, exactly what are you seeing?" Woo asked, no longer caring whom she was speaking to or who answered.

Brennan looked at Alex, who nodded. This moment was like so many of the others Brennan had experienced since arriving at Idona. "We're looking at a Haraken holo-vid, Tribune. It's a projected, three-dimensional display of whatever data is fed to it. In this case, it's a probe's view. I'm putting my hands into the holo-vid to expand the view, and now I'm rotating the view to focus on the admiral's battleship. This is incredible, Tribune. I can view every ship in the fleet closeup."

Woo was holding her head in her hands. *Bunaldi, why did you have to make enemies of these people?* Woo asked herself.

"Is there anything else you wish to convey, Tribune Woo?" Alex asked.

Woo racked her brain for whatever she might say to mitigate the horrendous oncoming clash of people, ships, and cultures. "Perhaps no one in the UE has said this to you, Mr. President, so let me be the first. On behalf of the government of Sol, I'm deeply sorry for the actions taken by our people in your systems and whole heartedly wish that we could start over."

"Apology accepted, Tribune Woo, but it does not erase the past. The UE has its work cut out for it, if you wish to earn our trust. I suggest you build it among your own people before you ever approach us again."

When Brennan returned to his quarters, Tatia regarded Alex, who was deep in thought, his chin supported by his hands. "Alex, there is a good argument for saying that what you intended to do, give the UE a reason to stay away from the Confederation, has been accomplished."

Alex glanced at Tatia and those others still in the room. *So many expectant faces,* Alex thought. "Not yet, Tatia, not yet."

-14-

After Woo's call to Idona, a thought occurred to her, and she looked over the comms table, locating the repeat call icon, and tapped it to start her call. "This is Tribune Woo for Julien."

"Yes, Tribune, how may I be of service?" Julien replied.

Woo shook her head in disbelief that communication to a distant planet could be this easy, and that the Haraken SADE could be so accommodating was disconcerting, to say the least.

"Julien, I need to speak to Captain Shimada, if you please." Woo couldn't remember the last time she had said please to someone and the thought was even more perturbing than her previous one. *How far we've drifted from even the courtesies,* she thought.

"One moment, Tribune, and I will connect you with the captain. You do understand that I will be monitoring your exchange."

"Yes, Julien, and I want you to relay to your president what I will be telling Captain Shimada."

Reiko Shimada was woken from a deep sleep by an insistent beeping from her comms console, and she struggled to tap the connect icon on her display "Shimada here," she said in a sleep-deprived voice.

"Apologies, Captain, but you have a comm from Tribune Woo," the comms officer on duty reported.

"Send the message to my console," Shimada replied.

"Captain, it's not a message. It's a comm call from Tribune Woo routed through the Harakens' FTL comms system. Julien, the Haraken SADE, is relaying her call."

Shimada was instantly awake. Her first thought was that it would be an audio-only comm, and she needn't dress. She grabbed a carafe of water by her bed and guzzled much of it to hydrate herself and help wake up. "Put it through, Lieutenant," Shimada ordered, wiping her mouth on her sleeve.

"Captain Shimada, while we've never met, I must take a moment to enjoy this sisterly occasion," Woo said. "We are the first UE woman-to-woman conversation across our solar system, excluding Julien, who is handling this comm."

"Do I understand you're still on Earth, Tribune Woo?" Shimada asked.

"Yes, Captain, I'm using the Harakens' FTL comms system, but let's get down to business. We have a big problem." Woo succinctly outlined Admiral Portland's message to Space Admiral Chong. "Before I continue, Captain, I have one important question. Have you witnessed any steps taken by the Harakens to move their fleet?"

"Negative, Tribune. Their three ships haven't moved since about two days after they took over the station."

"Thought as much, Captain. At this time, Admiral Chong and I consider Portland a renegade and his fleet movements as unauthorized.

"How may I be of service, Tribune Woo?" Shimada asked, her guts roiling at the possible requests the tribune might ask of her.

"I need you to offer your assistance to the Harakens in whatever capacity they deem useful," Woo replied.

Reiko Shimada was shocked. She expected to be ordered to abandon her post and retreat inward from the area. Her secret hope would have been just this, to support the Harakens, but it was a hope she could never have voiced.

"I have one concern, Tribune. Helping the Harakens will be viewed as treason by the judiciary."

"I intend to indemnify you, Captain. Record this next section separately," Woo ordered.

When Shimada readied a separate message file, she cued Woo and heard, "Captain Shimada, Admiral Portland is conducting an unauthorized fleet movement, intending to attack the Harakens at Idona Station. As the tribune representing the UE military contingent and with the approval of Space Admiral Li Chong, you are hereby ordered to lend whatever support, intelligence, or material that President Racine of the Harakens might request of you to defeat Admiral Portland's rogue military action. Tribune Woo out." Shimada closed the file and switched back to the open comm.

"Any questions, Captain?" Woo asked.

"Are there any conditions that apply to this order, Tribune Woo?" Shimada asked.

"None, Captain. Good luck. Tribune Woo out."

Shimada tapped off her comms console, but it remained lit. She tapped it a second time with no effect, and then the issue dawned on her. "Yes, Julien?"

"Greetings, Captain Shimada. I anticipate my president and admiral will prefer a face-to-face opportunity to discuss Portland's foolish foray."

"Understood, Julien. I presume we have time?"

"We do, Captain. First, I suggest you move your destroyer and patrol vessels outward of the station."

"What distance do you want me to maintain from Idona?" Shimada asked.

"Any distance you feel appropriate, Captain, but outside of the freighter transit lanes."

"We're no longer banished to the dark?" Shimada asked, a small smile tweaking the corner of her mouth. When Julien failed to reply, Shimada added, "We'll get underway immediately. I should be on station in a little more than two days."

"I'll let the president know to expect you, Captain. Your assistance is appreciated."

This time, Shimada watched the comm console wink off by itself. It would have been humorous if it didn't mean that with artificial intelligences there might no longer be any personal privacy. *Of course, your privacy would depend on the moral nature of the intelligences, which would depend on the moral natures of those who created them,* Shimada thought.

* * *

Shimada arrived at Idona much sooner than expected. Her destroyer was underway for about eleven hours when a Haraken fighter paralleled the ship. Actually, it suddenly appeared off the bridge's view shields while

Shimada was simultaneously hailed, causing the destroyer's pilot a momentary miss of a couple of heartbeats.

"Greetings, Captain Shimada. I'm Wing Commander Franz Cohen. Request permission to come aboard, Captain. The president would like you soonest at Idona."

Shimada made a quick decision. *Better start acting real nimble, Reiko, if you're going to keep pace with these people,* she thought. Command was handed over to her senior lieutenant, who had the coordinates for their new position off Idona Station. A quick call to her steward had him packing her cases and meeting her in the destroyer's bay.

A panicked flight chief called Shimada, wondering how to squeeze an enemy fighter into an already crowded bay.

"Let the pilot figure out what he needs, Chief," Shimada returned. "Just clear your people from the bay and get the doors open. I'm curious to see how well these fighters can maneuver."

Shimada and several of her crew crowded the airlock hatch's view plate, which looked into the bay. That officers and enlisted people were breathing down Shimada's neck for a glimpse of the Haraken fighter was something she could forgive today. The pilot eased nose first into the bay's opening, held steady for a moment, and then backed out to swing neatly around 180 degrees and reverse the fighter into the bay. Maneuvering his ship into the bay's corner, the pilot settled the fighter to the deck.

More than a few expletives filled the air of the airlock over the performance.

"So that's what we would be up against," the flight chief murmured to Shimada.

"Approximately 400 of them, I understand," Shimada murmured back. A soft, slow whistle behind her greeted her announcement. "Yes, good reason not to piss them off," the captain added. "Let's go, Chief. My ride is waiting."

The chief ordered everyone out of the airlock, closed the bay doors, and when the bay and airlock were equalized, Shimada strode across the bay and watched a hatch appear where there had been no sign of it before. But what truly caught her eye was the unusual hull. It was smooth, no angles in sight, and, instead of a metal sheen, it possessed a beautiful translucence in the ocean's colors.

Shimada was eyeing the steep steps inset into the hatch, which had folded down, when a mountain of a man, similar in size to the Haraken president, bounded down the half-dozen steps using only two of them. To her mind, the vid comms with the Harakens did not accurately portray their incredible size. After a quick greeting, the commander snatched up her bags in one hand and offered to assist her up the steps with the other. *For a big man, he's nimble,* Shimada thought, giving the commander a second look.

Inside, she was seated, and the commander disappeared. Shimada waited for the sensation of the fighter's launch, but it never came. Then finally, Commander Cohen came back into the cabin.

"We will be on station in ten of your hours, Captain. Relax and enjoy yourself," Franz said.

Shimada felt like a passenger on a luxury cruise. She was offered water and food, which she found delicious, but nothing matched her sublime seat. When it first shifted under her, Shimada found it extremely disconcerting, as if it should have waited for her permission. The next few times she moved and the seat responded in kind, she was merely annoyed. But, hours later when she sat drinking a marvelous cup of what the Harakens called thé, she thought of the chair as her personal masseuse.

Late in the flight, the commander returned to chat with her. "I was under the impression, Wing Commander Cohen, that this was a fighter. Am I mistaken? It appears to be a shuttle," Shimada said.

"Call me Franz, Captain," Cohen said extending his hand.

"Reiko," Shimada replied.

"You're not mistaken, Reiko. This is a fighter, but because it has the capability of traversing a system as many times as desired without refueling or rearming, we must travel with amenities."

"Is this your way of flirting, Commander Cohen?" Shimada said, her eyes staring hard at his. "Yes, I'm UE, and yes, I'm a woman, but does that give you the right to think less of me and tell me stories?" Shimada expected the chastised wing commander to become indignant and stomp back to his pilot's cabin. Instead, he gave her a good-natured smile.

"I won't deny you're an attractive woman, Captain, but you've been told no stories, as you put it. While I'm not at liberty to discuss how we achieve these extraordinary capabilities, I can tell you that some of the technologies are borrowed ... alien stuff, you see."

The commander winked at her and left to return to the pilot's cabin. Shimada dwelt on what the commander said until she was lulled to sleep in the oh-so relaxing seat.

* * *

The lights on board the Haraken fighter brightened, and Franz went back to the cabin to wake Reiko.

"We've landed at Idona?" Shimada asked.

"Yes, Captain, if you will follow me. We have a meeting to join."

Shimada stood up, stretched, and then dutifully followed Franz. But many aspects of her flight still disturbed her — the shortened flight time, no engine noise, no sensation of flight, and grav plating in a small vessel — to name a few.

After an eye-opening walk through a busy and bright main corridor, so unlike her last visit to the station, Cohen and she joined a meeting in the lobby of a sleepover, and Shimada was promptly introduced to the principals attending the meeting.

"Captain, we appreciate your help," Alex said. "We would like you to review each of the ship types in the approaching fleet and give us a summary of their capabilities."

"I have been ordered to assist you, Mr. President, but I believe this will work best if you are straight with me from the beginning."

"You have a reason to believe we won't be truthful, Captain?" Alex asked.

"If I may, Mr. President," Franz said. "The captain has taken offense to my statements about our travelers."

"Travelers? That's what you call your fighters? Interesting, but am I expected to believe they can traverse a system without refueling?" Shimada asked, staring at the faces surrounding her. "And that your travelers don't need to rearm?" she added, holding out her hands as if asking for sanity.

"Yes, Captain," Tatia said quietly.

Shimada looked around, and every Haraken, human and SADE, was nodding their affirmation. Her eyes landed on Franz, who wore just the slightest smile. "It looks like I owe you an apology, Commander. Sorry."

"One thing you should know about our Commander Cohen," Renée declared. "He's a most direct and honest individual."

"Apology accepted, Captain," Franz said graciously.

"Yes, well … it's not polite to overwhelm your associates on the first meeting. You should dribble out your extraordinary capabilities in small doses," Shimada said contritely.

"Noted, Ser, you would prefer me in small doses," Franz said, a wide grin spreading across his face, causing Shimada's cheeks to turn rosy.

"Well, now that intersystem relationships are well in hand, may we get down to business?" asked Alex, which caused Franz to grin wider and Reiko to blush redder. Alex turned on the holo-vid, and Julien connected the room's occupants with those waiting aboard the fleet's ships and the holo-vids. "Captain, we encountered the *Hand of Justice* in my home world's system. Are there any differences between that ship and this one?"

As Shimada peered at the image of the battleship, which filled only part of the holo-vid, it sprung to fill its entire width. "That's impressive. How much would it cost to buy one of these?" Shimada remarked, which earned her a round of chuckles and eased some of the tension in the room.

"This is the *Guardian*, the admiral's battleship, which will be the fleet's flagship. It's similar to the *Hand of Justice*, but not as powerful," Shimada began. For the next hour, she detailed ship type, armament, and capabilities, while the SADEs built models of the UE's fleet capabilities.

Once Shimada was done, she stepped back and watched the president's people use the holo-vid as a planning tool, formulating scenarios as the fleet came at them intact or breaking into various formations. The scenarios got more complicated and the holo-vid changed its display so rapidly that Shimada could not keep track of the myriad versions of their plans.

At one point, Shimada turned and whispered a question to Cohen. When the commander replied, he placed his lips next to her head, his breath warm against her ear. Despite her inclination to discourage the Haraken, she couldn't resist composing the occasional question for the commander.

"Okay, Captain Shimada, it's your turn," Alex said. "Help us with the nature of the admiral."

"You mean aside from the fact that he is one of the biggest butt-kissers and hard-asses in UE naval forces?" Shimada replied.

"You had to know that was coming," Tatia groused.

"Then a scenario for you, Captain," Alex said. "Suppose we demonstrate to the admiral that we have a dangerous tool that could annihilate his fleet. What would he do?"

"Could you give me more details about this tool?" Shimada asked.

<Negative, Mr. President,> Tatia sent in the open to the group. <We shouldn't share the details of our nanites solution.> Affirmations of Tatia's opinion poured onto the conference comm from every ship's captain and commander.

Renée volunteered a contrary opinion, privately to Alex. <You may tell her, my love. You find the woman intriguing, and you feel you can trust her.> When Alex hesitated in his reply, Renée decided to take the initiative.

"Captain, while my partner is still searching for the appropriate words, I will save us some time. The president has an uncanny intuitive sense, and he feels he can trust you, but his mathematically wired brain must still calculate the probabilities of whether responding to your question is beneficial or detrimental to our people."

Shimada hid her laughter behind her hand. It was obvious that the president's partner was having a good time at the man's expense. However, the president merely smiled good-naturedly and shrugged.

<Serendipity rules,> Julien sent to the group. He did so enjoy these moments that were in such contrast to the logic and order that dominated his crystal core.

"It's a demonstration of our nanites technology, Captain," Alex said. "The admiral would observe via his telemetry the disintegration of a small vessel."

"How long would this process take?" Shimada asked.

Alex looked over at Z, who said, "A vessel the size of one of your patrol ships would be absorbed in a few hours."

"And you could envelop the entire fleet if you wished? Dissolve the ships right out from under the admiral?" Shimada asked. When Z nodded his affirmative, Shimada replied, "Then it's foolish to show your hand with a demonstration. If you can defeat the fleet in one move, you should do it."

"And, at the same time, we would prove to the populace of Sol that Harakens are as proficient at warfare and murder as Earthers," Julien added.

Alex looked over at Tatia, who was smiling. "An officer made in your image, Admiral," Alex acknowledged. "Humor me, Captain. Suppose Admiral Portland sees this demonstration. What does he do?"

"Portland will realize that he is up against a dangerous weapon, and he'll abandon the sledge-hammer approach and divide his forces into squadrons for a multi-pronged attack," Shimada replied. Turning to the holo-vid, she said, "Idona and the fleet, please."

Julien manipulated the holo-vid display for her, and Shimada asked, "Can you add the traffic lanes for freighters and passenger ships, approaching from inward, at the same time as the fleet arrives?"

Both Julien and Z searched for arriving ships from the fleet's telemetry scans, calculating their velocities, arrival times, and comparing them to the UE fleet. Then Julien added colored lines, red for freighters and blue for passenger ships, to the holo-vid.

Shimada smiled and shook her head in wonder at the completed display. She studied the holo-vid for a while, and then said, "If you proceed with your demo, Portland will probably divide his command into at least three smaller fleets. His battleship will anchor the center contingent and will hide among these arriving civilian ships so you can't use your —"

"Nanites," Julien supplied.

"Yes, nanites," Shimada said, nodding to the SADE. "The other two groups composed mainly of destroyers, possibly a cruiser, and smaller ships, will circle left and right of the station to engage your forces. Meanwhile, his main force will come straight on until he has the station surrounded."

"Captain, how sure are you that Admiral Portland will use the civilian ships as a screen for his main force?"

When Shimada heard the voice issue from the base of the holo-vid, she mouthed the word "who?" to Franz. He whispered in her ear, "Wing Commander Ellie Thompson." It was odd to Reiko how quickly Franz's murmurings in her ear had shifted from disconcerting to pleasant.

"Quite certain, Commander," Shimada replied. "It's a tested and proven UE naval tactic, and one of Admiral Portland's favorites."

"Everywhere you go there's a Downing, a García, or a Bunaldi," Tatia grumped. "Must be a defect loose in the human genome."

Alex stared at the holo-vid and, as the silence dragged on, Reiko looked back at Franz, who signaled silence with a finger to his lips. She glanced over at the admiral, who had assumed a parade stance, and did likewise. The only one moving was Renée, who stood behind the president, her hands on his shoulders and occasionally stroking a finger lightly along his neck or ear. The intimacy of their connection so prominently displayed in public seemed out of place to Shimada, but glancing around at the other Harakens, patiently waiting, it was accepted, if not expected.

After a quarter of an hour, the Haraken president got a smile on his face that spread into a grin, and his people relaxed their stances and began smiling as well.

"We'll start with our demonstration here," Alex said, manipulating the holo-vid and pointing to a location. "It will give the admiral time to observe and make his next maneuver. Captain Shimada, I will need one of your patrol ships, with a pilot and a crew member. Both need to be EVA qualified for a spacewalk and able to follow our orders explicitly."

Shimada nodded her acceptance, confused by the sudden turn of events in the room.

"Commander Cohen, I'm sure that Captain Shimada hasn't had a proper opportunity to see the station's improvements," Alex directed. "Why don't you take the time to introduce her to the new face of Idona?"

Franz gallantly offered his arm to Reiko, and, when she accepted it, he steered her out of the planning room.

When the doors slid closed behind Franz and Reiko, Tatia eyed Alex. "Renée suggested you trusted her," she said, nodding toward the door Shimada had left through. "But I have a feeling you didn't share the entire plan."

"In fact, I do trust her, but we are surrounded by UE people, who are observing our every movement, most are curious, but some are definitely spies, based on comms the SADEs are monitoring. What Shimada doesn't know, she can't inadvertently share."

"So what's the real plan?" Sheila asked, her voice coming through the holo-vid.

"Oh … I told Captain Shimada the truth," Alex replied with a big smile for those around him. "We'll start with the demonstration, and that will be the bet that the admiral will focus on throughout his campaign."

Groans elicited from the holo-vid. Most Méridiens were not aficionados of Alex's card games, while many of the New Terrans loved to join Alex at his home for a few games with the ancient deck of cards.

"Okay … so we're playing poker. What's the bet?" Tatia asked.

"When do you win at poker, Admiral?" Alex asked cryptically.

Tatia knew the answer to this one, but didn't quite see how it applied. Nonetheless, she dutifully responded. "When you make the other players believe you have the winning hand, whether you do or don't."

Alex smiled at her, winked, and then left the planning room with Renée.

Tatia offered Julien a quizzical expression as if to say, "Help me out."

Julien smiled brightly in reply, and sent via the conference comm. <The unfathomable and unforgettable thoughts of our president — they make life interesting for the SADEs too, Admiral.>

* * *

In the corridor, Reiko slipped her hand out of Franz's arm, but he seemed not to take offense. "Is that typical of your president … his decision I mean? Ask his military advisors for their opinion, and then choose to do something entirely different?"

"It's an unusual relationship we have with our president, and it's a long story, best related over a meal," Franz hinted.

Reiko ignored the offer and continued her line of thought. "Your president seems intent on hearing what Julien has to say."

"Hmm … yes. I believe they're kindred spirits who've found each other."

"But Julien is an AI … I mean you speak of him as if he's human," Shimada said. When she realized Franz had stopped walking, she turned back to face him.

"No, Julien's not human, but maybe something better," replied Franz, his hands on his hips while he considered his reply. "You ask why the president listens to him. It's because Julien is probably the kindest, gentlest individual among us … he's our conscience, you might say."

-15-

The arrival of a UE destroyer captain on station had not gone unnoticed by the rebels. Her uniform incensed many among those whose families had suffered at the hands of the military forces. When word reached Vic, the opportunity for payback seemed too good to pass up. He rallied two cronies, who felt as he did about UE naval officers. The captain was reported to have attended the Haraken president's planning meeting, so they waited unobtrusively in the main corridor for her to appear.

When the captain exited the meeting on the arm of a Haraken commander, the three men slid out of sight and trailed the couple who appeared to be window shopping.

* * *

Reiko couldn't believe the transformation Idona had undergone. Her last visit to the station was about forty days before the Harakens arrived, and, at that time, she worried over catastrophic accidents that appeared imminent and might damage much of the station, to say nothing of the potential loss of life.

When Reiko was first posted to Idona, less than a year ago, she was shocked at the state of disrepair, the huge vacancy of shops and tenants, and the attitude of Major Lindling. Her first report up the chain of command was lengthy and detailed, and she waited for a response, something that would give her approval to take action and reverse the downward spiral of the station, but only a single terse reply was forthcoming.

As captain of the *Conquest*, her job, she was told, was to intercept rebel supporters and privateers, who preyed on the freighters and miners traveling between the belt and Idona, and nothing more.

The main corridor she walked today was everything she hoped Idona could become — the corridors were clean and bustling, the shops were busy — people were walking, talking, laughing, and spending their credits. Reiko heard of a small shop that opened on a smaller corridor two decks up, and Franz and she worked their way up to it.

The little storefront displayed beautiful carvings of small fantasy creatures, cut from rare mineral formations that miners recovered. Reiko heard the grandson of the original master craftsman had returned to Idona and opened the old shop. Her nephew loved exotic minerals, and Reiko promised the boy to send him something when she heard she was being deployed to Idona.

Some of the pieces were so unusual they required small chambers of pressure and exotic gases to maintain their environment, lest the crystals and minerals break down. However, the prices on the figurines were more than Reiko could afford to spend until she accrued more of her pay. After walking on not more than 100 meters, Franz asked her to wait a moment. He said he must have dropped something back at the figurine store's window.

Reiko wandered slowly ahead, pausing to stare into the windows of more shops. As she passed a utility corridor, a hand came from behind her, smothering her mouth, and she was yanked backward into the corridor. Three assailants hauled her bodily deep into the corridor, and, despite her diminutive size, Reiko fought back with every ounce of strength she possessed.

Freeing a leg, Reiko kicked the face of the man, who had held that leg. His wail and curse added to her will. She bit down on the hand over her mouth, and the assailant, who held her from behind, screamed and dropped her to the floor. Her back slammed onto the hard deck, knocking the breath from her, but a rush of adrenalin flooded her body, keeping her mind clear and focused. Spotting the leg of a third assailant by her feet, Reiko hauled her leg back and kicked his knee as hard as she could.

Another scream was added to her win column, and she felt a rush of momentary victory.

Then something hard slammed into Reiko's head, and she saw stars. Before she could recover, fists and feet began pummeling her entire body. Several strikes to her head created a numbness that dissociated her mind from the pain she knew her body was feeling, and she tried to curl into a ball to protect herself, but her arms and legs weren't responding to her efforts.

Suddenly, the savage beating was over, and Reiko slid mercifully into unconsciousness.

* * *

Alex and Renée were sitting down to a meal when Julien's urgent message reached them, and they rushed to the nearby medical clinic. When they arrived, troopers informed them that Terese and her team were still with Captain Shimada.

"What happened?" Alex demanded of a nearby Haraken.

"Three rebels ambushed the captain, Mr. President," the trooper replied. "They beat her so badly that Terese and her people administered to her on the spot before the captain could be safely transported to medical."

"Was anyone with her?" Renée asked.

"I understand Commander Cohen left her momentarily, and that was when she was attacked. He was the one who called for medical."

"Where is the commander now?" Alex asked.

A second trooper replied, "Commander Cohen is with the captain. He refused to leave her side … and —"

"And what?" Alex demanded.

"The commander is angry," the trooper replied.

"As he should be," Renée declared.

"No, Ser," the first trooper added. "The commander's anger is dangerous."

"Oh," Renée replied, looking at Alex.

"Have we located these three reprobates, and why are there so many troopers here?" Alex asked, looking around the front room of the clinic.

"We didn't need to locate them, Mr. President," a third trooper explained. "When we arrived, all three assailants were unconscious. Apparently, Commander Cohen caught them in the act. We carried them here to the clinic. Other medical personnel are presently working on them."

"Initial reports are that the three men suffered extensive damage," another trooper explained. "We're standing by in case Commander Cohen discovers the captain's attackers are here in the clinic … within easy reach, so to speak."

"Ah … understood … maintain your posts until I give you the all clear," Alex ordered, realizing the amount of damage an upset New Terran seeking revenge might deliver to injured men. "By the way, has the station director, Ser Fowler, been notified?"

"Immediately upon our arrival at the scene, Ser," a trooper replied then ducked his head.

"Immediately? Why?" Alex asked, noting many of the troopers seemed reticent to reply.

"One of the assailants is Vic Lambert," a trooper mumbled.

"No!" Renée exclaimed, clenching her fists in frustration. "After all the generosity extended to him and his people … he does this?"

Alex crossed to a far wall to sit and wait, his mood somber and dejected, and, after a few moments, Renée calmed down and sat beside him.

Hours later, with Alex and Renée having fallen asleep while waiting, a tired Terese poked Alex's foot with her toe.

"The captain will make it," Terese said when she had Alex's attention. "I don't believe I've ever worked on a person with that much damage. She received four doses of cell-gen injections."

"Not medical nanites?" Renée asked.

"Not fast-enough acting in the time we had. On the other hand, the cell-gen nanites were healing bones in the wrong positions. Several times, we had to realign them."

Alex and Renée winced at the medical euphemism. That the captain's bone structures were so damaged that the nanites reformed the bones improperly, forcing Terese to break them and realign them, told Alex and Renée how fully Terese was consumed with saving the captain's life — critical organs first — bones second.

"With food and two days' rest, the captain will be semi-mobile again. Some of the organ and skull damage will require six or seven days to completely heal. It was fortunate the commander was on scene. He preserved the eye for reinsertion."

"Her eye?" Renée asked, shuddering.

"Apologies, Ser, I thought you knew. The captain suffered severe damage to her head, most likely from an extensive number of strikes from the attackers' boots."

Terese, observing the blood vessels distending in Alex's neck and his fists balling, suddenly found a reason to be elsewhere.

Alex stood up and commed the twins. <Étienne, Alain, I need you to ensure the captain's assailants are kept safe. It will be crucial for this station to see they receive a fair judiciary hearing.>

* * *

Three days after Shimada's attack, the captain's three assailants stood before the station's judicial review board.

Captain Shimada was present with the help of the Harakens. Techs affixed a nanites-embedded chair on top of a grav-pallet. When Franz introduced it to Reiko with a sweep of his hand, she was horrified. "I'm not going to be seen hauled to the review board like a piece of cargo."

"Understood, Captain. That leaves us two choices. First choice, we delay the trial until you can walk under your own power, approved by Terese, of course. Second choice, I can carry you … which, by the way, is my personal preference."

"I don't doubt it is, Commander," Reiko shot back. She felt humiliated, traveling to the hearing on a pallet, even if it was Haraken technology and floating above the deck. On the other hand, she wanted the trial over with quickly. Then again, just ever so briefly, she considered riding in the arms of the huge Haraken, who had rarely left her side during the past two days. The medical technicians, while discussing her injuries and repair progress, included the details of the commander wreaking havoc on her attackers, calling for medical support, and even recovering her eye. Reiko was not medically trained, but any idiot could understand a person would have been dead without Haraken medical technology.

"I'll take the pallet," Reiko finally said. She was extremely sore and tired easily, and it required two female medical techs to ease her into her dress uniform. She struggled to stand up from the bed, and then in a sure and easy motion she was in Franz's arms.

"I get my wish, anyway, even if just for a short while," Franz said, settling Reiko into the nanites chair.

When a Haraken medical tech drove the pallet out of the medical center, Reiko was shocked to see a phalanx of Haraken and UE militia surround her. They were in full uniform and marched in step.

"The president?" Reiko asked Franz, who walked beside her chair.

"Most assuredly, Captain. I believe if the man could have found a means of transporting you to the trial in a traveler, he would have done so."

Reiko started to laugh, but her newly formed ribs couldn't handle the pressure and she coughed lightly. It brought her entire retinue to a halt. "I'm fine, people," Reiko managed to say. "Let's keep this parade moving."

Once in motion again, Reiko waved a hand loosely at her escorts and asked Franz, "So what's the president's point?"

"It's a personal message to the station, Captain. You would have to ask him for the translation."

In the militia's admin area, a room was set aside for the review board meetings. Normally, few attended these hearings. This morning, the room was packed with an assortment of station inhabitants, including many rebels.

The judges met briefly before the hearing of the captain's attackers, the only individuals to be tried today. Nikki Fowler recused herself as the presiding judge, and, by unanimous agreement, Desmond Lambros was selected to preside over the trial. In this circumstance, unanimous meant the four other judges elected Desmond — no one asked the businessman for his opinion.

When Desmond brought the court to order, he requested the charges be read, which Tatia stood to oblige. Before she could proceed, Reiko raised a hand to be noticed and called out, "Judge Lambros."

"Yes, Captain Shimada," Desmond said.

"As the victim in these circumstances, I want it known that I'm not pressing charges against these men. Enough damage has been done between my people and Mr. Lambert's people."

Murmurs volleyed around the courtroom, and Desmond called for order.

"I was about ready to read that part, Captain," Tatia replied. "You haven't pressed charges, but President Racine has."

"These men are guilty of my attack, and I know you will find them so, but I ask the court for leniency. I would ask President Racine for leniency," Reiko said, looking across the room where Alex sat.

Desmond was about to reply, but Tatia put a hand on his arm to still him.

Alex stood up and addressed the judiciary panel. "I must admit that I've been torn between marching these men to the nearest airlock and sending them to a belter's mine." His comment brought ugly noises from the rebels in the room. A lifetime in the asteroid belt mines was the de facto judgment handed down by the militia to any rebels they caught. "But I'm in awe of the captain's courage that she could forgive her attackers and ask for leniency. I withdraw my request for a maximum punishment and leave it to the court to decide."

Vic craned his head around and caught Reiko's eyes. His confusion was obvious. If he had a few more moments for the attack, he would have finished crushing the captain's head as he intended. Instead, the giant commander bounced him off a bulkhead and, for good measure, drove a fist into his chest as he fell back toward the Haraken. The pain of so many ribs shattering still frightened him.

"The details of this case are obviously conclusive," Desmond announced. "Video recordings obtained from Commander Cohen as he arrived on scene, confirm these three men are guilty of the attempted murder of Captain Shimada. Do the prisoners have anything to say before sentence is decided?"

Neither Vic nor his cohorts had a word to say to the panel. They had expected to complete their attack and disappear into the inner ring. With the captain dead and no cam evidence of the attack, they figured they would be safe. What they didn't know was that the Harakens would have eventually caught them — medical evidence and a relentless drive for justice notwithstanding.

The judges put their heads together for a moment. To the rebels in the courtroom, it appeared their ex-leader, Nikki, was arguing with the other judges, but finally, an agreement was reached.

"I have been asked by the panel to deliver the judgment," Nikki said, staring hard at Vic. "It's the judgment of this court that the three of you are to be shipped inward by working passage on the next freighter headed for Earth. You will receive no pay for your work aboard ship; you will be given 1,000 credits on a reader; and any other funds you've earned will be confiscated for the station's general accounts."

The faces of the convicted men reflected various reactions, since each of their accounts had amassed over 18K credits.

"Finally, no record of your conviction will be communicated to authorities, and your status on Earth will be as miners returning inward," Nikki added.

A raucous celebration issued from the rebels in the courtroom, and the militia and the shop owners displayed shocked expressions. Desmond called for order, and Haraken troopers set eyes on the most boisterous, which delivered the silence the presiding judge expected.

"It must be said that I heartedly disagreed with the court's judgment, but I was outvoted," Nikki continued. "I was a proponent of President Racine's first suggestion of an airlock to nowhere." Nikki bored into Vic's eyes, until he dropped his head. "Captain Shimada was stationed at Idona less than a year ago. Neither she nor her crew created any trouble for us, the rebels, when they visited this station. Vic, she was innocent of harm to our people," Nikki cried out, and Vic could only glance briefly at the burning anger in Nikki's eyes before he ducked his head again. "And worse, the three of you attacked a woman, a small woman at that, and tried to beat her to death. What were the generations of our fight about if in the end we act like those who persecuted us?"

Nikki looked around the room, locking eyes with rebels she knew still harbored deep anger against UE forces. "Don't you people get it?" she declared hotly. "If we want a better life for us and for our children, we have to be the better people. The Harakens have given us a chance to discover how to live together without hate, and some of you want to throw it away for misguided revenge." Nikki took a breath and let it out slowly. "And like any senseless act of revenge, the three of you couldn't even pick a deserving target. I could have wished Commander Cohen had finished the job on the three of you rather than face you today. Take the convicted men to their cells to await transport. Court dismissed."

The three men were led away amid a now silent courtroom. Nikki's statements had provoked a great deal of thought. The rebels, who were ecstatic at the light sentence, realized their ex-leader was the one who argued for the harsher sentence, but Captain Shimada's plea for mercy carried the day. For others, it had been a drama laying bare the underlying feelings that many had to work through if the station would continue to function once the Harakens were gone.

-16-

A week after the rebels' conviction, a fully recovered Shimada gave up one of her patrol craft for the president's demonstration to Admiral Portland. The captain of the patrol ship wasn't pleased by Shimada's order to dedicate his ship to some bizarre demonstration, but he insisted on commanding it to the required destination point. The copilot and bosun volunteered to join him, and the three men were startled when Captain Shimada wanted to affirm they were EVA certified.

A small group of Haraken ships exited the station to join the UE patrol craft and head inward toward the approaching fleet, still more than two days out.

Captain Shimada had shared with Tatia an indication of the battleship's telemetry quality, which gave the Haraken admiral an idea of how close to the fleet the demonstration must take place for Admiral Portland to understand what he was observing.

"An invigorating day, is it not?" Captain José Cordova announced to his guests, Ellie Thompson, Mickey, and Z, on the bridge of the *Rêveur*, the Méridien liner where Julien used to reside for the better part of two centuries. Tatia intended to ask Alex if he was going to request the elderly captain excuse himself from the upcoming mission, but then reconsidered. *Foolish question,* she thought.

Once the *Rêveur*, the accompanying squadron of travelers, and the UE patrol ship were headed inward, Julien used the station's comms systems to contact Admiral Portland aboard the battleship *Guardian*.

"Captain, Idona Station is calling," the comms officer of the *Guardian* announced.

Captain Shelley glanced at Admiral Portland, who nodded his assent, but before the comms officer could transfer the signal, the battleship's primary screen lit with a view of an enormous man, surrounded by a collection of both wide and slender people.

"This is Admiral Portland of the battleship *Guardian*. Whom am I addressing?"

"Greetings, Admiral. I'm Alex Racine, Haraken's president, and we know well who you are. Your poor reputation precedes you. I'm forbidding you to come any closer to Idona. In fact, I advise you to reverse course to Saturn. I believe your superiors, who I've recently spoken with, wish to have a word or two with you, Admiral. It seems your little foray toward our station is unauthorized."

"Let me point out to you, President Racine, that Idona Station is UE property. Now, I will give you one opportunity to vacate the station and exit our system, before I demonstrate the might of a UE fleet."

"I thought that might be your attitude, Admiral. I suggest you bring your fleet to a halt. A small group of my ships is headed your way from Idona. We've prepared a minor demonstration of Haraken technology for you. Do not allow your ships to come within 300K kilometers of this demonstration unless you want to lose them. Watch carefully, Admiral. It's my sincere hope that you are a more intelligent man than your superiors have indicated." Alex cut the comm.

* * *

Aboard the *Rêveur*, Mickey and his engineers loaded Ellie's Dagger with missiles armed with Z's latest invention, nanites minelettes. Harakens might be forgiven, thinking it was odd that a wing commander was flying the mission, but few of the planet's pilots were trained on the original New Terran Dagger, which Ellie learned on before escaping Libre.

Mickey signaled Ellie when all was ready, and the flight chief and crew helped load her into Dagger-1's cockpit. The bay was depressurized, and everyone aboard the liner awaited the mission's go signal. When the *Rêveur* reached its target point, Z signaled Ellie and the flight crew to launch the Dagger. Simultaneously, the UE patrol ship eased away from the shadow of the liner as both ships came to a halt.

Z signaled the patrol ship. "Captain, prepare your men to abandon ship."

"Seems a stupid idea to abandon a perfectly good vessel," the captain grumped.

"Captain," Z repeated.

"We're going, we're going."

The captain, second lieutenant, and bosun climbed into their EVA suits and cycled through the ship's small airlock, which barely accommodated the three men in their suits. The fourteen-year veteran bosun kept his eye on the junior lieutenant, who admitted that his spacewalk experience was limited to academy training. Tethered together, the three UE men eased out of the airlock. Once clear of the ship, they activated their suit jets, and the captain led his men toward the lights of the *Rêveur*'s open bay.

Gaining the bay, the UE men were drawn down to the bay's grav-activated deck. When the bay doors closed, pressurization quickly followed. The three UE men were debating whether to strip off their suits when the bay's airlock hissed open and three huge men came hurrying toward them. The young lieutenant went so far as to put up his hands in surrender.

"Welcome aboard the *Rêveur*, Sers, you may call me Mickey. Come, let us help you out of these suits and get to the bridge."

The patrol ship captain was surprised by the invitation. He expected to sit out the mission in some dim room, isolated and unable to inspect the Haraken ship. Instead, he and his men were escorted to the bridge, able to admire the corridors' clean lines and spacious width along the way.

On the bridge, the UE men were introduced to the Harakens. Isolated aboard their destroyer from before the Harakens took over Idona, this was their first view of the strangers' mix of body types — ultra-large, near Earth normal, and super slender.

"Why are there so many human types in your worlds?" the captain asked.

"There are only two types," replied Z, "Mickey's and Captain Cordova's.

"You're not a Haraken?" the bosun asked.

"I'm not human," Z replied. "I'm a SADE."

At that moment, Captain Cordova activated the holo-vid, displaying the nearby space, and the bridge's central screen, which showed Dagger-1 beside the liner.

"Where's our ship?" the lieutenant asked, staring into the holo-vid.

"We're 105K kilometers from your ship, Sers," Z stated.

The UE men exchanged astonished looks. There was no sensation of acceleration to indicate the Haraken vessel was accelerating that quickly.

Z signaled Julien that the demonstration was beginning.

* * *

Admiral Portland observed the small group of ships come close to his fleet, stop, and then retreat, leaving a UE patrol ship in their wake. Then a single fighter eased away from what appeared to a passenger liner and lined up on the patrol ship.

"Captain Shelley, I want eyes on that patrol boat and that fighter," Portland ordered. The monitoring screens of the battleship's bridge filled with images of the fighter and patrol ship in closeup, and a third screen contained an image of both craft, appearing as small dots.

"A twin missile launch from the fighter, Captain," a commander called out.

Portland eased away from the bulkhead where he was standing to peer closely at the third monitor. Two bright spots erupted from the dark, where the fighter was positioned and traced bright lines toward the UE ship.

"The missiles exploded," the commander announced. "Negligible energy recorded."

"That's it?" Portland asked, laughing.

"The president indicated we should watch carefully," Captain Shelley said.

"Continue observing, Captain. Call me if anything interesting develops. Otherwise, hold position."

A couple of hours later, long after the Haraken ships retreated toward the station, a first lieutenant called out, "Captain, there's something wrong with the patrol ship."

"Explain," Shelley commanded, coming awake from a snooze in his command chair.

"Here, here, and here," the first mate said, leaving his position to indicate various points on the ship on the screen, showing the vessel closeup.

Shelley left his command chair to peer at the monitor's image. "What are those?" he asked.

"I think they're holes, Captain. At first, I thought it was a glitch with our sensors, but everything checks out. Then I noticed that these dark spots were growing faster and faster like … like something's feeding on that ship."

"Comms, get Admiral Portland up here, now," Shelley ordered.

In the time it took Portland to gain the bridge, the holes in the UE patrol ship doubled in diameter, and where tens of holes were visible when the first mate noticed them, hundreds could now be seen, and more were appearing with the passing of minutes.

Shelley pointed to the screen when Portland came up beside him, saying, "Those two puny missiles that you laughed at seeded the space around that patrol vessel. Something in those missiles is eating that ship." While they watched, small pieces of the ship began floating away, and starlight began showing through the remaining hulk of the hull.

Z's missile warheads had sprayed hundreds of thousands of tiny globules of nanites surrounded by oxygen-impregnated thermite gel. When the globules struck the hull, the thermite compound was activated, aided by the embedded oxygen-transport compound. Once energized, the nanites began replicating by consuming the metal of the ship, creating an exothermic reaction, which supplied the nanites with additional energy. The process would continue as long as the nanites found native metal. To protect any other ship traffic, Julien and Z programmed the nanites with a short lifespan.

"Commander, get me Captain Tankerling on the *Dauntless*," Portland ordered the fleet comms officer.

"Captain Tankerling, Admiral."

"Captain, take your destroyer close to that UE patrol ship and ascertain what we're looking at. I need to know whether this is some sort of visual hoax or a weapon. Keep your ship at a distance of 10 kilometers from the vessel. That should be a safe distance." Portland ignored the glances aimed his way.

"Understood, Admiral, we're underway."

The *Dauntless* had closed to within 100K kilometers when the *Guardian*'s central screen lit up with an image of Alex. "I'm curious, Admiral. How many people are aboard that destroyer you're sending to investigate our demonstration?"

Portland briefly glared at the battleship's comms officer, angry that the Harakens were able to link full comms, audio and visual, at will. The harassed comms officer could only shrug an apology and work to regain control of his comms panel.

"I have plenty of destroyers," Portland replied arrogantly. "And I don't accept demonstrations at face value from anyone, especially not aberrant humans."

Alex didn't bother to reply and cut the comm.

Portland never left the bridge while the *Dauntless* reached the UE patrol ship or what was left of it. It was little more than pieces of non-metal material left floating in an ungainly clump.

"Admiral, call from the *Dauntless*," the comms commander announced. When Portland nodded, the connection was transferred to his bridge display.

"Go ahead, Captain."

"As best we can tell, Admiral, there was some sort of process at work on this vessel's metal, but we can't confirm whether the active material came from those missiles or was implanted on board the patrol ship before it was left here. It's our best techs' thoughts that it was the latter condition. It would have been easy for the Harakens to have sprayed the outside and inside with a compound that began breaking down the ship's metal components. The fact that we seem to be fine is probably a good argument for the techs' opinions."

"Understood, Captain. Good job. Return to formation." Portland chuckled to himself and then said to no one in particular, "And you thought you had me fooled, Haraken, with your weak magic show."

Portland assumed his command chair to develop scenarios for his assault on Idona, using the latest telemetry information on the Harakens when the commander signaled him of an urgent call from the *Dauntless*. On the monitor, a harried Captain Tankerling was issuing orders, while the sound of horns wailed the signal to abandon the destroyer.

"Report, Captain," Portland ordered.

"We were wrong, Admiral. The space around the patrol ship was seeded with the Harakens' weapon. We have tens of compartment breaches to vacuum and more happening every minute. I'm reversing course so that we don't contaminate the fleet. I intend to halt 100K kilometers spinward of the patrol ship's debris. My crew is filling the survival pods now. It's my hope that these aren't contaminated too. I have no idea when it will be safe to retrieve us, Admiral. I hate to suggest this, but maybe the Harakens can help."

Aboard the *Guardian*, they heard a voice on the destroyer bridge yell, "Captain, the bridge is about to be breached. We have to go now." Seconds after the destroyer's bridge was seen to empty, the comms signal was lost.

Over the next few hours, Portland, Shelley, and the bridge crew of the *Guardian* witnessed the destroyer and its survival pods fall apart. Cries for help from the crew could be heard by the comms officers across the fleet. After the pods broke apart, the nanites destroyed the metal rings on the crew's environment suits. Less than an hour later, when it was too late for any crew member, the nanites became inactive.

"Shall we continue to make for the station, Admiral?" Captain Shelley asked as neutrally as he could.

Portland swore under his breath. He had been anxious to teach the Harakens a lesson in UE military power. Now, his strategy needed rethinking. "Commander, what civilian ships are behind us?"

The commander consulted his screens. “We have three freighters and two liners on approach for Idona. They are spread about three and a half days apart.”

“Which ship is in the front?”

“A freighter, the *Shamrock*.”

“Signal our ships to reverse course. They’re to reassemble in fleet formation behind the *Shamrock*. Order its captain to slow to one-quarter present velocity. Then contact the other four civvie captains, and order them to form up on the *Shamrock*. They will be our shield.” Portland stared at the monitor for a minute, watching the scattered debris of the destroyer and the bodies of the crew floating in the dark and shuddered, wondering what kind of humans fought with weapons like these.

-17-

"Well, I didn't see that coming," Tatia commented to the group, who were on the conference comm and observing the demonstration via the holo-vids at the station and across the fleet. The struggles of the crew from the destroyer's failed pods ended with the breach of their disintegrating environment suits.

"You dissolved … everything … even the crew!" said Shimada, staring horrified at the holo-vid. "I thought the nanites would attack the hull or the engines or something specific."

"Technically, Captain —" was as far as Z got, before Cordelia's signal interrupted him.

"You were quite explicit about the safety distance, Mr. President," Julien commented, hoping to ease the heartache he knew his friend was suffering. He shared a glance with Renée, who stood behind Alex and kept her slender hands on the president's shoulders.

"The man just had to be sure it wasn't a trick, and he used an entire destroyer to discover the truth," Alex said sadly and switched the holo-vid's view to that of Portland's fleet. "The admiral is on the move. Captain, do you care to revise your estimate of what Portland will do?" When Shimada failed to answer, Alex shifted to a command tone, "Captain Shimada, will Portland change the strategy you suggested earlier?"

Shimada jerked as if she was shocked. "What? Um … I don't know. Wait." She took a deep breath and straightened her spine, her eyes focusing far away. Slowly the pain ebbed, and Shimada returned her attention to the room to regard Alex with an odd mix of emotion. A thought crossed her mind to tell the president what she thought of his demonstration, but her eyes wandered to Renée's face, and the thought fled. A woman she had considered a lovely companion to the president wore an expression that said, "Express that thought at your peril."

"You'll have frightened the admiral and most likely everyone in the fleet who had a view of the demise of the *Dauntless* and its crew."

"And by now the story has been circulated to every crew member and has grown exponentially," Tatia added.

"Undoubtedly," Shimada agreed. "Harakens will be viewed as monsters … waging warfare with inhuman weapons."

"Hmm … maybe we can use that," Alex said. "What about Portland's strategy, Captain?"

Shimada looked at the holo-vid. "I can't tell what direction the fleet is moving. How do you know?" She glanced at Alex, who tapped his temple. "Um … so care to enlighten this unenhanced individual?" asked Shimada, her tone revealing the pain and anger she was holding back.

"The fleet is moving to intersect a freighter, the *Shamrock*, Captain," Julien supplied. "There are four other ships on course for Idona behind the freighter. Undoubtedly, they will provide a substantial number of civilians for your good admiral to sacrifice, much as he did his destroyer and its crew."

Anger flared inside Shimada, and she pushed it into her eyes as she bored into those of Julien, who patiently regarded her in return. After a moment, her action seemed futile, and she glanced back to the holo-vid, a feeling of exhaustion overcoming her as if her rage was burning the energy out of her. A long sigh escaped her lips, and she gathered her thoughts to respond to Alex's question.

"As I said, Mr. President, you'll have scared the admiral, but he will depend on what's always worked for him. His main force will shield itself behind the civilian craft as Julien supposed. Since he favors a pincer movement, he'll probably expand that maneuver now by adding a third and fourth attack force. Two will come at your flanks on the ecliptic; two others will go over and under the ecliptic. It will divide your forces into five defensive groups."

"And the largest contingent of the fleet will be hiding behind civilians," Tatia added.

"Captain, Commander Ellie Thompson here. Do you have any idea how he will divide his forces?"

"The admiral favors using his destroyers anchored by a cruiser in the pincer movements. If he uses four attack groups, each escorting a cruiser, it would strip the main force of cruisers, which I don't think he'll want to do."

"Why not?" Ellie asked.

"He'll want to ensure that no matter what happens to the pincer forces, his battleship will be well guarded."

"A wonderful leadership style," Tatia commented.

"Criticism is easy, Admiral," Shimada said. "I'm sure your president has evaded the risks of battle as well." Shimada was floored by the huge swell of laughter that echoed around the room, including that issuing from the holo-vid's speakers. Even the twins and SADEs were smiling at her.

"People, leave the captain alone. Her day has been trying enough with the loss of her compatriots," Alex said and the laughter died instantly.

Shimada could feel the heat in her face and neck from the flush of embarrassment. It was the compassionate expression on the president's face that mollified her.

"So you've led from the front," Shimada guessed.

"Too far in front and too many times," Tatia acknowledged.

Shimada watched the heads in the room nodding their agreement and heard murmurs of assent from the holo-vid. She realized her failure in trying to find comparisons between her people and the Harakens. It wasn't that they weren't human; it was that they were a fundamentally different society — a society that bore little resemblance to that of the UE.

"Well, if the admiral does come at us in five groups with one hiding behind civilians, we are going to be challenged."

Shimada didn't know whose voice issued from the holo-vid, but she didn't understand the underlying problem. "What's the problem? You fire your missiles into the face of the four pincer groups and dissolve those ships away. Then you deal with the main force another way. Destroy the pincer forces, and you'll have cut his fleet's firepower by three-fourths or fifths."

"Z used a third of his nanites stock in the demonstration," Tatia replied. "It would take him much more time than we have to produce enough nanites to obliterate the four sub-fleets. But it wouldn't matter. We only have four Daggers, which would mean one fighter would have had to cover the spread of a UE squadron. Not going to be viable."

"You … you tried to bluff the admiral?" Shimada asked, staring at Alex.

"It seemed a good play," Alex replied.

"But I told you the admiral would not be impressed. Why waste showing your secret weapon when you have so little of it?"

"Captain," Julien responded instead. "Perhaps it has escaped your notice that we came here to prevent a war not start one. It was a calculated gambit that our president wished to try. He is usually quite successful with his inventive strategies. Just not today," Julien added, shrugging an apology to Alex.

<Not necessary, old friend,> Alex sent back.

"So what will you do now?" Shimada asked.

"That, Captain, is yet to be determined. Anybody hungry besides me?" Alex asked and headed for the room's exit.

What amazed Shimada were the good-natured smiles on the faces of the Harakens as they followed their president out of the room. *They've just learned their leader pulled their pants down in front of the enemy and admitted he doesn't have a backup plan, and they're all smiling and going to dinner,* Shimada thought in amazement.

"Come, Captain," Franz said taking Shimada's hand into the crook of his arm and guiding her toward the exit. "The universe will look a little better after some good food and hot thé."

Shimada's thoughts were in such a daze that she allowed Franz to lead her, never pulling her hand from his grasp. His powerful hand gently holding hers was a comforting touch in contrast to the enormously uncomfortable events she witnessed today.

* * *

Three days later, Shimada's prophecy proved true. Admiral Portland divided his forces and four pincers flared from behind the shield of civilian ships. A cruiser anchored each of the destroyer groups flanking on the ecliptic. It was squadrons of destroyers only that shot above and below the ecliptic to form the third and fourth attacking forces. The main group, tightly tucked behind a spread of civilian freighters and passenger liners, was composed of the admiral's battleship, two cruisers, and three destroyers.

The Haraken fleet officers were back aboard their carriers as were Cordelia and Julien. Z, Mickey, Ellie, and the only three other Dagger-qualified pilots were aboard the *Rêveur.* Shimada returned to her destroyer and was told explicitly by Alex to take no action in support of his people, regardless of what happened to them.

Alex, Renée, Julien, the twins, and squadrons of troopers stayed on station, with ten travelers in reserve. It crushed Alex not to be with his people, but he knew if he left the station, the fragile truce they created might collapse. He counted on his people to carry the day.

<Getting exciting enough for you, brother?> Étienne sent Alain as they strolled the main corridor in their leaders' company, ensuring the station saw them.

<These will be wonderful memories to recall, providing we are able to return to Haraken,> Alain sent back.

<Truth, but who knew the president would choose to take on an entire solar system of fanatics?> Étienne replied, a grin on his face.

<The madman does continue to surprise us,> Alain sent back, returning Étienne's grin.

* * *

Around the station, the air was one of nervousness. Station telemetry reported the maneuvers of the approaching fleet, and news traveled around the station faster than the speed of light. Captains and owners sought to launch their vessels as early as possible, but, on Alex's orders, all craft were denied exit from the station.

It was the Harakens' demonstration that curtailed the grumblings of captains and owners. Viewing the UE patrol ship and then the destroyer dissolve in a matter of hours, scared the station's populace. To most, the images of the destroyer crew's flailing arms and legs as they fought to repair their environment suits were horribly emblazoned in their memories.

Many of Idona's people changed their opinions about the benign nature of the Harakens, who had brought the station's people together. They had respected the strangers for their forbearance against the slights offered against them by the speaker and then the high judge, but most forgot that and suddenly saw their hosts as the aliens they first thought them to be. It was ironic that it took the death of their fellow UE citizens, despite the fact those people were commanded by an admiral intent on a war with the Harakens, to give the stationers, spacers, and rebels a common point of view.

* * *

Tatia was about to commit her entire force in the most complex battle she could imagine. That she would be following Alex's plan gave her some measure of hope, but the failure of the president's demonstration to intimidate Admiral Portland made her wonder if Earther minds were too convoluted to predict.

Time to stop worrying and act, Tatia told herself.

The Harakens needed to wait until the pincer forces came closer to the station to see which of the groups would rate first contact. As suspected, it was the two flanking forces on the ecliptic with destroyers escorting a cruiser.

<Z, let them fly,> Tatia sent.

The *Rêveur* was close to the station, the best equidistant point to the four encircling forces. From the liner's bays flew four of the aging Daggers the New Terrans first used to defend the Confederation. Each Dagger was armed with a full load of missiles.

In one of those rare moments of no communication, Z had requested Mickey supply the *Rêveur* with four Daggers and eight missiles. Mickey required a twelve-slot silo to hold the two missiles required at each fighter's staging point within the *Rêveur*'s twin bays. The master engineer saw no need to load empty silos and ordered the techs to load the silos' empty slots with Libran-X missiles. Considering past experiences, it seemed to Mickey the logical thing to do.

It was the edge Alex was looking for in the upcoming engagement. The Haraken travelers would have to close on the squadrons to engage them and would be susceptible to a powerful barrage of short-range missile and gunnery fire. But the Libran-X missiles were designed for a far more evasive and tougher foe than the Earthers' ships. When Mickey disclosed his bounty of full missile silos to the room's planners, it earned him a kiss from Tatia and then Alex, the latter buss making the engineer grin and flush red.

Z controlled the Daggers' initial flights, timing the fighters' arrival in the order required. The Daggers headed for the cruiser-anchored forces were pushed to max acceleration, and the other pair were lagged behind their sister ships so they would encounter their enemy squadrons hours later.

Since the Daggers required trained and experienced pilots, the tasks fell to Commodore Sheila Reynard, who with Admiral Tatia Tachenko captured the first dark traveler; and Commanders Ellie Thompson, Deirdre Canaan, and Darius Gaumata, three Librans who trained on the Daggers. The four pilots settled back in their seats for the ride, placing themselves in the hands of a SADE — something that caused a Haraken not one gram of concern anymore.

With most of the fleets' commanders piloting the Daggers, Franz Cohen and Lucia Bellardo found themselves in charge of the carriers' entire traveler force.

<If I had known what was coming when I gave up my shuttle pilot position, I wonder if I might have been so anxious to become a fighter pilot,> Lucia confided to Franz.

<Look at it this way, Lucia. If we mess this up, there won't be an opportunity for recriminations,> Franz replied.

<Not much light in that thought, New Terran,> Lucia said, <but probably a lot of truth.>

* * *

Ellie's controller signaled her helmet — Z had relinquished control of the craft to her. In her display, the UE cruiser came toward her, leading five destroyers spread out in a semicircle to its rear. As a child she yearned to fly and couldn't imagine anything more exciting than training in a fighter when the opportunity was presented. *One fighter against a fleet of warships ... can't get any more exciting than this,* Ellie thought with reservation.

Her Dagger carried a full load of missiles — two contained Z's precious nanites minelettes and ten were armed with Libran-X warheads. As Ellie bored in on the fleet, she set her controller's targeting sequence even as her controller signaled to her the launch of hundreds of enemy missiles. The last sequence she engaged was an evasion program to be activated the instant her pods were empty of missiles.

The UE missiles were approaching Ellie too quickly. Her controller's calculations warned there would be overlap — missiles arriving before her engagement sequence was completed. Ellie yanked another time on her seat harness. Despite the fighter's inertia compensators, it would be a wild ride, one she hoped to live to tell about.

At the Dagger's first engagement point, the controller fired the nanites missiles. Two points of white-hot heat marked their flight from her fighter. The two missiles flew toward the fleet's center and then angled apart, signaling the firing of the secondary stages. Twenty small warheads filled with nanites spread themselves across the front of the fleet.

The destroyers attempted to intercept Ellie's nanites missiles and were partially successful. They managed to destroy the expended first stages of the Haraken missiles. The second stages were well on their way to their targets. Only 15 kilometers in front of the fleet, the twenty heads burst in a wide spray of millions of nanites globules.

While the UE destroyers targeted Ellie's first launch and her fighter, her controller fired ten Libran-X missiles, which, instead of targeting the fleet, honed in on the cruiser. Alex and his people developed these missiles to defeat dark travelers with their high rate of maneuverability and incredibly hard shells.

The instant Ellie's controller fired her Libran-X missiles, it dove the fighter below the ecliptic, the abrupt movement catching Ellie off guard, and she grunted as straps cut into her environment suit. She closed her eyes and thought of Étienne as her controller fought to evade the missiles seeking her craft. Ellie was shaken and jerked, despite her inertia compensation, as her Dagger spun and twisted, often in multiple spirals. A peek at her helmet's display showed her fighter deep below the ecliptic, forcing the missiles to maintain their target lock and expend their fuel.

How much fuel can you have? Ellie thought. Several moments later, her Dagger's flight smoothed out and her display was clear of the trailing missiles. A giggle of relief escaped her lips. "Coming back, dear heart," she whispered into the dim cockpit.

* * *

Sheila had the honor, or so Tatia termed it, of attacking the other UE squadron circling on the ecliptic. She was not as fortunate as Ellie. Her cruiser was buried behind a wall of five destroyers. *Not so brave a leader,* Sheila thought, eyeing the cruiser in her helmet.

The squadron's formation presented Sheila with a thorny problem. Her job was the same as Ellie's, and her Libran-X missiles didn't have a chance of reaching the cruiser through the destroyers. *New plan,* Sheila thought and began reprogramming her controller's attack sequence. Once complete, she signaled the plan's activation.

Sheila received the same warm UE welcome as did Ellie — hundreds of missiles targeted her craft. At the first sequence point, her controller fired two nanites missiles. Both reached second stage, exploding into twenty warheads that burst into the millions of deadly metal-eating globules.

Immediately after launch, Sheila's fighter angled steeply upward, forcing the destroyers' missiles to chase her.

In time, the fuel-expended missiles lost contact with Sheila's craft and continued on into the dark of space. Then the controller executed the next program step, driving the Dagger back toward the ecliptic. Sheila's fighter was headed straight for the cruiser and into the teeth of a second launch of the squadron's missiles.

"Black space," Sheila mumbled when she eyed her helmet's display and realized she wouldn't reach an optimum launch point for the Libran-X missiles before the second missile wave would be on her. Sheila waited until the last moment before she signaled the launch of her warhead missiles and activated her evasion program.

The controller twisted and turned, spiraled and jinked, managing to dodge the majority of the second missile wave until one struck her engines. The explosion threw her craft onto a new vector that effectively allowed her Dagger to evade the last of the missile barrage.

The crippled fighter passed behind the squadron, angled down, and headed below the ecliptic. Unlike her fellow pilot, Robert Dorian, who had sat in a cold cockpit when his fighter was cut in half by a dark traveler, Sheila's Dagger was equipped with several of Julien's upgrades. Not the least of which was a crystal power backup in the cockpit that enabled the pilot's communications and telemetry even after engine power loss or, in this case, the loss of engines since Sheila's craft was about 4 meters shorter than when she left the *Rêveur*.

Good job, Julien, Sheila thought as she took stock of her situation.

-18-

Admiral Portland's first inkling of the disasters to come began with the simultaneous and nearly identical reports from his commodores aboard the cruisers circling the flank of the Harakens. The timing was eerily coincidental.

Portland listened to the commodores' reports of the Haraken fighters' launch of their first missile salvos at the squadrons and the odd twin missiles that veered across the face of the ships. One commodore reported that one of the fighters launched a second salvo and retreated, but the other commodore reported his fighter altered course to launch itself above the ecliptic.

Silencing the beta squadron commodore to concentrate on the comms of the alpha commodore, Portland heard the defense officer report a second missile launch from the Haraken fighter, and the commodore was calling on his escort destroyers to intercept the Haraken missiles.

"What just happened?" the cruiser captain was heard to demand.

A voice on a cruiser's bridge replied, "We counted ten missiles launched in the second salvo, Captain, but there's been a secondary stage launch. Now there are 100 warheads, and they're all coming our way."

The alpha squadron commodore was heard calling on the destroyer captains to intercept the incoming barrage, physically if necessary, and a distant voice, probably belonging to the cruiser's defense officer, was calling out something about spiral patterns.

What the UE officers couldn't know was that Haraken probes in the area were utilizing Cordelia's inventive algorithms to spiral the ten warheads of each missile in a complex pattern, first opening the complex interlacing pattern and then closing it on the intended target.

By pure statistical advantage, the UE missiles of the squadron managed to eliminate twenty-three of the elusive warheads, but the squadron threw more than a thousand missiles at the fighter's salvo to achieve that result. UE warships were designed to dominate colonies, stations, domed enclaves, freighters, and passenger liners. The officers and their ships never had to face an advanced naval adversary and were unprepared for it.

The remaining seventy-seven Libran-X warheads, designed to individually crack a hardened dark traveler's shell, tore through the hull of the cruiser like knives through paper. One missile punched through the hull, passed through a bridge officer, and entered the captain's quarters behind the bridge before it detonated. The subsequent explosion killed everyone on the cruiser's bridge.

The alpha squadron cruiser and its crew died quickly and violently. The Libran-X missiles blew out entire sections of the warship and ignited everything volatile. Within moments after impact, the Haraken missiles had dismembered the mighty cruiser.

Admiral Portland was absorbing the news of the loss of his cruiser when he heard the call from the beta cruiser's defense officer of the incoming fighter from above the ecliptic and its second salvo launch. When the defense operator claimed a strike on the fighter, Portland's bridge crew briefly cheered.

Multiple salvos of missiles from two squadrons to eliminate a single fighter, Portland thought dourly.

The beta commodore was aware of the loss of the sister cruiser and was warning his destroyer captains to eliminate the oncoming salvo before the secondary stage launch, but his cruiser captain was heard to report that he was too late and subsequently was ordering his pilot into evasive maneuvers when the comm went silent.

Portland glanced at his fleet commander, who said, "We've lost the second cruiser, Admiral."

"Two cruisers to their one fighter," Portland railed.

As the four squadrons continued to encircle Idona and the Haraken carriers, Portland thought he might have seen the worst of it. His self-assurance was slowly reviving when the destroyer captains, who had lost their cruisers and commodores, began reporting serious breaches in their hulls. It began with one captain, but soon, three more captains reported openings to vacuum through the hulls.

When a fleet officer highlighted the four destroyers on Portland's screen, they were seen to be the foremost ships in the two formations. The pit of Portland's stomach grew cold.

Within an hour, the two squadrons of destroyers were in shambles as crews fought desperate battles to prevent the disintegration of their ships, attempting to seal off the affected sections, but to no avail. Some captains, those most rearward in the formations, reversed course hoping to avoid contact with the contamination, little knowing that it was too late.

Crews were ordered to abandon ship, and Portland listened once again to the pleas for rescue until, on his orders, the fleet's comms officer filtered out their cries for help.

Slowly and inexorably the ten destroyers, which had been escorting the cruisers, deteriorated and were lost. Portland's losses now totaled two entire squadrons.

* * *

Deirdre and Darius were tasked with performing the same maneuvers as Ellie and Sheila on the two squadrons approaching the station from above and below the ecliptic. Each squadron contained four destroyers, and the two Haraken pilots fired two missiles that diverged in front of the enemy ships. Secondary launches from the missiles sprayed millions of globules at the squadrons — globules empty of nanites.

Tatia told Captain Shimada the truth. Z didn't have time to produce a sufficient quantity of nanites to arm all four Daggers. This was why the Harakens' attacks were carefully timed by Z, per Alex's instructions. The devastating effect of the nanites on the first two squadrons was relayed throughout the fleet. The destroyer captains in the squadrons facing Darius and Deirdre realized they faced the same type of fighters, launching the same type of attacks — two missiles spreading apart and separating into twenty warheads that burst before they reached a UE ship.

In Deirdre's squadron, a single rearward destroyer captain ordered his pilot to reverse course. That the captain's voice reached particularly high and strident tones could be forgiven. His pilot certainly didn't need any urging.

Moments later, another captain in the squadron retreated. The two remaining captains desperately fought the fighter's second salvo of missiles spiraling in on them, but they were unsuccessful in eliminating all of them. Both destroyers succumbed to the powerful Libran-X missiles that ripped through their hulls, igniting fuel and armament.

The squadron commodore who Darius confronted exerted tight command over his people, and his destroyers dived back toward the ecliptic to evade the deadly globules they thought were headed their way. Then, as the Haraken fighter's explosive warheads closed on the squadron, the commodore ordered the other destroyers into a tight shield, creating a field of overlapping fire. One destroyer was lost to the barrage, and the commodore was considering his good fortune when the officer holding down the bridge's defense position screamed, "Incoming."

With only moments to spare, the commodore was still issuing battle orders, when Lucia's 187 travelers swept past his three remaining destroyers, the fighters' beams cutting holes clear through the destroyers from hull to hull. Lucia's wing didn't require a second pass at the squadron. Two destroyers exploded, and their shrapnel tore through the third destroyer nestled tightly between them, igniting that ship.

Franz's wing came in on the ecliptic, searching for any of the destroyers that might have survived Deirdre's attack, only to find a field of debris and two destroyers in retreat. His admiral gave no orders concerning warships in retreat so Franz made a judgment call, probably more influenced by the image of a petite, Asian, destroyer captain than he would like to have admitted. He ordered his squadron to allow the two destroyers to abandon the fight.

* * *

"Two destroyers of delta squadron have survived, Admiral," the fleet commander reported to Portland. "The captains report no hull breaches, and the Haraken fighters aren't pursuing them. They're asking permission to rejoin the fleet."

"Tell the captains to quarantine their ships for twelve hours, approaching no closer than 500K kilometers until the time's elapsed. Any other responses to our hails?" Portland asked his fleet comms officer.

"Negative, Admiral. The guide's telemetry is back on all four squadrons. Only the two destroyers from delta survived the Haraken fighters."

The officer's words sent icy chills down the backs of the battleship's bridge crew.

"They had no capital ships?" Portland asked.

"None, Admiral. The Harakens sent only fighters against us."

Portland was considering his options when his commander called out, "Admiral, the civilian ships are diving below the ecliptic."

Right on the heels of the commander's announcement came the defense officer's warning, "Admiral, we have incoming … lots of incoming."

"Missiles?" the admiral asked.

"Hard to tell, Admiral. They're small, and they're coming fast."

The captain was in the process of calling the ship to battle stations when the defense officer yelled, "They've stopped."

"Clarify," Portland yelled.

"They're fighters, not missiles, Admiral."

"Position and distance?" the commander asked.

"Um … they're directly in front of us, Commander. Looks to be almost 400 fighters, 100K kilometers out, and they're just sitting there in a wall formation."

"Put it on the monitor," the admiral ordered.

The view of precisely spaced Haraken fighters was no sooner on screen than the ships began a strange dance. First two vessels moved, one sliding back and the other forward, and shifted to take each other's position. The movements were precise, mechanical, not as any human might fly. Then eight fighters completed the same eerie maneuver. Soon after, all the ships were participating in the dance without a missed step or collision. Just as quickly as it started, the maneuvers ended, and the effect on those watching throughout the UE fleet was as intended.

"Maybe they're not human," the ship's comms officer whispered to the female pilot beside him. "I mean maybe there aren't any pilots in those ships so they wouldn't care about their losses." The comms officer needn't have whispered. In the silence of the bridge, his comment was overheard by all, and it only echoed the same thought that was on the minds of every bridge officer and crew member.

* * *

<Lucia, you are diabolical,> Franz sent, his laughter following his comment.

<You think the admiral enjoyed our performance?> Lucia sent back.

<Let's wait and see what the admiral decides to do next,> Franz replied.

<Personally, I hope he runs for it. Even with this number of fighters, I have no desire to take on a UE battleship, two cruisers, and three destroyers.>

It wasn't long before Lucia got her wish. First the battleship, then the cruisers, and then the destroyers turned around and set a new course, which the Harakens determined was a vector for a return to Saturn.

* * *

The rescue of Sheila by the *Rêveur* was underway even before the battles were finished. With comms still operational in the fighter, Captain Cordova and Z were able to communicate to Sheila that they were en route to her. Sheila's terse reply is best left to the imagination. The tumbling of her fighter was wreaking havoc on her inner ear, and she was attempting to limit the effect through the use of her implant with some success.

Using the same method employed to retrieve Lt. Dorian's severed Dagger eleven years ago, the *Rêveur* was brought alongside Sheila's truncated fighter, and Mickey and his people caught the tumbling craft with beams and pulled it into a bay.

Once the bay was pressurized, the crew, composed mostly of Méridiens, took their time extracting Sheila, a New Terran who massed twice any one of the crew members, who was dizzy from her ordeal. When Sheila's feet were firmly on the deck, she waved off the support, and the three crew members released her. Sheila promptly pitched forward into Mickey's arms, fortunate that a New Terran was handy to catch a New Terran.

"Not often I have a woman fall into my arms, Commodore," Mickey quipped.

"Happy to be able to fall into anyone's arms, Mickey," Sheila shot back. "But don't let it go to your head." Sheila regained her feet and touched Mickey's face with her fingertips in appreciation.

While making her way to the bridge, a sense of the past overcame Sheila. Eleven years ago, she was a pilot aboard the newly repaired *Rêveur*, chatting to Tatia about the possibility of becoming a ranking officer, little guessing what the future held for her. Gaining the bridge, she walked up to Z and planted a long, full kiss on the SADE's mouth.

"Put that one in your crystal memory, my friend. Label it as 'a thank you from a grateful pilot.'"

Captain Cordova was wearing a gentle smile and a hopeful look in his eye, and Sheila laughed. "Yes, you too, Captain," Sheila said, crossing the bridge and delivering another kiss.

"One could wish for a third century," the white-haired captain said with a grin.

<As you are often commenting, Captain,> Z sent privately, while Sheila exited the bridge to change, <we have had a most invigorating day.>

-19-

The news of the resounding defeat of Portland's fleet circulated through the station like air rushing out through a hull breach. Over and over, the message was repeated: four UE warship squadrons destroyed and one Haraken fighter lost but the pilot recovered.

The population of Idona Station — owners, visitors, miners, militia, and rebels — were all having the same thoughts. The Harakens, for all their efforts to engender a peaceful environment for the prosperity of the station and its visitors, reacted with incredible ferocity against anyone who threatened them.

The arrival of the five civilian ships, which were drafted to be Portland's sacrificial shield, brought a different twist to the station's circulating stories, especially from the captains' viewpoints. They were the ones who received the threats directly from Admiral Portland and knew the consequences of disobeying them. As far as the five civilian captains were concerned, the Harakens could do anything to Portland's fleet so long as they rescued the captains' crews, passengers, and ships — all of which were the captains' responsibilities.

* * *

There were a few stationers who were indifferent to the demise of the UE fleet.

Z, returning to the station, exited an airlock to find his two admirers waiting for him.

"Welcome back, Z," Edmas said, extending his hand for the intricate thumb-lock the rebels used to identify one another.

"Greetings, Edmas," Z replied, twisting his thumb delicately in Edmas's grip.

"Milt … I mean welcome, Z," Jodlyne added, trying to encircle Z's waist in a hug.

"I'm pleased to see the two of you as well," Z replied, surprised yet pleased to be greeted in such a manner.

"Will you tell us about the battle, Z?" Edmas asked.

"No, my young friends, I'm not … proud of my achievements in this regard. Let us speak of other things," Z replied, guiding the teenage rebels down the corridor.

* * *

Once the travelers returned to the carriers, Julien and Cordelia transferred to Idona. They were walking the main corridor when they heard cries of, "Cordelia, Cordelia," and the rebel children led by Jason and Ginny raced up to them.

Cordelia snatched up Ginny as the other children crowded around her and hugged her body. The smile on her face was as wide as her synth-skin would stretch.

"I nere good," Ginny declared.

"I hear well," Cordelia corrected softly. Having been deaf for so long, Ginny was still mastering her speaking skills.

"Look," Jason said, indicating the initial growth of hair where his scalp was burned, the skin already rejuvenated, and Cordelia dutifully rubbed it and praised its growth.

One of the young boys, a sensitive child who rarely spoke, noticed no one touching Julien. He eased over to the SADE and reached up his little hand to grasp Julien's. The two, SADE and child, exchanged small smiles, while Cordelia and the other children chatted happily about the happenings on the station.

* * *

The great windfall for Portland's defeat fell to the salvagers, but most of them held back, frightened of the Harakens' diabolic weapon, the nanites, which they believed might remain in the salvage area.

One enterprising young man by the name of Jorre had made a good living in the asteroid field, but the lonely existence wasn't suited to him. Jorre took his small aggregate of funds and invested in a salvage tug. He had one initial success with a stranded yacht, but since then he was spending credits on ship services faster than he was making them. His station account was slowly but surely running out of funds, and it appeared he would soon be headed back to the mining belts if more work wasn't forthcoming. His problem was that much of his competition was well-established and had the inside track on notices of opportunities. When word of Portland's defeat reached him, Jorre sought the one kind of individual he thought could help him.

Cordelia was the first SADE Jorre located. "Excuse me, Ma'am," Jorre said, twisting his secondhand cap in his hand. "I'm a tug captain, and I'm wondering if you could guide me toward any potential salvage of Portland's fleet. I mean if it's safe to do so now ... what with the nanites out there."

The question halted Cordelia's processes for a moment. *Was this what it felt like, Julien, when you met your tug captain?* Cordelia thought, eyeing the nervous young man. "Of the four squadrons, Captain, two are no more than dust. However, two destroyer squadrons are available for salvage, and, yes, it is safe to retrieve them. The nanites were inactive within hours after the defeat of the squadrons. What is the name of your tug?"

"The *Homeward Bound*, Ma'am," Jorre replied.

Julien, you are not going to believe the impossibility of this coincidence, Cordelia thought. She located the vessel, surprised by its diminutive size, and transferred the relevant data to the ship's computer. "Your vessel has all the telemetry you require to reach the closest debris sections to the station, Captain. Good fortune," said Cordelia, bestowing a generous smile on the young man.

"Thank you, Ma'am. Thank you kindly," Jorre said, extending his hand.

Cordelia reciprocated and found her hand firmly gripped and shaken by both of Jorre's hands. *So young and so earnest,* Cordelia thought, watching the youthful captain hurry away.

Jorre was the first salvage tug on-site at the remains of Portland's delta squadron. But other salvagers would have taken note of his vector and concluded there was opportunity. The first section Jorre located was the entire bridge of a destroyer. It represented a tremendous find with its concentration of electronics and exotic metals. One voice in his head kept saying, "Don't be greedy, Jorre. This will be tough enough to haul by itself back to the ore smelting station, and competition is coming." But another voice said, "Think of the profits if we can recover another big piece."

And, as fortune would have it, Jorre located a destroyer's massive rear, engines and cowls, another great find. He towed the engine section over to his bridge piece, and reality sank in. His salvage had more mass than he had fuel to haul it for delivery. No credits were offered by the smelters on spec; credits were paid on delivery and only after careful evaluation of the salvage. Sitting on his tug's bridge, Jorre made his second smart decision since searching out a SADE.

"Idona Station, this is the *Homeward Bound*, requesting the Haraken SADE, Cordelia."

"Message received *Homeward Bound*, please hold."

Jorre didn't have time to sip his hot caf before he heard, "Greetings, young Captain. I see by your tug's data that you've made quite a haul. That's an enormous mass for your vessel, isn't it?"

"I think I might have gotten in over my head, Ma'am, but I was wondering if you would help me. Could you tell me which of these two sections would be the more valuable salvage?"

"One moment, Captain."

While Jorre waited, he checked his telemetry and saw seven good-sized tugs, each quite larger than his, making their way toward his position. The closest would arrive within another day and a half and then it might become an issue of who had the larger tug. He knew he couldn't hold on to both salvage pieces. Then it struck Jorre that he was no longer on the station, and the Harakens didn't hold sway out here in the debris field. There was the distinct possibility that he wouldn't be able to keep either section.

"Jorre, I have a freighter captain on the comms who is interested in your salvage," Cordelia said. "You can discuss your finds with him. Good fortune, young Captain."

Jorre sat up quickly to respond to the comm, excitedly discussing his salvage with Captain Liston. The old captain was a savvy negotiator and quickly realized that Jorre couldn't deliver the two destroyer sections with his small tug. But rather than take advantage of the situation, the freighter captain made a fair offer for the salvage on-site in the debris field. It was less than Jorre would have earned had he transported his salvage to the smelting station located 50K kilometers outward of Idona, but, under the circumstances, it was a generous offer. Of course, uppermost in the freighter captain's mind after learning of the opportunity from the Haraken SADE were her stern words, "I like this boy, Captain. Are we understood?"

Captain Liston did have some final words for Jorre. "Understand, young man, this offer depends on you having rights to those two sections when I arrive. That means you and only you and your tug are standing by those two sections. Do we have an agreement?"

Jorre readily agreed, even though he had no way of figuring out how to do that. The first of the large hauler-tugs that would arrive was captained by the notorious Tarek, a man known for intimidating salvagers into giving up their claims to him for small finder's fees. There was no asteroid field in which to hide his finds, and Jorre knew his tug and the two destroyer sections were already on Tarek's screen.

A day later, Jorre watched Tarek's gigantic tug slow as it approached him, and all thoughts of saving his prizes were gone.

"Well, Jorre boy, I thank you for guarding my bounty for me," Tarek said over the comm. "I'll just take a look at what we have here before I calculate your finder's fee."

"Captain Tarek, your claim to this salvage is refuted by the *Homeward Bound*, which was the first tug on-site."

"Who is this?" Tarek demanded. Unfortunately, for Captain Tarek, the answer became self-evident. Two Haraken fighters sat in front of his bow's windows, holding their positions, despite the forward velocity his tug still held. To Tarek, it appeared their deadly noses were pointing directly at his face. "Per … perhaps I was mistaken," Tarek stammered, ordering his pilot to veer off and hoping the Harakens would allow him to leave unmolested.

As Jorre watched Tarek's tug angle off, the two Haraken fighters holding pace with him, a huge grin slid across his face.

"*Homeward Bound*, this is Commander Cohen. We've been asked to keep you company until your salvage freighter arrives, if you don't mind?"

"Never been so happy to have company in my life, Commander," Jorre replied.

Franz smiled at the relief evident in the tug captain's voice. This story would circulate quickly among the Harakens for its ironic similarities to the events eleven years ago when a Méridien SADE was rescued by a New Terran captain piloting his tug, the *Outward Bound*. This time a SADE was reciprocating by rescuing a young tug captain, piloting a ship, of all the names, the *Homeward Bound*.

When the freighter eventually sailed close, Jorre watched the pair of travelers wiggle briefly and disappear back to Idona, no engine flares or emissions whatsoever.

"*Homeward Bound,* this is the freighter *Treasure Chest* approaching your position, Captain Liston speaking. Son, I had no idea you had friends in such high places. I just lost the bet with my first mate that you'd hold onto your salvage."

"Hello, Captain," Jorre replied, "Yes … yes, it's good to have friends." When Jorre signed his contract with Liston, he headed back to Idona a happy young man with enough credits transferred into his station account to last him six more years without needing to retrieve a single salvage.

Once back aboard Idona, Jorre would spend a week crisscrossing the station looking for a unique gift. A discussion with an ex-rebel would send him deep into the inner ring and the station's food banks, which were in full production. In a small bed of the banks, a dedicated horticulturist, a young dark-haired beauty by the name of Pauline, cultured her grandmother's prizes, strikingly delicate and exotic orchids.

"You want one of my orchids as a gift for a woman? A girlfriend? A wife?" Pauline asked, taking the measure of the young captain.

"Neither, really," Jorre replied, pretending to look over the orchids, but keeping the young woman in sight. Her smile was warm and inviting, and he had to work not to stare.

"So, do you often buy unusual gifts for women that you hardly know?"

Jorre knew he was being teased, but he didn't care. "I do when they help me land a salvage prize worth six years of income."

"Well, such generosity should be rewarded. I think this one should please her."

"How many credits do you want for it?" Jorre asked. He would pay any price, but being on his own since he was young had taught him to be prepared to negotiate at any time.

"A dinner at my choice of restaurant should suffice," Pauline replied, adding a bright smile.

Later that day, a Haraken trooper wearing a huge grin entered Alex's planning room. "Your pardon, Mr. President, but I was told that these required immediate attention. They're a gift for Cordelia."

Humans and SADEs turned to look at Cordelia, who smiled and said, "It's nice to be appreciated." She opened the top of the slender package as the trooper held it out to her, revealing delicate white orchids with fine pink and green lines that originated in the petals' outer rims and flared and softened as they traveled to the flowers' centers.

"And who is your admirer, Cordelia?" Renée asked eagerly.

A small handwritten note on paper, rare on the station, held the answer. "The captain of the *Homeward Bound*," Cordelia replied.

"There's mysterious symmetry in that I think," Renée replied, leaning into Alex's shoulder.

Cordelia kept Jorre's message to herself, which said, "I owe you my thanks twice. Once for the salvage and twice for your gift; the search for your present led me to a wonderful woman, the grower of these orchids."

Inside, Cordelia's emotional algorithms were rising and cascading. *You were in my care but for a moment, Captain,* she thought. *I wish you a safe journey and good fortune.*

* * *

Knowing Admiral Portland would send his own version of the truth to his superiors, Alex chose to preempt the admiral with a communication of his own. He assembled others to support the call.

Woo's lunch was interrupted and Chong's sleep received the same intrusion by their comms officers, who apprised each of them of the Haraken president's call. Chong was the last to join the conference, having hurriedly changed into fatigues rather than appear on cam in nightwear.

"Greetings, Space Admiral Li Chong," Alex said when the admiral sat down in front of his monitor. "Let me begin by updating you on the outcome of Admiral Portland's attack on the station. At this time, his fleet comprises only his battleship, two cruisers, and five destroyers, which are making their way back to Saturn."

"Are we to understand, President Racine, that you've disabled or destroyed sixteen destroyers and two cruisers?" Chong asked after some quick calculations.

"Unfortunately, that is the case, Admiral Chong," Alex replied.

"How many survivors were rescued?" Woo asked.

"There were no survivors from the ships you enumerated, Tribune," Alex answered simply. "Two destroyer captains decided to retreat, and we allowed them to do so."

"But how can there be no survivors?" Chong asked. He was incredulous and anger reddened his cheeks.

"If I may, Admiral Chong," Reiko said, stepping closer to the vid pickup. "I'm Captain Shimada of the destroyer *Conquest* stationed at

Idona. The Harakens demonstrated a powerful weapon to Admiral Portland in hopes of convincing him to withdraw his forces."

"What sort of demonstration, Captain?" Chong asked.

"The Harakens fired two small missiles toward an abandoned patrol boat, and what issued from the missiles dissolved every bit of metal in the ship. For some reason, Admiral Portland thought this was a hoax, and he sent a destroyer to investigate."

"And what did the destroyer discover?" Chong asked, already guessing the outcome.

"That it wasn't a hoax, Admiral. The destroyer was lost too … dissolved just like the patrol ship. Once the Haraken nanites hit metal, they continue replicating until all metal has been utilized … hulls, bulkheads, safety doors, escape pods, and the metal rings on the crew's suits." Shimada's voice dropped as she enumerated her list, barely whispering by the time she spoke of the environment suits. "In this case, there was no one who could be rescued. The space around the demonstration was contaminated until the nanites reached the end of their lifespans. The president was specific in the distance the admiral's ships were to remain from the demonstration site."

"Were all the ships in the battle … dissolved like this?" Woo asked, shuddering at the thought. She was struggling to wrap her mind around people who fought with weapons that ate a ship's metal.

"No, Tribune," Alex replied. "After two of the four squadrons received our nanites attack, the destroyer escorts succumbed to metal fatigue. In advance of those ships' demises, we eliminated those squadrons' two cruisers, and destroyed most of the other two squadrons, which continued to advance on the station. Unfortunately for your people, our weapons are much too powerful for your warships. Most of your ships detonated after a single pass by our fighters."

Woo and Chong were stunned by the president's words. Neither thought Portland would succeed against the Harakens, but they assumed there would be some sort of protracted battle with tremendous losses on both sides.

"Did you have any losses, Mr. President?" Chong asked.

"One of our older fighters was lost, but we recovered the pilot," Alex said.

"Not much of a fight for you, was it?" Chong asked. "I mean … not much chance for battlefield honors."

The muscles in Alex's neck flexed, and he fought to maintain control. "War is not about honor, Admiral. It's about death and destruction. The great accomplishments come when differences can be resolved and war prevented. Failing to achieve that goal, what follows is just fighting. But while we seem to be attempting to assign blame for the loss of UE crew and ships, why didn't you send recall orders to Admiral Portland?"

Chong looked completely uncomfortable with the question and even squirmed in his chair.

"We both sent recalls," Woo finally said. "Admiral Portland stated he was in possession of incontrovertible proof that your people were planning to takeover Saturn's moons."

"That's plasma vent," Brennan declared, speaking up for the first time. "The Harakens didn't move a ship until Portland's forces came close.

"My ship's officers have been monitoring Idona's space since the Harakens arrived," Shimada added. "Tribune Brennan is correct. The Harakens were not making any move on Saturn." Shimada knew that Woo knew this, but it appeared their personal conversation was to be kept private.

"For all the good that information does us," Woo said, "we now have to deal with the aftermath."

"Just for a moment, let's put aside Portland and consider the much bigger picture," Brennan said urgently, stepping toward the Haraken vid drone. "Tribune Woo, have you informed Admiral Chong of our conversations?" Brennan asked cryptically.

"Do I know that the UE is in danger of going broke? Yes," Chong declared angrily.

Shimada and the other Earthers couldn't believe what they heard, and the Harakens were signaling furiously back and forth.

"Yes, well … I wouldn't have put it so bluntly, Admiral," Brennan said, glancing around at the surrounding faces. "But now that we're all aware of the problem, let's talk about the solution." Immediately, Brennan had Woo and Chong's attention. "We have a model for the way out of our gloomy future right here on this station, but it requires us to stop thinking in black and white, right or wrong, the UE or nothing. On this station, it's compromise, tolerance, and goodwill that are working."

"Yes, with the Harakens as overseers," Chong challenged.

"Your pardon, Admiral, but that's not really the case," Morris piped up.

"And you are?" Chong asked, having noticed the lowly lieutenant's insignia.

"Lieutenant Morris, Admiral. I'm in charge of the militia," Patrice replied.

"Allow me to bring you up to date, Admiral," Alex said. "Major Lindling, the previous head of the militia annoyed me and has proven to have diverted huge amounts of funds from the station. At present, he's in a holding cell.

Chong glanced at his second screen to see Woo nodding her head in acknowledgment. At the moment, the conversation was too critical to divert his attention, but part of his mind was captivated that he was speaking in real time to a tribune on the opposite side of the sun from him and a station on the outer rim.

"I was informed that Captain Yun was a good fit to help the station director and assigned him there," Alex continued. "That left the militia's control in the hands of Lieutenant Morris, who's been doing a splendid job. Now, please allow her to make her point. Lieutenant?"

Patrice Morris suddenly felt like a sports ball between two formidable teams. She glanced at Alex who smiled encouragingly to her.

"The Harakens might have started the ball rolling, Admiral, by disarming the militia and convincing the rebels to come out of hiding, but since then it's been Earthers, as the Harakens call us, who've been doing the work and putting this station back on its feet. The militia operates as the station's policing and administrative force, but most of the troopers are on work assignment … maintenance on the station."

"Maintenance? Who trained them for that?" Chong asked, incredulous at the concept.

"That would be my people," Nikki supplied. "Since we maintained the inner ring for generations, we're the best qualified to train other personnel. And since you're probably wondering, Admiral, I'm Nikki Fowler, the station director and the ex-rebel leader. Personally, I like my new job much better."

Since Chong appeared to be busy trying to absorb the changes at Idona, Brennan seized the moment to drive his point home. "What these people are trying to tell you, Admiral, is that the old way … the UE way … wasn't working here. The station was suffering from poor maintenance and credit flow, not to mention unchecked theft of funds by the military. The Harakens offered these people the opportunity to work together and save the station. Then they stood back. It's the stationers who embraced the concept of cooperation, and it is working incredibly well.

"It sounds beatific, Tribune Brennan," Chong said, regaining his mental equilibrium. "So in your house of compromise you've had no lawbreakers?"

"Oh, yes, we have people, so naturally we have lawbreakers, Admiral," Nikki responded. "We have a panel of five judges, who review each case. But unlike the UE, our judgments are not innocent or guilty, where the guilty receive one of two sentences, a life sentence or death. That's a criminal waste of human potential. For instance, convictions for petty crimes receive station work assignments. This is tech work and requires training. A 50-hour sentence might be preceded by 150 hours of training. We've hired the majority of those who performed well in their training and sentencing hours."

"Even if what the bunch of you say is true, we won't have the Harakens around to set up each colony. Will we, President Racine?" Chong asked. The response he received was Alex's negative shake of his head.

"But do we need the Harakens?" Woo interjected. "Tribune Brennan represents the corporations that will embrace whatever model boosts their profits. As for me, I want to see a viable government with a future and not one collapsing into chaos. If the military takes the lead to make peace with the rebels and we create local and more flexible judicial panels, we might create a stable, economic future.

"I see two problems with your future, Tribune Woo," Chong replied. "The first is that Lucchesi and the enclave of high judges will resist the curtailment of their power."

"Undoubtedly," Woo said, nodding her agreement.

"And the other problem, Admiral?" Alex prompted.

"Not all naval officers are true to upper command. A good portion of them owe their allegiance to the enclave of high judges," Chong acknowledged. "But, President Racine, after Portland's debacle, I don't see the enclave or Lucchesi, for that matter, mounting another run at you. So, if anything, your people and Idona are safe.

"We didn't come here to be safe, Admiral," Alex replied. "We came here to find a peaceful way of preventing any more of your misguided fools from bringing warships to our space and forcing us to destroy them."

"So, if you can't find a peaceful means of achieving your goal, Mr. President, you'll resort to the subjugation of our entire system," Chong challenged.

Woo winced inwardly, but schooled her face to maintain a neutral expression. Her instincts told her Chong was reading the Harakens incorrectly, especially their president, but his decades of climbing the ranks under the UE's harsh methods put him at a disadvantage.

"Why are peace and stability so hard for you people to understand?" asked Alex, a disgusted expression on his face. "We have no intention of subjugating your system. If we wanted to limit your ability to harm us, we would simply flood your system with our nanites, programmed with a twenty-year lifespan, and let them enjoy an almost infinite meal of metal."

The Harakens knew Alex was bluffing, but the Earthers' reactions showed that they believed what Alex was saying was a distinct possibility.

"Wouldn't that be the UE way, Admiral?" Alex added. "Use your greatest weapon against your enemy. Well, Space Admiral Li Chong, you can thank your good fortune that it is not the Haraken way."

"We have several more immediate problems," Woo said, attempting to divert the impending head-on collision of Admiral Chong and President Racine. "News will reach the enclave and Lucchesi of Portland's failure, and it's not going to sit well with them. As Admiral Chong indicated earlier, the high judges have their pick of a good number of naval commanders who will gladly pick up the UE's judicial banner. In the meantime, word will have spread that Portland left his post at Saturn uncovered. By the time he returns, there will have been ample opportunity for freighters and privateers to land and offload supplies and arms to the rebels. There's every possibility that our militias on the colonies and domes of Saturn's moons are about to be overrun."

Woo and Chong waited for a response from Alex, but he was lost in thought, communing with Julien. Eventually, Renée stepped toward the vid drone and thanked the tribune and admiral for their time and promised to be in touch.

-20-

Woo thought there was plenty of time before Admiral Portland's report reached Lucchesi, which afforded her the luxury of carefully preparing the means to block his machinations when he did learn of the admiral's defeat. But she miscalculated. When she confronted Lucchesi about his complicity in directing Portland at the Harakens, the tribune's paranoia alarms were triggered and he took steps to protect himself.

A trusted security officer was turned and assisted Lucchesi in planting an application in Woo's comms console, which relayed her every conversation to him. Minutes after Woo's conference with Chong and Idona Station, Lucchesi knew of Portland's abject failure against the Harakens.

* * *

After listening to Woo's conference comm, Lucchesi wasted no time in vacating his residence at the Tribunal's retreat, ordering a shuttle for the trip to the Appalachian Mountains where he would attend an emergency meeting of the enclave of high judges, which he had called.

The last words of the enclave's spokesperson, echoed in Lucchesi's head as he sat contemplating what he would tell the fifteen member enclave: "If it fails, and it's our hope that it doesn't, then you will resign your position, citing ill health, and we will nominate another in your place. Are we clear?" The problem was the failure of their plan had developed unforeseen consequences, and Lucchesi had placed not only his future in jeopardy but possibly the future of the enclave and the high judges.

By the next morning, Lucchesi stood before the ornate doors of the enclave, waiting to be summoned. The same young man, who before had handed him the note with Portland's name, stood patiently waiting beside him. A twitch in the attendant's eyes cued his reception of a message via his ear implant. "Please enter, Tribune Lucchesi," he said as the massive doors swung open.

"What have you to report, Tribune?" the enclave's spokesperson asked without ceremony.

"Admiral Portland was repulsed at Idona," Lucchesi announced. He felt it was okay to use the admiral's name since the man was already outed as a judiciary underling. "Portland's forces were destroyed by the Harakens two days ago — two cruisers, sixteen destroyers, and an additional destroyer lost before the battle began."

"The Harakens' losses?" the spokesperson asked.

"One fighter, with the pilot recovered," Lucchesi said.

Murmurs circulated among the enclave's members, and the spokesperson briefly touched his ear implant. "The battle took place two days ago. How is it you are able to report it now?"

"I intercepted a communication between the Harakens, Tribune Woo, and Admiral Li Chong. It was facilitated by the Harakens' real-time comms capability."

"So your gambit failed, Tribune. Ready your retirement announcement."

"We have more pressing business than my retirement," Lucchesi replied and proceeded to detail the entire communication he intercepted. When he finished, he waited while the murmuring resurfaced and the spokesperson tilted his head to isolate his ear implant from the noise behind him.

"Leave us, Tribune. I suggest you enjoy lunch on us. We will call you when we've formulated our decision," the spokesperson said.

Lucchesi exited the room, and the attendant gestured down the corridor. "This way, Tribune. A meal is being prepared for you."

* * *

It was a longer wait than the length of a meal. Lucchesi was tempted to pace, but the thought of the effort kept him firmly seated in a most comfortable chair. Late in the afternoon, the attendant woke him and summoned him back to the enclave.

"Tribune Lucchesi, it's our decision to leave in you place while the next events play out. You will take no active part in what is to come, and any critical votes by the Tribunal will require our opinion as to how you will vote. Are we clear?" the spokesperson said.

"May I ask what the enclave plans to do?"

"No, you may not, Tribune. Leave us now."

Feeling evermore the chastened schoolboy, Lucchesi made his way out of the building for a private transport back to his waiting shuttle. Being taken out of the information loop scared him. He considered the possibility of continuing to report the conversations of Tribune Woo to the enclave, but the spokesperson was very clear. He was to take no active role.

Lucchesi came to the conclusion that it was time to activate one of his "retirement plans." Credits were stashed in hundreds of accounts across the system, but the difficulty would be in hiding his person. As much as he detested the idea, it looked to Lucchesi like it was an excellent time to schedule a week with a bio-sculptor.

* * *

Tribune Woo felt her reader hum in her hand and glanced down to see the sender. It caused her to misstep before she spun around and hurried to her private quarters.

Locking her quarter's door, she opened the message. It was short and written in open code. "Uncle Louie visited today. Don't think he enjoyed his visit. Mum said you should expect a nice gift. Look for it."

Woo did have a sister and a nephew, but they were estranged. The sender was masquerading as her nephew when in reality he was the attendant that Lucchesi met outside the enclave's door. It had taken years for Woo to place the lieutenant deep into the judiciary, and he was ordered to communicate only when critical information warranted it.

Reading between the lines, it told Woo where Lucchesi ran to yesterday morning. If he was unhappy, it meant the enclave had disciplined him and taken control. Not a good thing from Woo's point of view. The key phrases were the last two. "Mum'" meant the enclave, and "a nice gift" meant an overt military response. Finally, "look for it" meant soon.

Woo reread the message, committing it to memory, and deleted it. Within minutes, she was ensconced in the comms station, with the room to herself. "Hello, Julien," she said into the headset after setting Idona Station as her comm request.

"Greetings, Tribune Woo. How may I be of service?"

"It's vital that I speak with Admiral Chong."

"One moment, Tribune."

"Go ahead, Tribune," Chong replied as he sat down in front of his monitor.

"Is this a private conference, Admiral?" Woo asked.

"On my end, I make any comms facilitated by the Harakens private, or at least as private as the Harakens allow it," Chong replied, almost snarling the word "Haraken."

"Apologies, Julien," Woo said attempting congeniality. "This is Admiral Chong's usual demeanor." Woo didn't expect a response from the SADE and wasn't surprised when she didn't receive one. "Admiral, I received a message from my nephew today."

That caused the slouching admiral to sit upright. "And?" Chong asked.

"The enclave has cut Lucchesi out of the loop and is planning an imminent military action."

"Any more details?"

"None."

"What are the possible actions of the enclave?" Julien asked.

"As we told your president, Julien, we have suspected a significant number of warship captains and commanders owe their careers to the high judges," Woo replied.

"Would the crew follow an errant captain or commander?" Julien asked.

"That's supposing the crew knew that their commander wasn't following naval orders," Chong said.

"So the enclave could be considering anything from tactical strikes against their opponents, the two of you and Idona Station, to a massive strike against pro-naval forces," Julien surmised. "This has come quickly to light. How?"

"We just received a message from someone placed inside the enclave —" Woo began to explain.

"Yes, Tribune, your supposed nephew. This I understand," Julien said, interrupting. "But how did Tribune Lucchesi deliver his information so quickly to the enclave?"

Woo was about to explain the timeline when the heart of Julien's question hit her. "That overblown piece of waddling fat," she exploded.

It took a few more moments of expletives before Chong was able to ask a clarifying question of the tribune.

"On my private console, Admiral," Woo finally said. "Lucchesi must have a soft-tap on my lines."

"So Tribune Lucchesi and the enclave are now privy to the substances of our entire conference comm," Julien stated.

"You have my profuse apologies, Julien," Woo said.

"Apology accepted, Tribune. I understand that communications are a challenge in your society. Harakens prefer open communications, but we are considerably less worried about someone stabbing us in the back for what we say."

"Julien, we will need your real-time communications systems to give us an edge once the enclave's plan becomes clear. Can we count on it?" Chong asked.

"That will be the decision of our president. Did you have anything else to discuss?" When both humans said no, Julien closed the comm.

-21-

Julien located Alex with Renée and the UE scientists and decided his communication with Woo and Chong would be appropriate news for everyone present. When the group's conversation lulled, Julien casually announced that it appeared the UE was about to break out in open revolution.

"Julien, you're the driest wit I have ever met," Yoram said, looking the SADE up and down.

"You have no idea," Alex added. "So, my friend, would you care to elaborate or should we just start guessing?"

Julien smiled and then related everything he heard and surmised from the conversation with the tribune and the admiral.

Renée was the first to comment. "From what I've read of Earth's history, revolutions, once they're started, do not often achieve the goals of those who fomented them."

"In this case, Ser," Olawale said, "it might be more of a coup to divert the Tribunal from an undesirable path."

"You have to remember, Ser, the UE started from a grassroots swell of those seeking justice against the widespread criminality plaguing their communities. The institution of the high judges was the first leg and therefore the most entrenched leg of the Tribunal," Priita explained.

"At this point, the enclave members are probably well aware that they've taken their role too far, considering the economic conditions of the solar system, but they can hardly reverse course now. If they did, it might spell the end of their role in the UE," Edward noted.

"The question we must consider is how far the enclave might go to protect its position," Alex stated.

"My sons, before I lost them —," Boris began, drifting for a moment in his memories, and then refocusing his thoughts. "Um … my sons had officers' positions on the bridges with a variety of captains and often spoke about their superiors' affiliations. Often a captain would make it clear he favored the judicial branch of the Tribunal and expected his junior officers to fall in line with his sentiments. Over the course of their years of communications with me, I would surmise that those sentiments were shared by as many as one of every four commanders."

"Black space," Alex swore. "I was hoping for a much smaller number."

"What about senior command positions?" Julien asked.

"This has been going on for centuries," Nema said, looking at Boris.

"Quite right," Boris agreed. "Nema means that the enclave has had time to cultivate its initiates, insert them into officer training school, and support them attaining the highest positions … admirals, commodores, and captains of capital ships."

"Witness Admiral Portland," Olawale added.

"If the enclave felt sufficiently threatened, it would have two choices," Alex mused. "Tactical strikes against specific targets to decapitate the Tribunal's other two legs and then urge the pro-naval forces to capitulate or a massive, sneak attack against the pro-naval forces, hoping to catch them unaware and cripple most of their capital ships,"

"If the enclave's actions were to be successful, it means everything we've done for Idona will be for nothing," Renée stated angrily.

"Well, then I suppose we can't let the enclave win, can we?" said Alex, slipping an arm around Renée's waist and squeezing gently.

"I expect nothing less, my love," Renée replied, kissing Alex's cheek. "I'll leave you and your friends to it. Get busy," she added and swept out of the room.

"A most formidable woman," Yoram murmured.

"Mmm," Alex mused, his eyes following Renée's exit from the room.

"So, what are the weak points of both the enclave and its pro-judiciary forces?" Julien asked the scientists.

* * *

A collection of corporate heads selected their conference comm codes at the appropriate time as directed. Many wondered why the call occurred at such an odd time in their day, but it was at Tribune Brennan's request, and each one was anxious for an update about Idona.

"Greetings, as the Harakens say," Brennan began the conference. "And before any of you ask, this conference is systemwide, and I'm calling real time from Idona, courtesy of the Harakens." Brennan sat back in his chair, a huge grin on his face for Z, who was facilitating the comm call. "This is wonderful," he mouthed to Z.

After giving the corporate leaders an opportunity to discover that they were indeed talking to one another still sitting on distant planets and stations, Brennan called the conference to order.

"We have much to cover so I need your attention. First, let me say that the transformation of Idona is nothing short of a miracle, and if you thought it's entirely due to the Harakens, you would be wrong. They created the opportunity by removing the UE's overarching policies, and the Idona people did the rest. Leaders, credits are flowing through this station at 11.5 times what it was before the Harakens arrived, and it's still growing."

"Can this be replicated?" someone asked.

"That depends," Brennan replied, "and this is the reason for my conference call. Are we willing to change the way the UE conducts business ... specifically the way we manage our government?"

"What do you mean, Tribune?" another asked.

"UE judicial guidelines were suspended at Idona. This is probably the greatest impact the Harakens made after they freed the rebels and suspended the militia's authority. A review panel of five judges has applied an entire gamut of sentences to the guilty. Most petty criminals receive rehabilitation training, community service sentences, and then release."

"Is the format working?" was asked.

"Here at Idona it is. That's why I want to know if, as this system's commerce leaders, would you be willing to support a fundamental change in our governmental policies toward the rebels, toward the guilty, and toward our people in general?"

"I don't know about the others, but I believe this is something that would require careful study. It would take time to consider." The individual's statement created a flurry of comments as powerful people across the system attempted to make their opinions heard. More than once, Brennan tried to regain control, but he was ineffective. Finally, he looked painfully at Z, who smiled and sent a quick, harsh shriek across the conference comm.

"Now that I have your attention again," Brennan continued, "let me say simply that we are out of time. This is not a decision to be made after your accountants have analyzed the numbers. Circumstances are spinning out of control."

Brennan related the discovery of Tribune Lucchesi's plan to send Admiral Portland's fleet against the Harakens and his disastrous defeat. Next, he detailed the plan of the enclave of high judges to move against the Tribunal in some manner.

"So, what are you asking of us, Tribune?" came the question.

"It's simply a question. Are you willing to back the military that wants a change in the way the UE operates in regard to the rebels and the punishment of the guilty, or do you wish to back the enclave and keep the status quo?"

"What about our supply of the convicted to work in our factories?" another asked.

"If we back the military, that process would have to change. To what, I don't know, but you wouldn't have petty criminals serving life sentences anymore," Brennan replied. "All I can tell you is that the productivity of this station is incredible, and its governing rules, for want of a better term, are operating on entirely different planes than the UE's judicial system. I can tell you this, leaders; a decision has to be made soon. If we sit on the sideline when the judiciary moves its forces against the pro-naval forces, whoever wins will not take kindly to our having adopted a wait-and-see stance. I will convene the next conference call in twenty-four hours. At that time, I will ask for your vote by name and choice. I leave you with this final thought. It's time to get off our precious-metal asses and take an active role in the direction of our future, and I don't think this is a decision to be driven by data. It will best be made by addressing your conscience." Brennan looked over at Z, who cut the comm in the midst of hundreds of voices yelling to be heard.

* * *

Shimada exited her shuttle into one of Idona's bays and cycled through the airlock. A shiver slid down her spine. She had come and gone from the station several times since her attack, but entering the isolated, sub-level corridors of Idona forced her to remember the vicious moments, the pummeling and the kicking.

On exiting the airlock, she found Cordelia waiting. "My escort?" Shimada asked.

"No one sent me, Captain, if that's what you're asking. I thought we might walk together to the meeting."

Shimada studied Cordelia's face, but the SADE wasn't giving anything away. Finally, Shimada shrugged and indicated their direction with a wave of her hand. Not a word was shared between them during the entire time, but Shimada felt her shoulders relax and was able to enjoy the walk.

When the captain and SADE reached the meeting room, Shimada paused at the door, studied Cordelia for a moment, and nodded to her before joining the meeting.

You're welcome, Cordelia thought. An assortment of algorithm clusters underpinned Cordelia's love of creation, none more so than her empathy programs. She treasured them, nurtured them, and watched them develop as she gained her freedom and found her love beside her. Now, the interactions with the Idona children were adding a new dimension to these programs, which were gaining in hierarchy. It took only a moment to consider Captain Shimada's emotional predicament when returning to the station for Cordelia to act to mitigate the captain's anxiety.

They were the last two individuals to join Alex's meeting. The president had taken the image that Olawale and friends had drawn for him of the UE factions and brought that to this next stage of his planning, assembling Tatia, Julien, Z, Cordelia, Nikki, Morris, and, at the last minute, inviting Captain Shimada.

Alex spent the first part of the meeting summarizing the facts and the conjectures of the calamity about to befall the system of Sol, including the potential outcomes.

"Will you be staying to witness the outcome, Mr. President?" Nikki asked.

"That question has come up several times, not the least from my own people. My answer is the same. Yes. Imagine if the outcome of the upcoming conflict produces less than desirable consequences for the people of this system, and it takes years, even decades, to recover. How will the Harakens be remembered if we run after having propagated these events?"

"Not well," Nikki replied, nodding her understanding.

"As we have been told repeatedly, Nikki, once the cards are dealt, you have to play your hand," Renée explained.

"Cards?" Nikki and Patrice Morris asked simultaneously, which caused the Harakens to laugh.

"An ancient game shared with us by an Ancient," Renée added cryptically.

"Yes, well ... Captain Shimada, what are your thoughts on the direction the enclave will take?" Alex asked.

"Please, Mr. President, if she is Nikki, and she is Tatia, and she is Cordelia, then in such company, I can be Reiko."

"And I can be Alex. Welcome to the inner circle, Reiko."

"And I'm Patrice," Morris blurted, hiding her embarrassment behind a hand.

"Yes, you are," Alex said and laughed.

Shimada wanted to bask in the warmth she felt from the inclusion, but Alex ended the moment by reminding her of the question.

"If the enclave hadn't tried anything yet, I think it would have chosen subtler maneuvers that tried to weaken the other Tribunes and their key associates."

"But, Captain … I mean Reiko … how could the enclave weaken something as substantial as Tribune Brennan's associates, hundreds of industry leaders?" Tatia asked.

"That's what I was going to explain, Tatia. The subtle intrigues would have taken time, a great deal of time, but that's what the enclave likes … the long game, we call it. The enclave has the patience. But Tribune Lucchesi's gambit with Portland has unmasked the enclave members. They have no choice now. They have to move quickly and forcefully."

"So, Reiko, the enclave is forced to choose an overt move. Is it tactical assaults that remove key leaders or an all-out attack by pro-judiciary fleet forces?" Alex asked.

"Why let the enclave have a choice?" Z asked.

"Oh, isn't he the loveliest of individuals?" Tatia said, sidling next to Z and throwing an arm across his immense Cedric shoulders. "I agree. Why can't we go on the offense and take away the initiative?"

"A fascinating idea," Alex replied, "if we can figure out a means by which we remove the enclave member's choices and force them into the open. The narrower the window of activation of the judicial forces would mean they would have less time to play their games and that would be in the pro-naval forces favor."

"Agreed," Patrice chimed in, "if the enclave gets to choose, we are passive and on defense. If we take away the choice and force an open conflict, we will know which commanders are enclave lackeys."

Nikki stared at Patrice for so long the lieutenant shot back, "What?"

"You are UE militia, right?" Nikki asked.

"What I am is an Idona Stationer!" Patrice declared.

"Yes, you are," Nikki replied, offering her hand to Patrice, who shook it with determination.

<The fruit of your efforts, Mr. President,> Julien sent privately.

<Two down, and the remainder of the Sol system to go,> Alex returned. "People, I'm in favor of the idea, but it's lacking a key element,"

Alex said thoughtfully. "On many levels, this is a political battle as much as an engagement of forces. In part, it needs to be won in the hearts and minds of the people of Sol much as it's been won here at the station."

"If ... let me rephrase that ... *when* this escalates into open conflict, will the Harakens participate?" Reiko asked.

The room went silent, everyone waiting. For the Earthers, there was no understanding of whether the Harakens were communicating via their implants or whether they too were waiting.

"We will defend Idona Station and the surrounding space," Alex said. "It's the best neutral stance we can maintain after having initiated this system's dissolution."

Reiko glanced at Tatia, who was gently nodding her head in agreement with the president's decision.

"You realize that Idona will become a huge target for the judiciary forces, and I can think of one admiral, in particular, who will have it out for you and your people," Reiko challenged.

"Then we will need to be clever and pare down the judiciary forces before they gang up on us," Alex replied confidently.

Reiko started to offer a tart retort, but what Alex said gave her pause, and an odd thought crossed her mind.

Tatia was about to speak but Alex commed the Harakens to remain quiet, even hand signaling Nikki and Patrice to wait.

Reiko was about to speak once or twice, but continued to remain quiet, a deep frown forming on her face.

"Yes, Reiko?" Alex finally prompted.

"I have an idea, but I don't see how to implement it," Reiko replied.

"That's why we're here, Reiko," Julien said. "Share your idea and we'll help you discover a means of implementing it."

"Okay, be patient while I lay this out. It's our concept that we need to force the judiciary forces into the open to identify them. Suddenly, we'll have two opposing naval forces in a systems-wide battle, but what will every ship need?"

"Supplies ... personnel, food, water, servicing, armament," Z replied.

"Exactly, my huge friend," Reiko said, warming to her audience. "Both forces will need the stations, enclaves, and colonies to resupply them. And this is especially true for the outer rim."

"Why not the inner planets?" Renée asked.

"A lot more complicated loyalties there," Patrice supplied. "You have heavy industry and enormous populations, which will not take kindly to interference from either of the forces. It's hard to say which way things will go there."

"Right," Reiko agreed. "Besides, my concept will work best in the outer planets where the situation is a combination of colonists, militias, and rebels. I think if we can figure out how to recreate the cooperation that's developed at Idona, we can determine who gets supplied." Reiko beamed at the room's individuals as if she just hatched the most brilliant plan in the world.

"It took us a while to transform this one station, much less the enormous number of places you're talking about," Tatia objected.

"I know," Reiko said, her enthusiasm waning, "that's where my idea fell down.

"On the face of it, it has merit," Cordelia said. "The concept is one of bonding the militias, the stationers, and the rebels in a common cause, which could be used to deny services and supplies to judiciary forces."

"Let's not forget the opportunity for sabotage," Z added, enthused with the concept.

"Idona's bond came about by the presence of our people," Julien said. "Cordelia, this bond you speak of could only be forged on two conditions. The first is that the two long-standing enemies, the militia and the rebels, believe in a truce and a different future. They must be convinced of a fundamental change in UE policies."

"That could only come from the Tribunal," Patrice said. "On a change as fundamental as this, no one else's word would be accepted."

"And the second, my friend?" Alex asked.

"We will be asking people across the system to believe in something that they might have only dreamed of but have never experienced. It's a great deal to ask of the Earthers," Julien supplied.

"Unless, we don't ask them to believe in what's been accomplished. We show them," Nikki declared excitedly. "This system will have heard from sources on high or secondhand rumors, but they won't have heard from us."

"Yes," Patrice declared, laying a hand on Nikki's shoulder. "I heard from Z that Tribune Brennan conferenced systemwide to the commerce leaders, soliciting their support. Why can't we use the same concept and communicate to the system about life on our new community."

Alex glanced around at his associates, who were nodding their heads in agreement. "So we request the leaders of our pro-naval forces to proclaim a fundamental shift in UE policy, which will surely drive the enclave into the open. On the heels of that, we need a demonstration of Idona that will convince the people of the outer rim to forgive generations of strife and suddenly unite to deny services to capital ships of the judiciary. Sounds simple enough."

"So, no, we're not doing any of this," Patrice stated, after hearing the impossible laid out in such stark terms.

"On the contrary, my dear lieutenant," Renée explained with a big smile. "This is our leader's way of stating the ironic. We'll be doing exactly that."

"For the station presentation, Nikki and Patrice, work with Julien and Cordelia to prepare your presentation. You two will be surprised at the incredible, artistic skills of this one," Alex said, pointing to Cordelia.

"Our presentation?" Nikki asked incredulously. "You aren't intending to leave it in our hands to sell the entire rim on this plan, are you?"

"I can't think of two better people to sell it. Like you said … they've heard from admirals, commerce leaders, tribunes, station managers, and even the rumor mill, but an ex-rebel turned station master and a militia lieutenant standing together, what better imagery could you have?" Alex replied.

When the two women continued to stand dumbfounded, Alex said, "Go … get planning. Julien and Cordelia will join you shortly."

Reiko waited until Patrice and Nikki left the room, leaving only Harakens and her. "May I ask, Alex, exactly what your plan was when you came to our system?" Reiko was surprised when her question broke the Harakens up into laughter. Tatia was even laughing so hard she started choking.

Reiko stared at Alex in amazement. "You didn't have one?" she accused, and her answer was the shrug of Alex's shoulders. "What are you three laughing at," she asked, pointing to the SADEs. "You're supposed to be the geniuses, the cognitive intelligences, or whatever! How can you start out for a foreign system, with only three FTL-capable ships by the way, and no clear plan on how you intend to deal with an entire system, which has already proven to be your enemy?"

Julien stopped laughing and smiled at Reiko. "As illogical as it might seem, we bet on Alex." The room quieted and Reiko found herself the center of the Harakens, who were regarding her with steady eyes.

"Hmm … magic man," Reiko murmured.

"Careful, Reiko," Renée admonished, "We have enough trouble keeping his head to this size." She kissed the top of Alex's head by way of apology, but returned to staring straight-faced at Reiko.

-22-

Z facilitated Brennan's second conference call at the assigned time, and despite the protest of commerce heads who wanted to discuss the issue, Brennan proceeded to call roll and ask for the first vote. When the woman whose name was called, objected, Brennan said, "Sendra Deveening abstains."

"Wait," Sendra called out. Brennan waited, hoping he had made his point. "Sendra Deveening votes for the military."

After that first vote, Brennan moved quickly down his long roster, with minimal objections. The final tally was 87 percent in support of the military. Only a few of the remaining 13 percent said they supported the judiciary, while most attempted to sound neutral by stating they supported the status quo or abstaining.

Brennan stood up to go find Alex but stopped and adopted a foolish expression. "Could I speak with Alex, Z?" he asked.

"He's online, Tribune," Z said with a smile. "Go ahead and tell him your news."

* * *

Armed with Tribune Brennan's poll of the commerce leaders, Alex requested Z connect Woo and Chong to his comm with Brennan. It was Woo's turn to be interrupted from her sleep, which had been restless at best, but Chong was deeply annoyed at being pulled from his bath.

"Apologies, Sers," Alex began, noticing both of his contacts were dressed in robes and one was toweling wet hair.

"The pressure of the times," Woo acknowledged. "What news, Mr. President?"

"Good news, Tribune, Admiral; you have the support of Tribune Brennan's people."

"Do you have the numbers?" Chong asked.

"A solid majority of 87 percent, Admiral. The station's revival makes a compelling story."

"You taking the credit, President Racine?"

"For relieving these people of UE's crippling policies? Yes, I am, Admiral, but make no mistake, they did the work. We simply granted them the freedom," Alex said, bristling. A glance at Z caught the SADE wincing, and Alex shrugged an apology to him.

"Sirs," Woo interceded. "We need cool heads. With yours still being wet, Admiral, one would think that would be sufficient."

"Sorry," Chong grumbled grudgingly.

"You were saying, President Racine," Woo prompted.

"I have been listening to the scientists who fled your explorer ship at Hellébore and the stationers. The consensus is that the military faces an enormous problem with naval officers who owe allegiance to the patronage of the high judges, and the longer that we let these individuals remain hidden, the worse it will be for the pro-naval forces. I'm also told that the militia is solidly under your control, Tribune Woo. Is this true?"

"Yes, Mr. President. Any usurpation of the militia will be at an individual post level, not the commanders, as far as we know."

"So where is this heading?" Chong demanded.

"We force the judiciary commanders into the open. Get them to expose themselves."

For the first time during the call, the admiral stopped drying his hair, and tossed the towel aside.

"If we seize the initiative, the enclave will be forced to respond to us," Alex continued.

"So what's the plan?" Chong asked, more intrigued than angry. He could get his head around strategic maneuvering.

"The plan is simple. We make a systemwide announcement … more of a presentation. As tribunes, you are the hosts of the presentation, with a couple of special guests."

"That's it?" Chong asked, deflating.

"Hold on, Admiral," Woo said sternly. "What's in our announcement?" Woo asked, suspecting the president was waiting to drop the second boot.

"Ah … that's the good part, Tribune. The three of you begin the show by announcing several things: the decision of the military and corporate legs of the Tribunal to change the direction of UE-governing policies, the enclave's intentions to prevent this change, and a proclamation of amnesty for the rebels." Alex punctuated the end of his announcement with a bright smile. His audience was having a mix of reactions: the admiral was stunned; Woo seemed to be thinking; and Brennan was smiling.

"Let's take this plan of yours, piece by piece, President Racine," Woo said slowly. "We use your real-time communications system. I assume, Tribune Brennan, that you received systemwide coverage for your poll of the commerce leaders?"

"Systemwide, yes, Tribune Woo. It was fantastic," Brennan gushed.

"Do you expect your announcement to be received by the various systems, especially our encrypted military communications?" Chong asked, more comfortable with working through the details than dealing with the huge question on the table.

"Communication to any of your systems is not a challenge for my people, Admiral. Our SADEs have your comm protocols, your government and military encryption keys, and your systemwide addresses." Alex could see that with every question and answer he was angering the admiral more than encouraging him, but was unsure how to reverse course.

"So next question," Woo said, "what changes are we announcing?"

"They don't have to be detailed, but it must be a promise to shift from the punishing judgments of the high judges, the guilty receiving life incarceration or death sentences. I think you should present this shift as an opportunity to increase the economic opportunities for the entire system."

"And that's where the amnesty for the rebels ties in," Woo said, twigging to Alex's idea. "We use Idona as the model that will help the entire system … more freedom, forgiveness, fairer judgments … and everybody wins."

"Exactly, Tribune Woo," Alex declared.

"What makes you think people, especially the rebels, will believe us?" Chong asked.

"They won't believe you, Admiral, but they will believe the people of Idona. Our SADEs are helping our presentation guests, Nikki Fowler and Patrice Morris, put together a pre- and post-show of Idona Station," Alex replied.

Woo clapped her hands in appreciation of the idea. "An ex-rebel turned station manager and a militia lieutenant, and two women at that. Brilliant!"

"Not my idea," Alex said. "Credit goes to the two women."

"See, Admiral, I keep trying to tell you that we are the smarter sex, at least more likely to work together than kill one another," Woo said, laughing. "Wouldn't you agree, Mr. President?"

"No argument from me, Tribune."

"That's why you asked Tribune Woo if she had control of the militia," Chong said, catching up. "Once amnesty is declared, we need the militia to uphold it."

"It might be tenuous at best," Woo said thoughtfully.

"Which is why we give the rebels, the militia, and the colonists a common cause," Alex said. "And here comes the best part, courtesy of Captain Shimada."

"Don't say it, Woo … another woman," Chong grumbled, but without any rancor.

"Captain Shimada noted that once the judiciary forces were uncovered, it would be an all-out race for every ship to resupply."

"Yes!" Chong declared, grasping the concept. "If the people want the life they see on the Idona presentation and know that our pro-naval forces are on their side, they will fight to supply those ships. Yes … clever. We will need to ensure that we have a code system in place to help the people identify our forces. This could work."

"And what about your people?" Woo asked.

"You will have access to our FTL comms system for instant communication, and our SADEs, top commanders, and I will be delivering real-time intelligence on adverse forces your ship commanders will be facing. It will be critical in the early phases to get your ships free of the judiciary ships in their midst as they are identified.

"That could be an incredible edge," Chong acknowledged.

"And to answer your underlying question, Tribune Woo, my people will be protecting our investment … Idona Station and the space around it."

"A wise move, Mr. President," Woo acknowledged. "This is a UE mess. We need to be the ones to clean it up, although your help will be greatly appreciated. We will attempt to keep the knowledge of your assistance as close to the chest as possible."

"So, we have agreement … your future stance on UE policies, amnesty for the rebels, the station's presentation, and forcing the judicial commanders into the open?" Alex asked.

"I can't believe I'm going to say this, but I agree," Chong said.

"You have the vote of the corporate leaders and me," Brennan added.

"I am in agreement as well," Woo said.

There was a pause while Alex tried to think of a diplomatic way of phrasing what was on his mind, but Woo interpreted Alex's pause correctly.

"You needn't express your concerns or bother with threats, Mr. President," Woo said. "Whatever else you think of the UE, Admiral Chong, Tribune Brennan, and I have tried to live by our principles. You have our word, and we will do as agreed, including following through with the changes to the UE. Besides, after promising this Idona-like future, if we don't deliver there probably won't be a UE, anymore … just ashes."

"So be it, Sers. I'll contact you again once the presentation is ready. The sooner we intercept the enclave's move, the more its plans will be thrown into disarray."

"Just give us enough warning to get out of our beds and baths and get appropriately dressed, President Racine," Chong admonished.

"Certainly, Sers," Alex replied and closed the comm.

* * *

Less than four hours later, Alex was contacting Woo and Chong, and much to the relief of the UE leaders, each was fully dressed, just enjoying a repast.

"Is there a script for this?" Chong asked as he sat in front of his monitor and adjusted his uniform.

"I find it's better if you speak plainly and directly when talking to people," Alex said simply.

"Great, something that I'm terrible at," Chong groused.

"I'll take the lead, Admiral," Woo said and received Chong's appreciative nod.

Alex signaled the SADEs and across the system of Sol, communications were opened from Idona through every Haraken probe and into the comms systems of warships, freighters, passenger liners, private ships, stations, colonies, domes, and planets. Many systems resisted, and as fast as the SADEs could they hacked them. Per Alex's instructions, time wasn't wasted on those who resisted heavily. The message would eventually be dispersed to the people who depended on those systems. The goal was to reach the vast majority of people throughout Sol.

Across the system, the images of Tribunes Woo and Brennan and Admiral Chong appeared on monitors. Individuals who thought to interrupt what was considered a recorded message found there was too much resistance from those who were curious.

The opening remarks of the three leaders grabbed every viewer's attention when the leaders identified that they were individually located on Earth, Mars, and Idona and using the Haraken's real-time comms system for a critical announcement.

Tribune Woo was careful to couch her announcement as heavily influenced by the reports issuing from Idona Station as the primary reason the Tribunal was reconsidering its general policies. She focused on the social changes that had resulted in the incredible economic gains for the station, which she promised would be seen in more detail later in the broadcast.

After setting the scene, Woo went on to say, "To demonstrate the extent to which we are dedicated to these policy changes, which we hope will foster greater economic prosperity for the UE, as of the date and time stamp of this broadcast, where it is received live, all individuals previously labeled as "rebels" are hereby granted full and unconditional amnesty. Furthermore, all criminal trials are hereby suspended until the new policies regarding sentencing of the guilty are in place."

"To facilitate these changes," Admiral Chong said, "militia commanders are authorized to ensure that all trial proceedings are halted. Any judges unwilling to comply with this directive must be detained. Furthermore, you are to give any and all assistance requested by the rebels, who present themselves to you, including food, water, shelter, and medical aid. In no fashion must these individuals be treated with disrespect, regardless of past occurrences."

Brennan picked up the next part of the broadcast relating the details of his investigation into the transformation of Idona Station. "I've shared this information with our commerce leaders, and they are astounded by the productivity of the Idona Stationers, who are working together in a spirit of cooperation, unlike the policies that we at the helm of the UE have fostered. In this regard, I've received the overwhelming support of commerce to align itself with the changes embraced by Tribune Woo and Space Admiral Chong."

Leaning almost conspiratorially into the Haraken vid drone operated by Z, Brennan said, "And what, you might wonder, has been so great a transformation at Idona that it should engender such a change in attitude in your leaders? Well, have we got a surprise for you. Direct from Idona, here are Patrice Morris and Nikki Fowler."

Rather than starting with the two women on screen, Cordelia opened with stark black-and-white still shots of the station before the Harakens arrived. Nikki and Patrice's voices described the station's previous conditions from each of their viewpoints. Their story resonated with people across the system as many of those conditions still existed where they lived. The station's poor condition, lifeless corridors, and empty shops painted a scene of bleakness, and the two women talked of the unending and useless conflict between militia and rebels, without giving away their roles.

When Cordelia had made the initial point with her images, she signaled Julien, who cued the two women and switched to their vid drone. What people saw were two attractive women, one of them in militia uniform.

"I'm Lieutenant Patrice Morris, commander of the militia services on Idona Station."

"And I'm Nikki Fowler, ex-rebel leader and now Idona's station director. We are here to tell you that great changes are possible. It starts with forgiveness and grows with cooperation and collaboration."

"You might think the Harakens did all this," Patrice said, "but that isn't true. They set the stage, the stationers … all of us … we did the work. We made this happen."

Cordelia switched to bright, colorful shots of the station in real time, which was on the afternoon clock. The main corridor was crowded with pedestrians, shops were open, windows were filled with artful displays, and exterior shots, which previously had shown empty docks, were full with small ships waiting for bay access. In one artful shot, Idona Stationers were seen watching a monitor of the women's broadcast. When they recognized themselves on the screen, they turned to the cam pickup in the ceiling and waved.

The broadcast image reverted to Patrice and Nikki, who said, "You wouldn't recognize us now, would you? I won't lie to you. From the day of my exit from Idona's inner ring, I thought this idea of working together was going to be impossible, but every day we took one small step and then another. It can work if you want it to."

"For the militia commanders, I have some advice," Patrice said. "Lock up your stunstiks and crowd control rifles now. That way, you won't be tempted to do something stupid, like use them. Trust me. The rebels are going to emerge looking like wasted rats. You can take six of them with one trooper if they get rowdy," she said, grinning and gently punching Nikki's shoulder.

The image of a militia lieutenant teasing an ex-rebel, who now carried the responsibility for the station's operation, made a statement in itself—cooperation and collaboration between old enemies was possible. There was no reason that humans couldn't work together if they wished.

"But we have a word of warning for you," Patrice said, her eyes boring into the drone's eye. "The changes the tribunes and admiral promised are not going to be embraced by everyone. The enclave of high judges and their representative, Tribune Lucchesi, are firmly against these changes. They will seek to dismantle this process, which promises to grant fairness to the people of Sol. If you doubt this, be aware that it's already been tried. Admiral Portland, commander of the Saturn fleet, was sent by Tribune Lucchesi to attack the Harakens at Idona, much to his regret. But the enclave has many fleet commanders in its pocket. They aren't the majority of naval commanders, but they represent a significant number. Now, I'm not advocating that you put yourselves at risk, but these judiciary warships will need resupply."

"My fellow ex-rebels, you are skilled in resistance. Now would be a good time to share that knowledge with your fellow colonists," said Nikki, delivering a sly wink to the vid drone.

"Militia commanders, you'll need key codes to identify your naval friends. That will be forthcoming soon," Patrice promised.

Nikki had the last word. "To my ex-rebel comrades, I have this one important piece of advice." Julien closed the shot in on Nikki's face, nicely restored by the Harakens' medical nanites. "Put aside your grudges, and seize this opportunity with both hands. To put it succinctly, don't screw this up."

Admiral Chong, watching the broadcast closely, hoisted a glass of brandy to the monitor. "Clever, Mr. President, very clever. I'm glad you're on our side."

* * *

Nothing like the Harakens' broadcast had ever been seen or heard in the system. Not just the fact that it was a real-time, systemwide broadcast, but the admission by the UE leaders that their policies weren't working and needed to be changed. It created confusion and arguments among just about everyone until cooler heads managed to prevail.

Across the outer planets, rebels ventured out from their strongholds and hiding places. Some came out defiantly, hands on hips or cradling tools, which could be used as weapons. Others came out with their hands in the air, and the militia commanders with troops came out too. Not all was wine and roses. Often slurs were thrown and scuffles broke out, but in a great many cases colonists intervened. For every militia–rebel meeting that failed, nine survived their first meeting.

At those locations where an uneasy truce held, the question of how to aid the pro-naval forces and deter the judiciary forces was considered over a welcome meal for the rebels. The opportunity to plot some subterfuge against a common enemy did much to unite the old foes.

-23-

In his private suite aboard the *Guardian*, Admiral Portland's fork, with food dripping from it, froze halfway to his mouth when the tribunes' broadcast began playing throughout his battleship. Slowly the fork was lowered to the plate and the tasty meal went cold as did the sensation in the pit of his stomach. By the time the broadcast ended, Portland knew the strategic surprise was gone, the only solution left was all-out war, winner take all. He grabbed his tray and heaved it against the bulkhead. The food dripped down the wall, leaving an ugly smear.

Cursing the Harakens with every breath, Portland rang for his steward. When the crewman arrived and began cleaning up the mess, Portland yelled, "Leave that. I'm dressing. There's a war to fight!"

* * *

It was the most rancorous of meetings any member of the enclave could recall. Despite assuming their places in the chamber, the high judges were soon standing and shouting at one another.

Several times the spokesperson tried to regain order, but no one was listening to him. At one point, he walked out for a break and a drink, hoping to discover the enclave had calmed in his absence, but he was to be disappointed. It was hours before the room quieted, and only because several members left for a meal and others for an analgesic for their headaches.

The enclave did not reform until the following morning, and each member was challenged by the spokesperson to obey his request for order before they were allowed to enter the chamber. However, maintaining order did not mean the discussion was civil. It was acrimonious. Old wounds of votes lost resurfaced as the members sought to accuse one another of mishandling the enclave's role in the Tribunal.

At the heart of the debate was the election of Lucchesi to the tribune position. The minority had favored a hardliner, who they felt would enhance the enclave's power, but the majority felt that a less-aggressive personality was required, powerful rumblings by a populace disenchanted with UE policies having influenced their decision.

Lucchesi couldn't see the value of returning to the Tribunal's mountain retreat after the enclave's decision that he should no longer take an active role. He was unaware that upstairs, the enclave's debate on his fate finally reached agreement — his next shuttle trip would end in a disastrous accident.

The enclave's next order of business came to a swift decision, despite their anger over the subject. The high judges knew the Harakens had preempted their plans. There was only a single recourse left open to the enclave — activate their naval commanders and hope that surprise would win the day against the greater pro-naval force.

* * *

Woo and Chong worked intensively for the next few days following their broadcast to identify their resources. They knew they had a head start over the enclave. The high judges' first move would come only after they were assured that the great majority of their commanders were in receipt of their message, which must be sent cryptically through regular comm channels.

An entire company of top crypto-analysts, previously focused on rebel communications, was now sifting through mountains of messages, looking for the enclave's communications in hopes of identifying the judicial commanders.

In the meantime, Woo and Chong were making extensive use of the Haraken SADEs. It was Z's thought that the SADEs could assist the UE leaders by analyzing the commanders' historical communications, career experience, reviews, accommodations, and a host of other details to determine their possible affiliation.

The three SADEs sat in a single room where four Haraken troopers kept an eye on them. They were so subsumed in their analysis that for all intents and purposes they appeared as store mannequins. Stationed near the door, Étienne maintained his post. Alex sat next to the SADEs as stone still as them while he contributed to the top-down analysis.

Making use of the input from Woo and Chong, the group slowly separated the commanders into one of three groups — pro-naval, judiciary, and undecided. Trouble developed when Alex began asking questions related to recent senior officer transfers.

"I'm missing the point, President Racine," Chong said. "Please elaborate."

"Let me give you an example, Admiral. Z has identified Captain Charnoose, who was recently transferred from command of a destroyer to a cruiser, a form of promotion by increased responsibility, and we have identified him as a pro-naval officer. The captain had command for three-plus years of his destroyer, but he transferred to a cruiser that has had as many years under command of a commodore that Cordelia identified as sympathetic to the judiciary. To keep it simple … what happens on the cruiser when word of the enclave's declaration of hostilities reaches this commodore or our message reaches the captain?"

"If the enclave's message gets to the commodore first, our good captain could receive a fast exit out an airlock if the key officers are also loyal to the judiciary!" Chong exclaimed.

Woo added her own set of expletives as the problem occurred to her. "So, while we've been categorizing these commanders, we don't really know the loyalty of the lesser officers on each ship. We should be considering the possibility of mutiny by the officers or even the crew against the captain, and this might work in our favor or against us in any given situation."

"Well, that complicates the situation," Chong snarled. "How do we choose who to send what message to?"

"Each commander, captain, and higher in grade might receive an encrypted message, accessible only by that individual's personal key, might they not?" Julien asked.

"True," Woo replied.

"Then I suggest we personalize each message, based on our best interpretation of the commander's history, and send these to our groups of pro-naval and undecided," Julien replied. "This way we can even warn captains, commodores, and admirals of the nature of those in their command and the situation they might be facing."

"You're speaking of creating messages to thousands of officers, cross-referencing not only their loyalty but those within their command and composing personalized messages. This will take forever!" Chong exclaimed.

"Nonsense, Admiral," Z interjected. "I calculate we will complete the officers' review within 4.3 hours, Haraken time. Assimilation and cross-referencing of the data will be completed in mere ticks. We have the officers' encryption keys already in our possession."

"I'm sorry. What did you say about the encryption keys?" Chong asked.

<Is this an "oops" moment, Ser President,> Z asked privately.

"When Julien asked about the command officers' personal keys, Z assumed that we would need them and borrowed a copy from your secure storage, Admiral," Alex explained.

"While we were talking, that ..." Chong said, struggling to control his temper.

"SADE ... yes, Admiral ... decided it was expedient to acquire the encryption keys for your naval officers. Now, if you wish to make an issue of it, we can stop and talk about it."

"Admiral," Woo cautioned.

"Proceed, President Racine," Chong said, reluctantly relenting.

"I believe Z was speaking."

"Apologies, Admiral, your permission should have been requested. I was merely trying to save us time. I was saying that we can begin issuing the messages early this evening, Idona time. We need only to add an activation time for your orders."

"Well, Z, permission is granted, belatedly so. You're saying you will be ready within hours?"

"That's presuming all SADEs are able to be involved, Admiral. If the president —"

"Z," Cordelia cautioned, signaling that it was time for reflection on the part of the leaders, not time for them to hear extensive planning details.

"Well, Tribune Woo, do you have an opinion as to when we should start the war against our own people?" Chong asked with an air of sad resignation.

Woo was about to pick an arbitrary time when a thought occurred to her. "Sirs and lady … apologies, I'm unsure how to address you, the Haraken SADEs, as a group."

"Sers, will do nicely," Julien replied. "If I may anticipate your needs, Tribune, you're about to ask us to recommend an appropriate time, which will allow your commanders a sufficient window of warning to make preparations without placing them in jeopardy if the enclave's message already reaches those in their command."

"Yes, I was," Woo acknowledged, and her soft laugh followed.

"Mr. President?" asked Julien, which surprised Woo and Chong. They would have been more surprised if they had seen the flow of information between Alex and the SADEs.

Z pulled the ship assignment records from Admiral Chong's secure servers, without asking for permission this time either. Cordelia modeled the ship positions onto a visual matrix of the system. Julien added a timeline for the receipt of the enclave's message to reach 60, 70, 80, and 90 percent of the known judiciary commanders, if the transmission was to have occurred within hours after the leaders' broadcast. Alex created scenarios for captains and commanders to untangle themselves from the more dangerous positions, overlaying those timespans on Cordelia's visual matrix.

"Tribune Woo and Admiral Chong, giving the commanders thirty-six hours, by your clock, is sufficient preparation time," Alex replied. "If we add the time when we complete the sending of our messages and allow for the average lapse in time until the message might be read, we can round that time to forty-eight hours from now. I presume you have some sort of standard Sol time for your naval orders?"

"Yes, Mr. President," Woo replied. "As of this moment, it's 15:23 hours Earth naval time."

"So we will commence your war in two days at 15:30 hours Earth naval time. May the stars protect you and your people, Sers."

* * *

Captain Charnoose was doing his best to fit into his new command, but he seemed to be constantly butting heads with his commodore, and he was beginning to understand why. It was as if they reported to two different branches of the Tribunal, even though they received their pay from the same branch.

The captain finished his breakfast in his stateroom, took a deep gulp of his cup of caf, and pulled his monitor around to him. On the top of the queue was a private, encoded message, which could only be read on his monitor. Charnoose entered his key and begin reading. He reread the message several times, and his caf turned cold while he contemplated its meaning.

War between the branches was imminent. That part he understood. It was the notes about his commodore and his escort captains that took some thought. When he reread the message again slowly, it dawned on him that there were no orders, just suppositions about his compatriots to guide him in making a critical decision, which might save or cost him his life.

One thing was clear. His commodore and bridge officers were of a like mind. On this ship, Charnoose knew he was a dead man. The cruiser had four destroyer escorts, and the message indicated two captains were pro-naval, one captain was considered unknown, and the fourth was decidedly judiciary.

Since Admiral Chong's signature was affixed to the message, authenticating it, and the Idona broadcast was recently on his mind,

Charnoose decided to make a private call to Captain Darwoo, hoping the captain had already read his message.

"Captain Darwoo, I've been reviewing your readiness reports, and I have some concerns," Charnoose said after he asked the captain to take his call privately in his stateroom.

"Yes, Captain, what sort of concerns might those be?" Darwoo asked, wondering if this call was related to the message he read earlier this morning.

"I would rather discuss those in private, Captain … sometime within the next thirty-six hours let's say."

"I see," Darwoo said, his suspicions confirmed. "I'm having Captain Terrine over for a relaxed meal this evening. You could join us, and we can discuss your concerns afterwards."

"I appreciate the offer of a meal, Captain. I hear your steward has some skills in the kitchen."

"That he does. Dinner is at 18:30 hours, Captain. I'll tell the bosun to expect your shuttle. Feel free to pack a bag if our conversation takes us late into the evening."

Charnoose breathed a sigh of relief after the comm closed. Earlier, he had the suspicion that someone was testing him or he was becoming paranoid, but Darwoo confirmed that he had received the same type of message. "Pack a bag," meant Darwoo didn't expect Charnoose to return to the cruiser.

The dinner that evening aboard Darwoo's destroyer was made to look as casual as possible until the plates were cleared, drinks dispensed, cups of caf freshened, and the stewards retired.

"So both of you received messages," Charnoose confirmed, and the other captains nodded.

"You're a dead man if you return to your cruiser, and the commodore gets the enclave's message," Darwoo said.

"That I know. What do you two know about Captain Heywood?" asked Charnoose.

"I thought you knew? Heywood is a transfer request from the commodore," Darwoo replied.

"So much for the admiral placing him in the unknown column," Terrine groused.

"So what's the plan, Commodore?" Darwoo asked.

"What?" Charnoose asked.

"As I see it, we just became a two-destroyer squadron that needs a commander. You're the senior captain. So that makes you the acting commodore," Darwoo explained.

"And while we're on the subject of command," Terrine added. "I would appreciate you, Commodore, making my destroyer your flagship. As you know, I was just promoted six months ago from patrol ship to destroyer. You have a great deal more experience than me commanding a destroyer."

Charnoose looked at the expectant faces of his fellow captains and said, "Acting commodore it is, and I'll command from Captain Terrine's ship. Now, here is what I plan to do."

Captain Charnoose messaged his commodore the next morning that he was going to conduct some overlapping fire drills with a pair of destroyers to give the new Captain Terrine some experience with cruiser protection, which was heartedly accepted by the commodore. By 15:30 hours Earth naval time, the two destroyers were well away from the other ships in the squadron when they accelerated to full speed.

Cruiser contact came within minutes, but, per Charnoose's orders, the calls were not returned. The acting commodore announced to his two destroyer crews that orders had been received directly from Space Admiral Li Chong that pro-naval forces were now at war with judiciary forces.

An hour into their accelerated burn and wondering where to go, Charnoose received a comm call.

"Commodore, I have a call from a Haraken for you," Terrine announced.

Part of the message the captains received said that if they received directions or intelligence from the Harakens, they were to consider it as coming from the space admiral's office.

"Put him through, Captain," Charnoose ordered.

"Her, Commodore," Terrine corrected, "at least I think you call it a her. It's one of those intelligent machines."

"Greetings, Commodore Charnoose, and congratulations on your timely escape," Cordelia said.

"Thank you, Ms. —"

"You may call me Cordelia, Commodore. I have a destination for you and have already given your pilot the coordinates. We have a need for your two destroyers at one of Jupiter's moons, Callisto, where a destroyer squadron is about to be outgunned. We need your support, Commodore. Make haste. We will be in contact again soon."

* * *

Commodore Dahlia Braxton, standing on her destroyer's bridge, was startled by the image of a strange, broad-shouldered man that popped up on her central monitor.

"Greetings, Commodore, I am Z. I believe you are about to be ambushed, if I'm using the term correctly."

Questions flitted through Braxton's mind, not the least of which was asking the huge man how he had control of her destroyer's comms and, if he was a Haraken, was he typical of the humans, but she focused on his key word "ambush."

"We have comms with Callisto militia, Z. They would have warned us if there was danger," Braxton replied.

"The militia's comms have been compromised, Commodore, which we are attempting to correct. In the meantime, you're approaching Callisto from an inward direction, and there is a cruiser and two destroyers waiting in orbit on the opposite side of the moon.

The commodore swore under her breath for a moment, which Z couldn't hear, but he could read Braxton's lips. Several expressions were new to him, so he stored them in the appropriate directory

"My four destroyers can't take on a cruiser and its escorts, Z," replied Braxton, worried that she was going to be asked to do just that.

"That's why I'm requesting you halt your advance, Commodore. I'm sending you help, and I have a plan.

Z closed that comm and opened another, contacting Commodore Charnoose, who was approaching Callisto from outward of Jupiter and would have to swing around the planet to reach Callisto. "Greetings, Commodore, I'm following up on Cordelia's contact with you. Your pilot now has the telemetry on the situation developing at Callisto. Please regard your left monitor, Ser."

On the destroyer's bridge screen appeared a layout of the far side of Jupiter and its four largest moons, of which the farthest out was Callisto. "A cruiser and two destroyers are waiting to attack a destroyer squadron approaching from inward. You will aid them by taking this course." A dotted line illustrated the course, which allowed Charnoose's two destroyers to remain hidden until they broke cover from behind Ganymede, although the curve of Callisto would obscure their approach for a little longer.

"I see the judiciary has a cruiser and two destroyers against our six destroyers. It will be a close fight, Z," Charnoose allowed. The commodore wasn't a coward, but he was a practical man and liked the odds in his favor.

"Not to worry, Commodore, you will have further aid. Please follow the timeline and course, precisely. Good fortune, Commodore."

In the meantime, Braxton nervously paced her bridge, waiting for Z to respond with the help he promised her. The commodore's instincts were to retreat, but Admiral Chong's message on this subject was clear and explicit: "Do not underestimate the value of the Harakens' data. These are people who possess artificial intelligence and can defeat a fleet with mere fighters, suffering negligible losses on their part."

Many hours later, while Braxton had just begun a quick shower in an attempt to cool her impatience, the destroyer's comms officer hailed her. "Commodore, you're wanted on the comm." *Of course, now the Haraken calls,* Braxton thought with frustration. Throwing on a robe and toweling off her short, wet hair, she took the comm at her stateroom desk, but, to her surprise, the call wasn't from the Haraken.

"Commodore Braxton, this is Commodore Charnoose. I've been directed by the Haraken SADE, Z, to support you. I'm approaching Callisto from outward of Jupiter. Presently, I'm hidden behind Ganymede.

According to Z, your four destroyers will make a clockwise run at the hidden cruiser and its escorts. I will be attacking with two destroyers from about 135 degrees farther spinward from you."

"Is that man who contacted me one of the artificials?" Braxton asked.

"They refer to themselves as SADEs, Commodore."

"SADEs or humans … I have to tell you, Commodore Charnoose, if our messages hadn't come from Admiral Chong himself, I would say this is foolhardy, being directed by a … whatever … sitting over 3 billion kilometers from us."

"Your pardon, Commodore Braxton, but I owe my life to the timeliness of the admiral's message, which had to have been coordinated and distributed by the Harakens, probably by their SADEs. Our people certainly couldn't have done it. And I've been guided here by two SADEs to support you when you would have flown into a cruiser's trap."

"We're still six destroyers against a cruiser and two escorts, and militia comms is sure to warn them."

"According to Z, the comms have been reacquired, and they are fronting bogus communications to the cruiser. Also, Z promises us further aid, but he wasn't specific. I take it the SADEs are fairly busy if they are doing what they are doing for you and me all over the system."

"We are putting a great deal of trust in these people, Charnoose, but let's do this. Set your contact clock with the enemy to 8:35 hours, Sir."

"As the Harakens say … may the stars protect you, Braxton."

"Good luck to you too, Charnoose."

* * *

"You want me to do what?" the militia commander cried out.

"On my command, launch a full barrage of your asteroid-collision missiles against the cruiser. What part of my instructions were not clear, Ser?" Cordelia asked.

"That cruiser and its escorts will swat my missiles away like insects. Then that commodore will turn this moon base into debris," the commander wailed.

"You have control of your comms again, correct, Major?"

"Yes, we're doing as you've requested, Cordelia. The commodore is unaware that anything has changed."

"Excellent, Major. Fire your missiles when I command. The commodore will be too busy to attack your moon base."

* * *

The judiciary commodore, who was waiting for word when the pro-naval destroyer squadron made orbit, suddenly found his forces simultaneously attacked on two fronts. The crews aboard his cruiser and destroyer escorts raced to combat the six destroyers that threatened to bracket them.

Without warning from the militia that was supposedly operating as his confederates, a barrage of missiles was launched from the moon's surface. Although the missiles were small, there were hundreds of them, and in that number they were still dangerous to his ships. Unexpectedly, the defensive fire of the commodore's ships was forced to eliminate threats from three different directions.

The space around the cruiser began filling with the attackers' missiles and the moon base's defensive missiles. Unable to effectively mount a complete shield against the overwhelming fire from multiple directions, the cruiser was repeatedly struck until containment was lost on two of its three primary engines, and the capital ship exploded, taking one of its escorts with it.

The second escort captain immediately surrendered, which left the two pro-naval commodores with a problem, which was quickly solved by another comm call.

"Congratulations, Commodores, on your successful engagement," Cordelia said.

"Real-time visuals and comms," Braxton said, shaking her head at the concept that their engagement was monitored as it happened from billions of kilometers away.

"It appears that the captain who surrendered to you was one of the officers we placed in our unknown or undecided category. Whether you replace him as captain or not, I would take the precaution of changing out key bridge officers. You do need to add that destroyer to your squadron. I have need of all seven destroyers."

"Don't tell us … our pilots have the coordinates, and we should hurry," Charnoose guessed.

"Quite intuitive of you, Commodore Charnoose. One of us will be in touch soon, Sers."

-24-

Sol's war between the naval forces waged on for weeks, as fleets broke apart and reassembled with their compatriots. Although the judiciary forces were outnumbered, the enclave had worked diligently to promote its people into command positions aboard capital ships, primarily cruisers and battleships.

One critical aspect of the war was decidedly in the judiciary forces' favor. The pro-naval forces, discovering a rogue ship in their squadron, argued for the captain's surrender, which often cost their forces damage to their ships from the ensuing fight or a lost ship when the recalcitrant captain refused to surrender. On the other hand, the judiciary forces promptly dispatched an adversary in their midst — no questions asked, no quarter given.

The SADEs continued to assemble significant-sized pro-naval squadrons of destroyers, some of which were anchored by a cruiser or two. These large destroyer forces had the advantage of locating the judiciary's capital ships, and swamping them with horrendous barrages of missile fire, before they could rendezvous with other capital ships and present a formidable force of their own. Without the Harakens' technology and the SADEs, the pro-naval forces might have had to slog out a long war of attrition.

* * *

Soon after the tribune's broadcast, Admiral Portland sent requests to six commodores, ordering that they reinforce his fleet, and then waited weeks for their responses. Eventually, he received affirmative replies from five squadrons never hearing from the sixth, which he later learned had fallen prey to pro-naval forces.

As the five squadrons bolstered his beleaguered forces, Portland knew he needed to resupply his ships, and for that he depended on the moons and stations of Saturn — homes of the system's greatest concentration of rebels, with well-earned reputations as the most recalcitrant in the system. Even the local militia had operated in unstated truces — you don't bother us and we won't bother you.

* * *

"It's just a little subterfuge, Yelstein," Berko said. The militia major was working hard to convince the shuttle pilot to take part in his plot.

After the Idona broadcast, the rebels had come out in small batches from deep in the moon's enclave. Major Berko greeted each group with all the humility he could muster. Thankfully, his troopers supported him, and there were only minor incidents, which were eventually forgotten or, at least, put aside for the interim.

A squadron of destroyers, loyal to the judiciary, sat in orbit over Berko's base, and the major was seeking a means of supporting the cause — a long-awaited change in UE policies.

"You want me to dress up like a minute-chick and keep a bunch of Navy crew occupied while you screw around with their supply shuttle?" Yelstein asked. The major was nodding vigorously, like it would convince her to help. Lydia Yelstein knew she wasn't a beauty — a nice shape, if a bit on the slender side, but with a face that could only be considered handsome. "Major, I don't own anything much more attractive than a flight suit, much less face masks, nor do I know how to act the part."

"What if I found someone to help you with all that?" Berko argued. Actually, he already had someone in mind, having seen Trooper Marlene Elliot out one evening with some girlfriends. He wouldn't have recognized the young blonde if she hadn't hailed him. When Yelstein hesitated, Berko forged on, "This is our chance to help or don't you believe in what the tribunes are promising?" He narrowed his eyes at her as if to doubt where her convictions might lie.

"That's not fair, Major. You know I'm a supporter. Okay, okay, before you guilt trip me any further. Go find me some support."

A half hour later, Pilot Yelstein found herself in Trooper Elliot's cramped quarters, not much bigger than a militia holding cell. Marlene was working on her makeup, applying a face mask to Lydia from her wide selection, when a knock at the cabin door announced two of Marlene's friends, arms loaded with clothes.

The girls chatted happily while they sorted through pieces of clothing to see what worked. Lydia felt like a store mannequin as the girls spiked her hair with glow-pins and dressed her. Well, almost dressed her. Lydia was still waiting for the remainder of her clothes when the girls began having her try on footwear, finally choosing red, high-heeled boots that shifted through a rainbow of colors as her feet struck the deck.

Marlene quickly dressed and then turned Lydia around to look in the mirror with her. Lydia could hardly recognize herself. Marlene had achieved exactly the look Lydia feared — they were minute-chicks strolling for clients.

"You know the plan, Trooper" Lydia asked, trying to bring some order to the masquerade.

"Plan, Pilot? What could be easier? Your access level gets us to the shuttle bay where we find the destroyer's shuttle crew, who just happen to be all men!" Marlene said, cocking a hip, tossing back her blonde hair, and offering the mirror a brilliant smile.

Lydia felt ridiculous taking the lifts up to the shuttle bays located just below the moon's surface. It wasn't just her appearance that she had trouble with — she couldn't walk in the high-heeled boots and was forced to hold onto Marlene's arm the entire way.

"They're going to know this is a masquerade." Lydia grumbled.

"They will if you keep acting like that." Marlene shot back. "You have to loosen up. Pretend that any one of these guys could be a high flyer for the night. Just like you would pick up someone you liked in a date bar." When Marlene saw a frown form on Lydia's face, she stopped and turned

Lydia around to face her. "Pilot, tell me you've picked up a guy before for a one-nighter." When Lydia continued to frown and looked away, Marlene cried, "They gave me a virgin player … oh, we're dead. We're so dead!"

Lydia was forced to shush Marlene, whose voice had started to rise. "Okay, so I'm not experienced at this," Lydia said. "Think of a different scenario for us … one where you take the bigger role. The major says his people need about eight minutes, top."

Marlene was thinking furiously and came up with a variation of the plan before they reached the bay where the military shuttle was parked. They cycled into the bay's airlock, spotted the three crew members of the military shuttle they were targeting and waved at them through the airlock's plexi-window. The crew looked around for a moment to ensure the women were waving to them and then hurried to join them in the airlock.

"Hi there, boys," Marlene cooed as Lydia slid behind her and hugged her, nestling her cheek against Marlene's and smiling at the crew. "My friend here has a thing for uniforms … you know, military types, but she's a little shy. So we're looking for a brave man … someone who can handle two women at once."

Needless to say, the women had three takers, and Marlene spent the needed time chatting and pretending to interview each man as to who would get the opportunity. When the time was up, Lydia whispered in Marlene's ear and the trooper announced, "Sorry, boys, no winner today. My friend wants to try another crew."

Amid the crew's angry shouts, the two women quickly exited the airlock. The moment they made the first turn in the corridor, Lydia leaned against a wall and hit the vac-releases to slide off her boots. "You made that look so easy, Marlene," Lydia said.

"Yeah," Marlene acknowledged. "Too bad though. Two of them were cute, nice even, and they didn't even get a good send-off."

While the shuttle crew was entranced by the women, a militia sergeant and ex-rebel engineer slipped off a fuel line leading to the primary engines, inserted a coupling device, and reattached the line. They were in and out of the aging shuttle in five minutes. This shuttle was chosen because it was designed with an antiquated fuel system, and as such it was only in use in the moons' lighter gravities or for visits to stations.

The disappointed crew returned to monitoring the shuttle's loading and lifted off moments afterwards. Back aboard the destroyer, the shuttle engines were shut down and the small device, embedded in the line, was activated. It was a simple design. Once the engines were engaged and the fuel flowed on the moon base, a small plunger shifted forward. As long as the fuel flowed, the connection was secure. When the engine was shut down and the fuel stopped flowing, the plunger slid back and opened a hole in the device. Fuel began dripping from the line and formed a small puddle that wormed its way back toward the hot engines.

Ten minutes after the crew left and while the shuttle was still being unloaded, the puddle of fuel was ignited by the hot engines, and flame raced back to the leaking line. A massive explosion blew the shuttle apart, which ignited the fuel of the other two shuttles in the bay. They in turn ignited one of the primary missile magazines, which spelled the destroyer's doom.

The two women sat on Marlene's bunk. On her monitor, the moon's local media announcer was talking over images of the destroyer's destruction. Tears ran down Marlene's face, and Lydia reached over to hold her hand. They sat in silence, guilt over their part in the war burning deep into their hearts.

* * *

There was no shortage of individuals who wanted to do their part to help the tribunes redirect the policies of the UE. Unfortunately, most of them did not have the wherewithal to compete against warships. Sabotage was difficult at best. It took the subtle collusion of many people to successfully execute a plan, and more than one location discovered the error of devising a faulty scheme when judiciary forces retaliated against them for their ill-conceived efforts.

But, sometimes a simple plan combined with a dedicated individual was successful. One of Portland's new squadrons was stationed over Saturn's moon, Tethys. For weeks, the combined militia–rebel forces monitored the destroyers. Three captains were careful to constantly reposition their ships and kept their patrol craft providing screens. One captain was not so cautious.

One of the moon's young inhabitants was Weevil, a nickname given him due to the genetic disease that left the bones and muscles of his legs and arms atrophied but his joints swollen like an insect's. Weevil was approaching his seventeenth birthday, and the doctor's prognosis was that he wouldn't see his eighteenth.

Weevil sat on a heavy shelf to rest his limbs and listened to the discussion between a group of rebels and militia. Plan after plan designed to strike at the destroyer squadron stationed above was suggested, dissected, and discarded. The focus was on the errant captain, who hadn't moved his ship in a week.

"We need to be careful to choose an approach that can't be construed as anything but an accident unless you want to end up like Ceres Station," said a militia lieutenant, who was referring to a judiciary commodore, who chose to destroy the entire docking arm of the station simply because it was the location from where the saboteurs launched their small yacht.

The discussion droned on for hours without success, but one concept captured Weevil's imagination. It involved an abandoned mining grubber. The huge machine, used to scrape ore from the surface of large asteroids, was brought to the moon base for repair work, but was abandoned when the mining company went bankrupt.

During the discussion, the bare bones of a plan was laid, citing how easy it would be to aim the grubber at the idle destroyer and warn its bridge officers of the imminent collision when it would be too late for the warship to escape. But the key objection was that an unmanned grubber would not, by any remote stretch of the imagination, launch under full power and coincidentally be directed straight at a destroyer.

The plan to use the grubber wormed its way deep into Weevil's mind for days, until it was all he could think of when awake. After a night of restless sleep, his muscles and bones aching furiously, Weevil decided it was time to act. He dressed, took one look around at his meager belongings strewn across his tiny, cramped, single-room quarters, a gift from the base, and left without taking a single item.

Weevil made his way up to the landing bays, located just under the moon's surface. Every level up was a slight increase in gravity that dragged on his weak limbs and sent pain lancing through his joints with every step. Locating the correct repair bay, Weevil found the huge space a hive of activity, but no one paid him any attention. If anything, his deformities kept people from looking too closely at him.

The mining grubber sat abandoned on the bay's far side like some forgotten monster. Weevil lurched across the intervening hundreds of meters, hoping his limbs didn't fail him. They hadn't been subjected to this much stress in more than a couple of years.

Standing at the base of the grubber, Weevil stared up at the cab of the mining machine, some 15 meters in the air. Looking around, Weevil located a control system on the machine's skirt that overlapped the giant treads. It gave him access to the cab operator's conveyor. Weevil called the tiny car down from the cab, climbed in, and rode it back up.

Once inside the cab, Weevil activated the operator's panel, looked it over, and felt his hopes sink. He didn't have a clue where to start. During the planning discussion, the people said it was as easy as a child's toy to operate. Weevil smacked the panel, which sent a shock of pain up his arm and into his brain. "Stupid, useless machine," he cried out in frustration.

"Welcome, operator, the help menu is ready," the machine replied. "Please state your name."

"Uh … Weevil," the boy stammered in reply.

"Welcome, Uh-Weevil, please state your help request."

Weevil could have hugged the panel in joy. "The help menu is not required," Weevil intoned officially. "Prepare the machine for launch."

"Preparing for launch, Uh-Weevil," the machine replied. A series of operational steps popped up on the panel, which the machine proceeded to perform: sealing the cab; activating the air scrubbers; bringing the fusion engines, which were never deactivated, online; checking power levels; and examining its exterior conditions.

"Launch on hold, operator. Humans in proximity and ceiling detected overhead."

"Please recommend next steps for launch from the bay," Weevil requested.

"Announce launch conditions, enabling humans to clear the bay, and prepare the bay for exit."

"Execute the announcement of launch conditions," Weevil requested.

"The machine's horns wailed for several moments, and in the following lull the bay's speakers announced the departure of the grubber. The bay's work crews looked around in confusion, but when the horns sounded a second time, they scrambled for the airlocks.

"All humans have safely exited, depressurizing the bay, Uh-Weevil," the machine announced. The boy glanced through the cab's windows to watch the bay's giant overhead doors slide aside. Parked in a corner of the bay, the grubber wasn't going to be able to execute a vertical takeoff.

"Can we liftoff safely?" Weevil asked nervously.

"Affirmative, Uh-Weevil. Starting launch."

The increase in gravity from the shove of the engines came close to making Weevil pass out from the pain. He was saved from the engines' maximum thrust as the machine was required to slide sideways to angle itself through the open bay doors.

"Destination required," the machine announced as it slowed its ascent a few hundred meters above the moon base and waited for instructions.

"Display ships in close proximity," Weevil requested.

A monitor above the panel detailed over fifty ships in the machine's 180-degree arc of visibility above the moon. Again Weevil was momentarily stumped until he had an idea and requested a display of only UE warships. Immediately, the monitor refreshed and only four ships remained, but Weevil was unsure which of the destroyers was supposed to be his target.

"Visual call, line one, Uh-Weevil" the machine announced.

"Accept," Weevil said.

"Who is this … Weevil?" the bay operations director began before he recognized the boy. "What do you think you're doing?"

"Choosing how I go out, Sir," Weevil replied.

"Weevil, I know it's been hard on you with your … ailment, but this isn't safe … this thing you're doing."

"Sir, you need to talk to Lieutenant Provo now. I'll wait for his call," Weevil replied, reaching out to the panel to tap the call off. While Weevil waited, he peered at the monitor, wondering how to deduce the ship with the lazy captain. "No use getting blown into space debris before you even get to the target," Weevil mumbled to himself and chuckled, his nerves getting the best of him.

When the machine announced the next call, Weevil found the lieutenant's face on his monitor.

"Weevil, you heard us discussing this plan. It won't work," Provo said.

"Yes, it will, Lieutenant. I've thought about it. We just need to do a few things first," Weevil replied. For the next ten minutes, Weevil laid out his plan, unaware militia and rebels were gathering around Provo.

The boy's plan had heads nodding in the operation director's control room, and finally even Lieutenant Provo was convinced. "Are you sure you want to do this, son? There's no turning back. Those destroyers will either blow you out of space or —"

"Or, I'll die a year earlier than scheduled and in a lot less pain," Weevil replied flatly.

Provo reluctantly accepted Weevil's answer, and set about executing the steps necessary to carry out the boy's plan. Operations sent the grubber the coordinates for the target destroyer, an irregular set of flight vectors, and an order to override its safety protocols. Then the machine was requested to switch communications to an open channel and deliver a med-display of the operator. A rebel doctor looked at the med-display when it came online in operations and shook his head sadly at the boy's weakened biometrics.

"Activate the programmed flight path," Weevil requested of the machine.

With massive engines firing, the grubber launched itself away from the moon base. Immediately, Lieutenant Provo launched into the masquerade, hailing the unknown mining grubber and the rogue operator.

A media announcer, sympathetic to the cause, was prepared to ride the story as breaking news. She colored the narrative as a joy-riding teenager, who desperately wanted to fly, before succumbing to an incurable illness. It wasn't far from the truth.

While the lieutenant seemingly attempted to convince the boy to return, the teenager's anxious voice was heard to announce that the engines were stuck on full power, and he was unable to shut them down. The operation director's voice was heard yelling in the background that the grubber was in for repairs to its control panel among other things. A cacophony of voices allowed the listeners on the moon and in the surrounding space to understand that bay operations was trying to wrestle control of the machine's panel, and, barring that, change its course to protect shipping.

The media announcer kept selling the tragedy of a lonely, ill boy in trouble aboard a rogue mining grubber. Relief flooded through her voice when operations told the boy, who was now identified as Weevil, that the trajectory of the grubber was now safely pointed away from surrounding ships.

Actually, the preprogrammed vector change on the machine's panel coincided with the announcement from operations. The grubber was now paralleling the line of judiciary destroyers.

In the final moments before the grubber passed the last destroyer in line, Weevil knew it was crucial he sell the story to protect his people on the base, but the machine's heavy acceleration and hard course changes had battered his weakened heart. He felt weak and lightheaded, but the panel was displaying an unobtrusive countdown to the final course change, and he struggled to play his part and present a reasonable excuse for the abrupt change.

Over the media channel, the announcer switched to an image of Weevil's med-display, pointing out the irregular and slowing heartbeat. She lamented over the grubber's new direction, which would take it far out into open space, with rescue possibly coming too late for the boy. Switching back to the machine's visual comm, it appeared to everyone watching that Weevil was near death.

With the countdown to the course change only seconds away, Weevil summoned his last ounces of strength and lurched out of his seat to slump over the operator's panel. In the operation control room and the media channel, Weevil's med-display flatlined. The announcer's plaintive whisper of, "Oh, no," was heard by all.

The lieutenant glanced at the operations director, who shrugged his shoulders. It was their plan to flatline the med-display at this critical point, only neither had done it.

The huge grubber suddenly changed course, and the lieutenant broadcast an emergency request to the destroyer squadron to move their ships out of harm's way. Three of the destroyers were immediately underway, their captains and bridge officers having been intently monitoring the unfolding event.

A lieutenant was on bridge duty on the fourth destroyer, the last ship in the line, and he began issuing emergency orders. A steward ran to wake the captain, who preferred to turn off his comm when he went to sleep. The lieutenant punched the imminent collision icon on his panel, which began an insistent wail throughout the ship, and bridge officers scrambled to prepare the destroyer. Crew secured hatches against decompression. Engineers were yelling at one another in an effort to bring up emergency power on the primary engines. The lieutenant had enough presence of mind to use the docking jets to try to turn the warship aside. The jets' meager efforts saved the ship from total disaster.

At full speed, the giant ore excavator, several times larger than a shuttle, slammed into the top of the destroyer, about one-third back from the bow. The grubber glanced off the destroyer, and its fuel tanks ruptured and exploded moments after passing the warship. The impact crippled the destroyer, but, with emergency doors sealed around the ship, the loss of life was minimal. However, another of Portland's destroyers was out of action.

As for Weevil, the cab's cam couldn't get a view of the boy's face after he slumped over the panel. His med-display indicated the boy died at that point. What the populace watching the newscast and those in the operation room couldn't see was the smile on Weevil's face. He did get to fly, and he got to leave the world on his terms.

-25-

Alex and the SADES were connected in conference with Tribunes Woo and Brennan and Admiral Chong.

"Mr. President, I wonder if one of your SADEs could update us on ship status," Chong requested. It was evidence of the small changes the Harakens' war effort had wrought on the hard-edged admiral that he was politely requesting the SADEs' help.

"Every warship is now clearly in the pro-naval or judiciary category, Admiral. There are no more unknowns," Cordelia said. "I have just dispatched the most recent code updates on the remaining warships to all militia stations and pro-naval warships."

"And where do our forces stand?" Woo asked.

"Overall, the UE's effective naval forces have been reduced by 38 percent," Z summarized. "The pro-naval ships and crew represented by that percentage have been completely lost. The enemy is not offering surrender. On the other hand, many judiciary ships have been crippled either through battle or subterfuge and will require extensive repair. The combined militia–rebel sabotage has been quite effective, although the judiciary forces are becoming more vindictive in their reprisals."

"How have the numbers shifted?" Chong asked.

"Favorably," Julien replied. "At the start of the war, we identified the pro-naval forces at 53 percent, with a significant percentage of unknown vessels, either due to unknown commanders or commanders facing unknown situations. The pro-naval forces now compose 72 percent of the remaining ships. However, if you factor in armament power, the ratio comes closer to 50–50.

"The situation is ever-evolving," said Alex, which was an understatement. It was chaos. For the first time in their long lives, the SADEs were overwhelmed. It was all they could do to guide the war efforts of their side, much less help with the other communications the tribunes and admiral were constantly requesting.

"It's not as dire as it might sound, Sers," Alex continued. "Our prime asset is our system of FTL probes, which allows us to strategically maneuver our greater number of smaller ships to take on the capital warships the high judges have under their control. An example of our success is Commodore Charnoose. Originally a captain, Charnoose was warned of his predicament and successfully abandoned his cruiser position to take charge of two destroyers, which Cordelia teamed with a squadron of four destroyers. The two squadron leaders with the help of Z and Cordelia ambushed a judiciary cruiser and two destroyers. After destroying the cruiser and one of its escorts, they added a seventh destroyer to their combined squadron."

"As the senior of the two commodores, Charnoose took command and led his destroyer squadron against a judiciary force comprising a cruiser and three destroyers and defeated them with the loss of only one of his destroyers. Credit for that particular ambush goes to Julien, who orchestrated the battle."

Julien didn't respond. The deaths of the thousands of humans from just this single battle still weighed on his conscience, something some Méridiens still doubted SADEs possessed.

"In summary, you must have patience, Tribunes and Admiral. You are winning the war, but it will be a costly one for your naval forces," Alex said. "Perhaps the good news is that the rebels and the militias have found a common foe and are working in concert against the judiciary forces. They are anxious to see the UE evolve into a kinder society. You might not have need for such an extensive military force in the future."

With little else to discuss, Alex closed the conference comm. He picked up the next battle scenario on the master list, but his focus wavered.

Julien noticed the subtle signs that indicated Alex's failing mental acuity. He had been paying close attention to his friend for days. Alex wasn't a SADE, even though sometimes he tried to act like one. He was flesh and blood in need of nourishment and rest. Cordelia picked up on Julien's concern, and the SADEs made a quick decision.

Alex requested telemetry from a probe located outward of one of Uranus's moons, but received no response from his request. His thoughts were sluggish enough that he repeated his request without considering any other reason for the lack of response.

<You will not get a response, my friend,> Julien sent.

<Time for some food and rest, Ser President,> Cordelia added.

<You shouldn't have to take on the burden of these fights and the resulting loss of lives by yourself,> Alex replied.

<If one was to be interested in the finer points of that argument,> Z interjected. <By my estimates, you are responsible for more deaths than any one of us.>

<Z!> Cordelia scolded.

<Not this time, Cordelia,> Z sent back. <Our president is a skillful tactician, who has done more to help win this war than any one of us, but he works to the point of exhaustion when he will be of little use to any of us. This is not logical.>

<It is not a question of logic, Z, although your numbers are correct,> Julien sent. <It is a question of conscience and heart, and we appreciate your intentions, Mr. President. Renée and Terese are waiting outside. I believe it would be a wiser decision on your part to go to meet them rather than receive them here.>

Alex tabled his battle plan and linked it to the central database on board the *No Retreat*. He stood slowly to let his bout of lightheadedness clear, and as he passed behind each SADE he laid a hand on a shoulder, squeezing lightly. Cordelia briefly touched Alex's hand in return.

<Someday, our president will have to realize he isn't a SADE,> Z shared.

<You do him a disservice, Z,> Julien replied. <He knows he isn't a SADE, but that will never stop him from preventing you or any of us from having to take on the dirtiest of moral chores by ourselves.>

<Even if it means endangering his well-being?> Z asked.

<Even if it might mean his death,> Cordelia added. <It's individuals of good conscience who are determined to protect others and see the doors of opportunity opened for those they protect. Witness us free of our boxes.>

* * *

Tribune Woo was hunting the enclave. While the exclusive committee of high judges wasn't in real-time communication with its naval forces, it still represented a danger to the UE's future. Militia forces had halted trials across the globe and, in most cases, on the inner planets. The freeing of the rebels in the outer zone ensured trials on the moons and stations were discontinued until a new judicial structure and sentencing laws were in place. It was Woo's hope that the judges in the rim weren't floating in space in retaliation for their harsh verdicts.

Woo reached out to her "nephew," Lieutenant Gardia, several times despite her own prohibition that contact should not be initiated by anyone but the lieutenant. She had never received an answer.

A militia colonel that Woo placed in charge of tracking down the enclave's headquarters used the lieutenant's messages to locate the originating server, which led him to the enclave's hidden location. The stone entrance was embedded in a granite mountainside, making it almost invisible from the air. The colonel reported finding the location deserted, except for the mutilated body of Lieutenant Gardia. It was surmised from the extent of bruising and partial healing of his wounds that he was tortured for days.

"How do you wish me to proceed, Tribune?" the colonel asked.

"Find them, Colonel. Find every one of them. This is a priority. Request as many people and services as you need."

"And when I find them, Tribune Woo?" the colonel asked.

Woo knew what the colonel was requesting. It would be a lot less trouble for the new government if the enclave's members simply disappeared. Instead, she said, "I don't think it would be an auspicious start to our new society, Colonel, if we behaved as they have done. Arrest them."

"Understood, Tribune." The colonel was relieved to hear his orders. He was looking forward to the policy changes as much as most of the other militia officers he knew. The changes were needed and long overdue. *And to think it took a bunch of alien humans to force us to do it,* the colonel thought.

* * *

Idona Station became a haven for much of the outer rim's shipping. Small freighters and passenger liners, fearful of making the trip inward, lingered at the station, despite the loss of revenue. A little poorer in credits was a lot better than dead.

Refined ore and solid gases piled up at Idona's refining stations, waiting shipment inward. But the opinion was the same for the freighters' captains and on-board owners alike; there was no safer place in the entire system than where the Harakens were stationed.

That was proven when two judiciary destroyer captains foolishly decided to attack Idona. Captain Shimada was readying her destroyer for battle, when she received a comm.

"Stand down, Captain," said Franz, who filled her monitor.

"The last time I checked, I don't report to you, Commander."

"No, you don't, Captain. Not unless you wish to," Franz said with a winning smile, which made Shimada's cheeks color. One of the female ensigns ducked her head to hide her smile. "Let's consider the practicalities. Where is your rearmament supply store, Captain?"

Shimada knew Franz had her there. There were few of the precious supplies for her destroyer at Idona. Rearmament supply for a ship-to-ship battle was not seen as a priority by command, until this war showed the error of that decision.

"Be my guest, Commander," Shimada relented. The captain's directive to stand down was gratefully heard by the crew, who had no wish to take on two destroyers. Instead, they watched while two squadrons of Haraken travelers made short work of the destroyers, spreading out in an arc of 120 degrees for the attack. The thirty-two fighters forced the UE warships to spread their defensive fire too thin, allowing the travelers an easy time navigating through the small number of missiles targeting each fighter. The

Haraken pilots expertly excised the engines from both destroyers, one of which suffered secondary fires and explosions, but the great majority of the crew was able to evacuate in time.

Despite the fear of what was transpiring across the system and the station receiving real-time news of the major events, including every battle, life aboard the station was reasonably comfortable. For the first time in generations, the rim people at Idona were at ease with one another.

Interior repairs on the station were nearing completion, and Nikki Fowler had sufficient funds for purchasing upgrade equipment. The refinery stations were overjoyed to receive her order for new hull plating and were busy fulfilling her order from the stockpiled reserves awaiting loading onto the freighters standing by, and owners and captains alike were ecstatic to be selling their goods without having to transport them inward.

Some of the station's unhappy people were the orphan children, who were denied access to their favorite people, the Haraken SADEs.

* * *

Another unhappy person in the outer rim was Admiral Theodore Portland. In the early days of the war, his battleship, cruiser, and destroyer escorts had eliminated a handful of destroyers, and the success had buoyed his confidence. Squadrons continued to join his nascent fleet until he was well on his way to being stronger than when he first attacked Idona.

As the days and weeks passed, the admiral began receiving reports of battles that took place throughout the system. Early news was encouraging, but slowly the reports indicated successes on the part of the pro-naval forces, even against the judiciary's capital ships.

Then Portland began losing destroyers, one after another, by sabotage. This ignominy was occurring on top of his inability to consistently resupply his ships without threats. His shuttles were forced to land under the heavy guard of patrol ships, which left his destroyers under-protected.

In the past ten days, all the battle reports Portland received were negative for the judiciary forces — two battleships, four cruisers, and fifteen destroyers lost. The writing on the bulkhead was plain. The judiciary forces were going to lose the war, if they hadn't already done so.

Portland came to the decision that sitting at Saturn was a losing proposition. Eventually, the pro-naval forces would aggregate and come for him, the last of the judiciary forces, but there was no place for his fleet to hide. He considered making a run at Earth or another heavily populated, inner world and taking it hostage, but the odds were against him successfully crossing that much space without engaging in numerous running battles that would weaken his fleet.

As Portland reviewed his opportunities, one thing was clear. If he was captured, it would mean a death sentence, a kinder UE or not. Any of his several crimes was punishable by death. After weeks of deliberation, Portland felt he was left with only one option — revenge.

-26-

The SADEs were close to winning or rather they were close to helping Admiral Chong's people win the war. The judiciary forces had congregated into two massive fleets, one in the inner zone, hiding in the asteroid belt outward of Mars, and Portland's fleet in the outer zone. The majority of the pro-naval forces' capital ships were concentrated in and around the three worlds of Earth, Venus, and Mars.

Woo was negotiating with Admiral Ullman, who was in command of the judiciary forces in the inner zone, and was hopeful his unconditional surrender could be achieved. What was helpful was the real-time telemetry feeds detailing the extent of the pro-naval forces still in play. Ullman was constantly updated by Woo on the tide tilting in favor of the pro-naval forces and that he was the last of the inner world judiciary forces.

Portland wasn't so accommodating. He refused every entreaty by Admiral Chong and Tribune Woo to talk, and the more evidence they presented that the war was lost for the judiciary, the more convinced Portland was that he had only one choice. He would not let Admiral Chong's people take him alive, and if he was going to die, he would take the Harakens with him.

* * *

"Good news, President Racine," Woo enthused to Alex. "We've negotiated the surrender of Admiral Ullman. His forces are disbanding, and his squadrons are making for separate locations where the crew will be taken into custody. That clears the inner zone of all judiciary forces."

"Wonderful news, Tribune Woo," Alex replied.

Julien was managing the comm, and Cordelia and Z, with no more need to direct battle maneuvers, much to the joy of the orphans, were free to do as they wished. The stationers were enjoying watching the two SADEs walking the corridors surrounded by the chattering young orphans, healthy and happy.

"That leaves just one judiciary fleet remaining. Unfortunately, it's one of the largest fleets assembled, as you know. Portland's at Saturn," Chong said.

"Before we discuss Portland, I'm curious about people's opinions, since the two of you are on the two most populated planets in the system," Alex replied.

"Yes, I'm curious as well," Brennan chimed in.

"On Earth, opinions have been overwhelming and extremely positive," Woo replied. "My staff, which I've expanded, is filtering thousands of messages every day. Many are constructive, offering opinions of better judicial systems and a variety of punishments to fit the degree of criminality. And many are asking for case reviews of family and friends who have been sentenced."

"It's the same here," Chong said. "Most of my messages urge me to finish the war so that the UE policy changes might proceed, but far and wide, they're positive and supportive of the pro-naval forces and our efforts to further Tribunes Woo and Brennan's promises of change."

"I'm pleased to hear this. It was always my hope that Sol was populated by people who wanted something other than that offered us by High Judge Bunaldi," Alex said.

There was silence on the comm. To the UE leaders, High Judge Bunaldi and Admiral Theostin were a lifetime ago. Alex's mention of why the Harakens came to Sol was a harsh reminder of the terrible events that led to the UE's war, despite the enormous potential for the people of Sol.

"Well," Alex continued, "for other news … Portland's fleet left Saturn eight Earth hours ago. It appears he's headed for Idona."

Alex waited while Woo and Chong tried to shout over each other so that their questions might be heard. Suddenly, a sharp whistle pierced the noise, issued by, of all people, Tribune Brennan.

"Apologies, Mr. President," Brennan said. "Was there anything else you wanted to add to your announcement?"

"I don't need to summarize Portland's fleet. We all know what warships he possesses and how heavily weighted he is in capital ships. We've directed every pro-naval warship to Idona that can possibly arrive before Portland reaches us. In warship count, the pro-naval forces will be at a great disadvantage, and in armament your ships will be virtually unprepared to engage the admiral's fleet."

"It's not that bad, Mr. President," Woo said. "Let Portland have Idona. We'll be able to combine our forces and come for him in a few weeks."

"It won't work, Kwan," Chong said gently. "Portland knows it's the end for him. He's a dead man if he's captured. If the Harakens pull back, he'll take his anger out on Idona."

"How far do you think he would go, Admiral?" Brennan asked.

"I think Portland could convince his people to turn Idona into space debris."

"That's my assessment of the man, Admiral," Alex agreed.

"I still think you should pull back, President Racine," Woo said, "but hear me out first. I said at the beginning of this war that this was our fight. We wronged your people in the first place. They don't deserve to die on our behalf as well."

"Your sentiments are appreciated, Tribune Woo, but perhaps you misunderstand my role as Haraken's president," Alex replied. "I serve at the pleasure of my people and on their behalf, not for my pleasure or gain. If I was to tell my people that we're abandoning Idona's defense in the face of Portland's massive fleet to a severely underpowered pro-naval force, they would laugh at me and rightly so. No slight intended, Tribune, but that's not who we are."

"So what is your plan, Mr. President?" Chong asked.

"Strategically, defend Idona Station. Tactically, I have no idea, yet. The planet positions are in Portland's favor. There is a substantial pro-naval fleet at Jupiter, but it can't reach us in time to help. A small squadron of destroyers at Uranus is on its way."

"What will you choose to do, Tribune Brennan?" Woo asked.

"If the president is staying, I'm staying," Brennan blurted defiantly. "I'm tired of hiding behind the mantle of my office. If I can help to save this station in any way, no matter how minor, I intend to do it."

Alex closed the conference comm and eyed Brennan, who ducked his head in embarrassment over his declaration. Alex extended a hand and Brennan shook it tentatively until Alex said, "Welcome to the fight, Ian," then Brennan pumped Alex's hand enthusiastically.

* * *

Alex's team plus others, such as Nikki Fowler and Captain Shimada, spent an entire day without success considering ideas on how to defend Idona from Portland. Finally, Alex called it a night, scheduling the next meeting to start after morning meal.

The next morning, Shimada brought her tray over to Tatia and Sheila's table. "May I, Admiral?" she asked, motioning to a seat with her tray.

"Be my guest, Captain," Tatia replied.

The three women ate in companionable silence until the burning questions in Shimada's mind would wait no longer.

<Here it comes,> Sheila sent to Tatia, who covered her smile with a meal cloth.

"Pardon me, Admiral … and I don't mean these questions to sound accusatory, but I could use your help trying to understand the situation," Shimada began.

"Proceed, Captain," Tatia said.

"If your people's purpose in coming to Sol was to find a way to prevent a war with the UE, haven't you done that?"

"I suppose we have, considering the changes in your governing body and this war to ensure those changes will be enacted," Tatia replied.

"Then if you've succeeded in your mission, why not pull out … save yourselves?"

"Can't we have more than one purpose, more than one mission?" Sheila asked.

"Yes ... you mean Idona Station. But why take on the burden? Our people attacked you and killed many of your pilots without provocation on your part."

"Do you believe in what you are asking us to do, Captain, or are you just trying to understand us?" Tatia asked.

"I'm not sure anymore. Maybe it's just my distrust of altruistic motives. The UE might have beaten it out of me."

"It's an understandable reaction to the constant social pressure of distrust. Are you wondering whether our commitment stems from our leaders or from our people?" Sheila asked, beginning to understand Shimada's questions.

"That question had occurred to me," Shimada admitted.

<She's wondering if Franz is real or a puppet,> Sheila sent to Tatia.

<Aha,> Tatia sent back. She stood up and announced to the room, "Please stand." As one, the room of Harakens stood. "This is a vote and you are asked to vote your conscience, as would be expected of you. Please sit if you think we should abandon Idona Station to Portland's forces."

No one moved. Every man and woman stood awaiting the next request.

Tears appeared at the corner of Shimada's eyes, and she wiped them away. She stood and faced the room, delivering the manner of thanks she had seen the Harakens use in important moments, placing her hand over her heart and bowing her head. Across the room, implants coordinated the Haraken response and heads as one nodded their acceptance of Shimada's honor for their efforts.

"You'll excuse me, Admiral, Commodore," Shimada said immediately afterwards and walked quickly from the room.

"Are we really that hard to understand?" Sheila wondered out loud.

"Or is it that our captain wants to be a believer and doesn't trust us to be true to the image we present?" Tatia replied.

* * *

Tatia and Sheila were the last to join the planning session and arrived in time to hear an unusual suggestion by Cordelia.

"It might mitigate Admiral Portland's anger if he could believe he won a victory."

"Pardon our lateness, Alex," Tatia said. "An important Haraken–UE relationship needed attention. What's your idea, Cordelia?"

"We pretend to let Portland win by sending our travelers at him unmanned. He destroys them, and we retreat in defeat."

"How many of our travelers would we have to send?" Sheila asked.

"It would require the majority, Sheila. The admiral is aware of the number he fought before."

"Can you control your travelers to the extent that their actions in combat would appear realistic?" Shimada asked.

Alex looked over at the SADEs for an answer.

"Negative, Ser. We might have sufficient processing power at this end," Julien replied, nodding to his fellow SADEs, but our probes couldn't manage the bandwidth of communications and data transmissions to realistically fly hundreds of travelers in believable attack and evasion patterns."

"Then Portland won't buy it," Shimada declared. "He'll presume a trick, and, when you pull back, he'll hit Idona Station to force you to reengage, and, at that point, you'll be short a lot of travelers."

"Rather tough to predict the actions of a madman," Sheila mumbled.

"By the way, congratulations, Commodore," Alex said, staring at Shimada. "Admiral Chong's confirmation came this morning. The destroyer squadron is yours."

"But I don't have seniority. Is this your doing, Alex?" Shimada asked. She still felt odd with the nature of these intimate meetings, but it would have appeared even odder to be the only one calling Alex, Mr. President.

"The admiral might have asked my opinion, Reiko, but it was his decision," Alex replied with a slight shrug.

While everyone congratulated Shimada, she was heard to mumble, "Now I only have to live to enjoy it."

"Okay, people, back to work so that the only ones who will suffer in this fight are Portland's forces," Alex said.

Planning proceeded for the next several hours without producing a single viable option. Even the ideas that sounded good ran afoul of the SADEs, whose analyses predicted heavy losses for the Harakens and Shimada's squadron.

<Should we be considering evacuation of sensitive personnel to the *Rêveur*?> Cordelia sent to Julien.

<Who do you think would volunteer to go?> Julien sent back.

<Alex could order them to leave,> Cordelia said.

<And our president would learn just how far his authority extends when he was refused. This is, of course, even if he did agree to give the order, which I doubt he would,> Julien replied.

Cordelia knew Julien was correct, and if she had allowed herself to calculate the possibilities, she would have realized it too. But her emotional programs were overriding her analyses programs. She had been thinking of the children.

The frustration in the room was growing, not the least for Tatia, who considered herself the master of tactical solutions for the Harakens. "With the numbers we're facing, Alex, we might just as well be throwing rocks," Tatia declared.

Alex's mind produced a silly image of giant rocks flying at Portland's fleet, and he was suddenly galvanized. "Yes, that's it. We throw rocks," Alex declared and grabbed Tatia, planting a huge kiss on her.

"I always wondered if he preferred bigger women," Renée said, throwing a wink Tatia's way.

"It's nice to be appreciated," Tatia replied with a grin, "but as the admiral, don't you think I should know why I'm being appreciated?"

Alex pulled up the holo-vid and requested the position of Portland's fleet, his approach vector to Idona, and the outer asteroid belt. He studied it for an hour while all around him patience was wearing thin, but before anyone could voice their frustration, Alex said, "I'm thinking an asteroid storm is headed Portland's way … an asteroid storm of big rocks … rocks big enough to hide a traveler."

"He'll just move his fleet aside," Sheila objected.

"I would expect nothing less," Alex agreed.

"But that would place our traveler squadrons next to him, in the middle of him, or right behind him for an ambush," Tatia said, grinning hard.

"Now, all we need is an asteroid storm," Z said drily.

"We make one with the carriers," Sheila said excitedly. "We launched the travelers outside the Méridien system. Why can't we do the same thing with these asteroids?"

"I know a bunch of miners and ore haulers who would love to see their livelihood defended against that madman, Portland," Nikki added.

"Julien," Alex said, looking at his friend.

"One feasibility study for one asteroid storm coming up, one hopes," Julien replied.

-27-

The SADEs shared the responsibilities for the feasibility study among themselves. From the most recent probe telemetry, Cordelia quickly determined the amount of time they had to implement the plan if it could be determined to be viable. The time period appeared more than adequate, but no one knew what problems were still to be encountered.

Z set about determining the physical characteristics of the asteroids they would use. His initial thought was to consider the lighter ice asteroids, containing frozen water and gases, but this was overruled by Alex and Tatia in case Portland tested the oncoming storm by firing missiles at the asteroids.

Next for consideration was the diameter of the chosen rock asteroids. The larger the rock, the easier to hide the traveler, but the more mass the carrier would be required to accelerate. In the end, Z decided on two key parameters. The first was the minimum and maximum width of the rock. The second was a request that, if workers could be found, the rocks should be heavily carved out on one side to form a thick, parabolic shape — minimizing mass and creating the greatest shield dimensions to hide a traveler. The latter condition would require the carriers to load the rocks in precise positions to allow the travelers to catch and hide behind them.

Julien took Z's calculations and determined that his fellow SADE's suggestion of carved-out asteroids was going to be a requirement not an option. Otherwise, the mass would be too great for the carriers to accelerate and return to launch a second barrage within a reasonable period of time. A corollary of his decision was that the staging point for the launch would need to be located far outward of the station. If not, the carriers would be passing inward of the station before launch, exposing them to Portland's fleet telemetry, and the ruse would be over before it started.

Cordelia was tasked with working out the details of a coordinated launch between each carrier's barrage of asteroids and travelers, which was proving to be more complicated than imagined. In simple terms, a carrier was capable of launching an asteroid. A traveler was capable of catching the asteroid from behind after its launch. These elemental steps were a given, but Cordelia had to figure out how to coordinate a sub-wing of travelers racing after a barrage of rocks and selecting a rock that no other pilot had selected.

To solve the dilemma, Cordelia decided to tag each asteroid with a transponder, and the SADE tasked Mickey with rounding up hundreds of miner transponders and updating them to communicate with a traveler's controller. After the carrier's launch of each barrage, the programmed controller would seek its own rock, thereby preventing a mad scramble for an uncontested hiding place in the short time available before the rocks passed inward of the station.

It was about this time in the planning process that Z halted his primary decision algorithms in mid-calculations and said, "Yes, I apologize."

Cordelia was searching for the error that Z must have made, but her partner, for some reason, was smiling at her.

"It would be prudent to leave Idona Station in the UE's hands, although I would have been quite displeased with that decision," Z said. "Our president has chosen not to do that, which, on evaluation, is an illogical decision, since our forces are woefully inadequate. Then he seeks to counterbalance our weakness by conceiving a strategy to throw rocks at the enemy. I still have much to learn about humans," Z admitted.

"Especially about this one," Julien said, smiling at his compatriot.

* * *

The SADEs shared their concern with Alex about the visibility of the carriers and travelers during the barrage launches, an exposure necessitated by the longer run time the carriers required to accelerate the considerable mass of the asteroids. To solve the problem, Alex contacted Nikki for help.

"I need a screen, Nikki, a large amount of metal, but something that could be explained away when seen from a distance," Alex said.

Nikki was stumped by the request, but fortunately, Captain Yun was in her office and Alex was on Nikki's speaker.

"How about derelict ships, Mr. President?" Yun replied. "There's a graveyard of older ships at each of the refining stations, waiting processing. The metals and materials of the ships are valuable, but the labor to dismantle them is expensive, so the stations are waiting on lean times when the smelting work of ore shipments from the belt slows."

"What's their condition?" Alex asked.

"Some are bare hulks, but others are in fairly decent shape. They would pass as freighters or other ships waiting at the station."

"Perfect. Nikki, I'll get back to you."

Alex decided that a screen of derelict ships would serve his purpose admirably. There was the distinct possibility of accidents, such as strikes of the derelict ships by the asteroids just after release by the carriers, so it would take some careful placement to make an effective screen to minimize impacts. The pilots would require a warning to allow time to abandon their hiding position before impact. It was just another factor for the SADEs to figure into their calculations.

Cordelia considered the problem of asteroids striking the derelicts. There would be no time for the pilots, with their human reflexes, to respond to an imminent impact. So she adopted her previous concept by requesting that Mickey tag the derelict ships with transponders. She updated the fleet's traveler controllers with the frequencies of the new transponders and added an evasion routine. When the controller received a proximity warning, it would pull the traveler out of the asteroid shell before impact.

Woo and Chong were surprised to get Alex's request for access to a credit stream, as he called it. Alex was being polite. He could have had Julien transfer the funds. The leaders gave their approval, wondering just what the Haraken president was up to and hoping that it would be something that would successfully counter Portland's fleet.

"Nikki, I've set up a station account for you under the title 'Rocks,'" Alex said and heard her giggle. "It seemed an appropriate name, at the time," Alex said, laughing at himself.

"How much is in the account and what is it for?" Nikki asked.

"You'll be hiring all the help we need, anything to do with the preparations for this fight."

"Mr. President," Yun interrupted, "who might we consider recipients of these credits?"

"Anyone reasonable and any amount that is seen as market price ... stationers, miners, ore haulers, freighters, reclamation ships, even yachts if they're serving a purpose."

"How much money is in this account?" Nikki asked, looking it up in her finance application. "None," she said, confused.

"It doesn't work that way, Nikki. Just enter the amount, the payee, and service notes. The account is linked to one of Tribune Woo's primary accounts. The debit will be replaced with a credit from her account. Any problems with it let me know."

While Nikki was trying to process access to an almost limitless account as far as a station director was concerned, Yun had a practical concern. "Mr. President, we could add an enormous amount of debit to this account, practically bankrupting the station, before the transfer of credits from Earth arrives weeks later."

"Negative, Captain, the transfers are accomplished through our probes. They will be real time. When this fight is over, you will have some time until we leave your space to process any late charges."

When Alex closed the comm, Nikki and Yun grinned at each other. Nikki contacted Cordelia, per Alex's instructions, for the ship placement and the type of ships she preferred. Yun commed the refining stations and told them he was borrowing their derelict hulks. Most objections were overcome when Yun explained that the cost of transport from the graveyards to the station and back would be at Idona's expense. Any other objections were silenced when Yun added that the Haraken president ordered the transfer.

* * *

Finally, the SADEs pronounced the plan feasible and distributed the extensive requirements to the databases of the fleet and the station.

After spending most of the night reviewing the plan's details with Yun, Nikki arranged a conference comm with the mining concerns in the belt for first thing in the morning. It proved to a most unusual conversation.

"Let me get this straight, Fowler, you're ordering asteroids to the size specifications you've sent us, and you want them hollowed out?" one owner asked.

"That's correct, Sir," Nikki replied.

"What in the dark of space are you going to do with all these rocks?" another asked.

Nikki laughed, even though it probably wasn't the most appropriate time to do so, and said, "The Haraken president is going to throw them at Portland's fleet."

There was dead quiet on the comm, and Nikki was sure that she had blown the request. Then she heard laughter, small at first and then a bellowing that was followed by several coughing fits. Finally, someone leaned into their comm and said, "Well, break a shaft, Nikki, why didn't you say so in the first place? Can do for the Harakens."

When the owners regained control of themselves, Nikki added, "And one more thing, you're getting paid for your work, and it's coming out of Tribune Woo's account." Nikki wouldn't have been surprised to know grins were forming on owners' faces across the belt.

Later, as the owners contacted their underlings to begin fulfilling the strange order, one field manager said to his owner, "This is crazy, boss, getting paid to carve out rocks to help the Harakens defend the station with asteroids against UE forces."

"I can't say I can argue with that sentiment, but think on this," the owner replied. "If the president's gambit isn't successful, it might not matter. We probably won't have a station around to ship our ore through or spend our credits at."

* * *

The establishment of a staging point for the rocks, outward of the station, created a huge demand for services of all kind. Freighters, small yachts, a couple of liners, and numerous ore haulers and reclamation vessels headed for the coordinates Nikki distributed. Each owner or captain was required to register their ship and the services they would be providing with the station to gain approval first. Patrice had her militia personnel dive in to help Nikki and Yun coordinate the enormous effort.

The liners became small oases of food and rest for the people who were working as many hours as they could manage. The freighters were supplying reaction mass for larger vessels, fuel for smaller vessels, and supplies of all type, and the yachts were acting as shuttles, luxurious shuttles, but shuttles nonetheless.

Jorre piloted his reclamation tug into a holding position alongside several other tugs. He glanced toward the copilot's seat, which until today had been empty since the day he bought the vessel. Pauline sat there, smiling shyly back at him. Jorre had heard the announcement from the station director for work at the staging point, and his first thought was to find Pauline and ask her to accompany him. To his surprise, she said, "Yes," adding, "it's not every day you get an offer to save your home." She had kissed him on the cheek and run to pack a bag.

Cordelia calculated that in the time they had before Portland arrived, the asteroids would have to be moved from the belt by the carriers. Miko Tanaka and Edouard Manet piloted their ships, the *No Retreat* and the *Last Stand*, to the belt's staging position. They had expected to wait while the miners organized themselves. Instead, they found double rows of ore haulers waiting, with carved-out asteroids in their grips. The miners were skilled blasters, and within minutes of selecting and surveying a choice rock they knew where to set charges to crack the rock in half. Then they had used various processes to carve out the excess material to create the parabolic shapes requested.

The carriers maneuvered into positions, the bays opened, and the tethering beams activated. Immediately, the haulers and tugs began pushing their loads toward an open bay, coordinating with the bay's crew chief. Within an hour, the *Last Stand*, the smaller carrier, was on its way to the station's staging area, and the *No Retreat* followed soon after.

At the station staging point, Jorre eased his tug forward to grasp an asteroid from the *Last Stand*, his face screwed up in concentration. On his comm, the carrier's flight chief signaled when the beams were cut, passing the load off to Jorre, who was excited to see that he had retrieved his load first, but then he realized he had no drop location to head toward.

"Anxious as always I see, young captain."

"Cordelia," Jorre exclaimed.

"The coordinates are in your computer, young captain. Drop your load there and ensure it has zero velocity relative to the station."

"Ser Pauline, my thanks for the beauty you grow," Pauline heard in her comm headset.

"You would be the recipient of the orchids, Jorre's benefactor," Pauline replied. "The way he gushes about you is enough to make a girl jealous."

"And yet *you* sit beside him, young Ser. It might help you to know that I'm a century too old for your young man. Good fortune to you, Pauline."

When Cordelia closed the comm, Pauline looked at Jorre in astonishment. "You didn't tell me you had a thing for older women," she teased, much to Jorre's confusion and consternation.

* * *

Tatia wondered at Alex's forethought. He'd ordered a probe launched in Sol's outer belt when they first crossed the field headed inward to Idona Station. The probe saved them days of time that they would have lost sending the *Rêveur* out to communicate with the miners. At the time, she couldn't see the value and asked Alex why.

"I have a fondness for asteroid fields and miners, Tatia. Harvesting them was the reason I met the Méridiens," he said to her.

Tatia's question to Alex this time was, "How many rocks do you want us to get?"

Alex's equally odd response this time was, "Haul them out until our time is up. You can never have too many rocks."

* * *

For days on end, the people of Idona space — Harakens, stationers, miners, captains and crew, and visitors — labored to fulfill Alex's crazy plan. Despite the long hours and hard work, the mood was generally upbeat.

It wasn't that the people didn't know that this was one of the strangest ways they had ever heard of to take on a dangerous UE fleet and that there was every possibility it would fail; it was the fact that the people, for once in a long time, were united in a common cause. They were working to save a place that had been transformed from a derelict outpost to a home for most and a safe haven for others.

Previously, to most stationers, Idona was a place to exist. Now it was a place to prosper, but more important, it was a new way of living, of existing together without the stifling stress the UE policies had created, and they, most of all, were adamant about protecting it from some egomaniac of an admiral bent on destroying it.

So they mined asteroids, carved them, loaded them, unloaded them, tagged them with sensors that were wedded to traveler controllers, and settled them into discreet groups that related to the side of a particular carrier and the order of launch. The groups of asteroids grew as myriad small ships — tugs, ore haulers, and reclamation vessels — any craft that could safely move an asteroid piled them up. And just as important, each small ship was required to adopt the asteroids they transported. It would be their job, at the appropriate time, to repeat the exact process. For each barrage's preparation, the haulers would have to attach the same asteroid to the same bay's beams on the same ship's side from where they had originally unloaded it.

The key to this carefully crafted routine was to allow the sub-wing of travelers to chase their assigned rocks once the barrage was released by the carrier. In any human endeavor, this type of precision without rehearsal would have been fraught with errors, some of which might have led to the death of pilots, but the SADEs depended on the Harakens' technical infrastructure.

The carriers' and travelers' controllers were at the heart of the complicated procedures. Movement of an improper asteroid toward a bay at loading time, and the carrier's controller, receiving the asteroid's transponder signal, would notify the vessel operator and redirect the operator to the proper bay. This and innumerable other crosschecks gave the Harakens a chance at succeeding with Alex's plan where others would have stalled at the first barrage.

-28-

Tatia, Sheila, and Reiko were locked in an intense discussion for hours. Alex, Julien, and Renée were nearby and could often hear the women raising their voices. At one point, Julien inquired of Alex if he shouldn't be assisting them with the barrage computations.

Overhearing his question, Renée replied, "This isn't a question of computation, Julien, it's a matter of intuition … work best left to women."

Alex grinned at Julien and walked away, refusing to touch Renée's comment.

It would leave Julien wondering if SADEs could be intuitive until he reached the point where he decided that if he survived the upcoming fight he might have centuries to discover the answer to that question.

The women's discussion centered on Portland's reactions to different barrage formations, but the permutations were too many to consider. So the decision was to proceed in a manner that limited the admiral's options.

"Portland will surround his battleship with other capital ships, which will be commanded by his most loyal people," Reiko said. "The perimeters of the fleet will be manned by destroyers, captained by the admiral's camp followers, if you will. Send the first bombardment directly at the extreme perimeter ships, and there is a high possibility of them shifting away from the fleet."

"Away from the fleet, not closer?" Tatia asked.

"Say you're a destroyer captain, who has been going along for the ride with the admiral, until now. You're out on the periphery of the fleet because you aren't one of the committed. You're sailing to attack the Harakens and Idona Station again, where Portland lost most of his fleet last time. Now, all of a sudden and very mysteriously, a great number of huge rocks comes flying past the station at your warship."

"Oh … I get it," declared Sheila. "We're the mysterious aliens of the deep dark. Who knows what we're capable of? And closing toward Portland's battleship might not be the safest place to be."

"Excellent," Tatia said. "Instead of a barrage with travelers behind the asteroids, we can start with launches of just rocks to force the fleet apart, perhaps even creating avenues." *You can never have enough rocks,* Tatia thought, recalling Alex's words. "I like this concept," she added. "If the fleet sees successive waves of asteroids sailing past, it won't be expecting our travelers when we launch an armed barrage."

"Does this mean that we'll have to reprogram the travelers to mate with later groups of rocks?" Sheila asked.

"No, not if we just take some of the surplus groups of asteroids and have Cordelia program them as the initial launches," Tatia replied.

"You know, I wanted to ask you about those extra asteroids," Reiko said. "What made you expend the extra effort to haul them out in the first place? I mean it's great that we have them, considering the changes to our plan, but I'm curious as to your reasoning." When Tatia and Sheila started chuckling, Reiko became a little miffed and exclaimed, "What?"

"Alex," the two Harakens said simultaneously and started laughing.

"Oh," Reiko said, "forget I asked." Then she joined in the laughter.

After the women settled down, Sheila considered the upcoming change and said, "When we add the empty barrages at the front of the queue, we'll have to tag the new rocks and reorder the links between the tugs and the asteroids."

Her comment caused Tatia and Reiko to groan. It would be the fourth time that the plan had a significant strategic change that necessitated a revamping of the data and the order of battle.

"At some point, people are going to think we don't know what we're doing," Sheila joked.

"Throwing rocks to defeat a UE force led by capital ships doesn't constitute that already?" deadpanned the diminutive Reiko.

Sheila clapped her hands in front of Reiko's face, creating an explosive sound. "Squish like bug," she said, and the women broke into laughter again.

* * *

Positioning of the derelict ships to use as screens for the carriers' launches turned out to be a nonstarter. As Z put it to Alex, "It's analogous to aiming a weapon. The projectiles are thrown by the carrier. The target is the fleet; its position we can't anticipate. How do we set up a screen to hide our weapons when we don't know where our targets will be in advance?"

Alex pulled up the holo-vid, which was loaded with the carrier's staging position, the stock of carved-out asteroids, Idona, and Portland's present position. He pulled up a chair, sat down, and stared at the holo-vid before he closed his eyes.

Reiko took a breath to raise a question, but felt Sheila's big hand on her arm, signaling her to wait. She looked around the room and saw the three SADEs in frozen positions. It made Reiko wonder again what an implant would feel like and what she would be able to do with it. An image of Franz flashed through her mind. Noticing that Tatia and Sheila had adopted parade rest positions, she copied them.

"We're trying too hard. Forget the idea of a screen as a wall. What we need is simple camouflage," Alex said, a few moments later, opening his eyes, and the SADEs were nodding in agreement. He approached the holo-vid and images of ships began appearing. "Lay the ships out in an expanding cone at various distances from the carrier staging points up to and past the station. In fact, throw in a few ships behind the staging points. The UE warships have simpler telemetry returns with their guides. It will be difficult for them to distinguish the barrages as anything more than a storm originating in the belt and speeding past the station."

* * *

Aboard the station, Nikki Fowler was inundated with requests from the stationers asking to help with Idona's preparations. She organized work crews under engineers to ensure every emergency decompression door was operable, could seal tight, and actuated at the slightest drop in pressure. Food and water were distributed and stockpiled in each section in case people were trapped by the decompression doors.

Nikki spent hours with her engineers planning for various catastrophes. What helped her peace of mind was the fact that thousands of stationers would be aboard the ships, helping the Harakens prepare for Portland. At the same time, that meant there was little opportunity for evacuation of the station's remaining residents and visitors, who were represented by a significant proportion of children.

Arrangements were made to begin moving people from the outer ring to the inner ring and core, which stood greater chances of surviving any errant missiles. It saddened Nikki that such a wonderful, social experiment as Idona Station, post the Harakens' arrival, which had proven to be so successful might soon become space debris because of one man's undying anger.

* * *

On the trip from Saturn's moons, Portland regained much of his old assurance. He entertained thoughts of destroying the Harakens and Idona Station then proceeding on to the belt where he would use the mining hubs as bases, while he ransacked stations in the outer rim until the tribunes granted him immunity.

Portland's great weakness was his assumption that he was a leader with absolute power, but that confidence was severely misplaced where it concerned his commanders. The admiral's battle at Idona Station was a well-known event. Every commander in Portland's fleet was aware of the beating he had taken, losing entire squadrons to the Harakens' superior technology.

The senior officers possessed little information about the Harakens' strange fighters, and that in itself was both odd and troubling. The question they often asked one another was, "Shouldn't we have specifications and performance analysis of the enemy's ships?"

Shimada was correct in her evaluation of Portland's captains, especially those on the periphery of the fleet. To say they were nervous was an understatement. Most were wondering if the same fate as that of Portland's lost squadrons was awaiting them in the upcoming battle. It caused them to consider it might be more prudent to abandon Portland and throw themselves on the mercy of the newly heralded UE policies.

Portland decided that his mistake in the first battle was to divide his forces. This time he would keep his fleet together, not spread along a thin line but stacked several ships high — a wedge formation. His winged battleship was securely nestled behind a front shield of ships with cruisers in close proximity.

Another of Portland's decisions was to ignore any Haraken provocation, as he thought of the traditional-looking fighters that first attacked his squadrons. His plan was to strike at Idona and force the Harakens to defend the station, denying them their maneuverability and speed. *Let's see how your technically superior fighters operate when pinned in place,* Portland thought. *And, if you run, I'll demolish the station, and everyone will know you're cowards.*

-29-

The Harakens were ready for Portland as his fleet approached Idona Station on the ecliptic. The carriers were loaded with asteroids. The pilots were waiting in their travelers, formed up in squadrons, vessels of all sorts were gripping their second load of rocks in claws, and the station was as secure as Nikki could make it.

A full sub-wing of travelers, commanded by Franz Cohen, floated next to Commodore Shimada's destroyer squadron. They were the last line of defense against Portland if the fighter wings under Sheila, Ellie, Deirdre, and Lucia failed to stop his warships.

"What a coincidence, Commander," Reiko replied to Franz when he arrived. "I knew the battle plan assigned me a sub-wing of Haraken fighters, but imagine my surprise that they're commanded by you."

"Are you really surprised, Commodore?" Franz asked.

"No … no, I'm not. Quite pleased actually," Reiko replied, and her bridge crew heard the lift in their commodore's voice.

"So, after the fight, Commodore, dinner?" Franz asked.

A spate of snickers and chortles broke out on Shimada's bridge, which even her glare failed to extinguish entirely. The thought of a witty barb in reply evaporated before it could even take hold. "Dinner together would be enjoyable. I look forward to it."

When the comm closed, Shimada eyed her bridge crew and squadron officers and announced in a firm voice, "Okay, people, you heard. I have a dinner date. Now see that you do everything possible to ensure I get to my date."

* * *

Edouard and Miko were comparing notes. Both spoke to Alex independently, questioning the possible actions to take after the bombardment and traveler attacks were launched. Their greatest concern was that Alex had committed every traveler to the fight. There wasn't a single Haraken ship left aboard the station. Julien and Z were each aboard a carrier, while Cordelia chose to remain on the station, and Renée and the twins were with Alex, as anyone would have expected.

The captains found that Alex's answer to each of them was the same. "After the bombardment, take a position off the station for the travelers' return." Alex's answer bothered both of them, and they sought out Julien with their concerns.

"I'm not sure it matters whether our president is on the station or aboard a carrier," Julien replied. "If the station's people are lost, he might be too. The stationers are the innocents, the everyday people who are disregarded by those represented by Downing, Bunaldi, and Portland. To our president, the stationers are the people who matter the most."

"Too many fights in a young life," Miko said sympathetically.

"Or by staying aboard the station, he indicates that it's time for us to take on the burden of the fighting," Edouard said.

"Perhaps," Julien said, "I, of all people, am forced to accept his stance since my partner has chosen to remain on station as well. The children of Idona, especially the orphans, have become precious to Cordelia, and their loss would be devastating to her. So they stay, saying to the people of the station, 'Your fate is our fate.'"

Alone in their thoughts, Julien sought to shift the mood. "So, Captains, let us ensure it's Admiral Portland and his ill-conceived minions who meet their fate today, not the good people of Idona."

As the comm closed, images of Cordelia, the children of Idona, Alex, Renée, and the twins flashed through Julien's crystal memory. *So many fragile treasures at risk,* he thought.

* * *

<It's confirmed, Mr. President,> Julien sent on open comm to the Harakens, Nikki Fowler, Patrice Morris, and Reiko Shimada. <Portland's fleet has deployed into a wedge formation and is making directly for the station.>

Julien's report was for the allies since every Haraken was watching the fleet's movement via controllers and holo-vids in real time, and if any single individual could be banished to their worst nightmarish afterlife by an entire population, Portland was being sent there by the people of Idona for his cowardice.

Z and Julien were linked and sharing calculations at an intense pace, forcing their internal cooling systems into overdrive. Data on the carriers' loads, acceleration rates, velocity of the asteroids, angles of attack, warship positions, and, most critical, Tatia's strategy against the fleet, combined and flowed in a continuous stream as Portland's fleet closed on the station.

There were no wild shouts urging troops into action or even commands sent to the carrier captains. Exacting precision required direct control. On the required tick of time, Julien sent the *Last Stand* surging forward, and soon after, Z did the same for the *No Retreat.*

The engines of each carrier were pushed to their limits to accelerate the ships and the massive rocks tethered outside their bays. At the instant required by each SADE, the ship's controller slewed its carrier and cut the beams holding the asteroids along one side of the ship. Like a child's ancient sling, the metal-rich rocks were whipped forward, sailing past derelict ships to race through the dark of space toward the enemy fleet.

The carriers were returned to the staging point to start a second run, shooting forward to sling the asteroids tethered on the other side. Once having loosed both sides, the carriers reset at the starting point, and myriad vessels jumped into action, offering their rocky cargo up to flight chiefs, who activated the beams when the asteroids were in position.

Once loaded, the SADEs signaled the carriers forward twice again to let loose each side of their loads. The *Last Stand* sent four staggered barrages of sixteen dense, rocky asteroids each, and the *No Retreat* threw twice that number in four of its own barrages.

* * *

"Admiral, the guide identifies an asteroid shower coming our way," the battleship's navigator announced.

"Origin?" Portland asked.

"Directly ahead, Admiral. The shower just passed the station."

"Now, isn't that a coincidence?" said Portland, his mind racing.

"A second wave of asteroids incoming, Admiral."

"Show me where both waves are headed." Portland demanded.

On the admiral's central monitor, the ships of the fleet were laid out in textbook wedge formation, which gave Portland a surge of pride before he examined the incoming waves of asteroids headed at the flanks of his fleet. "How big are these?" he asked.

"Huge," the navigator replied. "The guide estimates them at around 8 to 10 meters across."

"What? Are you telling me these asteroids are the same size? That's statistically impossible," Portland yelled. He knew it was the Harakens again, but for the life of him he couldn't figure out how they could be sending asteroid showers his way. *What is your game this time?* Portland asked himself.

"Commander, have the lead destroyer in each of our flanking squadrons target an asteroid with missiles. I want four strikes against each asteroid. Let's see what these accursed Harakens are hiding," Portland ordered.

Moments after the commander relayed the order, he reported, "Missiles away." Time ticked by until he added, "Direct hits," and finally, "The asteroids broke into large chunks, Admiral. They seem to be nothing but heavies … metal-rich ore formations."

"This makes no sense," Portland mused out loud.

"Admiral, the flanking squadrons are asking permission to spread out," the commander said.

"Yes, yes, permission granted," Portland said absent-mindedly, waving a hand at the commander in dismissal. He was desperately trying to understand the purpose of the asteroids. "Commander, I want eyes on those asteroids as they pass by our ships."

"Yes, Sir," the commander affirmed, and later reported, "Nothing behind the rocks, Sir,"

"Incoming, Admiral. Two more waves. Identical in makeup, count, and direction," navigation stated.

"That tears it. It's the Harakens doing this!" Portland shouted angrily.

"To what purpose, Admiral?" the commander asked.

"That's the right question, Commander. I think it's some trick of the Harakens to make us unsure of our actions, but it won't do them any good. The squadrons have permission to move out of formation to evade the swarms, but check those rocks as they pass."

Twice more navigation announced incoming waves of asteroids, and twice more the admiral had the passing rocks checked for evidence of extraneous structures or fighters hiding on the back sides. "Nothing," was the answer in each case. Again and again, the fleet separated to allow the huge rocks to pass through their formation, which no longer resembled the admiral's textbook wedge.

The first three double waves separated the wings of Portland's wedge into six groups of warships. Then the final double waves of asteroids came directly at his battleship and surrounding cruisers, forcing two of the cruisers to one side and Portland's battleship and a third cruiser to the other side.

After the first waves, Portland was tempted to reform the wedge, but the subsequent waves convinced him he was right to wait. What these initial barrages accomplished was the disruption of Portland's formation and the undermining of his command. Captains were wondering what type of humans they faced that had the technology to dissolve warships and hurl asteroids, and they were taking the waves of giant rocks as a warning sign to retreat.

-30-

<Now we test the limits of our skills,> Z sent to Julien.

The carriers were reloaded with asteroids, but this time the SADEs had to launch both sides of their carrier in quick succession, with the travelers chasing each barrage to hide behind their rocks. The Harakens had just the one opportunity to surprise Portland's fleet. After that, it would be open warfare.

The SADES ran the calculations of mass and forces on the carriers prior to and during each launch in an effort to estimate the danger to the carriers, which must first twist one way and then the other. It was Z, who was the first to admit that there was insufficient data and a lack of time to consider all ramifications.

<Time to face the possibility of our own fallibility, brother,> Julien sent back.

This time, the SADEs accelerated their carriers on the same tick of time, hurtling them toward the station. The carriers slewed first one way, rocks were slung, and then the carriers slewed the other way to launch the other side's asteroids. Warnings hit both controllers from numerous breaches in the hull seams. Had the bay doors been closed the stresses would have been insignificant, but the open bays did much to weaken the carriers' overall strength. But the crews were safe. They were deep in their ships, ensconced comfortably in environment suits.

Four groups of rocks hurtled past the derelict ships, and the travelers shot forward to give chase. With Franz Cohen allied with Shimada's squadrons, the fighters were led by Sheila, Ellie, Deirdre, and Lucia. Each traveler controller tracked its transponder tag, and quicker than the eye could follow, the fighters nestled behind their assigned rocks, maintaining a 1-meter distance from the inner curve of the asteroid.

<Well done, boys,> Tatia sent to Julien and Z after the travelers successfully caught their asteroids before the rocks passed the station.

<Boys?> Z queried.

<Better than saying congratulations, you old guys,> Tatia shot back.

<As for me, I will accept my compliment with grace,> Julien replied, and sent a vid of a poorly dressed fop sketching an exaggerated bow to a pompous, heavy-set queen, with her crown askew, seated on a faded and tattered throne.

<I must practice replying in this manner,> Z enthused.

<All joking aside, boys, it's time for the next act of this play,> Tatia sent.

* * *

The *Last Stand* launched thirty-two asteroids, and the *No Retreat* threw sixty-four rocks. The original concept called for a total of ninety-six travelers to hide among this set of barrages. But it was Tatia's estimate that this number of fighters would be insufficient to engage the fleet in a head-on fight.

"We can't take on Portland's entire fleet; but we can take on parts of it. If we can count on demoralizing some of the captains, then maybe parts of the fleet are all we will have to fight," Tatia had said to her commanders and Shimada.

Ellie had pulled up a closeup view of one of the asteroids on the holo-vid, adding a traveler, which she tucked into the hollowed-out shell. It hid beautifully. She then added a second traveler, bow to the aft of the first traveler, but it stuck out way too far. Next, she moved the first traveler up in the shell, which pushed its aft slightly farther out of its hiding spot, and then tucked a second traveler under it.

Tatia and the other commanders crowded around to look at the concept, grins breaking out on their faces, fierce expressions Portland would never wish to see.

So 96 asteroids flew again at Portland's fleet, but 192 Haraken fighters hid in their rocky shells.

When Tatia saw the fleet formation break apart after the first barrages and not reform, Shimada's words rang through her mind. Portland's fleet was a fragile political arrangement. In a quick decision, Tatia ordered Julien and Z to send the travelers down the paths of the middle sets of the first series of barrages.

Sheila inquired of Tatia why they weren't targeting the more peripheral portions of the fleet, and Tatia replied that she needed to undermine some of the confidence of the capital ship commanders.

Sitting nervously in their travelers, the pilots were relayed detailed images of the fleet's formation by their controllers, which were gaining carrier and probe telemetry.

As fast as she could, Tatia assigned targets to her commanders, who were then sharing them out among their wings. Each traveler would execute its own individual attack, but Tatia issued overarching commands to her pilots. They were to make one pass and one pass only, reforming into squadrons and ranks well behind the fleet, and they were to target the engines of the warships.

"Admiral, why not target the bow … try to take out the captain and bridge crew?" Deirdre asked.

"I want to whip up fear, Commander. Target their engines. If you're successful, that's one warship out of the action. If not, you'll still have made them feel vulnerable," Tatia replied. "Remember, people, this fight is as much about psychology as weapons."

Both Sheila and Ellie, whose wings would pass on the nearer lines of the divided wedge, assigned several squadrons to target the cruisers. No one would be able to reach Portland's battleship.

The pilots scanned their telemetry in detail, searching for UE missile launches as they approached the fleet, hoping that they weren't discovered early. The size of the fleet ensured the launch of enough missiles so that there was no way a controller could evade every one. Short of diving below or above the ecliptic to float out into weak gravitational space, where they would have to wait for rescue, which would defeat the entire battle strategy, surprise was their singular asset while the travelers were still in front of the fleet.

Time dragged slower and slower, despite the constant velocity of the asteroids, until the travelers reached the midpoints of the enemy's squadrons. Then the Harakens' fighters broke from cover and ambushed Portland's warships.

Unlike UE fighters, which required locks on their targets before the release of missiles, the traveler controllers were programmed to hunt heat signatures. Once free of their hiding places, the controller launched its fighter at full power toward its assigned target, sliding sideways to fire its beam at the warship's engines at deadly close range, and then send its pilot and craft speeding into the dark beyond.

As the Haraken fighters uncovered, alarms sounded throughout the warships, and crews searched for targets even while their vessels took hits. Some missiles were fired in panic, and the defense operators were forced to detonate them prematurely. Several missiles reached fellow warships to inflict friendly damage. Overall, the enemy fleet's actions were inconsequential; the attack was over before the judiciary captains could react.

* * *

In their wake, the travelers left shaken and disturbed fleet commanders. Portland was yelling to reform the wedge, and his order was relayed throughout the fleet. In the meantime, damage reports flooded into the fleet commander's panel.

"Admiral, one cruiser and thirteen destroyers have lost primary engine power. They are drifting out of formation and requesting assistance," the commander said.

"Forming the wedge is a priority, Commander. Rescue is secondary," Portland ordered. The admiral missed the winces and frowns evidenced by many of the bridge officers at his comment.

"Admiral, another cruiser and five more destroyers are reporting they have significant damage to their engines but are still able to form ranks but not at full power. The slowest will make only about one-third power."

"Too slow! Have any ship that can't maintain 70 percent power fall back to help those without power," the admiral ordered. Moments later, when Portland heard his commander's voice rising, the words catching his attention, he yelled for a report.

"Sorry, Admiral," the commander replied, "eight destroyers are refusing to join the formation."

"Refusing?" Portland yelled in anger. "Put the ship positions on the central monitor."

Portland's fleet was in shambles. Fourteen ships were veering off on whatever tangents they had taken during the attack when they lost power. Three more ships were maintaining velocity, but were not rejoining the fleet. Then the admiral's eye caught the eight destroyers the commander highlighted in red. They were making for the destroyers in trouble. Portland knew the commodore who was at the center of that outrageous disregard for his order. "Bleeding heart," Portland grumbled to himself. His wedge was reduced by half, with two capital ships lost to him.

"Admiral, please regard the left monitor," the commander called, his voice rising.

On the monitor, the admiral saw a formation of the Harakens' own and swore under his breath, not wanting to add to the fear he could feel eating its way through his officers.

* * *

Deirdre and Lucia commanded sub-wings of fighters and floated in space facing the remainder of Portland's fleet. Tatia was tickled to learn of Franz and Lucia's performance at Hellébore when they faced the UE explorer ship. The effect of their machine-like maneuvers, beautifully executed by their controllers, impressed her, and she gave her commanders freedom to perform their own brand of intimidation when they faced Portland the first time.

For this fight, Lucia volunteered some schemes of her own, but Deirdre voted for something that would add to the fear that Tatia's tactics were generating.

The two sub-wings totaling 128 fighters sat in a wedge, imitating Portland's fleet. It was a jest in the face of the admiral's vaunted UE naval formation. In an instant, the two sub-wings split, hurtling for the flanks of the fleet's foreshortened wedge. The controllers executed the spiral patterns programmed by the two commanders. It wasn't a fighter that was spiraling; it was the entire sub-wing that spiraled like a child's streamer toy. On the monitor of any warship, it would be a chilling display of sophistication unmatchable by any UE pilots and their fighters — otherworldly, if not alien.

The Haraken fighters continued their spiraling through the fringe warships, cutting and slicing with their beams. Warship missiles, attempting to target one fighter, would lose contact; attempt to lock on to a second, only to lose that one. Missiles were still in flight searching for targets in front of them when the Haraken fighters were already past the fleet.

Behind Deirdre and Lucia's sub-wings were more damaged destroyers. Tatia's orders were the same as those for Sheila and Ellie; make a single pass and attack the engines.

* * *

Among the commodores of the destroyers, damaged ones and rescuers, there was a brief but terse conference. Not one of them had missed the fact that in the second pass of the Haraken fighters none of their ships were targeted. Commodores and captains alike knew that they would have granted no such largesse to their enemy, which before the war was often a rebel freighter or privateer.

The consensus of the commanders was the fleet was outmatched, and they had just been granted a moment of clemency. It was a quick agreement among the commanders to abandon the fight and afterwards to surrender to the Harakens or the nearest pro-naval forces. It was better to fall on the mercy of the new courts, naval or civilian, than expect certain death at the hands of the Harakens.

The few remaining destroyer captains in Portland's diminished wedge eyed the now dwindled ranks and decided the odds were against them. Ship after ship pulled out of Portland's formation until the admiral's battleship was accompanied by two lone cruisers.

-31-

"Cowards," Portland ranted at the icons of the destroyers on his monitor as they left his meager wedge to go to the assistance of the damaged ships. The three icons on the screen, representing his capital ships, were all that was left of his fleet.

The fleet commander dutifully collected the damage reports and loss of life. He couldn't believe the figures, the number of disabled and damaged ships should have tallied deaths in the tens of thousands. Instead, the dead counted a mere 181. *The Harakens are sending us a message, and the admiral isn't receiving it,* the commander thought.

Portland was livid. All his thoughts of redemption, or at least forgiveness at the hands of the new UE, had evaporated. One opportunity remained. Idona Station was dead ahead. He would soon reach missile range of the station. At his present velocity, it would be difficult if not impossible for the Haraken fighters to catch him from behind. *Just a few paltry destroyers to annihilate first,* Portland thought.

"Commander, signal the cruisers, continue to make for Idona. Destroy it as we pass and then make for the belt," Portland ordered.

"Admiral, surely this is unnecessary —" the battleship's pilot began to object, but he never got to finish.

Portland holstered his needler, an unauthorized weapon among naval personnel. "Captain, you need a new pilot," Portland said in a strangely calm voice.

The captain ordered another pilot to the bridge and waved to the bridge security personnel to haul the dead pilot's body away. A female pilot hurried onto the bridge and stuttered to a halt as security dragged the body of her friend past her. A harsh nod from the captain toward her position sent her scurrying to take a seat.

"Now, we may proceed," Portland stated with an air of satisfaction. "Commander, send the signal. The cruisers are to stay tight to me. We'll pass the station on our port side. I want a full salvo of missiles ... hold nothing back." When the commander hesitated, Portland stared at him. "Commander," he repeated in his deadly calm voice.

"He's lost it," the navigator whispered to the new pilot. His words were unnecessary. She was still wiping specks of blood from the previous pilot off her panel.

* * *

"Black space," Tatia muttered under her breath, echoing Alex's favorite words of frustration, when she realized Portland was still advancing.

"Commodore," Tatia said, sending via comm and implant simultaneously to Reiko and Franz, "I'm sure you can see by your telemetry that you've won the wager."

"Much to my regret," Reiko replied. She told Tatia and Sheila that they would have to destroy the *Guardian* to stop Portland himself, but the Harakens were sure he would turn around if they could strip his fleet from him, and the women had placed a small bet on their opinions.

"Portland will be within missile range of the station before our travelers can catch him from behind," Tatia said. "My apologies, Franz and Reiko, but it's fallen to you to stop the madman."

"Cheer up, Admiral," Reiko said, "I have a good feeling about the outcome of this fight. I have a dinner date, and I intend to keep it."

"May the stars protect you," Tatia said and closed the comm.

There was some good news for the two commanders. The *Guardian* was not the monster battleship, Bunaldi's *Hand of Justice,* the Harakens faced at New Terra. This ship possessed three decks instead of five, and its bays were loaded with patrol ships not fighters. Built in the winged-shape of the FTL-capable battleships, its engines were traditional, but would be capable of retrofitting, in the future. Still, it possessed two tubes housing the UE's ship-killer missiles, or, in this case, perfectly suitable missiles for destroying a station.

Five destroyers were able to join Reiko's command before Portland arrived at Idona. Watching Portland's remaining ships approaching, she paired her destroyers into three groups, two destroyers to target each capital ship. Reiko and a second destroyer occupied the center of her simplified wedge and targeted Portland's battleship.

Franz spread his sixty-four travelers along the destroyer line, choosing to place his traveler off the bow of Reiko's destroyer. This would be an open fight with no possibility of ambush. The destroyers and the Haraken fighters would interweave their fire to protect their ships. The destroyers possessed extensive antimissile defense, and the travelers were deadly accurate with their beams for shorter range contact.

"Comfortable out there, Commander?" Reiko commed to Franz. "Sure you wouldn't like to tuck back along the rear where it will be safer?" Reiko heard more snickers from her bridge personnel, but, at this moment, she didn't care. If she was going to die in the next hour, she wanted to feel alive, and bantering with Franz made her feel just that way.

"Just looking out for my date, Commodore," Franz riposted.

"Let's get this done, Commander. I'm getting hungry."

Reiko ordered her squadron forward at one-third acceleration. Closing the gap on Portland's capital ships and moving away from the station would gain her destroyers more room to maneuver, and proceeding slowly would prolong the engagement window. It was contrary to her tactics training, but then again she didn't intend to allow any one of Portland's ships past her forces.

If Reiko was worried about Franz's fighter, hanging just meters off her bow, she needn't have been. Each Haraken pilot programmed their controller to maintain the fighter's position from the nearest destroyer. It was the simplest of routines for a traveler's controller to execute no matter how fast or hard a destroyer maneuvered.

Within a half hour, the forces were closing on each other, and missiles from both sides were launched, filling the intervening space. The bigger missiles were targeting ships; the smaller ones were targeting the bigger missiles.

Despite the six-to-three ship majority that Reiko's forces enjoyed, the armament ratio was unequal. Portland's ships could load and launch more missiles faster than Reiko's destroyers. It was the Harakens, who turned the odds in Reiko's favor. More than one destroyer captain was shaken to hear their defense operator yell, "impact," warning of a missile that had breached the destroyer's defenses, only to see a bright flash ahead of the ship as a Haraken beam intercepted it.

Reiko's bridge crew watched Franz's fighter flip from one side of the bow to another, almost faster than the eye could follow, and, an instant later, two flashes from closing missiles lit up Reiko's bridge screen. Her navigator, a burly, middle-aged first lieutenant said breathlessly to his fellow officers, "That man must really want his date."

The battle continued to rage. With the defensive capabilities of the two sides fairly matched, little damage was being inflicted on either force. But the traveler controllers weren't just tracking UE missiles. These SADE-built tools were running analyses programs and had detected a weakness in the enemy's tactics. Once Portland ordered the initial missile launch, the capital ships continued in lock step, loading and launching further salvos at the same time.

Franz's controller updated him on the missile launch pattern and the relevant interval. Soon after, a harried Reiko contacted him.

"Small problem, Commander," Reiko sent. "We're running low on missiles, all types."

"By 'we' do you mean you or all the destroyers?" Franz asked.

"I shared our armament stores evenly before we left the station, Commander. We're all running low."

Franz glanced at the enemy's missile cycle in his helmet display. His hope was that the capital ships that had been throwing more missiles, faster than the destroyers, might be running low on reserves as well.

"Commodore, Captains," Franz sent on open comm to the destroyers, halt your missile launches for a count of five on my mark. Immediately, he connected with his pilots and readied them for the attack.

"All destroyers 'mark,'" Franz sent. It was the same signal for the Haraken fighters, which launched at the capital ships at full acceleration, eliminating the latest salvos of judiciary missiles to be launched at the destroyers.

Franz's sub-wing's orders were different from the other commanders — protect the station — but he didn't want a prolonged fight for his pilots either. The Harakens' single-pass technique was proving devastating to Portland's ships. The judiciary crews had no time to target the fighters at their incredible velocities. So Franz ordered his sub-wing to make a single pass and target not the engines of the capital ships but their bridges.

The fighters closed on the enemy ships. Franz expected their next missile launch at any moment, but it didn't happen. By the time it did, twenty-one travelers had struck each of the capital ships, targeting the bridge. The first half of the travelers to strike the cruisers' bridges eliminated the entire ship's command structure, and the remaining fighters burned deeper into the cruisers' main bodies.

The massive size of Portland's battleship withstood the attack much better. The *Guardian*'s gunnery defensives destroyed five travelers at the front of the Haraken vanguard just after the fighters fired on the bow. Two travelers ran afoul of their compatriots' debris and were demolished. Seven more travelers were struck by gunnery fire and debris, losing power and veering off course to be rescued later. The devastation of the fighters immediately in front of the remaining travelers targeting the battleship caused the controllers of the last seven fighters to seek secondary targets, veering off to cross over and under the battleship's wings, swiveling the travelers around and firing on the ship's four pairs of engines.

Then, as quick as they had launched, the travelers were past the capital ships, leaving behind two destroyed cruisers, one battleship without primary engine power, and a single traveler. Franz remained floating off Reiko's bow.

* * *

Admiral Theodore Portland finished closing his helmet's face plate and checking the seals of his environment suit, before he stepped from his emergency cabinet. When the fleet's commander screamed his warning of the fighters' attack, Portland dived for the small, protected unit at the rear of the bridge just before the first fighters fired on his bridge. The explosions shook his bolt hole, but the triple-layered, reinforced cabinet held.

Portland stepped into a view of the deep dark. The majority of his bridge was gone. Looking down, he could see stars through the multiple decks. Creeping along the side of the cabinet, Portland reached an emergency comm unit on the wall. Its green light told him he was still connected to functioning crew locations.

"Engineering, this is Admiral Portland. Give me a status."

"Admiral, this is Ensign Torres. We have no primary engines … auxiliary power only. Most of engineering is dead."

Portland clicked off the connection, swearing to himself. As he stared at the stars through the mass of twisted and chopped bulkheads, a familiar image resolved — the twinkling lights of Idona Station — and an ugly grin could be seen through the admiral's faceplate.

"Missile Command, this is Admiral Portland. Status on our inferno missiles!"

"Admiral, Lieutenant Hawkins here. Both infernos are secure, and we have power to launch them."

"Excellent, Lieutenant. Target the station, and launch when ready."

"Yes, Sir," Hawkins enthused. The lieutenant was a believer, and the thought of delivering a blow against the Harakens appealed to the stoked anger he harbored for the aliens.

Portland stood staring into the dark void when it was suddenly lit by the bright burning exhausts of the twin launches of his battleship's inferno missiles. At that moment, surrounded by his devastated ship, he was a happy man.

* * *

"Missile launches ... two infernos," was announced by bridge officers across the destroyer squadron.

"Three starboard destroyers, you have the missile on the right. Three port destroyers, we have the left missile. Empty your magazines until you light them up. Now!" Reiko ordered.

The destroyer captains began expending their meager missile reserves at the giant ship-killers, but these weren't ordinary missiles. They carried sophisticated spoofing mechanisms, tricking many of the destroyer's defensive missiles into targeting false images and echoes of their locations.

When the left missile came within range of Franz's beam, he fired, destroying the warhead, which left tons of shrapnel racing toward Reiko's destroyer. His traveler dodged the mass of debris, but her ship suffered damage to its rear third when the pilot tried to turn the destroyer out of the way.

The right inferno missile was exploded by the destroyers' defensive missiles but only just in front of the ship on Reiko's wing. Huge chunks of metal ripped through the bow and side of the ship, igniting explosions that tore the destroyer apart.

"Navigator, get me a close view of that battleship," Reiko ordered after she absorbed her squadron's damage reports. Her engineering reported that the destroyer's engines were offline, and they weren't repairable without a station's dock.

Reiko studied the ugly monster coming toward her. The initial strikes by the lost travelers cut heavily into the battleship's bow and central fuselage, and their subsequent impacts ignited local explosions, which continued to damage the central support structure. The lights from the battleship's engines were gone. The judiciary capital ship was dead and toothless, but it was still moving. "Navigation, I need a vector on the *Guardian*. Where's it headed?"

"Directly for the station, Commodore," the navigation officer reported.

"Of all the luck," Reiko groused. "Destroyers, target the central fuselage of that battleship. I want it cut in half. Maybe that will nudge the wings off course enough to pass the station."

Reiko listened to the reports coming in from her four remaining captains. Like her ship, they hadn't a single missile left among them. She stared at the image of the destroyer, hating the admiral more than she had hated anyone in her life.

"Captains, make for the station. Standby there to be of aid in any manner the president requires," Reiko ordered. "Pilot, do we have maneuvering power?"

"Yes, Commodore. We have docking jets."

"Push us around until we are directly on target for what's left of that battleship's central section," Reiko ordered, and then hit the emergency evacuation icon on her panel. The warbling sound of electronic klaxons sounded throughout the destroyer, and Reiko's bridge crew looked at her in confusion. "Since when do you not know how to perform an emergency evacuation, people?" When no one responded, she yelled, "Jump!" and the officers and noncoms fled the bridge.

"You okay in there, Commodore?" Franz asked, watching the four destroyers on Reiko's flanks swing out of formation and head for the station.

"That hulk is headed for the station, and not one of us has a missile left. Worse, my engines are offline."

"So what's the plan, Reiko?" Franz asked in a husky voice. He was watching the emergency pods jettison from the front half of Reiko's ship, while he was still talking to her on the bridge.

Reiko liked the sound of her name on the commander's lips. Franz had a way of saying it that felt more like a touch than a sound. In a voice that told Franz that Reiko was reminiscing, she said, "My grandfather hated the digital games but loved anything that was physical, especially if it involved subtle hand skill and strategy. One of the principles he taught me in his games was to employ your ball's velocity to separate two of your opponent's balls when they are close together."

"So you're the ball?" Franz asked, inputting a query to his controller, which responded that, factoring in the recharge time, the beam of his fighter would require more time than was available to cut through the remaining sections of the battleship. Worse, the controller estimated that the neatly slicing beams would impart insignificant forces to move the wings aside.

"That's the idea," Reiko replied. "If I hit that weakened central structure of the *Guardian* just right, I should be able to separate the wings and impart enough inertia to shift them onto trajectories that will miss the station."

Reiko was waiting for Franz's response when his traveler disappeared from her bow view. It bothered her that Franz wouldn't be staying around for the end, but, in a small way, she understood. Reiko eyed her telemetry data every few moments. Her young pilot was excellent, and she had placed the destroyer dead on target.

* * *

Franz slipped his traveler into the destroyer's open bay. A shuttle was closing its hatch and preparing to launch, and he edged his fighter to the far side of the bay and settled it to the deck. One more shuttle remained inside.

After checking his environment suit, Franz cycled through his airlock, an upgrade to the travelers by Mickey's engineering team, three years ago. Exiting the traveler, Franz hurried across the bay to an airlock, which more of the crew was cycling through. It dawned on him that the damage to the rear third of the destroyer had taken out a good number of emergency pods, and the crew was using the shuttles to evacuate the ship.

When the officers and crew piled out of the airlock, Franz's arm was yanked on by a female officer, who was struggling to pull him inside the airlock. He barely cleared the airlock's doors, when the officer smacked the actuator to close the bayside doors and cycle the airlock. When the corridor-side doors flashed green and opened, the officer snapped up her faceplate, revealing a youthful face.

"The commodore's this way, Sir. I'll lead," she yelled and took off at a run.

Franz pounded after her, grateful for the guide. With the twists, turns, and level changes, he would have been still searching for the bridge about the time the two ships impacted each other.

The bridge door opened as the pilot neared it, triggered by her ID implanted under her shoulder's skin.

"I said evacuate, Lieutenant —" Reiko yelled, but the next words died on her lips when she saw Franz run in behind her pilot. "You … you can't be here," Reiko said in a whisper, tears beginning to blur her eyes.

"Are you on course?" Franz demanded, his chest heaving from the exertion.

When Reiko failed to answer, the pilot leaned over her panel. "Dead on course, Commander," she replied with a grin, proud of her work.

"Time to go," Franz announced. He didn't have to tell the youthful lieutenant twice. She bounded off the bridge, intent on making the bay and an exodus before the impending crash. Reiko drew breath to say something, and Franz never gave her the opportunity. He slung the diminutive commodore over his shoulder and chased after the lieutenant, who was getting too far ahead for eye contact, so Franz concentrated on her footfalls.

"What if there's no one to correct our trajectory?" Reiko yelled from Franz's back. Her mind was racing to decide whether to fight to go back or stay across Franz's shoulder and possibly live. In an odd tangent, the thought crossed her mind that the commander could move extremely fast for such a huge man.

"You've been underway for about half the distance you have to close. You like your trajectory; your pilot likes your trajectory. I don't think another asteroid storm is expected any time soon that might throw you off course, Commodore," Franz yelled through ragged breaths.

At the airlock, the lieutenant was holding out the lower half of an environment suit, and Franz neatly dropped Reiko's feet into the suit's legs. After that, Reiko was all business, strapping into the suit as fast as she could. The three of them closed faceplates, cycled the airlock, and dashed across the bay toward Franz's traveler.

Reiko was out of the airlock first, but both Franz and the pilot beat her to the traveler. The lieutenant scrambled up the short, steep stairway into the ship's tiny airlock. When Reiko arrived, Franz grabbed her and launched her up to the lieutenant, whose grin he could see through her faceplate.

The fit in the fighter's tiny emergency exit airlock was tight. Both women were squished tight against Franz while he signaled the airlock cycle. His controller was relaying the countdown to him, and it was this SADE technology that saved them. While in the airlock, Franz signaled the controller to exit the bay and depart at max acceleration for the station.

The airlock's inner door opened into a dimly lit interior, and both women stared at Franz as he took his time extricating himself from the airlock. He stepped into the corridor, sank into a passenger seat, popped up his faceplate, and dragged in huge breaths.

"Uh … Commander," the pilot hesitatingly began.

"We're good, Sers," Franz replied. "We're on auto-pilot, so to speak."

"The auto-pilot launched us out of the bay and determined the proper course?" Reiko asked, sinking into a nearby seat. "Sit down, Lieutenant," she added.

"If we're going to be technical, I gave the orders and the fighter's controller followed them." Franz tapped his temple by way of explanation.

"That would be so great to have one of those," the pilot enthused.

"And the plan … did it work?" Reiko asked, trying to act casual, but a knot was forming in her stomach.

Franz closed his faceplate, viewed the telemetry in the display, and popped it back open. "The destroyer hit the battleship … perfect placement. Cleaved the wings in two."

"Yes!" the pilot shouted. "Um … sorry, Commodore."

"No need, Lieutenant. You set a good course. What about the aftereffect? Did we move the wings far enough?" Reiko asked.

Franz closed his helmet again. His telemetry was unable to define the vector change, at this time, so he commed for Julien and Z, getting both, and Julien linked in Cordelia.

<You're having an exciting day, Commander,> Julien sent.

<Defending your destroyers against a superior force. Dodging the remains of an enormous missile, which you detonated just at the last tick.> Z added. <Although, there was that awkward moment when the missile remains slammed into your date's destroyer.>

<Who he subsequently rescued,> Cordelia said, defending Franz.

<Do you think that was the commander's diabolical scheme?> Julien asked. <Damage Commodore Shimada's destroyer so that he might rescue her at the last moment? It would make the woman feel quite indebted to the man.>

<Okay, okay,> Franz sent, trying to end the SADEs' banter. <I take it from your festive mood, at my expense I might add, that the *Guardian*'s wings will miss the station.>

<By several hundreds of meters,> Cordelia said happily. <My congratulations to you, Commander, and to the two Sers in your company.>

Franz closed the comm, opened his faceplate, and removed his helmet. "Success," he announced to the women.

The pilot cheered, and Reiko smiled warmly at Franz.

"Pilot, why don't you check out this fighter's cockpit? It might be your only chance," Reiko said.

The lieutenant grinned and hurried up the aisle, and Reiko stood up and came over to Franz to settle herself into his lap. "Too bad about these suits," she said, staring at Franz with soft eyes. "You'll just have to settle for a more cursory thank you for now," she added and kissed him.

* * *

Reiko's anger at Portland for his fixation on destroying Idona and the Harakens dissipated on the flight back to the station, especially while enjoying Franz's attentions. However, knowing Portland's final moments might have gone a long way to relieving her anger.

Anchoring himself to the emergency cabinet with one hand, Admiral Theodore Portland's stare was fixed on the twinkling lights of Idona Station as they drew slowly closer. A gleeful smile was painted on his face, but his eyes appeared blank. It wouldn't have surprised observers if they saw the admiral begin to drool. Suddenly, a huge, dark shape loomed out of the void headed directly for him. "No," was all Portland had time to utter before Reiko's destroyer slammed its millions of metric tons of mass through him and his battleship's central fuselage.

-32-

As the battle raged, Alex, Renée, the twins, Cordelia, and her orphan band of children chose to sit around the planning holo-vid. The winking off of the ships' icons meant little to the younger children, who were preoccupied by Cordelia's lovely voice as she sang song after song to them. Edmas and Jodlyne would glance at Alex, whose stolid expression would be broken by a small wince when the icons were representative of Haraken fighters. There was no need for the teenagers to look Alex's way when Shimada's destroyer was hit and her wing ship exploded. Even Cordelia's song faltered.

After that loss, Alex slipped Renée off his lap and hurried to the holo-vid, enlarging the image until the admiral's battleship stood in relief against the stars. He shifted the holo-vid's viewpoint continually until he recognized the danger to the station from the battleship's dead hulk. The four destroyers returning to the station confused him until he saw Shimada's tortured ship turn slowly toward the *Guardian* and Shimada's people begin to evacuate.

<Julien, what's Commander Cohen doing?> Alex sent as he watched Franz's traveler abandon its post and head for a destroyer bay.

<Commodore Shimada is still at the *Conquest*'s helm, Mr. President.>

<Oh, black space,> Alex complained, trying to imagine what would keep Reiko at the helm.

<The commodore is directing her flight via the destroyer's maneuvering jets. Her engines are offline. My presumption is that the commodore is allowing nothing to interfere with her impacting the target,> Julien replied.

<Calculations on success, Julien?> Alex asked.

There were moments of silence as Julien and Z shared their data. <The commodore's concept is simple and brilliant, Mr. President,> Julien responded. There is a high probability of the commodore's ship destroying the central supports of the battleship, but whether it will be sufficient to push the massive wings far enough off course to miss the station is unknown.>

Alex shifted the holo-vid to the myriad ships that were stationed at the staging point and gauged the distance to the station, comparing it to the *Guardian*'s distance to the station. His groan was heard by the SADEs, who were monitoring his efforts.

<It was an idea worth considering, Ser President,> Z acknowledged when he realized Alex wanted to use the tugs and ore haulers to intercept the battleship, but the distance was too great in the time they would have.

<The commander has exited the destroyer,> Cordelia announced. <He has the commodore and the pilot … the last two people aboard.> She and Renée exchanged smiles, having enjoyed observing Franz and Reiko slowly circling each other.

Julien, monitoring Reiko's destroyer, sent <Impact … clean separation of the wings.>

Alex began pacing and the children's eyes intently followed him. Renée and Cordelia, who moments ago enjoyed a small moment of celebration, now traded worried looks. Inside, Alex wanted to scream for a status, but he knew the SADEs would need time to collect the data.

<Miss … the wings will miss, Ser,> Z announced excitedly.

<Tugs and haulers have been notified, Mr. President,> Julien said in a much more controlled voice, but he was as relieved as Z, probably more so. Cordelia was safe.

"Well, children, who's hungry?" Alex announced swinging his arms wide.

Edmas and Jodlyne whooped in joy.

"We're save-ed?" Ginny asked when Cordelia picked her up.

"Yes, we're save-ed, little one," Cordelia said hugging the child. Tears weren't incorporated into a SADE's avatar, but that didn't mean Cordelia's emotional algorithms were processing smoothly as she smiled at the children, chatted with Ginny, and shared her happiness with Julien.

* * *

The Harakens' travelers returned to their carriers, which had made for the station — all but fourteen of them. Seven pilots and their fighters were lost. Seven more pilots were headed away from the ecliptic in damaged shells, which couldn't charge the drives sufficiently to return.

Captain Cordova and Mickey were standing by during the battle and lost no time in pursuit of even the first lost traveler, zeroing in on the controller's signal. Fortunately, every pilot obeyed the standing order to dive below the ecliptic if in danger of losing charge, which foreshortened the collection distance for the *Rêveur*.

Strangely, the time-honored passenger liner resembled its original derelict appearance when it returned to the station. There was room aboard the *Rêveur*'s double bays for only three travelers, which necessitated the last four fighters, in some cases just half a ship, to be tethered outboard of the bays by the beams. One young New Terran pilot, comfortable in his environment suit, whose half-ship was tethered with its aft end facing toward the *Rêveur*'s bow, sat in the aisle of his traveler, staring out at the deep dark and the twinkling lights of Idona Station, never so happy for the view.

* * *

The station celebrated for days following the defeat of Portland's fleet. Stationers and visitors aboard various liners, freighters, tugs, haulers, and yachts poured back into the bays and docks of Idona from the staging point.

Julien connected Brennan and Reiko to Woo and Chong to share the news — the last of the judicial forces was no more. Woo directed Shimada to round up the able, enemy destroyers and have her squadron accompany them to Mars.

"I want the commodores and captains under arrest aboard your destroyers, Commodore," Woo stressed. "Put lieutenants in command. And, as for you, Commodore, stay put on Idona. Captain Irving of the *Challenge* will be promoted to acting commodore to escort the group back to the inner zone."

Reiko's confusion must have been evident, wondering what she would do without a ship and what she had done to deserve the loss of her destroyer.

"Remove the sad face, Commodore," Chong said. "The cruiser, *Daedalus*, your new command, is on its way to you with a pair of escorts, newly commissioned destroyers. You keep that new experiment of ours safe."

"Yes, Admiral," Shimada said excitedly.

Reiko commed her four remaining captains, congratulated Captain Irving on his temporary promotion, and sent them to help rescue the men and women of the damaged destroyers. The senior judiciary officers were grateful for the help, especially when they saw that their rescuers were unaccompanied by Haraken fighters. The specter of the strange fighters would forever haunt the memories of those who fought them.

Commodore Irving communicated to the defeated commodores and captains that Tribune Woo and Space Admiral Chong guaranteed that the death penalty and life sentences were off the table for any convictions. Officers would be tried and the judgments would range from suspended sentences up to twenty-year work terms. Enlisted crew members would be interviewed and either reassigned or dismissed from service, no charges brought. The news relieved much of the anxiety of the defeated personnel.

* * *

Woo and Chong had news for Nikki Fowler.

"You have a tremendous amount of space junk out there that belongs to the military, Station Director Fowler," Woo said. "Maybe we can make a deal and hire you and your people to process it."

"That depends, Tribune Woo. What sort of proposal do you have in mind?" Nikki asked. She was enjoying her newfound authority and meant to ensure that her station wasn't on the wrong end of the stunstik when it came to any deal.

In the end, Nikki received the claimant rights to any warship debris. The smelting stations were anxious to get their hands on the high-grade materials used to build the warships, and Nikki used the proceeds to pay the tug and reclamation captains. A significant portion of the profits was earmarked for transfer to Admiral Chong's reclamation accounts, but Nikki was ecstatic over the opportunity for the station. She began devising schemes on how the station might be expanded.

* * *

Following the celebrations, stationers got back to work, and an incident occurred that marked a turning point in rebel–militia relationships, which had progressed from a fragile state of truce in the first days to working relationships.

The rebel engineers and techs, who had adopted the militia youths they first saw screwing up the resurfacing of the station's bulkheads the day the rebels came out, were breaking work for midday meal.

As a habit, the militia youths expected to return to the station's administration offices for their food. This time, the engineers decided they didn't wish to wait while the boys traveled halfway around the station when one of the Haraken food dispensaries was near at hand.

Stepping into the meal room, the militia boys stumbled to a halt when the room of rebels stopped eating and stared at them. But one of the quick-witted engineers slapped his fellow rebel's shoulder and declared in a loud voice, "See. I told you those medical nanites are making us look so pretty we'd stop traffic." His comment broke the room up in laughter. The two engineers took the moment of levity, linked arms with the militia youths, and headed toward the food dispensers.

Thereafter, many of the rebels seized on the jest of being pretty as the excuse to dine with militia personnel. As one rebel engineer put it to a pair of sergeants at morning meal, "With my nanites, I will look even more handsome if I sit next to you common people."

The militia veterans didn't have the heart to tell the rebels that they had resembled wasted refugees when they emerged into the outer ring. The medical nanites were of great help to the rebels — but only to return to the land of the living.

Whatever the excuses, the Méridien concept of dining together to prevent isolation due to their implants was serving to heal the generation-old rifts between rebels and UE militia.

-33-

Franz finally got his date. With a smile on his face and a kick in his stride, Franz made his way to pick up Reiko at the temporary station quarters extended to her by Nikki. Her squadron, in the command of Commodore Irving, had left the station days ago. Franz expected Reiko to be wearing her uniform. It was the only clothing she possessed — all she had on her when she was carried from the destroyer.

But as Reiko's cabin door slid aside, she stepped out to greet Franz wearing sky-blue, thigh-high boots in a soft material and a cream shirt dress that just met the top of the boots. The top was cinched at the waist by an integrated belt, dialed to a blue-green that complemented the boots. Her short hair was styled in soft, spikey curls.

"You're staring, Commander," Reiko said self-consciously, trying not to reach up and touch her hair.

"As any man should be, at this moment," Franz said gallantly, recovering his wits. "I must say, Commodore. It's a marvelous improvement over your environment suit."

Reiko's laughter, recalling the moments she spent in Franz's lap after they escaped her doomed ship, eased the knot of tension inside her. "You better, approve, Commander. This is the result of two hours of efforts by two militia women, who insisted on helping me. If I didn't know better, I would say our date is anticipated by the entire station."

"May I, Reiko?" Franz said, offering his arm.

A small thrill ran through Reiko's body at the sound of her name on Franz's lips. She took his arm, grateful for the extra support. High heels would never have been permitted on a warship, and a little extra help keeping her balance in the unfamiliar boots was appreciated.

The couple took a short lift down to the main corridor for the walk to the restaurant Franz chose. Stationers, recognizing the pair, cleared their path, standing respectfully to the side. It made Reiko uncomfortable, but Franz was smiling and nodding, a happy man.

Just short of their destination, two figures blocked their way. For a second, Reiko flashed back to her assault, and her grip on Franz's arm tightened. But, recognizing the twins, she relaxed. The Haraken escorts slowly and as one lowered their heads and crossed their arms to place palms over hearts.

Reiko was embarrassed that the Méridien honor was being offered to her, and she almost told the twins it wasn't necessary.

Franz recognized Reiko's hesitation and her moment of discomfort. "Reiko, you were willing to sacrifice yourself to save those on the station, and their loyalty is to the president, who was waiting on the station for the outcome of the battle."

Despite Reiko's belief that the honor wasn't due her, she chose to treat the twins' offer with the greatest respect. She released Franz's arm, came to attention, and bowed gently from the waist, in a manner she remembered her great-grandmother doing. The twins immediately adopted their usual cautious stances and flowed around Franz and her like water.

"You know, Franz," Reiko said, enjoying the opportunity to call the Haraken by his given name, "I've wondered about that. If your president is such an important man to you, why let him stay on the station? I mean, if worse came to worse, haul him aboard one of the carriers."

"You have no idea what that would entail, Reiko," Franz said, laughing at the idea.

Seated in a quiet corner of the restaurant, where the owner and his staff seemed intent on ensuring the couple received every courtesy, Reiko pursued her question. "Why risk your president?"

"It's not a question of risking him. He chose to make a statement in this manner, and it was respected. Besides, your suggestion is fraught with danger."

"Danger … from an unarmed man?"

"Who said he's unarmed?" Franz replied, thinking of Alex's twin implants and his abilities to link with his people even down to the nerve and musculature levels. "Besides, you would have to get past the twins, and I know of no one foolish enough to attempt that."

Reiko let the subject drop. Franz's comments just added to the mysteries surrounding the Harakens. She had seen the president in more than one skintight outfit, which the Harakens preferred, and there wasn't a place to hide a weapon. Truth be told, she had to admit that she had looked. Well, maybe not for a weapon. The enigmatic twins were another matter. Quiet and slight did not seem to equate to dangerous, but then again, even the Harakens, save Alex, Renée, and the SADEs, deferred to them in matters of security.

The couple enjoyed a quiet conversation throughout their meal, and Reiko found the food and drink delicious. She was amused by the difference in proportions they were served. The owner appeared to anticipate Franz's needs, which were similar to those of the president.

When they finished, Franz stood up and offered her his hand. With the effect of the evening's drink, the high-heeled boots were becoming an exceptional challenge, and Reiko worked to stifle a giggle. She almost asked Franz to carry her, although not as he had when they ran though her destroyer.

"We haven't paid the bill," Reiko objected. She glanced at the table. The table's screen was clear — no bill showing.

"Don't look at me," Franz replied. "When I made the reservation, the woman who answered my call asked if I was dining with Commodore Shimada, the hero of Idona."

"She did not," Reiko exclaimed. Franz held up his hand to her in some manner that meant nothing to her but apparently meant he was telling the truth.

At the door of the restaurant, the owner asked if everything was to their satisfaction, but he was focused on Reiko.

"Yes, it was excellent," Reiko replied, a warm glow from the dinner and Franz's company infusing her.

"It was our pleasure to serve you, Commodore. Nothing is too good for the hero of Idona."

In the couple of moments, during which Reiko's mouth hung open, Franz was able to intervene and move Reiko along before she could think of a reply.

Feeling the best she had in a couple of years, Reiko was holding Franz's arm with both hands while they walked back down the main corridor. At one point, she pulled on his arm to attempt to bring Franz to a halt, saying, "This is us." It was a good thing Franz was attentive to her because she was sure her pull had no effect on his momentum.

Franz looked over Reiko's head at the signage of one of the nicest sleepovers on the station, known for its elegant suites which were favored by yacht owners. He grinned as Reiko held up a key pass, realizing she had already rented a room.

The suites were as advertised, having been remodeled after business returned to the station. Inside, Reiko pointed to the luxurious bed and said, "Sit." She strolled toward the door, turned, slowly undid her belt, and then dropped the shirt dress and her undergarments to the floor. Picking up the room's controller, she dimmed the lights, saying, "How do you like your heroes, Commander … with boots on or off?"

* * *

While a feeling of contentment settled over the station, the notorious privateer Dimitri Agaloo, landed the luxury yacht, *Bon Vivant* in a bay at Idona Station. He and his crew had pirated the yacht forty-two days ago at the height of the turmoil.

Dimitri calculated the yacht was good for perhaps another thirty to sixty more days before he would be pressed to procure another ship once the rim's databases were updated with the reported loss of the *Bon Vivant.* Such was the life of a privateer — take a ship, dump the passengers, maybe keep some women or pretty boys, and stay ahead of the militia and naval records.

It would have been smart of Dimitri to disguise his appearance, but he was a vain man, and he was in love with the images of ancient pirates, wearing his beard in braids and decorating them with semiprecious stones. Dimitri assumed that his reputation would protect him. His last visit to Idona was over a year ago and the pickings at that time were slim, to say the least. Since then, Dimitri and his crew spent the time roaming the moons of Saturn and Uranus.

Word reached Dimitri that the Harakens would soon be leaving Idona and the station was prospering, which had brought the privateer prospecting. Walking through the sub-level corridors and taking a lift to the station's main corridor demonstrated to Dimitri just how much Idona had changed. It was clean, bright, and credits were flowing, making Dimitri's hopes of some valuable scores soar.

What the privateer was unaware of was how much Idona had changed — shop owners and stationers were no longer the divisive and frightened individuals of a year ago. They had rebuilt their station and their lives together, adopting Idona as their home, and were willing to defend it.

Calls, originating along Dimitri's path, flowed into militia administration headquarters, and when the privateer turned to enjoy a shop display, the reflection revealed four militia noncoms behind him. Dimitri attempted to brush off the militia with an innocent statement, while reaching to his ear implant to warn his crew, but swift hands pinned his arms and a metal-braided bag was slipped over his head, blocking comm calls to and from his ear implant.

Moments later, a squad of Haraken troopers and Lieutenant Morris surrounded the *Bon Vivant* and the crew was ordered to exit the yacht one by one. As they came down the gangway ramp, each was searched and taken into custody. The interior of the ship revealed three traumatized individuals, two girls and a boy, who had been severely used by the crew, and Terese and her team were called to attend the victims.

Lieutenant Morris requested the Haraken troopers march the privateer down the main corridor in full view of the stationers, and people came out from the shops, sleepovers, and restaurants to applaud the capture. More than one individual called out "well done" to Lieutenant Morris, who realized how much the station had come to mean to her.

* * *

Patrice Morris sat down at her small multipurpose desk and stared into the mirror. She had stripped out of her uniform and taken her three-minute allotted shower. It was her thought to go out tonight, to celebrate, but not as a militia officer — as a woman.

Since arriving at Idona, Patrice faithfully followed Captain Yun's first day's advice. He said, "Wear your uniform at all times, Morris, when you leave your cabin. It's your best defense. Nobody bothers a militia officer, not even the rats." It was days before Patrice learned that the rats were the rebel teenagers.

Every day, morning and night, Patrice donned her uniform — the cloak of the militia, as she thought of it, and was loath to be without it despite the fact that Reiko was wearing her uniform when she was attacked. In Patrice's mind were burned the images of Reiko after her beating, and, to this day, she couldn't believe the Harakens not only saved the commodore but restored her looks.

But people's attitudes on the station were changing, had changed, and Patrice was still a young woman and not too bad looking, if she said so herself. Making up her mind, Patrice pulled out her face kit, which hadn't seen the light since she moved into the assigned, utilitarian, and oh-so depressing cabin. She selected her favorite mask, positioned it on her face, and triggered it. The mask was a young UE woman's favorite form of makeup — instantly applied — in this case, bright, fluorescent colors with the sparkles that Patrice favored while at the naval academy.

Looking in the mirror, Patrice could hear her mother saying, "Oh, dear, you look like a 200-credit an hour girl," and Patrice had to agree this time. She reached for the bottle of de-mask, sprayed it over face, waited a minute, and brushed the light powder off.

At the bottom of her face kit was an unused mask, an academy graduation present from her mother. Smiling to herself, Patrice opened the package and applied the mask. She kept her eyes closed, a little afraid to look in the mirror — reluctant to think she was leaving the vibrant days of the youthful academy cadet behind.

When Patrice did open her eyes, she was surprised. It wasn't the boring makeup application she expected. The colors were subtle, blended, but artfully highlighted her features, and there was a touch of soft sparkles at the corners of her eyes that her mother knew she loved.

"Mom, who knew you had so much style?" Patrice said to her mirror then hurried to change. She dressed in a pair of skin-tight, black, dragon-scale motif pants, pulled on a pair of black, calf-high, spike-heeled boots, and slipped over her head a dark-red top with balloon sleeves but with an open back and daring, drop front.

For her first venture out, Patrice chose an upscale bar frequented by shop owners, captains, and officers as a place to meet and talk. When she stepped through the door, a maître d' guided her into the dim but tastefully lit interior. Conversations stilled the deeper into the bar Patrice walked, and she was tempted to spin around and exit as quickly as her spike-heeled boots could carry her. While that thought was rolling through Patrice's mind, the bar's customers, who had been staring at her, begin politely applauding and then broke into cheering. More than one sharp whistle of appreciation cut the air, and Patrice blushed.

A liner captain and a sleepover owner hurriedly stepped beside Patrice. The two men eyed each other for a moment and then seemed to reach a simple agreement, each extending an arm to her. Patrice smiled and took both of the offered arms. Walking toward a vacant table, the two men were grinning as if they had won the evening's grand prize.

-34-

After a half year at Idona, the Harakens began the process of disentangling themselves from the affairs of the station. Their advanced technology had to be replaced with UE substitutes or reclaimed — financial applications, controllers, upgraded transponders, security sensors, holo-vid, nanites chairs, and food dispensers with stock. It was acknowledged that the recovery would be incomplete. For instance, the upgraded transponders were embedded in large metal-heavy rocks headed inward just waiting to be recovered by some inquisitive individual.

As for the stationers, they wanted to resume a life punctuated by normalcy, perhaps even boredom. Most of them were emotionally drained by their experiences with the Harakens. Life-and-death struggles tend to do that.

Julien was with Alex when the president asked the scientists if they wished to stay at Sol or return to Haraken. The scientists struggled momentarily with their implants but managed to form a conference.

<Did I look that bad when I was learning?> Alex sent, watching the dull-faced fugue settle over the scientists' faces and a few pairs of eyeballs roll up in heads.

<Much worse,> Julien replied

<And I was foolish enough to help you gain mobility,> Alex shot back.

<The greed of a simple human seeking superior technology,> Julien riposted.

* * *

Later, Olawale sat with his friend, Francis Lumley, telling the captain of his decision to return to Haraken, when the ex-administrator came to the critical question he sought to ask. "What do you say, old friend, do you have one more adventure left in you?"

Lumley couldn't say he was surprised by the offer. Since he arrived at Idona with Tribune Brennan, the thought had surfaced many times. Like Olawale, Lumley was without family, and his closest friend was telling him that he had decided to return to a faraway star.

"You would need to gain the permission of the president, correct?" Lumley asked cautiously, not wanting to get his hopes up unnecessarily.

Olawale's bright white smile flashed. "I have already asked President Racine, and he said, 'Men of Captain Lumley's qualities are always welcome on Haraken.'"

* * *

Before the scientists and Lumley left for Haraken, they requested an opportunity to speak with the tribunes, and Julien hosted a conference between the two tribunes, the scientists, and the captain.

"I'm not sure what your intentions are for the Tribunal's structure now that the high judges are in disgrace," Olawale began, "but we have some suggestions for you."

It took a bit of effort for Woo not to comment. She thought the ex-administrator was taking advantage of the situation, but she recalled it was due to the scientists' analysis of the UE's intentions that Alex Racine chose to journey to Sol instead of waiting for the UE to come to him with an armed fleet.

"We would ask you to consider a five-person, governing body," Olawale continued.

In the quiet that followed, Boris added, "We have witnessed balanced and considered opinions by the court judges here at Idona, who are more representative of the span of people."

"That's true, Tribune Woo," Brennan agreed. "I have been impressed by the quality of judgments handed down by the panel against those who are convicted."

"How do the judges at Idona relate to our Tribunal?" Woo asked, unsure of the comparison.

"By representing a greater cross-section of the people of Sol," Nema explained. "Your Tribunal consists of three individuals, who represent the most powerful entities in the system. We would suggest eliminating the judiciary, and ask you to consider adding two positions, filled by representatives of the people, one individual elected from residents of the inner zone and the other from the rim people."

"So, if the military, commerce, and two representatives from the people occupy four positions, who do you suggest occupies the fifth seat?" Woo couldn't believe she was asking the question, but then again, she thought, *Why stop now?*

"That's why you're the tribune," Lumley said laughing.

"Careful, Captain, you still report to me," Woo said, feeling that the conference was exceeding her patience.

"Actually, no, Tribune Woo," Brennan said. "Captain Lumley resigned his commission. He's chosen to accompany his friends to Haraken."

"I meant no disrespect, Tribune Woo," Lumley apologized. "I believe if you look at the trial transcripts you will see what we are trying to tell you — the fundamental concept is balance. No one represented group having sway over the others. You have commerce and the military represented. When you add two representatives of the people, you have balance."

"So I ask again, who are you suggesting for the fifth member of this body? We must have someone to break the deadlocks," Woo said.

"Tribune Woo, Yoram Penzig here. Please, do not consider that I'm being facetious when I say a perfect fifth member would be a Haraken, human or SADE."

That did produce an extensive period of silence.

"Someone who doesn't have a stake in the outcome, a neutral," Brennan finally said, understanding dawning.

"But who would that be in our system?" Woo persisted.

"That's where you misinterpreted my laughter, Tribune Woo," Lumley said. "We have no idea, but you are considered one of the UE's most brilliant women, and we hope that through your efforts you will discover who that fifth person, that neutral person, should be."

"I must say, your ideas have merit. Julien, could you — never mind. I just received notice that the court transcripts are on my console. Thank you, Julien." The thought crossed Woo's mind that she would accept Julien as the fifth individual, and the realization took her aback. *Seven months ago, I didn't know AIs existed. Now I want one to help us govern our system.*

"People, if you think of who this fifth person might be before you leave, please don't keep it a secret," Woo said as she signed off.

* * *

After the conference call with the scientists and Lumley, Woo connected briefly with Brennan.

"The enclave's high judges have been accounted for," Woo announced. "Two bodies were discovered when the judges chose to commit suicide. Three judges with their security personnel attempted to fight their way past the militia when they were discovered. Those three are dead. The remaining ten high judges were taken into custody."

"What about Tribune Lucchesi?" Brennan asked.

"The tribune seems to have met with an unfortunate accident … and before you ask, it wasn't me."

"The enclave?" Brennan suggested.

"I would think so. Lucchesi outlived his usefulness to the enclave and probably became an embarrassment."

"What are your intentions with regard to the high judges that you've arrested?"

“I think we’re done with those types of questions for criminals, Ian,” Woo said, the tiredness in her voice evident. “If we intend to make a clean break of our past procedures, then I don’t think just because the enclave had a habit of conveniently making people disappear means that we should take the easy way out.”

“Why not announce that the high judges are being held for trial, but that these trials will not commence until the new laws are in effect for the courts?”

“You took the words right out of my mouth, Ian … you’ve been hanging around the Harakens too long,” Woo said, a small laugh escaping. “I think the new laws have to be our priority, and the records of Idona’s judicial panel might just be our guidelines.”

“Announcing this systemwide while we have the Haraken probes will give the incarcerated hope. It would go well to keeping a lid on emotions while we shift our policies,” Brennan suggested.

“We will need that. The Harakens have set our people’s hopes for the future very high, and it will be our undoing if we don’t live up to those hopes.”

* * *

Catching Brennan in the main corridor before the tribune caught his naval clipper for the trip back to Earth, Alex wished him good fortune and offered a final word of advice. “Please do your best to see that the UE leaders keep their word to the people of Sol. You wouldn’t want us to come back.”

Brennan saw the polite smile the president added, but it didn’t appear to reach the man’s eyes. But rather than take umbrage at the implied threat, Brennan grinned. “Thank you, Mr. President. That’s just the sort of message that I will be pleased to deliver to anyone foolish enough to resist the implementation of the changes we expect to make.”

Alex extended his hand, and the two men shared a warm handshake and conspiratorial smiles.

After Brennan left, Alex contacted Woo with Julien's help.

"Greetings, Tribune Woo," Alex began when the tribune answered her comms console in her bedroom.

"Mr. President," Woo replied, "I understand you are days away from leaving our system. I can't say that I will regret your departure, despite all you've done for the UE."

"Without trying to be argumentative, Tribune Woo, everything we did was for your populace."

"And that is most appreciated. It's just that we have a great deal of work to do to stabilize our situation, and it will best be accomplished without the Harakens' presence. No offense."

"None taken, Tribune Woo. However, the reason for my comm is to tell you that we are leaving you a present. We have done our best to sweep the Idona space clear of our technology, but we have decided to leave our system's probes in place. They are set to deactivate if tampered with except for one."

"Let me guess," Woo replied, "the one on the Earth's moon."

"Correct. I suggest you recover it soon and protect it. When your scientists figure out how to communicate with its systems, you will have access to the entire system of probes. Short of that success, perhaps your people can reverse engineer our technology."

"Quite the gift, Mr. President. Perhaps, I haven't sounded grateful enough for what you've done for the UE … for us."

"Understandable, Tribune Woo, you have had a great deal to juggle and will have much more in the future. Oh … by the way, if your scientists are successful communicating with our probe, they will be challenged for a password."

"It's not going to be some unintelligible set of Haraken characters we can't create so that you can get the last laugh, will it?" Woo asked. Personally, she was grateful to the Harakens, but the system of Sol had been turned upside down by their visit, and Woo knew she would be spending the rest of her time as tribune, and perhaps the rest of her life, trying to restore some sense of stability and balance to her people and the government, especially since everyone now knew there were powerful aliens out there — even if they were human aliens.

"You're overthinking this, Kwan," Alex said, using the tribune's given name for the first time. "Have your people input, using their own letter keys, the word "friend."

Woo smiled to herself. Even the Haraken president's final message was trying to teach a different way of thinking.

"Good fortune to you, Kwan, and may the stars guide the people of Sol," Alex said closing the comm.

-35-

Almost 30 percent of the station's militia members boarded various vessels headed inward on deployment to other locations. Sol's militia was receiving new marching orders. In addition to their general policing practices, which were now termed colony or station security, they were to support civilian projects and relieve the strain on civil administrators. Chong and Woo repeatedly stressed to the militia commanders that they must be prepared to roll up their sleeves and get to work. An often-repeated phrase to the commanders was "make your location shine like Idona."

Captain Yun boarded a passenger liner headed for Earth. His traveling companion was Major Lindling, who he was delivering for trial on charges of corruption. Yun took a little pleasure in confining Lindling to his cabin for the duration of the trip — he never did like the man.

To Chong's surprise, the resignation of Patrice Morris crossed his console. The lieutenant's high profile rated it flagged for the admiral's attention. For a moment, he was perplexed, thinking that the lieutenant was a strong supporter of the changes at Idona. It was the note attached to her file by his adjutant that made him smile.

* * *

After transmitting her resignation to the naval headquarters offices on Mars, Patrice Morris, now a citizen, dropped into the station director's office looking for Nikki Fowler. She found Nikki bent over her desk panel studying income flow matrixes.

"I'm looking for employment," Patrice said without fanfare.

"I heard you resigned your commission," Nikki replied.

"Word gets around fast now that everyone is talking to one another. I like this station and what it's becoming. I'll take whatever position you have available."

"Any position?" Nikki said, raising an eyebrow.

"Any position," Patrice said with resignation. She envisioned ushering a fleet of scrubbers down the corridors at night.

"Well … Captain Yun is headed inward with Lindling so I could use an assistant station director," Nikki replied, grinning when she saw Patrice's mouth fall open.

"Sure … I mean yes," Patrice replied, breaking out her own grin and extending a hand to Nikki.

"Done," said Nikki, shaking Patrice's hand. "Let's get started," she added, dropping into her chair and indicating another for Patrice. "With the Harakens leaving, station security is going to become a top priority. You'll be taking on that role until you hire a chief of security."

* * *

Knowing the Harakens were soon leaving, Nikki asked to meet with Alex and, of all individuals, the three SADEs. The group met in a small room next to one of the meal rooms.

"This is going to sound a little unusual, but I'm going to come right out and ask," Nikki began. "Would you consider taking some of the children with you? I'm speaking of the orphans … the ones who've become attached to the two of you," Nikki said, pointing to Cordelia and Z. "When we were in the inner ring, everyone took care of them, but they have no relatives. Now, out here, with all that's going on, I'm worried that they won't have the guidance they need, and, truth be told, I'm concerned that they could end up being sent to a UE orphanage."

"What about the children? What do they think?" Cordelia asked. "Edmas and Jodlyne are teenagers and have grown up on this station, and Jason and Ginny have their six friends."

"That's the ten I'm talking about," Nikki replied, "and as far the children go, I talked to them yesterday about the possibility of them leaving with you. Early this morning, all ten showed up at my cabin door with an assortment of carryalls and bags, with one question among them: 'Had I talked to the Harakens yet?'"

Nikki sat back against the edge of the desk, watching the SADEs transform into inanimate figures. "Must have stumped them on that one," she whispered to Alex. "You're not included in this one?" she asked, noticing Alex's relaxed posture and visage.

"And happy not to be," Alex replied, smiling.

"Why are you smiling?" Nikki asked.

"It's a long, long story, Nikki," Alex said, laying a companionable hand on her shoulder. "Someday, when it's possible, visit me, and I'll add this tale to the other ones I've promised to tell you."

"Now, how can I refuse an offer like that?" Nikki said, laughing at the idea of traveling to meet the Harakens.

"You never know what the future might hold for you, Nikki. Believe me … no one knows that better than me."

Nikki stopped laughing and regarded Alex. They appeared to be about the same age, but his eyes said that he was lifetimes older than her.

While they waited, Alex's mind drifted over the years with Julien from their incredible introduction aboard the derelict liner, to the day Julien transferred into his avatar, to Founding Day when Julien and his beloved showed up in their inventive costumes at Alex's offices in the Assembly, and a lopsided smile softly formed on his face.

The SADEs returned to the here and now. "We will speak with the children," Cordelia announced. "If they are still willing to go after our discussion, we will take them. They would live together with Julien and me. Z will visit Edmas and Jodlyne, but his avatars often take him where the children can't go."

"Fair enough," Nikki agreed. "They're waiting for you in the next room," she added, pointing to a connecting door.

The SADEs would not have agreed to someone accusing them of being nervous, but, at this moment, they might accept words like concern and trepidation. This was appropriate because algorithms drove their reactions. However, in humans, it would be called fear — perhaps a lower level of the emotion, but fear nonetheless.

The children were assembled at a long table in the empty meal room, their small bags of possessions clutched in their arms and wearing expectant expressions.

"Are we going with you, Cordelia?" asked Ginny, her little face contorted in confusion and angst.

"Remember, Ginny," Edmas said, "we're supposed to wait to hear what they have to say first."

"Oh," Ginny said quietly.

Over the course of time, since the freeing of the rebels, Edmas and Jodlyne had taken on the responsibilities of care and wrangling of the eight younger orphans. This was entirely due to Z's influence. The two tunnel rats began following Z for the protection the huge individual represented. When it was announced that Z wasn't human, instead of being repulsed as some rebels were, the teenagers were utterly fascinated by the discovery. But in the end — human or SADE — it made no difference to the teenagers. He was Z, and slowly but surely the two tunnel rats copied the manner in which Z treated others. It was during this time that Edmas and Jodlyne recognized that the eight small orphans needed the attention that the adults were too busy to give them.

"You do realize that you will probably not return to your people for many years, if ever," Cordelia said.

The children all nodded their understanding, and the SADEs continued to present reasons why the children should stay on station.

"Excuse me," Edmas finally interrupted. "What we want to do most of all is stay together." The children nodded their heads vigorously to Edmas's statement. "That won't happen here," he continued. "Families might take one or two of us, but they can't take all of us. If we chose to stay together, then it's a UE orphanage for us, which is a guarantee that we won't be staying together for long."

"I want to swim with the aliens," one little boy said.

"Can you swim, little one?" Julien asked with a smile, knowing the answer.

"No," he admitted, "but I can learn. We can all learn. We're smart." This was greeted with another round of adamant nods.

"Edmas and Jodlyne," Z said, "you know that much of my work takes me to places where humans can't travel."

"Yes, but you'll come visit us," Jodlyne challenged, making it a statement rather than a question. "And we can ride your horse and hear about all the places you went."

"Z, you've taught us that it's important to help others. We can best help by being with these little ones," Edmas said. "We want to go with you to your world, but we want to stay with them."

Despite their intentions to appear human as much as possible before the children, subtle fugues worked across the SADEs' faces as they ran the possibilities through their crystal minds and shared their conjectures with one another. That they couldn't reach a logical decision, despite their attempt to do so, was a foregone conclusion. This was the messy world of humans.

<Since analysis seems unable to reach a logical conclusion,> Cordelia sent to her companions, <I have chosen to use emotion as my guide. I want them.>

Julien instantly agreed with her, and the two SADEs waited for Z.

<I find it frustrating that this can't be resolved through deductive reason to determine the best possible outcome,> Z sent. <But how can you quantify the values of the myriad possibilities of their futures?>

<And so?> Cordelia asked.

Z looked at the pleading faces, intently watching them, especially those of Edmas and Jodlyne. <We are SADEs. Do we have the right to raise human children?> Z sent.

Cordelia once asked Alex the same question, and she played his response for Julien and Z: <Cordelia, I believe that children should be loved and cared for above everything else. If you can do that for these children, then you have as much right to raise them as any human.>

<I want them too,> Z said, still confused by his inability to resolve the question in the manner he approached all problems. <If the two of you are willing to raise all ten of them, I will do my best to assist when available.>

"Come, children," Cordelia said, opening her arms to them.

With whoops and squeals of joy the children raced to embrace the SADEs, hugging whatever chest or leg they could comfortably reach.

"I'm a Haraken," Ginny announced to Cordelia.

"Yes, you're all Harakens," Cordelia said laughing.

* * *

"I understand you've become a father," Alex said to Julien later that day. "Quite a feat … you having ten children at once."

"Yes, I will need some parenting tips. I was hoping to ask your mother what difficulties she failed to overcome in your upbringing," Julien shot back.

The two friends sat together, alone with their thoughts. The stars outside the station's view window twinkled and, far in the distance, the dim light of the star of Sol fell on Idona Station.

"Perhaps, your eminence," Julian said, "it's time to leave for home unless it has been your true intent all along to adopt Sol as your new kingdom."

"You wound me, my friend. I intended to give Sol to you as a gift. You'd be the first SADE to rule a system." Alex said and sent Julien an image of the SADE wearing a shining gold crown.

Julien melted the crown, let it flow down his body, and transform into amoeba-like protozoa that chased a screaming Alex.

And so the two of them, human and SADE, threw images back and forth until their ritual restored a sense of equilibrium for both. Their desperate mission to save their worlds from domination by the UE was over, and they had won a peace.

"Home, my friend?" Alex asked.

"Home," Julien agreed.

-36-

<Be patient, my love,> Renée was sending to Alex. <I know both of us are anxious to return to Haraken and see our son again.>

<We're two days away from leaving this system, and she's requesting a special conference?> Alex sent back.

<She must have a good reason. Just hear her out,> Renée cautioned Alex.

At Terese's request, Alex and Renée were on their way to one of the station's clinics with the twins bracketing them. They found Terese in the clinic's administration office, which was overly crowded with the addition of Pia, Mickey, Z, Captain Cordova, Nikki, and Reiko.

<Maybe I spoke too quickly,> Renée sent. <Isn't this where we're supposed to hear Tatia's warning of "incoming"?>

<Too late now,> Alex sent back. He took one look at the determined faces, the crowded small room without chairs for Renée and him, and made an about face.

Nikki and Reiko were momentarily confused, but the Harakens were dutifully following Alex. So the two Earther women presumed the implants were in play. Alex returned to the planning room, where everyone found seats around a large table, and he gestured to Terese to begin.

"Ser President, we have seen some incredible changes here at Idona and across the UE, and we wish to help the people who have suffered at the hands of some of the unconscionable policies. On this point, I wish to revisit your edict that the medical nanites not be given to anyone but the ex-rebels of Idona."

Terese felt her jaw tightening. She was ready for an argument and was determined not to lose her temper, something Pia Sabine repeatedly warned her about if they were to win Alex over, which is why she wasn't ready when she heard Alex say, "Go on."

"The plan, Ser President," Pia said when Terese appeared stunned, "is to use Idona as a manufacturing site for our medical nanites. We would program them for a one-year cycle and distribute them across the solar system."

"Go on," Alex prompted.

"I showed images of my attack from Terese's files to Tribune Brennan," Reiko added, "and asked him before he left if the UE would support the manufacturing cost of your medical nanites for the people, Mr. President. Julien and Z supplied me with raw material costs, which the tribune agreed to fund. He did ask for the technical specifications for creating the nanites, which Terese forbid. The tribune was okay with that, just saying he had to ask."

"Z, will you be able to obtain the necessary materials to set up the manufacturing process?" Alex asked.

"The station has facilities for us, Ser President," Z explained. "My analysis of asteroid samples indicates a rich supply of the minerals we require. I included the mining costs in the procurement estimates I gave Commodore Shimada. The three-tiered GEN machines are on board the *No Retreat* ready to be offloaded. I will remain to facilitate the manufacturing process and provide additional security."

"I take it the Harakens at this table are volunteering to remain at Idona while our carriers return home?" Alex asked and received nods from everyone.

Alex leaned back in his chair and stared up at the overhead while he thought.

<It's incredibly generous of them, my love,> Renée sent to Alex, <I am proud of their gesture.>

<I am too,> Alex replied. <I just don't want to be seen giving in to Terese too easily. It would make it even tougher next time around, and I'm sure there will be many next times!> Finally, Alex focused on Terese, who he could see tensing up. "There are some conditions." The moment Alex said that, smiles went around the room.

"First," Alex began, "the manufacturing site does not leave this station. Second, Haraken personnel do not leave Idona Station or the nearby space, if local travel is required. By extension, all UE medical personnel, who will be responsible for distributing and administering the nanites, will be trained at Idona Station."

"Mr. President," said Reiko, "I have Admiral Chong's word that my cruiser command will be permanently stationed at Idona as long as the Harakens are here. It would be my job and my honor to protect your people and this station."

Alex nodded to Reiko, hearing the strong commitment behind her words.

"Let's continue with the conditions," Alex said, eyeing Z. "The GEN machines do not leave Idona Station under any circumstances until they leave with you as you exit this system. In fact, they do not leave our people's care at any time. Furthermore, Z, you are to ensure that if the machines are tampered with they will permanently disable themselves. If and when you determine this has happened, the job of medical nanites manufacturing will be considered concluded and all of you will pack up and come home. Am I understood?" Alex waited for everyone's nod of agreement, especially that of Terese.

Looking at Captain Cordova, Alex asked, "Is this why you're here, Captain?"

"Yes, Ser President, I will ensure our people get home safely, and I would not wish to miss another adventure," he added, a youthful smile lighting up the aged face.

"Then the *Rêveur* remains at Idona," Alex said. "It's here, Captain, for our people's safe return and not for touring the solar system."

"Understood, Ser President," the captain replied, knowing Alex's words were meant for many at the table.

About this time, a rushed Franz Cohen hurried into the meeting.

"Ah, Commander, I was waiting for someone to show up about now," Alex said, and he eyed Terese, who took the opportunity to shrug her shoulders in Alex's inimitable style and then let loose her own trademark laugh.

"Let me anticipate your request, Commander," Alex continued. "Yes, you may stay, and four travelers will be at your disposal. I presume you've selected your pilots?"

"Yes, Mr. President," Franz replied, "I was waiting to request permission of Commodore Reynard for three other pilots and me, if you approved Ser Lechaux's request. Am I premature?"

"No, Commander, I think we are in the negotiations stage. And you, Ser Station Director, what is your role in this plot?" Alex asked Nikki.

"Ostensibly, Mr. President, it's to provide assurance that Idona Station will provide a manufacturing base for the Haraken medical nanites at no charge. However, the thought that some of your people might be outmaneuvering you made it impossible to stay away." Nikki punctuated her last sentence with a cheeky smile.

"Rebel," Alex grumbled. "Mickey, you have your flight crew picked? Captain, you have your crew?" In both cases Alex received a nod of acknowledgment.

"So you believe you have it all covered?" Alex said to the room. His question was greeted by satisfied smiles, which slowly waned in the face of Alex's own smile. He waited, knowing implant comms were burning with questions and reviews of checklists.

"So what did we miss, oh great one?" Terese asked grudgingly.

Alex looked over at the twins, who nodded to him without his asking the question. "Which troopers were asked to stay to provide security?" A short round of expletives greeted his question. "Étienne and Alain have volunteered to stay to manage security, and I'll have Tatia request volunteers," Alex said. "You people and the GEN machines are to have around-the-chronometer protection. Now let's talk about how long this might take."

The meeting dissolved into the minutiae of UE medical personnel travel, manufacturing, training, and other assorted details. When Alex got ready to leave, he put a hand on Franz's shoulder and whispered, "Let me know how Reiko likes her first turn in the cockpit of one of our travelers, Commander."

"Certainly, Mr. President," Franz agreed, embarrassed at being so easily read.

* * *

Renée took a moment to talk to Reiko before she left the meeting.

"I hear that Franz asked you to return to Haraken with him when he leaves." Renée said.

"Not much privacy among your people," Reiko replied, but the wry smile she offered was meant to take the sting out of her remark. "Yes, he did," she finally admitted. "But, I was serious when I said I wanted this cruiser command to protect this station and your people. It's important to me.

"And your commitment is appreciated, Reiko," Renée replied. "I know Alex can think of no one else he would choose to trust the welfare of his people to than you."

"I did tell Franz that there's the possibility of getting a ride on the *Rêveur* when he returns home, but I also said that I wanted a guarantee of a ride back to Sol if things didn't work out on Haraken," Reiko said and laughed self-consciously at her words. The idea of leaving with Franz excited and scared her and probably in equal amounts, if she was honest with herself.

"We'll see you within the year, Reiko," Renée said, giving the commodore a quick hug.

"You seem sure of your opinion," Reiko called after Renée.

"Oh, I am. There is a sort of adventuresome woman, who finds a certain type of New Terran male irresistible," Renée said, adding a conspiratorial wink.

Reiko cracked up, laughing at the thought that the alluring Ser de Guirnon, partner of the president of an alien world, and she might have similar personalities.

* * *

Terese and the Harakens who were supporting her efforts would spend the greater part of the next year at Idona. The Haraken probes made it possible to get the call out to everyone immediately, but a lengthy time was needed to allow the medical teams to journey from the farthest rim across the solar system.

If it weren't for the tremendous impression Haraken technology already made on the people of Sol, the visiting UE medical personnel wouldn't have believed the instructions they were receiving. The administration of the medical nanites was simple. More difficult was the pre- and post-surgical procedures required if the individual had artificial material in the body, such as metal implants in the bone. That material would need to be removed before the initial injection, and the patient maintained in a stable position until the nanites repaired the body.

The objections from the doctors were always the same. "We don't have room to hospitalize our population for long periods of time." The answers were always the same. "The period we are discussing is at most several hours for the more radical operations, provided nutrients and fluids are immediately supplemented.

It was an important item stressed over and over in training — the need for superior nutrition. The body would require tremendous amounts of calories and nutrients. This would be especially true for those who had been restricted to poor diets, such as the rebels and those people serving life sentences in the corporate and government factories.

Supply of the medical nanites would represent a huge boon for the station. Miners were kept busy procuring the exotic raw minerals Z required, and the station's sleepovers, restaurants, and shops were constantly filled by medical teams and, of course, visitors, who were anxious for a sight of the Harakens before they left the system.

Terese became a notable personality for her efforts, and it wasn't long before she realized why Alex preferred not to attract public attention. But for Idona's visitors, if Terese wasn't available, a look at the exotic twins or heavy-worlders, such as Franz, was always worth the trip.

Scientists from outer-rim locations made the trip to the station to speak with Z, who good-naturedly entertained their questions. The influence of the Miranda persona did much to balance Z's replies to their more awkward questions. Most went away shaking their heads in awe. They expected some sort of indication of robotics or hybridization, but after hours of conversation, they couldn't detect anything but human physiology and responses. Some even suggested that Z might be just an incredibly large heavy-worlder. At which point, Z would often smile and say, "But that's the purpose of any SADE human avatar, Sers, to have it appear indistinguishable from its intended purpose."

Idona was inundated by the arrival of so many liners that docks were often unavailable, necessitating the use of shuttles to transport passengers to and from the station. It was not long before Nikki Fowler was able to realize the dream of her great-grandfather, whom she never met. She would have the credits to expand the station.

The great gift Nikki received, although not the one she expected, started with a long conversation with Mickey and Z, who after listening to her ideas volunteered to design the expansion. Nikki spent hours talking about how she thought it should function and appear.

One day when Nikki was asked by Mickey and Z to join them, Nikki anticipated attending another planning session. In Alex's old planning room, their design slowly revolved in the holo-vid left behind for Z's use. Nikki was upset that apparently her suggestions were ignored, but the engineer in her began studying the design, and she began asking questions.

As Nikki was nodding her approval of their achievement, elegant solutions beyond her capabilities, her final question became, "This is nice and all, but can UE technology build this?" When they told her that the detailed plans using UE technology were on her servers under the title, "Nikki's Dream," she hugged both of them.

-37-

The leaves of the collector closed around a group of crystals surrounding the brightest and tallest of the specimens. The robotic explorer retracted the collector, tucked it into its rear end, and started working its way back to the moon's surface. Time was of the essence. The moon, in its elliptical orbit, was making a near approach to the planet, and tidal forces would begin disrupting its surface.

Already the cylindrical explorer was halting, extending its burrowing arms, spinning them at high speed, and reopening the pathway back to the surface, which was slowly closing from the shifting surface.

Sitting on the moon's surface, three miners, Stremski, Willard, and Lister, were pacing, sweating, and swearing. Their explorer was struggling to reach the surface, and if it failed to reach them in time, they would have to abandon it and the prizes it held in its collector.

The men specialized in locating unusual mineral formations and were exploring deep inside a moon of metal ores covered by a thick layer of frozen gases. It was a risky venture, but Lister had a feeling, and Lister's intuition was the team's good luck charm.

Deep crevices in the surface were expanding toward the mining cab when the robot popped up not 200 meters away, having chosen an alternate pathway up. Slapping one another on the back, Stremski piloted the cab over to their exploration tool, Willard snatched it up, and Lister employed the comm to ready their ship, which was maintaining a geosynchronous orbit above their cab.

Once aboard, the men locked down the cab in the ship's bay, unloaded the collector, and hurried to exit the space, ridding themselves of the planet's increasing gravitational forces.

Stremski and Willard were in the pilot's cockpit when Lister yelled to them on the comm. Locking in the autopilot, they hurried back to the specimen analyses room where Lister was examining the robot's last collection. They piled into each other in front of Lister, who was wearing an extraordinary grin in what was normally a taciturn face and holding up an enormous crystal column, a beautiful specimen exhibiting a delicate blend of pinkish orange light.

"It can't be," said Stremski, staring at the 30-plus centimeter long specimen. "Is it a pad?" he asked, referring to the ultra-rare padparadscha sapphire.

"That big? It can't be," said Willard.

"Spec machine says it is, boys," replied Lister. That his heavily lined face was still wearing a broad grin convinced the others of what he was saying, and a victory dance by Stremski and Willard proceeded to pound worn boots into the ship's aging deck.

When the two men stopped dancing, having run out of breath quite quickly, Lister deadpanned, "You two done yet?" He waited a couple of heartbeats and broke into another ear-splitting grin before he asked, "You want to see what else we got?"

Days later, Stremski, Willard, and Lister marched into Nikki's office and placed the cleaned, brilliant, crystal column on her desk.

Patrice regarded the exquisite crystal and said, "Happy birthday, Nikki!"

"It's gorgeous," Nikki replied, "but it's not my birthday."

"It's a pad," Stremski said, beaming. "A rare pink-orange sapphire … a padparadscha," he plowed on when Nikki and Patrice only stared at him. "It's worth hundreds of millions of credits."

"Congratulations on your find, men, are you looking for us to protect it for you until you find a buyer?" Patrice asked.

"It's not for us," Willard said excitedly. "It's for Idona … for the people of the station, the miners, the captains, the crews … everyone in this rim space."

"Perhaps, I'm a little slow today," Nikki said, dropping back into her chair. The Haraken president had left her a gift, a nanites chair, and she couldn't resist enjoying it every opportunity she got. "Explain this from the beginning."

"It's like this," Lister said. "All three of our families were on this station when Portland, may he find torment wherever he is, tried to demolish it. Everyone in this rim space pitched in to help the Harakens … and we won."

"Okay, all true … and this ties into your magnificent crystal, how?" Nikki asked.

"We won," Willard said, "and we don't have a commemoration of what went on here."

"Yeah, my wife was telling me about how people used to commemorate big events in the old times, and I told Willard and Stremski here that it was sad that we didn't do anything," Lister explained. "I mean handing the high judges their heads has to be one of the greatest days across the system, and we stopped their admiral right here at Idona."

"So, are you saying you want to make this crystal into a commemoration, a memorial, for the events of that day?" Patrice asked.

"That's it, Lieutenant … I mean Patrice," Stremski exclaimed. "A pad sapphire this big, this clear, is unique in all the system, and that's what we are out here … unique." The three miners puffed up, displaying pride in their faces and stances.

"You sure you don't want to sell it?" Nikki asked. "That's an enormous gift you're talking about … an incredible gift."

"It's what our commemoration deserves," Lister said.

"Besides, Nikki, we had a pretty good run out there," Willard added and the three miners shared grins. They had a really good run. Inside the collector and nestled with the huge pad were numerous smaller specimens, each of which would fetch tremendous prices from collectors. After decades of just getting by on the rim, the miners had struck it rich.

"Okay, men," Nikki said. "Patrice, please take possession of this crystal and take note of these men's names. I want credit given for their gift. We have a memorial to design."

As the three miners exited the office, Nikki looked at Patrice and said, "Did that just happen?"

"You mean did three loopy miners walk in here, dump a priceless and rare gemstone on your desk, and call it a memorial stone to our independence day. Yeah, I think so. And you know what, Nikki, I'm proud to have been here when it happened.

* * *

Two days before the last Harakens were due to leave Idona, an unveiling ceremony took place in the central rotunda located in the main corridor just outside the station's administration offices.

Present were the miners, surrounded by their wives and children, Nikki Fowler, Reiko Shimada, the Harakens, and over 1,000 stationers and visitors. The station's media department was broadcasting the event to the rim, and Z was transferring the signal to the probes across the system. Nikki would have been a great deal more nervous if she knew billions of people were watching the commemoration.

"I'm not an eloquent speaker … having not had much practice while hiding in Idona's inner ring my entire life," Nikki began. "But today, as Idona's station manager, I'm truly proud to be present at this event. These three miners," Nikki said, gesturing to the beaming men at her side, "reminded me that something momentous happened at Idona almost a year ago, and we did nothing to help us and our children remember those days. They convinced me that we needed a memorial, and they donated something so rare, so unique that it will command the attention of anyone who passes by this memorial for as long as this station or its next iteration occupies this space."

Nikki nodded to Patrice who pulled off the covering of the memorial, and a gasp went through the crowd. A designer of mineral displays, the one whose works Reiko had admired, was commissioned to craft the memorial. He used a dark, embossed, black metal hexagon base to lift the gem into the air and then wrapped a deep, copper-colored band around the top of the base on which to inscribe the dedication. The beautiful sapphire crystal column stood on its own base at the top. It was encased in display glass, which passed light from inside the base and into the gemstone from all directions. The pad sapphire shone, its delicate pink and orange colors mixing as if the light came from within it.

"This memorial commemorates the extraordinary period during which Idona Station changed, beginning the moment the Harakens arrived," Nikki continued. "We've heard some people call the Harakens aliens, and some refer to them as our distant human cousins. On Idona, we will always call them our friends. Our miners, Stremski, Willard, and Lister, said it best. This crystal is unique in all the system, and that's what this memorial called for, because that's what we are out here ... unique."

Nikki stepped back and the media department's cam drone closed in on the gem for a better view. Then it dropped to the engraving, which circled the base, and slowly followed the words to allow the people of Sol to read it too. The inscription read: "In the year 837 UE, 253 men and women of Sol sacrificed their lives to preserve the dignity, opportunity, and freedom humans should grant one another as a matter of course. They did so because seven alien humans gave their lives to show us we should. Idona Station extends its deepest gratitude to our friends, the Harakens."

Two days later, the last Harakens on Idona Station packed up and said farewell to their hosts, leaving the system of Sol much better off than when they found it — a valued tenet of the best of visitors.

— Alex and friends will return in *Espero* —

Glossary

Haraken

Alain de Long – Director of security, twin and crèche-mate to Alain, partner to Tatia Tachenko
Alex Racine – President of Haraken, partner to Renée de Guirnon, Star Hunter First (Swei Swee name)
Assembly – Haraken government representatives
Cedric Broussard – Z's New Terran avatar
Central Exchange – Haraken central bank, directed by the SADEs
Cordelia – SADE, Julien's partner
Darius Gaumata – Fighter/traveler captain and pilot
Darrin Hesterly – *No Retreat* chief medical officer
Deirdre Canaan – Wing commander
Edouard Manet – *Last Stand* captain, partner to Miko Tanaka
Ellie Thompson – Wing commander
Espero – Haraken city
Étienne de Long – Director of Security, twin and crèche-mate to Alain, partner to Ellie Thompson
First – Leader of the alien Swei Swee hives
Founding Day – Celebration of the founding of Haraken
Franz Cohen – Wing commander
GEN – Machine designed by Julien to help New Terran technology
Hive Singer – Mutter, SADE, who sings to the Swei Swee in their language
José Cordova – *Rêveur* captain
Julien – SADE, Cordelia's partner
Libran-X – Powerful explosive discovered and made by the Librans
Lucia Bellardo – Wing commander
Michael "Mickey" Brandon – Senior engineer, partner to Pia Sabine
Miko Tanaka – *No Retreat* captain, partner to Edouard Manet
Miranda Leyton – Z's femme fatale avatar
Mutter – SADE, Hive Singer to the Swei Swee

Nua'll – Aliens who imprisoned the Swei Swee before they became Harakens
People – Manner in which the Swei Swee refer to their collective
Pia Sabine – Assembly member, partner to Michael "Mickey" Brandon
Renée de Guirnon – First lady of Haraken, partner to Alex Racine
Robert Dorian – Assembly member, commander of military pilot training school
SADE – Self-aware digital entity, artificial intelligence being
Sanders – Traveler copilot to Darius Gaumata
Sean McCrery – Deceased fighter/traveler captain, friend of Darius Gaumata
Sheila Reynard – Fighter commodore
Star Hunter First – Swei Swee name for Alex Racine
Swei Swee – Six-legged friendly alien
Tatia Tachenko – Admiral, partner to Alain de Long
Terese Lechaux – Medical expert
Z – SADE

Méridien

Con-Fed – Méridien language
Confederation – Collection of Méridien worlds
Independents – Confederation outcasts, originally exiled to Libre, rescued by Alex Racine

New Terra

Clayton Downing – Former president of New Terra, convicted and imprisoned
Maria Gonzalez – New Terra president
Sol-NAC – Language of the New Terrans
Tara – Computer on board Alex Racine's *Outward Bound* explorer-tug

United Earth (UE) and Earthers

Alicante – Captain of the *Lazy Pleasure* yacht
Antonio García – *Reunion* mission commander, UE speaker
Berko – Militia major on moon base
Borden – Captain of the *Vigilance*
Boris Gorenko – UE scientist, medical background, immigrated to Haraken
Charnoose – Pro-naval captain, later acting commodore
Dahlia Braxton – Pro-naval commodore
Darwoo – Captain, pro-naval
Desmond Lambros – Sleepover owner aboard Idona Station
Diaz – Militia sergeant aboard Idona Station
Dimitri Agaloo – Privateer
Edmas – Teenage rebel boy aboard Idona Station
Edward – UE scientist, lead physicist, mathematician, immigrated to Haraken
Enclave – Fifteen-member group of high judges who elect the three Supreme Tribunal members
Faring – Militia major aboard *Vigilance*
Fliklight – Luminescent tags for the tunnel rats aboard Idona Station
Francis Lumley – *Reunion* captain
Gardia – Lieutenant undercover against the judiciary enclave
Ginny – Deaf child aboard Idona Station
Giuseppe Lucchesi – Supreme Tribunal member, judiciary
Guide – Generic name for the controlling computer on UE ships
Hanford – Militia sergeant aboard Idona Station
Hawkins – Lieutenant in Missile Command on the *Guardian*
Heywood – Judicial force destroyer captain
Ian Brennan – Supreme Tribunal member, corporate
Irving – Pro-naval captain promoted to acting commodore
Jason – Burn-scarred child aboard Idona Station
Jorre – Tug captain of the *Homeward Bound*
Jodlyne – Teenage rebel girl aboard Idona Station

Kwan Woo – Supreme Tribunal member, military
Li Chong – Space admiral, supreme leader of the UE naval forces
Lindling – Militia major in command aboard Idona Station
Lister – Miner out of Idona who donated Idona Station's memorial
Liston – Freighter captain of the *Treasure Chest*
Livingsworth – Militia lieutenant masquerading as wealthy traveler
Lydia Yelstein – Shuttle pilot at moon base
Marlene Elliot – Militia noncom at moon base
Needler – UE personal weapon fires high-speed poisonous darts
Nema – UE scientist, immigrated to Haraken
Nicolette "Nikki" Fowler – Rebel commander and granddaughter of Idona Station director
Olawale Wombo – *Reunion* lead UE science administrator, immigrated to Haraken
Patrice Morris – Militia lieutenant aboard Idona Station
Patricio Bunaldi – *Hand of Justice* mission commander, UE high judge, killed at New Terra
Pauline – Idona Station horticulturist and friend of Jorre
Priita Ranta – UE scientist, immigrated to Haraken
Provo – Militia lieutenant in league with Weevil's plan
Reiko Shimada – Captain of the UE destroyer *Conquest*
Sendra Deveening – UE commerce head
Shelley – Captain of the UE battleship *Guardian*
Stremski – Miner out of Idona who donated Idona Station's memorial
Stunstik – Militia weapon that stuns with darts
Supreme Tribunal – UE highest political system
Tankerling – Captain of the UE destroyer *Dauntless*
Tarek – Notorious hauler-tug captain
Terrine – Captain, pro-naval
Theodore Portland – UE judiciary admiral aboard battleship *Guardian*
Theostin – UE Admiral aboard the *Hand of Justice,* killed at New Terra
Torres – Ensign in *Guardian* Engineering
Tribune – Member of the Supreme Tribunal
Ullman – Admiral in command of last judiciary force in inner zone

Vic Lambert – Rebel second-in-command at Idona Station
Weevil – Sixteen-year-old dying boy who steals an ore grubber
Willard – Miner out of Idona who donated Idona Station's memorial
Yoram Penzig – UE scientist, philosopher, immigrated to Haraken
Yun – Militia captain aboard Idona Station

Planets, Colonies, Moons, and Stars

Callisto – Moon at Sol's Jupiter
Ganymede – Moon at Sol's Jupiter
Haraken – Home of the Harakens in the Hellébore system
Hellébore – Star of the planet Haraken
Libre – Independents' ex-colony in Arno system, now home to the remaining Swei Swee hives
Méridien – Home world of Confederation
New Terra – Home world of New Terrans, fourth planet outward of Oistos
Niomedes – New Terra fifth planet outward
Oistos – Star of the planet New Terra, Alex Racine's home world
Sol – Star of solar system where Earth is located
Tethys – Moon at Sol's Saturn

Ships and Stations

Bon Vivant – Luxury yacht pirated by Dimitri Agaloo
Ceres Station – Site of a rebel launch, resulting in docking arm destroyed by judicial forces
Challenge – UE destroyer, Captain Irving in command
Conquest – UE destroyer, Captain Shimada's first command
Daedalus – UE cruiser, Commodore Shimada's new command
Dauntless – UE destroyer
Guardian – UE battleship under Admiral Portland
Hand of Justice – UE battleship under High Judge Bunaldi, destroyed at New Terra

Homeward Bound – Reclamation tug captained by Jorre
Idona Station – Crossroads station located near Sol's Neptune
Last Stand – Haraken carrier
Lazy Pleasure – Hijacked UE pleasure yacht, captained by Alicante
No Retreat – Haraken carrier
Outward Bound – New Terra explorer-tug, originally captained by Alex Racine
Reunion – UE explorer ship
Rêveur – Haraken passenger liner
Shamrock – UE freighter
Travelers – Haraken fighter-shuttles built with Nua'll technology and Swei Swee shells
Treasure Chest – UE freighter captained by Liston
Vigilance – Renegade destroyer interdicting the *Lazy Pleasure* yacht

My Books

The Silver Ships series is available in e-book, softcover print, and audiobook versions. Please visit my website, http://scottjucha.com, for publication locations. You may also register at my website to receive email notification about the publish dates of my novels.

If you've been enjoying this series, please consider posting a review at your favorite retailer, even a short one. Reviews attract other readers and help indie authors, such as myself.

Alex and friends will return in the upcoming novel *Espero, A Silver Ships Novel.*

The Silver Ships Series

The Silver Ships

Libre

Méridien

Haraken

Sol

Espero (forthcoming)

The Author

I have been enamored with fiction novels since the age of thirteen and long been a fan of great storytellers. I've lived in several countries overseas and in many of the US states, including Illinois, where I met my wonderful wife thirty-seven years ago. My careers have spanned a variety of industries in the visual and scientific fields of photography, biology, film/video, software, and information technology (IT).

My first attempt at a novel, titled *The Lure,* was a crime drama centered on the modern-day surfacing of a 110-carat yellow diamond lost during the French Revolution. In 1980, in preparation for the book, I spent two wonderful weeks researching the Brazilian people, their language, and the religious customs of Candomblé. The day I returned from Rio de Janeiro, I had my first date with my wife-to-be, Peggy Giels.

During the next thirty-four years, I outlined dozens of novels, but a busy career limited my efforts to complete any of them. Recently, I've chosen to make writing my primary focus. My first novel, *The Silver Ships*, was released in February 2015. This first installment in a sci-fi trilogy was quickly followed by books two and three, *Libre* and *Méridien*. *Haraken* and *Sol*, the fourth and fifth books in the series, continue the exploits of Alex Racine and company in a two-part story. *Espero*, the sixth book in the series, is forthcoming.

I hope to continue to intrigue my readers with my stories as this is the most wonderful job I've ever had!

Printed in Great Britain
by Amazon